Wisher, wisher, by the water
Come and seek your heart's desire

Offer your blood and a whispered oath,
To call forth the lady from Salfar's smoke

But be cautious, little wisher
Wishes granted are often bitter.

PART ONE
A Garden of Thorns and Teeth

CHAPTER ONE
The Caveat

EARTH
After the Rising, 334

The Spotters swept into the alleyway like sinister shadows that had left their hosts behind to go hunting. The trick to catching sight of them, barely visible as they were in their dark blue uniforms, was to track their weapons. The piercing hum of magic the guns emitted always gave them away. It wasn't a sound meant for human ears.

From where Thorn crouched behind a rubbish bin, its rancid stink making it difficult to focus, she could count ten Spotters at least. There were likely more searching adjacent streets and alleyways. Like mould, more Spotters always hid just out of sight.

Squinting, head now splitting from the hum of magic, Thorn could just discern the chrome plates of the trackers on their forearms. The devices were capable of detecting human presence with magic. While the blockers she and Thistle wore on their wrists kept them from being discovered on radar, given how many Spotters there were, it wasn't much of a comfort.

The distant booms from the now burning Speak Softly that she and Thistle had been in mere seconds before floated across the air like a warning. As if the magical green flames licking up the sides of the building like a thousand venomous snakes wasn't enough, the Spotters who'd shut the venue down were now doing their utmost to reduce it to ashes. Unfailing in their hatred of mixed revelling, the Spotters burned down every Speak Softly they discovered.

Louder than the crackling fire, louder even than the building's interior creaking and snapping its way to collapse, thunder rumbled in the distance. But the rain both Thorn and the building so desperately needed was holding off. And until the rain arrived, the still night air left them exposed and vulnerable.

It wasn't a good night when her own lungs felt like traitors.

The Spotters weren't alone, either. The *tch-tch-tch* of approaching drones sent shivers down Thorn's spine, reminding her that up was also a bad option; worse, the charmed metal Scuttlers appeared at the head of the alley, moving with quick, jerky motions across the cobblestone road, closer with every second. If the machines had another name, Thorn didn't know it. Shaped like large arachnid-type monstrosities, the Scuttlers were made of metal, fired bullets as far as lasers, and could easily outrun a human.

'Shit,' she mouthed soundlessly. When the Spotters came in force, all their machinery came along with them.

A little behind Thorn, Thistle was on her knees, searching through her bag as quietly as she could. She produced a shiny black canister and held it up, eyes glinting in the dim glow of the streetlamps overhead.

Thorn deliberated. The drones had disappeared around the corner, drawn by the sounds of another human who'd been at the Speak Softly, but the Scuttlers were almost done searching the bins not twenty paces away. The Spotters were kicking in the doors to the surrounding buildings and conducting sweeps.

Thorn's eyes flicked over Thistle and her heart sank. *Where's your gun?* she signed frantically.

Thistle shook her head. *I didn't bring it*, she signed. *Sorry.*

The movement of her jewellery as she signed made the hair all over Thorn's body stand on end. Thorn had never worn jewellery a day in her life, but in recent weeks, the gifts had been coming in constantly from Thistle's latest boyfriend, and now her outfit might be the very thing that gave them away. The fact that she hadn't brought her gun only made matters worse and it took a concerted effort for Thorn not to roll her eyes at her best friend.

Sorry, Thistle signed again.

Resigned, Thorn gestured to the canister. Thistle pulled the pin, threw, and Thorn ducked down, hands over her ears as the explosion rocketed through the alley.

Debris instantly shot every which way with violent wrath. Some of the buildings lost plaster and brick; a few windows shattered, Scuttler parts blasting through. Catching the light of the neon signs, the debris looked like falling stars, and was likely just as dangerous.

With chaos as their cover, Thorn and Thistle shot to their feet and bolted across the road, around the mess of Suriia body parts and metal flotsam and jetsam, somehow making it to the stairs which led down to a lower street.

Thorn was barely around the corner when the sounds of more Scuttlers reached her ears. She drew out her gun, turning in the same step.

'Go!' she hissed at Thistle before firing at a Scuttler that had locked onto them.

She managed to catch its leg and the chrome machine crackled and zapped, magic and metal bouncing off each other, but it continued to stumble towards them, discombobulated, electrics snapping. She fired again before turning and bolting after Thistle, who had stupidly lingered.

'Go!' Thorn shouted again.

They shot down an alley and then scaled a rusted, rain-slick fire escape. Atop the buildings, they jumped from rooftop to rooftop, the shimmering lights of Courtenz illuminating their path as they sprinted to the outskirts of the city.

When they reached the last building of the street, they dropped onto the road and darted into the trees. Slowly, the sounds of machines above and below – an ever-hum of a city that thrived on distortion and wealth – began to fade, and Thorn slowed to a walk.

'That was close,' she groaned, clutching her side. Her chest burned with every breath and there was a rattling wheeze in her lungs from a cough she never seemed quite able to shake. It'd been a long time since she'd been able to draw a full breath, though she didn't like to think about it. Humans couldn't go to doctors unless they were on the Register.

'I'm so sorry,' said Thistle. She, too, was gasping. Her shoulder-length black hair that had been styled artfully an hour before now hung in a messy disarray. Beads of sweat dotted her brow, her lipstick had faded, and her eye makeup was smudged. Yet even dirty, wet and tousled, Thistle cut a stunning sight.

Thorn, however, was too busy wheezing, trying desperately to slow her heartrate, to answer. No matter how many times they escaped, no matter how fast she knew she was, she could never shake the panic.

The distant rumble of thunder followed by a flash of bright lightning signalled the rain, drawing Thorn from her racing thoughts.

'Figures,' she grumbled, pulling up her hood.

Ten minutes later the pair reached the park. It sloped downhill and traversing the thicket was especially tricky at night. Several of the bushes sprang to life and puffed out breaths filled with seeds and petals. The plants were alien to Earth, but had become far more widespread in the centuries under Suriia rule. Thorn didn't know any of the proper names for the invasive flora, but she knew the ones to avoid. She and Thistle had come up with names for those: the black ones that made you sleepy were Blackbreath; the scarlet ones that made you hallucinate were Red Crazies; the poisonous cerulean ones were Deathshade. There were also the purple ones with yellow vines that Suriias used the buds of to make Hazies, a popular party drug. Hazies even appeared at the Speak Softlies, which was a large reason Thorn and Thistle never drank or ate anything while they were out. That, and discerning what did and did not have magic inside was tricky.

On the other side of the park, through the corner of a forest that carried on towards the mountains, down a hidden path, through a hole in a fence, and then across a garden, was the shed they had been living in for a few months now. The pair stole across the lawn like ghosts and slipped inside without a sound.

The shed smelled like rot and mould and soil, but the roof only leaked a little, and they'd done their best to make it habitable. The location was too good to pass up. The shed was obscured from the main Suriia house on the other side of the property and they had been able to stay longer than Thorn initially thought.

Doublechecking the lock on the door, she kicked off her ratty boots and dropped heavily onto a moth-eaten chair, exhausted by the night's events. They didn't dare turn a light on at night, but years of trying to see in the dark had left her with a keen sense of things in the night-time and she had no trouble tracking Thistle's movements as she traded her dress and jewellery for soft trousers and her father's old sweatshirt. Littered with holes and stains, and at least four sizes too big for Thistle, it made her look even smaller than her already petite frame, and the night's close call weighed all the more on Thorn's shoulders.

'So,' began Thistle, curling up opposite Thorn and drawing her spindly legs into her chest. 'I've got news.'

Thorn waited silently, too tired to muster the will to enquire. Nothing good ever came from going to a Speak Softly and she already dreaded the answer.

'He asked me to marry him.'

Thorn laughed lowly. But when she realised Thistle wasn't joking, she went stiff. 'Tiz, tell me you're not actually considering this.'

'He said if I marry him, you can live with us,' said Thistle cheerfully. Like marrying a Suriia was somehow remotely normal. 'It's not a bad trade, Tor,' she continued. 'That's what he was asking. That's why I was late. He asked me to marry him.'

Thorn wrinkled her nose, thoroughly disinclined. It was illegal for humans to marry amongst themselves or own property, but if a Suriia wanted to marry a human and accept responsibility for them, it was allowed. Sometimes Suriias bought humans off the Register, sometimes they 'found' them – often at a Speak Softly – and, upon registering them, could marry. Sometimes they bought them from off the continent and trafficked them over. However it happened, Thorn found the whole idea monstrous. She wasn't sure when humans lost all rights – sometime after the rebellion – but it was long before she was born. Long before her parents or their parents. And the one rule she'd always lived by was to never trust a Suriia.

'Humans don't marry,' she said flatly. 'We're not allowed.'

'We're allowed to marry Suriias.'

'Oh, how *generous* they are.'

'I don't mean forever.'

'You don't?'

'No, just for the snowy months. To get out of the cold.'

Thorn made a face.

'We'd be safe, Tor,' Thistle urged.

But this entirely true and accurate point failed to resonate with Thorn. 'We'd be owned,' she argued, the mere words making her feel like maggots had laid siege to her flesh. 'And I've been owned before. No.'

'Nithin's not like that.'

'Because he says he's not?'

'I trust him.'

'You don't know him.'

'Just think about it,' Thistle pleaded. 'He lives near the city. He's rich enough to keep us safe and fed and warm, Tor. Winter's on its way. We almost died last year. And your lungs sound like a lawn cutter.'

Thorn longed to call Thistle out for being dramatic, but pride and survival were often mutually exclusive and sometimes even she knew when to cave.

'I'll think about it,' she grunted. 'I'm not saying yes.'

This small concession was enough for Thistle's entire face to light up. They got into their warmer, thicker sleep clothes and drew their hole-filled, well-worn blankets up to their chins. Thorn wrapped one arm around Thistle, her other hand resting on her leg, fingers curled around the hilt of her father's knife, and fell into a restless sleep.

The world was still shrouded in darkness when Thorn was torn from her nightmares, a scream in her throat and sticky with cold sweat. Yanking her sleeve up, exposing the scar tissue that was too deep to ever heal properly, she covered the teeth marks with her hand and squeezed, willing the memory away. She had thought, often, of hacking her arm off simply to be rid of the reminder.

'You okay?' Thistle sounded groggy and a yawn eclipsed the question.

'No,' said Thorn, trying to think of anything else. She glowered at the wall until she felt calm enough to force a smile to her face. The result was likely something akin to a contortion. 'I'm hungry,' she announced, needing desperately to distract herself. 'You hungry?'

'Always.'

Thorn stood and stretched. She tried to inhale fully, but her lungs seized, and she ended up coughing violently into her hand.

'Have you thought about what I said last night?' asked Thistle, clearly not in the same mindset of Suriia-free conversation.

Resisting the urge to groan, Thorn searched around for her boots, which were somehow never where she'd left them.

She found them under the sofa, still wet from the night before. A rather unpleasant smell emanated off them and they soaked her socks seconds after she stamped them on.

'Tor?'

'About getting married and moving into a city filled with our enemies? Yeah, I heard you.'

Thistle dropped her head back dramatically. 'It won't be like that. I promise.'

'Why do you trust him?' Thorn held out her hands. 'What makes this one different from the others who just wanted a human to buy?'

A dreamy cast glazed over Thistle's dark eyes and she inhaled slowly, seemingly bracing herself for something, and then produced a ring from her pocket. It was thin, silver, ordinary.

'A ring?' said Thorn, thoroughly stumped.

Thistle was smiling in the strangest way, like a thin silver ring was something extraordinary. 'Nithin gave it to me.'

'Why?'

'He says humans used to wear them back when we were allowed to get married.'

An odd feeling crept over Thorn's skin and her eyes lingered on the ring, disquiet spreading through her veins. 'I've never heard that.'

'He said there's old human books that talk about it. And he wanted to do it our way. Something I'd be comfortable with. Not Suriia at all.'

Thorn forced a swallow and stood. Her head spun a little from lack of food and her bad mood only worsened as she swayed on her feet. 'If he's making that up, he's an absolute prick.'

For the first time since she'd brought up Nithin's proposal, Thistle appeared angry at Thorn's reticence. 'He's not making it up.'

'How do you know?'

'Because I believe him.'

'Why?' She was starting to get the feeling she'd ask the same question at least a dozen more times before the conversation wore itself out. 'Wearing a ring to show you're married couldn't sound more made up. What good is a ring?'

'What would you give someone if humans were allowed to marry?'

'A knife,' said Thorn bluntly. 'It shows you care about them. It shows you want them to live.'

'That is *utterly* unromantic.'

'As opposed to sleeping with the enemy to stay alive? Golly, where am I going wrong?'

She knew the words were harsh, but Thistle's ability to compartmentalise it all had long bothered Thorn. Was solidarity against their enemies too much to ask for?

Thistle crossed her arms. 'That's so mean.'

'It's true.'

After a moment's heated scowling match, Thorn turned and stomped outside. The blast of icy morning air did nothing to improve her mood. Thick fog hung low on the ground, obscuring most of the surroundings. The air smelled like rain and felt heavy from the previous night's thunderstorm, and dew kissed her boots as she darted across the grass towards the house.

She hated arguing with Thistle more than anything. Her life only worked when Thistle was happy with her. That was how it had always been. She kept Thistle alive, she made Thistle happy, and when the world around them crumbled to dust, she could look at her best friend and be assured that there was still some goodness left.

That didn't mean she didn't sometimes feel like throwing a pillow at Thistle's face for her unending naiveté when it came to trusting their enemies.

The shapeshifters who owned the house were already out for the day and, after checking that the coast was clear, Thorn jimmied a window and crawled inside. The house smelled like fragrant candles and a lingering blend of coffee, breakfast meats and bread.

She only ever took what there was an abundance of so that the Suriias wouldn't miss it. Two of the sons also stowed food in their rooms that they didn't think anyone but them knew about. When she stole from them, they always argued about it, neither believing the other when they claimed not to know where the chocolate had gone to. Thorn had eavesdropped on so many of their fights she felt like she knew them at this point.

The meal hadn't been totally cleared away and she ate the leftovers and scraps happily.

After grabbing a backpack's worth of food and bottled water, along with a few medical supplies, a candle, and some old books, Thorn slipped out of the house the same way she entered.

Back in the relative safety of the shed, she bolted the door and dragged in several breaths, her eyes seeking out Thistle immediately.

'All good,' said Thistle.

Thorn let out a rattling breath that ended in a whistling wheeze. 'Here,' she rasped, tossing Thistle her bag mid-cough. 'Make us food.'

Deftly catching the bag, Thistle said, 'You could say please, you know?'

'Please, baby.' Thorn dropped down on the hole covered, half-broken sofa, slinging her legs over the armrest. 'You know a growing girl like me needs sustenance.'

With an exasperated smile, Thistle set about cooking. But there was only peaceful silence for five minutes before she once again brought up the subject of The Annoying Suriia Who Liked to Make Up Stories About Human History.

'He says that most of his friends abhor the treatment of humans and want accords signed,' said Thistle, briefly pausing her cooking to pour Thorn a cup of tea. She also added a few spoonsful of honey once it had steeped.

Thorn took the tea gratefully when Thistle offered it. 'Nithin sounds like an amazing lie,' she muttered, cradling the mug close, glaring at the dark brown liquid. She'd found the peppermint in the garden a few weeks back, and the sharp scent helped clear her nose and lungs.

'Stop it. He really does like me.'

'He's using you.'

'I'm using him. And both of us are aware of that. But he's offering us something no one else has. Nithin's the first one to offer me anything – and he's offering us *everything*. Please. I'm so sick of hiding and running all of the time. I want a hot bath so badly.'

'I didn't come to the city for you to get laid, Tiz. I came to find Veryn, which you've barely wanted to do. I thought you were with me on this?'

'I am,' said Thistle vehemently. Although how much revenge she'd ever wanted was something Thorn often dwelled on. But then, it wasn't Thistle who'd buried their parents. It wasn't Thistle who'd seen the damage done to them.

With characteristic determination, Thistle continued, 'Nithin's home is a short walk to the city, not a four-hour hike through the backwoods. He's got more connections than any Suriia we've ever met. He's rich. We'll be in the best place to find Veryn and if we find Veryn, we can steal supplies and go. How much better off will we be with proper clothes, some fat on our bones? What about weapons? Suriia weapons would be amazing to have. They never stop to consider what'll happen if it's their guns we're aiming back at them.'

The glint in Thistle's eye was conspiratorial and it was hard not to be seduced by it. Thorn hugged the cup of tea closer to her chest, thoughts of killing Veryn, the one who orchestrated the deaths of their parents, swirling around her mind.

But still—

'What if the Spotters catch us?'

Thistle winked at her. 'Jailbreak, baby,' she drawled.

They always said that to each other when they talked about being taken. Sometimes the only way not to truly panic at the outcome was to laugh about it.

Thorn's eyes flicked to the ring around Thistle's finger. It was a thin silver band, nothing impressive. Nothing gaudy. If Nithin was going to concoct a lie to buy her, he was going about it in the strangest way.

'Okay,' said Thorn after a long stretch of silence. 'Okay. But only until we find Veryn. We use Nithin, we find Veryn, and then we run. Deal?'

Her words took a second to register with Thistle. Then, with a squeal, Thistle tackle-hugged her onto the sofa, giddy with delight. 'You're the best!'

'I don't want to be there more than a few weeks,' said Thorn pointedly. 'Until we find Veryn.'

'Until Veryn,' said Thistle, cuddling Thorn close, smothering her in that comforting way only someone who loves you can achieve.

'If we kill Veryn before you marry the Suriia, you'll leave, right?'

'Of course. But there'll be beds! And heating!'

Rather begrudgingly, Thorn told Thistle to send Nithin a message on the phone he'd given her a fortnight beforehand, informing him that they would meet later that night.

'He says he can pick us up here,' said Thistle a minute later.

Thorn's head snapped up. 'Did you tell him where we are?'

'Of course not,' said Thistle hastily. 'He just offered to come get us directly.'

'We'll meet where it's safe. Tell him Easting Forest, the south road by the river.'

'That's so far away.'

Thorn blinked at her.

'Fine,' said Thistle. 'You're right, it's safer.'

It was also a location that Thorn knew like the back of her hand. If Nithin betrayed them – or brought a contingent of Spotters along – they had more chance of escape in those woods.

Long after nightfall, the pair snuck out of the shed and headed into the backwoods. The neon shimmer of the Suriia city in the distance, its great skytowers blotting out the moon, obscured the stars with menacing showmanship.

Thorn's grip on her gun didn't slacken as they made their way through the trees, ears keen for sounds that didn't belong to the forest.

The constant rain and freezing temperatures meant several areas were slick and perilous. More than a few times they slipped on patches of ice they hadn't even seen, and Thorn was nursing multiple bruises within the hour.

The forest brought them to the edge of the city, the sea on one side, Courtenz looming in the distance on the other. At the base of the hill, where the river rushed out into the ocean, was a long disused backroad. Thorn triple checked that there were no incoming coaches or drones in the sky – or Spotters or Scuttlers on the ground – before she led the way down the steep hill, Thistle trailing just behind. The tall grass and bramble-filled underbrush made it a slow, tricky descent that was made all the worse by the thick, salt-laden breeze whipping at their necks.

Midnight had swallowed the sky by the time their footing finally evened out, and Thorn checked the dial she'd attached to the leather strap on her wrist where the blocker was also sewed on. 'Your sbura is late.'

'By two minutes,' said Thistle, clutching her side and gasping. 'Calm down.'

Thorn shot her a warning look. 'We linger, we get caught. We get caught, we die. You know that.'

'It's going to be fine,' said Thistle, waving a hand in a manner that was slightly grating. 'Nithin promised we'd be safe.'

The word of a Suriia meant less than nothing to Thorn.

She had just kicked a rock into the darkness when a coach appeared in the sky. The roar of the wind on the ocean made the noise of its engine a dull burring. The coach flashed its lights twice as it descended. It was an expensive model, likely running off solar power and Suriia magic, and Thorn's irritation skyrocketed at the mere sight of such wealth. She hated the whole plan already.

A shudder of fear jolted through her as Nithin lifted the door of the coach and stepped out. Thorn had seen him from a distance several times already, always keeping to the shadows of the Speak Softlies, eyes on Thistle, a hand on her knife. She'd even seen him before Thistle ever had.

Whether it was instinct or sheer coincidence, Thorn tracked him the moment he entered that first night, somehow just *knowing* he would go for Thistle. He was tall, refined, dark in that annoying, perfect way that made her skin crawl. She didn't trust perfect.

Nithin had bypassed every look sent his way and went straight to Thistle's side. He'd held out his hand to her and said, 'May I cut in?'

That was the first thing which registered for Thorn. Politeness from a Suriia was a rarity.

She watched Thistle take his hand; she watched them dance and talk and laugh. One night after another. She watched Thistle fall in love.

It was a strange thing, Thorn thought, falling in love. Abstractly, she understood it. She remembered her parents being in love. How happy they had been. What she couldn't – and would never – understand was falling in love with their enemy.

The sight of him emerging from his sleek coach, dressed in a suit that undoubtedly cost more than all the money Thorn had stolen in the nineteen years she'd been alive, only showcased just how very different he was from them. City born, oozing wealth and power, magic dancing on the tips of his fingers and in the depths of eyes far too green to be human, Nithin Summons was nothing like them.

Without any hesitation – or any conversation – he went to Thistle's side, took her hands, drew her close in a fluid motion, and kissed her. He kissed like some kind of actor, tilting her head back, his hands coming up to cradle her face. Everything about it seemed like a production, although Thorn couldn't fathom who he was trying to impress.

When he finished kissing Thistle, Nithin finally acknowledged Thorn's presence. 'You must be the caveat.' He kept his arm around Thistle's waist possessively, but his gaze lingered on the gun in Thorn's hand. 'Trouble?'

'You tell me,' she retorted.

Rolling his eyes, Nithin kissed Thistle's cheek. 'You're right, she's *charming*. So charming I almost cut myself.'

'Tor's just worried,' said Thistle, patting his chest placatingly. Like they were an old married couple. 'We had a close call with the Spotters last night.'

The humour vanished from his face and his body went stiffer than stone. 'Why didn't you call me?'

'I … I never even considered it, honestly. Sorry.'

Thorn couldn't figure out why her words clearly bothered Nithin. As if he took personal affront at not being Thistle's port of call. Instead of saying anything, however, he cupped Thistle's face between his hands and kissed her again.

The wind picked up, icy, rain-filled and painful, and water slithered down Thorn's skin behind her collar, chilling her to the bone. Somehow it did nothing to Nithin and Thistle.

'Get a room,' Thorn muttered under her breath. Louder, she called, 'Tiz, time to move. A drone could come by.'

'No reason to worry,' said a new voice.

She whirled around, gun in hand, and found herself pointing it at a Suriia. One so quiet, so encased in shadow, she'd not realised he was even there. And that was the most terrifying kind of Suriia.

'It's okay,' said Thistle, suddenly appearing at Thorn's side and putting her hand on the barrel of the gun. 'That's his friend.'

'I'm sorry—*who*?'

'Kol,' said Nithin nonchalantly. 'We live together.'

It was like being smacked in the face with a bucket of ice water.

Utterly dismayed, Thorn grabbed Thistle's hand and pulled her away from the coach. 'We're not moving in with *two*,' she hissed. 'Are you kidding?'

'They've been best friends for years,' said Thistle in a low voice. 'They both like humans.'

'You *knew*?' Thorn's hands went to her head. 'You knew there was another one and you didn't tell me?'

'Look, Kol—'

'There's no way you just *happened* to stumble across two Suriias who like humans and want nothing from us. Use. Your. Brain.'

Thistle held out her hands placatingly. The weather was growing worse by the second and they were both trembling, but Thorn was willing to stay all night outside if that's what it took.

'You promised you would give it a chance,' said Thistle.

'Yeah, when we only had nympho-boy to contend with.'

'If we're going to start name calling, I'd much prefer something less juvenile.'

Thorn turned to see Nithin and Kol watching them. Neither appeared bothered by the downpour. They were leaning against the sleek coach like they had all the time in the world, water droplets rolling off their expensive, waterproof coats.

Kol nudged Nithin with his elbow. For some bizarre reason he was wearing sunglasses in the middle of the night and she couldn't tell if he was a sbura like Nithin. 'I did suggest Lord of Lust,' he said.

'Somehow even "nympho-boy" is better than that,' said Nithin dryly. He inclined his head towards Thorn and gestured to the coach with an almost mocking flick of his hand. 'Didn't you want to leave?'

Hatred was not a strong enough word for how Thorn felt about the Suriia in front of her. Gun still in hand, she moved between Thistle and the Suriias. She wasn't opposed to shooting them both and stealing their coach.

Clearly nursing a death wish, Kol stepped forward, hand outstretched. 'I didn't catch your name.'

She stared at his hand.

'Hi,' he prompted, somewhat questioningly. 'You don't have a name?'

'I'm the caveat.'

'I'm the roommate.' When it became clear she wasn't going to shake his hand, he finally lowered it, a frown reversing his smile.

Thistle stepped closer and put her hands on Thorn's hips. 'Please,' she whispered in her ear, the slightly sweet smell of her breath close enough for Thorn to detect. 'Remember what we said?'

Thorn could not have wanted to leave more, but her desire to find Veryn trumped almost every other feeling inside of her. They'd left the relative safety of the northside of the island to be near Courtenz. To find him. Finally.

Grinding her teeth together, Thorn let Thistle walk her over to the coach and clambered inside after her. Once they were both seated, Thistle reached out and took her free hand, interlacing their fingers.

The coach hummed to life and slowly rose into the air. Thorn's heart leapt into her throat.

'Do you like music?' Nithin asked Thistle as he fiddled with the dial.

'Sure,' said Thistle.

'What do you like?'

'I, ah …' Thistle let out a laugh. 'I don't actually know.'

'No?' This question came from Kol.

'It's not safe to play music,' she explained, a slight edge to her upbeat tone. 'So we never really have.'

The silence following this apparent revelation was only broken by the thrum of the engine and the whipping winds outside the coach.

'I think you'll like this,' said Nithin, finally breaking the awkward spell that had taken hold.

A gentle tune filled the coach, covering the hammering of her heart, and Thorn fixed her attention on the dark countryside passing by. So high above the ground, everything looked small and harmless. But she couldn't enjoy a second of it. Thorn had never been in the sky and she couldn't stop gripping the door handle. Her gut tightened excruciatingly, as if someone was wringing her intestines out inside of her like laundry.

With practised ease, Nithin diverted the coach away from the ocean and forest, making for the distant twinkling lights of the city. The great sky towers of Courtenz, hundreds of storeys high, carved dark, unnatural shapes into the horizon. A vast city made of magic and technology, it cast its shadow upon all below. The few times Thorn and Thistle had been in the heart of it, they'd seen gambling arenas, street fights, human and animal markets, magic shows, coach parades and races in the sky. There were exotic dancers who could fly, and billboards with offers to hunt down the tastiest humans. It was a mad, spine-chilling, chaotic city and Thorn felt sicker by the second.

Her eyes swept over the frenzied horizon around them: the coaches in all shapes and sizes, swerving between each other with astonishing speed and precision; the flying Suriias – mostly frai – with their great, terrifying wings that did not belong on Earth, flitted in between the coaches at lower levels; and the metallic drones and other machinery that flew this way and that, each with a different destination and purpose.

To Thorn's immense relief, Nithin flew over the outskirts of the massive city and kept on towards the forested areas. He descended onto a smooth road minutes later and drove the rest of the way up to a fenced-in house where a figure in a high-collared suit opened a gate. There was a flash of magic that signalled a spell of some kind.

Thorn glanced at Thistle with a raised eyebrow. *How rich is he?* she signed.

Thistle put a hand over her mouth as she giggled with muffled glee.

The driveway was long, with manicured lawns on either side, flowers and shrubbery done up with obsessive perfection. Thorn didn't know if the designs and creations were amazing – or insanely overdone.

Nithin parked in front of the house and everyone got out. It was a modern home, with security systems and doors which opened of their own accord. Nithin gave them both the code to the front gate and door, and Thorn memorised them as he led the way up a great stone staircase and into the entrance hall.

'You can come and go as you please,' he continued, his deep voice resonating loudly in the chamber of the hall. 'The guard at the gate won't stop you.'

'Is it safe?' asked Thistle.

'This is one of the safest parts of Courtenz,' he assured her. 'And no one will touch you if they know you're with me. But I wouldn't wander into the city alone.'

Thistle kissed his cheek. 'Trust me,' she said. 'I won't.'

'We can see the city together,' said Nithin, wrapping his arm around her shoulders.

Thorn averted her gaze from their couple-ness and took in the interior of the mansion. While the outside was white, almost shiny marble, the inside was accentuated with darker tones. The walls were scarlet, the floor wood or covered by an area rug.

There were paintings on some walls, photographs in frames on others. Scattered throughout the place were plants in pots, sculptures that likely cost more than a human, and books. So many books. An entire wall was made of ancient-looking tomes that begged to be picked up and devoured. But, as a whole, the house was too large to be necessary. It was large only for show, and it infuriated her. Humans ate out of bins or cast-off scraps, or bargained what little they had, chancing death. This was just tacky.

'Kol,' said Nithin, drawing Thorn from her judgements, 'take the caveat upstairs. Show her the spare room.'

Thistle whacked his arm with affectionate sternness. 'Don't call her that. Her name's Thorn.'

'She has all the delights of one, too,' he retorted, kissing Thistle's ear.

Thorn didn't bother responding. She signed to Thistle – *Yell if you need me* – before trailing after Kol. Photographs lined the stairwell in fancy frames, broken up only by various awards and plaques, all with inscriptions in the Suriias' native language, which she could only read because her mother had painstakingly taught it to her as a child. All the humans she knew spoke English, but Suriias spoke Enesh, too. Long before the war, Suriias adopted English while living in hiding from humans, but their own language took precedence following the rebellion and their victory. Most everyone now spoke in a mix of both languages in day to day life, but written English was disappearing.

Trailing after Kol at a purposefully slow pace, she took in each room, door, window and closet. He stilled outside a room halfway down the long hall and gestured for her to go in.

She had been sleeping on the ground for so many years, she didn't even know how to react to the sight that awaited her. The bedroom smelled wonderfully of flowers and the windows were open. There were no bars and it was an easy drop to the ground. The fence wasn't far, either, and appeared climbable. Walking over to the window, she glared out into the night. The lights of Courtenz were visible, but thankfully she couldn't hear any of the city's sounds.

'You're quiet,' said Kol from behind her. 'Not much for words?'

'I'm here for Thistle. Not because I want to be.'

'Oh,' he said, slightly taken aback.

'Can you go?'

He drifted away, hands in his pockets, but he didn't leave the room. Instead, he leaned back against the doorframe and propped one of his legs up. 'I didn't mean to offend you.'

She scoffed.

'What?' he asked. As if he was genuinely confused.

The sheer ridiculousness of his confusion left her flabbergasted and she opened and closed her mouth several times before formulating a reply. When it finally came, the words were harsh and biting, and her anger escalated with every breath. 'Are you serious right now? "Offend me"?'

He grimaced and straightened up. 'I feel like we should start over. I'm—'

'Suriia.'

'Yes,' he said, still seemingly bewildered by her reaction.

Thorn threw out her hands, barely restraining the urge to punch him. 'When was the last time you saw a human that wasn't either dead or bartered?' she demanded. 'Slave, food or toy. That's all we've ever been to your kind. I'm not fucking *grateful* we got a bargain not to be killed. I'm not thanking you for not buying me or capturing me. Go buy a brain.'

Kol exhaled slowly and she braced herself for him to attack or laugh or even storm off. To her great surprise, he only offered her a tentative smile. 'I'm sorry if it seemed like I was making light. I'm really out of my depth on this one, honestly. I don't know what it's like. I grew up in a house. I've never been hungry. Can we both agree that this world can be awful and try to be friends anyway?'

A noise of utter derision left her before she could rein it in. 'Why?'

He ran a hand through his inky black hair and tugged absently before shrugging. 'I live here too,' he said, 'and they're going to be nauseating. It'd be nice to have someone to hang out with while they're banging their brains out.'

'Lovely.'

A deep, rumbling laugh sounded in his chest. 'Well, why do you think I want a friend?'

'No Suriia friends?'

'Plenty. Always room for one more.'

'Not for a human caveat.'

'I disagree.'

While she doubted that immensely, he did sound oddly genuine. 'You're not sbura,' she noted, having a hard time gauging what kind of power he had. Ghuls and vrykos had pointed ears and teeth to give them away; shapeshifters were often remarkably tall. But most Suriias looked like humans until their magic came out. It was how they had hidden amongst humans for so many years before the war. But the legends differed on when and how it all changed.

He exhaled audibly and, after a pause, removed his sunglasses. 'Frai.'

She took a step back automatically, instantly unsteady on her feet. She'd really been hoping he was a prico or sbura. But his eyes, gold with vertical pupils like a cat's, gave him away. Frai hid their wings like pricos hid their fangs and claws, but the eyes were always honest.

'Sorry,' he said, holding up the sunglasses. 'I didn't want to freak you out before. But you're safe. Honestly.'

A shrill, strangled sound tore out of her without permission. As if her disbelief simply refused to be contained.

Vrykos, those blood-and-soul suckers with their mouthfuls of jagged teeth, terrified her. But where they were the grotesque brutes in her nightmares, the frai were the puppeteers of the whole show. Frai formed the bulk of the Spotters; they were the ones in charge, for they were the most cunning, and by far the most sinister.

Kol's face fell at her reaction. 'Have you met another frai before?'

For the briefest of pauses, the sort that felt in its moment like a small eternity, she considered lying, but he'd know instantly if he aimed to.

Forcing a swallow, her hand twitching towards her gun, she said, 'The frai run the death camps.'

'Not all frai,' he said firmly. 'And not me.'

It was an easy move to the window, but she wasn't about to leave without Thistle. 'Why would I ever believe that?'

Seemingly surprised by her unguarded distrust, his eyebrows shot up. 'Do you think we brought you two here to play with?'

'It's happened before.'

'To a friend of yours? If you give me their names—'

'Not to a friend,' she spat. 'My friends are all dead. My family are all dead. It happened to *me*. All those sad little rumours you hear? Well they've all happened to *me*. So give me a better reason to trust you than "I'm not like the others", because only a moron would believe that. Your kind hunt mine for *fun*.' With the hand that wasn't hovering over her gun, she yanked her shirt collar to the side where the scars Jared had left marred her skin.

Kol's gold-black eyes, so like a cat's but decidedly more striking, took in the wound for a long moment before meeting her gaze. 'What we can do and what we choose to do don't have to be the same, you know? Like I said, we *can* be friends despite all the world telling us it's impossible. Like a rabbit and a wolf. I'm not playing you. I really want to be your friend. It honestly just sounds exhausting living in the same house with someone who hates me. If I prove you wrong, I'm giving you my full pardon and permission to stab me with iron. Honestly, anywhere will do. Stab me in the gut, the shoulder, the leg. Go for a toe, even. That would be really embarrassing for me. Death by toe. Can you imagine? I don't think my father would ever acknowledge my existence after that. But that's beside the point. What was the point? Oh, yeah: iron in me and I'm dead.' He snapped his fingers for effect.

Thorn opened and closed her mouth twice. 'I thought iron was a myth.'

'It's not,' he said. 'They want humans to think it's a myth. There is no iron on Salfar. There's no gold, either, actually. In fact, most of the metals differ. Something about iron doesn't like our blood, though. It's poisonous. Corrosive.'

'Why would you tell me that?'

'Consider it a peace offering.'

Now more puzzled than bothered, she asked, 'Why would a rabbit ever trust a wolf?'

'Because perhaps the wolf is lonely and won't let the lions or tigers – I'm not really sure how far we're taking this metaphor but I'm digging it – anywhere near the rabbit. Perhaps the wolf doesn't see so great a difference between them.'

'Rabbits bleed.'

'Wolves bleed, too.'

Finally, Thorn moved her hand away from her gun. And held it out to him. If for no other reason than to see where he was going with this, and why. 'If you're lying, I'll cut off all your toes with iron and shove them down your throat.'

He grasped her hand and, to her astonishment, winked. 'For the sake of my dignity, you have a deal.'

When she let go, Kol stepped around her and gestured to the other side of the room. 'The bathroom's in there. Water's always hot. Dinner in a few.'

'What do you eat?' she asked cautiously.

'Do you think we eat raw flesh or something? Cos I can promise that one is definitely a myth. I'm not a rare meat kind of frai.'

She pursed her lips. 'I've seen more disturbing.'

When he realised she wasn't joking, he blanched. 'Where?'

'Ghuls.' Her mother told her years ago that the ghuls had lived underground for centuries before the rebellion and it changed them. Turned them into something wild and untameable. They preferred to come out at night even now that the Suriias were in charge. And they liked human flesh. They also liked *fresh* human flesh, which meant Thorn had heard more than a few stories of humans who'd been kept alive for months on end, sliced away piece by piece.

Kol's nose wrinkled, although what stories he knew about ghuls she didn't care to ask. 'We were thinking burgers. Or do you not eat meat at all?'

'I eat anything that's not people.'

'Duly noted.'

With that, Kol left her alone, closing the door behind him. The animated way with which he spoke and carried himself made the silence that followed his departure that much more pronounced. He was the first Suriia she'd ever met who acted … almost human.

Not sure what to make of the strange encounter, Thorn spent a few minutes testing the locks on the windows before she wandered into the bathroom. She'd never been able to take a hot shower that wasn't filled with panic at the thought of being caught and killed.

Turning the tap and finding that the water was indeed hot, she stripped quickly and stepped in. After cleaning herself from top to bottom, she set about cutting first her fingernails, then her toenails, and finally her hair.

Her hair was more a tangled mop than anything else, hanging past her waist and full of knots. She cut it to her shoulders with ruthless efficiency. It was a hack job, but she didn't have the energy to care. Exhaustion had seeped into every fibre of her being and at this point all she wanted was to feel clean.

A quick glance in the mirror showed how deep the circles under her brown eyes had become. Scars on her cheek and neck from Jared stood out against the surrounding skin almost like a crude attempt at artwork. Then there were the bite marks on her shoulder, arm and torso from one of Veryn's gang; and the gouges across her ribs and back from a ghul. Her body was a canvas of what Surilas did to humans.

There were bags by the door when she stepped back into the bedroom. There was also a note on her table in Thistle's messy, untrained scrawl.

> *I told Nithin what to get. It's all your size and no colours you won't like, I promise!*
>
> *There's also food in one of the bags in case you don't want to come downstairs. If you do, just save it. I know how much you like to snack. And now we can!*
>
> *You're the best, baby.*

The words niggled unpleasantly at something in Thorn's chest. It had been years since Thistle had been so happy about anything and knowing her joy was the result of one of their enemies didn't sit well with any part of Thorn.

Throat tightening with emotion, she set the note on the dresser and picked out a few items from the bag, examining them one by one. In all her life, she'd never had new clothes. Thistle got the odd gift from whatever Suriia she was wooing, but Thorn had never received anything. Having an option not just of what to wear, but all in pristine condition, was a marvel.

She opted for a pair of warm trousers and a thick jumper. Then, checking her gun, she put it in the bedside table drawer. Bullets were hard to come by and she'd never felt comfortable having a gun out when it wasn't in her hand for a specific purpose. Instead, she always kept her knife close at hand. It had been her father's before the Suriias killed him.

Buckling the sheath to her calf, well hidden by the baggy trousers, Thorn tied her now much shorter hair back from her face, took a steadying breath, and exited the bedroom.

In the immaculately clean sitting room furbished in décor that cost more than Thorn was worth at the Blood Market, she found Thistle on the sofa watching television. An advertisement for lipstick was playing a Suriia dancing on the screen as she did her lips in a horrid shade of azure that was apparently meant to be chic.

Ignoring the commercial, Thorn dropped down beside Thistle, worry spiking as she took in the pale cast to her friend's already alabaster skin. Contrasted against her ebony hair and bewitching hazel eyes, Thistle looked all the more fragile.

'You okay?'

'I'm fine,' said Thistle firmly, and, in truth, she did sound fine. 'Nithin's making me something to eat.'

'I'll make you something.' Thorn didn't trust Nithin to do it properly. She kissed Thistle's forehead before standing and walking into the kitchen where Nithin and Kol were preparing dinner. The smell of cooking oil mixed with onions, potatoes and cheese hit her immediately upon entry. Mixed with the soap scent from the sink and the aroma of their two half-drained glasses of beer, the kitchen gave off the impression of being safe. Contained. Calm enough to relax in. The allusion wasn't one Thorn trusted, but it had been a long, long time since she'd been in a clean, warm kitchen with such abundance that there was both food and beer on offer.

Without a word to either of them, she began to root through the cabinets and refrigerator. Finding the right ingredients took no time at all and she quickly set about making Thistle a smoothie.

'Can I get some of that?' Kol leaned back against the counter beside her and flashed an unfettered grin. 'Looks good,' he added as she added two bananas to the blender that was already half filled with strawberries, raspberries and cranberries. 'You like smoothies?'

'It's not for me.'

Kol's wolfish grin only broadened, as if he was incapable of detecting standoffishness in all its forms. 'Any other hidden talents?'

'Yeah.' She finished the smoothie and poured two glasses to the rim. Handing him one, she said, 'I have a knife I know from experience can cut through bone,' before she turned and walked out.

Thistle looked up as she walked in, a sleepy smile plastered across her delicate features. Thorn held out the glass. 'Drink,' she ordered. 'You look sick.'

'I look beautiful.'

'Beauty can still look sick. Drink.'

Meaning pooled in Thistle's eyes and she took Thorn's free hand. 'This is a home, Tor,' she whispered. 'We're safe here. We don't have to run.'

Not wanting to agree, but not wanting to argue, Thorn leaned against her, staring unseeingly at the television. Their hands remained loosely intertwined and Thistle sipped at the smoothie obediently; as the minutes passed, Thorn felt slightly less sick.

When Nithin and Kol joined them, they came bearing plates. Steam rose off the surface of each one and Thorn's stomach growled loudly.

Now that Thorn could see them side by side in the light, it was hard not to laugh at how different they were. Where Nithin was dressed in a black suit, his hair brushed, his beard impeccable, Kol wore comfortable looking clothes: a high-collared, long-sleeved shirt and jeans, his black hair messy and tousled. They looked as different as Thorn and Thistle.

'What are we watching?' asked Kol, sitting beside Thorn and handing her a plate with a burger, salad and chips.

'Some mystery,' said Thistle, taking the plate Nithin offered her and moving over slightly so that he could claim the space beside her. 'It's really good.'

Really good was not how Thorn would've described watching Suriias moan about their problems.

Kol looked at Thorn encouragingly. 'Do you like movies?'

'Sure.'

'Very enthusiastic,' he teased, nudging her with his elbow.

'Thorn steals books whenever we find them,' Thistle supplied unhelpfully. 'Her mother taught us both to read. Most humans can't.'

Thorn almost choked at the sudden tightness of her throat and took a second to steady herself before continuing to eat, the ache for her mother almost crippling.

'What kind of books?'

'How-to manuals,' said Thorn, barely finding her voice. She sounded raspy and choked. 'Smoothie instructions.'

Whether he noticed or not, Kol chuckled.

'We have a library down the hall,' Nithin interjected. 'You're welcome to it.'

Thorn looked down at her plate. Despite her lack of words, the prospect made her heart flutter. As a child, she would sit in her father's arms and listen to her mother's soft-spoken stories until the light from the campfire burned too low to read by. Thorn never fell asleep first. When she thought of books, she thought of family.

The rest of the night passed in a strange, suspended unease. As soon as the movie finished, Nithin suggested they turn in, and Thistle hugged Thorn goodnight before disappearing into Nithin's room like it was a perfectly normal thing to do.

Thorn did the dishes on reflex, unable to leave a mess for someone else to pick up. To her surprise, Kol joined her by the sink and dried the dishes as she went. He stayed blessedly quiet, only bidding her a quiet goodnight when they finished.

She had only brushed her teeth when there was a knock on the door.

It was Nithin. He had taken off his suit and was wearing a short-sleeve shirt and sleeping trousers. He looked almost unkempt, and for the first time he didn't make Thorn's skin crawl in disgust. She settled for remaining expressionless and waited to see what he wanted.

He held out a set of keys with jarring abruptness. 'To the house and coach. Don't fly it if you don't know how. I like my coach.'

'Oh.' She took the keys, too stunned to form much of a response. 'Okay.'

Nithin turned to leave, only to pause. 'Whatever you think of Suriias, Thorn, I do love Thistle.'

Thorn didn't believe him, but she nodded anyways. Better to play along. Better to let them think she was complacent while she learned their weaknesses. And Thorn fully intended on finding out Nithin's weaknesses.

Just in case.

CHAPTER TWO
Caution: Unlikely Friendships May Occur

Thorn had always had a somewhat tenuous relationship with sleep and rest, unable to fall asleep and stay that way for longer than a few hours at a time. If that. The first morning at the mansion, she was more on edge than she'd been in years and barely closed her eyes.

She was wide awake when the sky lit up with a cascade of reds and oranges and yellows, like someone painting across the horizon with blood and honey. There was no rain or thunder, making the quiet of the estate all the more noticeable. And yet, for the first time in a long time, she didn't have to listen for sounds from a nearby house. She didn't have to wait to see what the weather would be like before food could be determined. She wasn't cold from a lack of heating, or dirty because she'd not found a shower for months on end. Hard pressed to enjoy any of it, Thorn drew back the blankets with an irritated sigh and got out of the bed, half-expecting something underneath the large bedframe to grab her ankles and yank her beneath.

In the bathroom, she inspected a few nasty-looking cuts on her leg and thigh that hadn't been healing right. Finding disinfectant above the sink, she treated the wounds methodically. It hurt, a lot, and holding in a slew of expletives that likely would've woken the whole house took a concerted effort, but within five minutes the throbbing had mostly stopped and she was able to leave the bathroom.

She dressed in warm clothes, secured one blade under her sleeve, and another under her trouser leg, and left her room. She spent the better part of an hour wandering through the house, learning all the exits and hiding places. Despite its modernity, the house did not seem like the cage she'd expected.

She explored the grounds next, then the garage and the garden, finding *far* more flowers in the garden than was normal. The gardener clearly had an odd obsession with kaleidoscopic displays.

As she wandered between the rows in the garden, taking in the massive variety of flowers, vines, fruit trees and berry bushes, petals cascaded down from trees that seemed to have an abundance of them and coated her like snowflakes. Somehow, even as the blossoms fell, the trees did not look bare.

She pulled some of the petals out of her hair to examine. They were white when they fell, but as she held them, the petals turned indigo, then lilac, then burgundy. They danced out of her palm and floated back onto the tree they'd fallen from, folding into the stems like they'd never left at all.

She stared at the magical plants and found herself admiring them. There was nothing sinister in the garden. Nothing creeping. Reaching up, she traced her fingers over the petals, prompting them to shudder and change colour three times. Dropping her hand, she gazed at the flowers for another minute, a strange feeling burgeoning in her chest, before carrying on.

Once she felt like she had the whole place figured out, she returned to the kitchen and rummaged through the shelves and refrigerator until she found all of her favourite foods. If there was one nice thing she could say about Nithin, it was that he knew how to stock a kitchen. Although she supposed Kol probably had something to do with it.

She knew little of Suriias, and less about their social interactions, so she had no idea if it was normal for a sbura and a frai to live together, but Thorn reckoned they had been friends for a while. Photograph after photograph of them lined the shelves and adorned the walls: them standing in fine attire, glasses in hand, smiles wide; on the mountainside, covered in mud, Kol in the midst of pulling Nithin to the ground; in front of a coach, both appearing to be admiring its paintjob; at some meeting with a group, both formal and unsmiling. But no matter the setting, it was clear that they were always together. Like brothers.

Coffee in hand, pastries baking, Thorn meandered into the library and slowly perused the shelves. Adventures, mysteries, thrillers, romances, histories and more besides. She traced her fingers over the titles. There was something almost hypnotising about being around books. She'd never had the luxury of having her pick before.

With an appreciative sigh, determined to inspect them all later, she headed back to the kitchen. Picking up all the food she'd left out, she made a bowl of mixed fruit and sat on the table, staring out at the garden and thinking of the petal plants. It was hard not to feel like a traitor to her own kind just for wanting to know what the plant was called and why the petals danced.

'Don't get used to it,' she muttered. 'It's all for show.'

A sudden creaking on the stairs made her stiffen and she watched the doorway with narrowed eyes.

Kol walked in seconds later. He was dressed casually, in a grey shirt and jeans, his black hair brushed back from his face. But even so casual, Suriias carried themselves differently. It was innate. They knew they were the dominant species and walked as if they had nothing to fear. He shuffled into the kitchen barefoot and unbothered, clearly half-awake, and smiled dopily at her as he poured himself coffee.

'How'd you sleep?' he asked as he added almond milk to his coffee. 'If it's too warm, I can show you how to adjust the temperature.'

'I slept fine.'

'See the library?'

She nodded, lips pursed. She'd preferred being alone.

'I thought we were going to try and be friends,' he said, leaning against the counter and blowing on the surface of his coffee. 'Come on. Am I really that bad?'

'You're okay,' she allowed. 'For now.'

A bark of laughter tore out of him, but he seemed pleased, rather than put off, by her acerbic response. 'Do you want me to show you the city?' he asked. 'Nith's going to be occupied with Thistle for a while.'

Thorn barely tampered down the urge to gag.

'Come on,' he pressed. 'You can bring that knife you're poorly hiding if you want. But I suggest you don't stab anyone with it.' The quirk of his lips and glint in his cat-eyes told her he was teasing.

A day in the city was not an appealing suggestion, but if she knew the city, she'd be able to find Veryn. And finding Veryn was one of two things she cared about. Thistle being the other.

'Even if Nithin's name weren't enough to keep you safe – which, for the record, it is,' he added, 'I won't let anything happen to you. You're not a human runaway anymore. You're one of us. Not even the hunters will touch you.'

'Hunters?'

'The Unit of Prestigious Hunters,' he said, somehow packing a remarkable amount of sarcasm into the name. 'That's what they call themselves.'

'Blue uniforms?'

He nodded.

'We call them Spotters.'

'Not inaccurate, I suppose. And definitely less obnoxious,' he mused, more to himself than to her. 'Although perhaps they deserve their ridiculous name.'

'You're not that intimidating. Spotters and vrykos are scarier.'

'No. They really aren't.'

'Do you know many vrykos?' she asked, pulse quickening.

After a beat of deliberation, he nodded and shrugged. 'I don't care what anyone is so long as they're decent.'

'Lucky you.'

He set down his mug. 'I'm not taking you into the city to throw you to the vrykos. I won't let anything happen to you.'

She thought about that for a moment before pushing aside her empty bowl and standing.

'Fine,' she grunted. 'Let's go.'

'Awesome,' he said, pumping his fist back.

She trailed after him with all the excitement of one about to get their teeth pulled. They paused in the hallway to put on their shoes, and it was only when she'd finished lacing her boots that she realised he was staring at her feet.

'What?'

'First coffee, and then shoes,' he declared. 'You can't walk around in those.'

'These are fine.' She'd found them in a donation bin a few years before. They had seen her through some of the worst runs of her life. The previous pair had caused her heels to bleed.

'They're held together by tape and luck. Stop being stubborn. Nith's going to insist upon it anyways. People will think we're mistreating our guests if you walk around like that.'

Not remotely troubled by her choice of footwear, Thorn stepped around him without bothering to reply and walked out into the brisk winter morning. It was a damp, grey day, with a bite in the air that went straight through her nose to attack her lungs.

They took Nithin's shiny coach and flew into the heart of Courtenz. For a time, the flight was almost peaceful, but the closer they got to the inner city, the more air traffic increased. The sky was soon far too filled with humming coaches for Thorn's liking. She missed the solitude of the mountains so much already.

'Does it scare you?' she asked abruptly.

'What?' he enquired. 'Shopping? Absolutely. I hate queues. And crowds.'

'Flying.'

'You mean the coach?'

'No, the tree.'

'Don't go in coaches often, I'm guessing.'

'Yesterday was my first.'

'Really?'

'Where would I get a coach?'

'There are stories of humans who have dozens.'

'Those are lies. Humans don't have anything.'

He let out a long sigh, but instead of responding to the biting remark, he said, 'Do you want to drive?'

It was her turn to be surprised. 'What?'

'Here.' He clicked three switches on the dashboard and then slid the wheel over to her with all the confidence of someone sure that their companion was up to the task. Breezily, he added, 'Just don't fly us into anything. Insurance is a nightmare.'

Thorn, who had never driven or flown once in her life, gripped the wheel so tightly her bones began to ache. Yet she felt oddly giddy at the prospect of flying and sat up straighter, eyes flicking from the ground below to the approaching city in the distance.

The group of islands were collectively known as the Kassiterides, although Thorn was sure her ancestors had once called them something else. She knew the island they were on was Itannera, with Courtenz, the capital city and most populated area, but she knew little else about the geography of where she lived.

Courtenz was an old city, renamed after the Suriias overpowered the humans in the Red Sky Rebellion. Much of the architecture dated back to the height of human might, but it was the first time Thorn had ever really been able to appreciate it. Most of the time she ran past buildings. She never got to admire them. Yet doing so now filled her with bitter longing for a life she had never known.

The closer they flew to the high-rise buildings and colourful mass of flying coaches, the more uneasy Thorn felt. More and more Suriias began to pop up on all sides, too, and seeing them fly past the coach was beyond unnerving.

As they passed the first skyscraper, Kol took over driving again and she sat stiffly, fingers curled into the fabric of her jeans, anxiety spiking in her chest.

When they landed and parked beside the river, Thorn couldn't bring herself to get out. She wanted to vomit, and she was far too aware of every Suriia on the street who would happily see her dead.

Kol came around to her door and opened it. He bent down and held out his hand. 'I meant what I said,' he whispered. 'You're safe with me.'

She eyed his hand dubiously. 'You're really scarier than a vryko?'

'The first vryko who comes near you will be dust. I promise.'

He was either the world's best actor or an anomaly of some kind, because she couldn't spot a single trace of dishonesty in his face.

She didn't take his hand, but she stepped out of the coach. The cold air hit her lungs sharply and she started to cough again, unable to fully shake the itching, seizing feeling, like spiders had made webs inside her lungs.

'You okay?'

Forcing herself to breathe through her nose, she put a hand over her face to warm the air. 'Fine,' she choked out behind her hand. 'Got a cold.'

'That sounds worse than a cold.'

'I'm fine,' she reiterated and walked past him toward the café.

The architecture of the building was jagged and crude, industrial and magical. The vibrant sign above the entrance kept rewriting itself to advertise different specials.

A gust of coffee-scented air wafted over Thorn as the doors opened before them. The stifling humidity that came from multiple stoves being utilised at once instantly relaxed her lungs, and she dragged in a rattling breath.

'Well, well, well,' crowed a voice to her right, making her stiffen. It was a ghul. Yellow eyes and elongated fingers gave him away. 'I love when humans deliver themselves.'

Kol stepped between them. 'Watch it,' he warned. Suddenly, his eyes were black, his teeth fanged, his fingers sharp, deadly talons.

The rapid change in his appearance drew the notice of the entire café and silence swallowed the previously animated chatter. Thorn's gaze flicked from onlooker to onlooker curiously. The patrons seemed to be collectively on edge, but she could not have said why, only that it was Kol they watched, not her or the ghul. It was like walking into a room of dogs and realising she stood beside the wolf king.

After a moment's staring match, the ghul sat back down. Hatred filled his beady eyes and left Thorn feeling queasy and exposed. When Kol glanced back at her, his eyes reverting to their normal gold-black, the ghul licked his teeth menacingly. Kol didn't notice, and she didn't bother to tell him.

'Want to leave?' he asked, sotto voce.

'Let's just get coffee and go,' she muttered.

'Okay.'

No one else said anything as they joined the queue of patrons, all grumbling about the early hour and how much they wanted to be anywhere else. When the pair reached the counter, Kol gestured from Thorn to the prico behind the till, who looked bored out of her mind. Pricos were an offshoot of vrykos and vylkas, although Thorn didn't know what that meant in actuality. She could only tell because of their eyes: blindingly cerulean and often swirling with magic.

The eyes gave away most. Even humans.

'Asa, this is Thorn,' introduced Kol, gesturing between them. 'Make sure the staff know she's with us. Nithin's fiancée is also going to be coming by.'

Asa nodded. 'Of course, Kol.'

Thorn looked over at him as Asa turned away, thoroughly nonplussed by the ease with which he existed. 'Do you have a tab or something?'

'Nithin does,' said Kol. 'Bless him for it. I've a monstrous coffee addiction.'

Their coffees only took a minute and when he suggested they go for a walk, she agreed with dizzying relief. The ghul leered at her as she passed by, but she managed to ignore him.

The city air felt painfully cold after the café's warmth and Thorn cradled the cup close to her chest as they walked toward the park. She tried not to look up and notice how many coaches filled the air above her, how many Suriias walked the streets.

Thankfully, a few minutes later, Kol led her off the main footpath and onto the lane that led into the park. It was a tranquil, blessedly serene section of the city. Leaves dotted the ground, crunching underfoot, and the number of Suriias lessened the further they walked. And as the trees enveloped them, she was finally able to breathe enough to take a sip of coffee.

They meandered down a winding path with flowers and trees dotting the sides until they came to a picnic table in the corner of a small field.

Kol gestured for her to sit, which she did, belatedly.

The wooden bench was worn from years of use and bearing the brunt of heavy rains, yet determinedly sturdy; a few previous occupants had carved characters into the wood. She glared at the words until her eyes burned and she turned her attention towards the pond. If she tuned out the city around the park, she could almost pretend she was just in some valley in the mountains.

'You're so quiet,' Kol remarked, drawing her attention back to him. 'Am I that boring?'

She shrugged and fidgeted with the lid of her coffee.

'Stop being so cynical, Rose. We're not all bad.'

'My name's Thorn.'

'I know.' He took a sip of his coffee, a roguish smile on his face. 'But you're not so thorny all the time. In exchange, you can call me whatever you want.'

'Fine, *Charcoal.*'

He choked on his coffee and liquid sprayed out of the corner of his mouth. Wiping his lips and chin, cheeks somewhat reddened with embarrassment, he said, 'You should tell Nith that one. He'll love it. He called me Holey Koly for years.'

'Why?'

'I got impaled on a fence in one of my more spectacular flying mishaps. I was drunk. I should clarify that. I'm normally a fantastic flier.'

'How was the coach?'

'Oh, no coach,' he drawled with a broadening grin. 'Just me.'
'Wings?'
He bobbed his head.

Although he'd clearly meant the story to be funny, the prospect of wings sent a curl of foreboding through her, and she tried not to imagine what his wings looked like. 'Is there much more to this place?' she asked, casting about for a change of topic.

'Want to explore?'

'Sure.'

They stood in unison and set off down an empty, tree-lined path. Birds chirped above and a small hare thumped past.

Thorn watched Kol, still remembering the change in the café. Despite her fears, a part of her was curious about something.

'Why do some Suriias change but others look mostly human?' It had always bothered her. Surely if Suriias had come from another world, they wouldn't look so similar to humans?

'Do you want to know what my mother told me?'

'There isn't a straight answer?'

'Does there need to be?'

She rolled her eyes.

Laughter left him at that, and he carried on without missing a beat. 'My mother says life is lived in levels.'

'Levels?'

'Yeah, like, one over another.' He put his hand over his coffee cup, then his cup over his hand, and then his hand back on his cup. 'Way she explained it to me is that there's a life before Salfar, too. And a life after this one. In the one before Salfar, souls are in their rawest, most volatile forms. When they die, they are reborn on Salfar, echoes of the old life still inside their soul. So, you have two forms. One in which you are the most powerful, but with less control; the other your most rational, but with less power.'

Thorn thought about that for a second and found herself completely annoyed by the implication. 'Going by that logic, when a Suriia dies on Salfar, their soul becomes human.'

Kol inclined his head, as if he believed the ridiculous story.

'That is the most ludicrous thing I have ever heard,' she said scathingly. 'Humans don't come from Suriias.'

'Humans come from Earth,' he countered. 'But souls come from the universe.'

'No, they don't.'

'Fine.' He held up a hand pacifyingly. 'I did preface it as a non-straight answer, you know? It's just one belief. It could be complete crap.'

'It's crap.'

'And you're thoroughly entitled to that belief. There are others.'

She scowled, but the anger ebbed ever so. It was a stupid idea and there was doubtless any truth to it. Suriias probably had to tell themselves bedtime stories to make their atrocities seem less awful. 'What are the others?'

'Beliefs?'

'Yeah. We know that one's crap, so what are the others?'

Kol overlooked her derision. 'Some think Salfar's in a parallel universe that cut into this one. Some think it's just a distant planet in this universe and one day our technological advances will enable us to travel there without the Tear. So the choices we've got so far are: it's a before-world, it's an after-world, it's a far away world or it's a parallel universe.'

'Helpful.'

He chuckled. 'I think the possibilities make it so much more interesting. Who needs confirmation anyhow?'

Thorn. Thorn wanted confirmation. 'The Tear?' she asked.

'The way to Salfar,' he said casually, as if this wasn't the most horrifying piece of information he could have possibly relayed. There was a way to Salfar *open*?

'Are Suriias still coming and going?'

'No.'

Thorn's hysteria hit a snag and she narrowed her eyes. 'Why not? You guys commit genocide there first before starting here?'

'No,' he corrected gently, 'we can't go back because the Tear isn't an open doorway between Earth and Salfar. It was a bridge that a group of Suriias broke through centuries ago. We're their descendants. But there is no way back. For some reason, the secrets of magic never came with an instruction manual. We can bend the world around us, sure, but no one has, like, a spell to go back.'

'You can't go back through the Tear?'

'I mean, it's not a doorway, it's now a deadly magical river that leaves this world. Do you feel like sailing across an ocean into starlight? Because I don't. And it's impossible to traverse without magic and a map. So no one really knows what happened on Salfar or why our ancestors left. They just settled here in hiding for a century and then the war broke out.'

'The war they started.'

'That is what happened, yeah.'

'There aren't stories?' she pressed, her thirst for knowledge getting the better of her.

'My mother thinks that the immortals on Salfar wanted to experience mortality. So they came here and got trapped.'

'And apparently decided to play dice with human mortality instead,' Thorn grumbled to herself.

Kol grimaced in agreement.

'Are you not immortal, then?'

'Frai are,' he said. 'But we're the only ones now. Trust me when I say it's a delicate issue. I had my head shoved into more than a few toilets when I was a kid because of it.'

Thorn wasn't interested in Suriia politics, but the limited immortality was new information. As far as she'd been aware, all Suriias were immortal.

'It's why the vrykos consume blood and souls,' he added, and he had the grace to look ashamed. 'It extends their lives to near-immortality. Same with ghuls and the consumption of human flesh. It wasn't like that on Salfar. I have no idea why or how it's different here, but it is. We've only been here three hundred years and are still figuring out the differences between the worlds. Took the first hundred for anyone to even realise their immortality was gone.'

Her blood was thrumming with anxiety at the mention of vryko consumption habits, but at least she was finally understanding why.

'Do any of you want to go back? To Salfar.'

He bobbed his head. 'But, as I said, it's a touchy subject. And if anyone knows how to get past the Lady of the Tear, they aren't telling.'

'The Lady of the Tear?'

'An ancient Suriia who can walk between the worlds.'

'How?'

Kol shrugged. 'And I've no interest in dying to find out. Apparently the forests surrounding the river are treacherous and filled with monsters that have come out of the Tear. Most who go don't come back. So Suriias largely leave the past in the past. This is home now. We just need to share it with humans.'

Thorn's stomach twisted into knots just imagining what kinds of monsters Salfar could come up with. 'Tell me something,' she said abruptly. 'You talk like you get it. Actually, you talk a great talk, I'll give you that. So how can you associate with those who kill us?'

'I don't.'

She didn't bother to smother the contemptuous snort that cut its way out of her at his claim.

'I'm serious.' Kol stopped short, a hand out. But he didn't grab her or move closer, he held his hand out in earnestness. As if he truly sought her understanding. 'Look, humans are being screwed over, but there's a lot of us who have tried for years to reverse the crap they're doing. There are countries on the continent that have made it illegal to hunt humans and have made accords. Suriias who believe humans are less than, are food or toy or whatever else, are not my friends. They have never been my friends. Okay? I want a world for everyone.'

Thorn didn't know how to process his intensity – or the claims that came with it – and instead walked on, biting the rim of her cup. But his words played over and over in her mind. Was there really a place on Earth where humans weren't hunted?

They wound their way through the gardens, the noise of Courtenz becoming distant as the inner city was swallowed by the trees.

At one point, Kol picked up a running commentary on the different types of flowers and trees they passed. He seemed especially keen to tell her about the medicinal use of each plant, root, seed and whatever else. Whether he was doing his best to keep from talking about anything problematic, or he was just weirdly fascinated with botany, Thorn found it interesting all the same. Listening to him was easy, interesting even. She had never been to a real school and she'd always wanted to learn. One of the happiest times of her and Thistle's lives was living behind the garden centre.

Listening to Kol, the park seemed a sort of contained paradise. Great bushes with blooms of every colour burst from the ground at random. There were blossoming trees with gently falling petals, flowers larger than her torso, and trees which turned out to have trick fruit that took flight and proved to be colourful birds.

He was telling her about something called a qillow tree, when a group of Suriias appeared on the other side of the path. Two vylkas and a prico. There was no missing the change in their stride when they spotted her, or the looks they exchanged with each other.

'Walking your pet?' one of the vylkas asked Kol. 'She's cute. Most look like leather.'

Kol's expression hardened. 'You want to run along.'

The vylka turned to his fellows. 'We were just admiring the new plaque,' he said, nodding to a stone pillar further ahead. 'In honour of the Sacrifice of Traitors and the end of the war.'

All three watched her, gleeful with anticipation, and Thorn's breath caught in her throat.

Kol looked from the trio to the plaque behind them. To his credit, revulsion darkened his features.

The second vylka inched towards Thorn and Kol stepped between them succinctly.

'Don't do it,' he warned, voice quiet and filled with a confidence that Thorn envied deeply. 'You're about two seconds away from ending up in jail because you touched a registered human.'

Her eyes snapped to him, dismayed. The Human Register kept track of every human claimed by a Suriia, thereby making them off limits. And, purportedly, safe. But the only way she could be on the Register was if Kol had put her there. If he'd told every Suriia that she belonged to him.

Sick horror crawled through her like a parasitic invasion and she had to force herself not to run yet. Not with the other Suriias still there.

The nearest one seemed to be weighing Kol's words. After another few seconds, he scoffed, shrugged, and carried on, his fellows falling in step beside him.

When the trio disappeared, Kol turned to her. 'Thorn—'

'Fuck you and fuck your kind.'

'Please just—'

'Leave me alone,' she snarled, turning on her heel and tearing off into the trees.

'It's not safe!'

Years of dodging Suriias meant losing Kol was easy enough. Only when she was several streets over did she slow to a walk. Her cough started anew, and she gasped and wheezed for several minutes.

But the distraction cost her.

She didn't realise how exposed she was until the sound of metal on stone made her stomach drop.

A Scuttler.

Before Thorn could even move, gunshots rang out and she ducked behind a bin. The Scuttler began to fire at the rooftop, distracted from its pursuit of Thorn. It only took her a few seconds to figure out where the shots were coming from.

A hooded figure atop the adjacent roof beckoned to her frantically; beside them, another fired back at the Scuttler with remarkably good aim.

Thorn bolted across the road and scrambled up the fire escape and onto the roof. Darting to the edge of the building, she jumped onto the adjacent roof.

Not two paces away stood a pair of humans, hoods now down, smiles welcoming.

'Thank you,' she gasped. 'Seriously. Amazing timing.'

'You should see what we can do when the bullets aren't homemade,' said the girl with a wicked laugh.

Coughing and spluttering, her lungs in complete rebellion, unable to rid herself of the relentless need to wheeze, Thorn held out her hand. 'I'm Thorn.'

The man shook it first. 'Jinx.'

'Jade,' said the woman. 'We saw you run away from that Suriia in the park and tracked you. Are you okay?'

'I am now.' Thorn brushed sweaty hair out of her eyes and grinned at them. 'It's good to see people.'

The pair were similar enough and Thorn guessed them twins, or at least remarkably identical siblings. Both had dark curly hair, hazel eyes and long lashes; they wore similar threadbare outfits and were as scarred as she was. Jade had jagged marks on her neck and cheek, and a fresh bruise on her forehead; Jinx had two sharp lines through one of his eyebrows that carried on down to the corner of his eye.

It had been so long since she'd met new humans she wanted to cry, and Thorn fell a little in love with them both in those first seconds.

'When did you last?' asked Jinx, holstering his gun in a belt that had seen better days.

'At the Speak Softlies, mostly. And I live with my best friend, but that's it.'

'Were you there the other night? The one that got busted?'

Thorn did a doubletake. 'I didn't see you there.'

'We were scouting for people in the corners,' said Jade. 'But finding renegades is harder than it looks. Most want a Suriia who'll treat them right and keep them safe.'

Thorn and Jinx both made sounds of disgust, and they exchanged looks of solidarity.

'Do you live in Courtenz?' he prompted.

She nodded. 'Can't say it's my favourite place, though.'

'Where are you from?'

'I was living in a shed on the north side outskirt borough.'

'We lived on the north side two years ago,' said Jade. 'Good hiding places.'

'What made you come here?'

'We've been gathering others like us,' said Jinx, and the way he said it, the conviction in his voice, sent a honey-like feeling straight to Thorn's bones. 'Finding them all around the city. Once we get enough people, we're going into the mountains up north. Leave Itannera. There's enough land there to get lost. To start over. To live away from the Suriias. You want to come?'

The offer ignited such an instant sense of comradery that Thorn felt something not far from heartbroken at the prospect of leaving them. Of having to return to the Suriias. But Thistle was still there.

'I can't come with you until I sort things out here,' she said, wishing so much that she could.

'Sort out what?' asked Jinx.

'We're using two Suriias to find the ones who killed our parents.'

Jinx nodded without judgement. 'Our parents were murdered too. The ghuls that did it then sold us. It took years for me to find Jade.'

'But you found each other,' said Thorn thickly, chest constricting with the rush of emotion.

Jinx wrapped an arm around his sister and kissed her temple.

'Do you want help?' said Jade, reaching out and squeezing Thorn's hand. 'We can do our best.'

'I'd love help.'

'We'll be around for a few weeks. Jinx has some buildings he wants to take care of.'

'Try and do a little damage,' he added with a wink. 'Where are you staying?'

'The obnoxiously large mansion that's up the hill from the river.'

'Which river?'

Thorn thought a moment. 'It forks at the western side of the city.'

'Soshing.'

'That's it!'

'We'll see you soon,' he promised.

'We should go,' said Jade, nodding towards the dancing lights of an approaching drone.

As they turned to leave, Jinx paused. 'It was nice to save your life, Thorn.'

'It was nice to be saved,' she replied, a smile spreading across her face.

With a last look at them, she climbed back down the fire escape and dropped into the alley. Rain was drizzling down by now, the ground slick and the sky prematurely dark.

When she got to the end of the street, she ran headlong into Kol. He was breathless, flushed and wide-eyed.

'There you are!'

She stepped away from him, good mood dying a fast death. 'I'm on the Register?'

He winced. 'Okay, I know that sounded bad.'

'Sounds really creepy.'

'It's the only way to keep you safe,' he said flatly. 'Nithin registered Thistle and later that night she messaged to say that she was bringing you. I wasn't looking for a human, Thorn. But we can't have you in the house without registering you.'

'Fine.'

'It doesn't mean anything,' he barrelled on, as if he cared enough about her opinion to bother explaining his thought process. 'Just a name. If you're caught or arrested, they won't bring you to the camps – they'll send for me.'

'So you basically own me?'

'I never said it wasn't disgusting. I said it would keep you alive.'

'You didn't have the right.'

'You're right,' he agreed. 'And I'm sorry.'

Still far from appeased, she crossed her arms over her chest. She felt unsteady on her feet, like her legs had become butter and wouldn't hold her up for long. 'I'm not your pet.'

'Good,' he said with surprising vehemence. 'You look like you'd suck at playing fetch.'

She didn't realise he was joking until his lips twitched, and then it was hard to stay furious at him. Instead, she settled for glowering.

As the truce between them grew more apparent, Kol relaxed somewhat. But then he froze. He looked her up and down, his body stiffening with a strange kind of fury. 'Why do you smell like gun powder?'

'You can smell that?' She tried not to cringe at the idea of him smelling her.

His eyes shuttered black and she thought his teeth looked sharper, though it could have been a trick of the gloom. 'Were you attacked?'

'A Scuttler.'

This admission turned his pale skin paler still. 'Are you okay?'

'I'm fine,' she muttered.

Gold returned to his eyes, and he looked passably human once more, but to her surprise, he seemed distraught.

'Thorn,' he said, oddly urgent in his delivery, 'I'm so sorry.'

'Let's just go,' she said, voice clipped. 'I want to see Thistle.'

With a grim nod, he gestured over his shoulder and led the way back to the coach.

The lights were on in the mansion when they pulled up a short while later. Kol nodded to the guards, who nodded back, and the gates opened before them.

'Why not fly straight over?' she wondered.

'We have wards up. Coaches can't just fly in. They'll be electrocuted if they try.'

'You really feel safe with someone watching you all the time?'

'We employed those guards a week before you two moved in,' said Kol, tone low and pointed. 'We never needed them. They're here for you. To protect you and Thistle.'

Thorn had no idea what to say to that, nor did she know if she was angry or appreciative. She did not want anyone spying on her, whatever the reason.

The instant they were inside the house, Kol shouted for Nithin.

'In the kitchen!' came the reply.

They wandered into the adjacent room to see Thistle sitting on the counter, her legs around Nithin's waist.

Resisting the urge to roll her eyes, Thorn looked deliberately at her face. The cut that had been throbbing must have been apparent, because Thistle instantly hopped off the counter and hurried to her side.

'You okay?'

Thorn took her hand. 'Come on.'

Kol gave her a tight smile as she passed by, but she ignored him.

Alone in the bedroom she was staying in, Thorn told Thistle about everything that had happened. But to her surprise, Thistle didn't seem as excited about it as Thorn was.

'Things could be really good here, Tor,' she said. 'Nithin's done nothing but help us. I don't want to mess that up.'

Thorn huffed. 'Yeah, because he gets something out of it.'

'As do we.'

'I thought you wanted to leave?'

'After Veryn. Not with random humans we don't know.'

'We can be with people again. *People*, Tiz. I want to be with people.'

Something she said seemed to get through and Thistle nodded after another few seconds.

'Okay,' she said begrudgingly. 'But not until we're sure they're going to help. I want a better option, Tor. Not a worse one. I'm sick of hiding.'

'That's fair,' said Thorn, hugging her tightly. 'I just hate that you have to do this. Be with Nithin.'

Thistle stepped back abruptly. 'I want this. I picked this. If you can find us something better, okay, but I like Nithin. I could even love him.'

The idea was laughable. 'Tiz, please.'

'What?'

'You can't love our enemies!'

Thistle crossed her arms. She was so thin and small; it was impressive how much defiance she could pack into one look. It also emphasised her fragility. Even now, Thorn thought of Thistle as breakable. Someone Nithin could easily overpower. But her next words packed a punch.

'I'm sick of your close-mindedness, Tor.'

Rage made Thorn bristle and it consumed her fear like an inferno. 'Think of our parents and say that to me again.'

Tears brimmed instantly in Thistle's eyes. 'That's not fair.'

'Yes, it is.'

Thistle threw up her hands. 'Why do I have to suffer in street corners and shadows because vrykos killed our parents? I hate them too, Thorn! Nithin's not like that. Kol's not like that. I found us two perfect options and you're determined not to even give them a chance.'

A sudden knock at the door made them both start.

Thistle let out a stilted, shuddering sigh and wiped her eyes before walking over to answer it.

Nithin and Kol stood in the threshold. Nithin took one look at Thistle's tearstained face and brought her into his arms.

'What's the matter?' he asked in a soft tone Thorn had never heard him use before. Thistle didn't say anything and he looked to Thorn. His eyes narrowed, as if he were making a million observations and turning them over one by one in his mind. Then, rather than voice them, he said to Thistle, 'Do you want to get out of here?'

Thistle nodded, clearly taking comfort in his presence. For her part, Thorn stared at Nithin's hands on Thistle's arms, the violent urge to remove them burning through her like an inextinguishable wildfire.

The pair departed without sparing either her or Kol a moment's more of attention, leaving Thorn feeling hollowed out and indignant. Her body still roiling with tension from the fight, she shoved away from the wall and walked over to the window. Scowling down, she watched them cross the stone pavement towards Nithin's fancy coach. Nithin kept his arm around Thistle's shoulder the entire time, whispering in her ear. From so far away, they were picture perfect.

Kol joined Thorn and leaned against the glass, cutting off the view of the coach. 'I'm sorry,' he said again. 'I knew it had happened, but I didn't know there was a plaque. I'll send a request to have it taken down. Perhaps it means little, but I hope it's something.'

Thorn weighed the sincerity in his tone and found it right there on the surface, not hidden behind platitudes or excuses. 'Okay,' she grunted, suddenly doubting her words to Thistle not seconds before. 'I don't want to go there again.'

He bowed his head. 'I promise I'll never take you there again.'

Strained silence followed this exchange. Kol didn't leave, but nor did she ask him to.

'Do you want to watch a movie?' he asked after almost a minute of strange quietude.

'I don't like Suriia movies.'

'I figured. C'mon.'

Curious, she trailed after him, down the spiral staircase and into the luxurious, yet remarkably cosy sitting room. She claimed one of the squishy chairs, drawing her legs into her chest. But she didn't relax. She couldn't. She remained stiff-backed and counted Kol's every breath out of habit. She'd know the second he moved.

He pulled a box from the closet and gestured for her to peruse it.

'Vintage human films,' he elaborated. 'Pick one.'

Thorn gaped at him before springing from the chair. She set upon the box like it was filled with buried treasure and began rooting through it. The covers all had vibrant, colourful images; some were drawings, some were photographs with graphics. The fonts were all different shapes and sizes, but the language was mostly English. Some were in Polish, a language she'd never heard with her own ears but knew existed on the continent. She recognised one of the words from a book her mother had owned in the language, a remnant of the world before. There was a third language too, one she couldn't guess. But they were human films. Every one of them.

'How do you even have these?' she asked, aghast. 'I thought they'd all been burned.'

'They weren't burned. Most are in the libraries and museums, but plenty of collectors have their own collections. My brother-in-law loaned these to me.'

Not sure how she felt about Suriias hoarding human films, Thorn plucked one at random from the pile and handed it to him. The photographs on the back told her it was a black and white film, made centuries before. He grinned and put it into the player. They took opposite sides of the sofa and Kol turned off the lights.

She watched each scene with almost religious dedication. It was a lovely story. Beautifully overblown and dramatic, but in a world so simple, so utterly foreign to Thorn, that she stared at the screen and wondered what it could possibly have been like to live at a time where humans ruled Earth. To be able to travel at will, to see the world, to marry and go to school. To be able to sleep in a bed at night without having to strike a bargain and clutch your knife. Thorn couldn't imagine it – not really – but she felt addicted to the notion, and hardly allowed herself to blink.

When the film broke for intermission, Kol threw a piece of chocolate at her. It tumbled into her lap. 'Would you relax?' he urged. 'We're not watching a horror movie.'

She picked up the piece of chocolate and smashed it between her fingers. 'The last time I relaxed, three vrykos broke into our shed and attacked us. They almost raped Thistle before I managed to kill them.'

Clearly expecting anything but this, his whole body went stiff and whatever quippy retort he'd had ready seemed to die on his tongue.

'The worst thing,' she continued, not sure how she felt about his astonishment, 'is that's not even notable when you compare it to everything else that's happened. There was a time I didn't kill them fast enough … and all I can think is, "What if I can't get to her this time?" Nithin's making that more unlikely by the day. I know you want to be friends, and on some level, I can appreciate that. But you scare me, okay? You scare me and I can't relax. If that bothers you, I can go upstairs.'

He turned to fully face her and held out his hands. 'I'm sure it won't mean anything to you,' he murmured, 'but Nithin and

I both voted for the death sentence for Suriias who rape, kill or eat humans.'

That took her by surprise. 'Did it pass?'

'No.'

'Of course not.'

He sighed heavily and then cleared his throat. 'I'm sorry.'

'For throwing chocolate at me? You're forgiven.'

'No,' he said pointedly. 'I'm sorry you went through that. I'm sorry Thistle did. I'm sorry you've been hunted and abused. It's not all right. It's not fair. I hate it and I wish it was different. So, I'm sorry.'

For a long time, they gazed at each other, both weighing the uncertainty in the eyes of the other.

And then Thorn said, voice barely louder than a whisper, 'You're the first Suriia who's ever apologised to me.'

'I mean it.'

'Thank you.'

With a determined nod, he clapped his hands on his legs, stood, and disappeared into the kitchen. He returned a minute later with a bar of chocolate and two cans of fizzy drink.

'Come on,' he said, holding out a can and the chocolate bar. 'A movie's not a movie unless you're eating.'

She eyed the chocolate for several seconds before taking it.

The movie ended an hour later, but rather than suggest they turn in for bed, he put on another and went to fetch more chocolate.

'I know you won't believe me,' he said when he returned, voice low as the credits rolled and the orchestral background symphony picked up a tranquil tune, 'but I couldn't imagine killing you. I look at you and I see someone worth knowing. I don't blame you for hating me, but just know that I don't hate you. Even if we disagree on things, even if we ever have a fight,

I won't hurt you. I won't turn you in. I swear. And I hope one day you believe that.'

If words could have a physical impact, those had somehow punched and cradled her at the same time. They left her breathless and sick and hopeful.

Hopeful.

With slow, methodical bites, Thorn finished the chocolate bar, not taking her eyes off the screen. For some reason, she didn't want to leave it at that. Hesitant, she looked at him. Wondering.

He glanced over. 'All good?'

'If it's any consolation,' she muttered, 'I've had nightmares about everyone and everything all my life. Even Thistle hurts me in my dreams. Last night I dreamed that Nithin raped us both before tearing out Thistle's throat. And then he killed me as I screamed.' She picked at the corner of her nail, stomach in knots. 'But, weirdly, you weren't there. So, for now, the only one who's never killed me in my sleep is you. You probably will tonight, but you haven't yet.'

He held out another bar of chocolate succinctly, a soft, sad smile gracing his lips. 'I hope your only dream of me involves chocolate.'

To her irritation, the smile she gave him in return was entirely genuine.

CHAPTER THREE
The Tangled Vines of Dreams

A sennight at the mansion passed before Thorn suggested they go into the city to find Veryn. To her disappointment, Thistle declined, saying there was no way to sneak out without Nithin knowing and asking questions. Questions neither of them could or would answer. Thorn agreed, but Thistle's refusals kept up as the nights went by. Until, one night, Nithin and Kol left on a business trip and they were alone in the mansion for the first time.

'Will you come tonight?' she asked as they ate dinner on the floor of the sitting room, one of Kol's human movies playing on the television.

Thistle nodded after swallowing a mouthful of pasta. 'Of course.'

Relief slammed into Thorn and she felt better than she had in days. The niggling feeling that the Suriias would convince Thistle to join their side increased daily, and the verbal confirmation that they were still on the same team meant everything to Thorn.

They waited until the sun had fully set before sneaking out of the mansion and setting off down the road that led to the city. Thorn hadn't come up with a good excuse for Kol and Nithin if they were caught leaving the mansion, but she supposed she'd say she wanted to go to a Speak Softly.

'I'm sorry about the other day,' said Thistle as they meandered along the roadside, their breaths forming clouds around them. 'You're right. I know you're right. But I do think Nithin wants to help humans.'

'Maybe,' said Thorn, although she had trouble believing it. 'But we have to find Veryn and then we have to find people. We owe our parents that much. Don't we?'

Thistle sighed heavily. 'You're right.'

Thorn took Thistle's hand, lacing their fingers together and squeezing her apology. 'Is he really that good?'

Thistle let out a hysterical giggle, delighted by the subject change, and launched into a far too graphic description of Nithin's capabilities with his tongue. Thorn blushed six shades of red just listening to her, but Thistle's happiness made her heart light, and things felt back to normal by the time they reached the city. Thistle's joy was one of the only things she cared about. She didn't want to be the reason it diminished.

'So,' said Thistle, drawing her hood up as they stepped down a side path that had a blessedly abundant assortment of trees to obscure them from view. 'What is the plan?'

'Find a vryko, ask him, kill him after.'

'Simple enough.'

'I hate complicated.'

Thistle slung an arm around her shoulders. 'This I know.'

Silence took hold as it always did when they reached the side streets, moving through the shadows like the night incarnate. Thorn's mother used to tell her that she'd been born with dark eyes and dark hair because the universe wanted to protect her. She could blend in with the forest during the day and fold into the darkness like a child of the moon.

An alley appeared up ahead and Thorn signed to Thistle to follow her. At the end of the alley, they crouched low and surveyed the road ahead. The main street was littered with Suriias of all types.

Thorn didn't think she was ever going to get used to the activity of the city. To the neon lights and the bright advertisements and the constant smoke that filled the air. Music spilled out of buildings, clashing with the endless hum of the coaches above them and the crackle of magic from all around, and the heady smell of potions that mixed with the salty smells of food and drink only added to the noxious mixture.

What was perhaps most surreal were the rampant signs of poverty that cropped up in the corners of the shimmering urban landscape, like a secret incapable of being contained. Thorn didn't know what to make of it. Suriias hunted humans like animals and yet it was clear, judging by life on the ground level of Courtenz, that there was disparity amongst Suriias, too. She and Thistle gave a wide berth to more than one figure sitting or sleeping on the ground.

I can't wait to get back to the mountains, she signed to Thistle when they finally found a road that was empty.

Thistle nodded thoughtfully. *Got to love the food.*

I'll give you the food, she signed back. *Especially the chocolate.*

They grinned at each other and carried on, hiding whenever they heard approaching footfalls or the rattle of metal. Thankfully, the vryko bar wasn't hard to find.

Vryko bars were the stuff of nightmares. According to her father, they'd been worse when there were more humans around. Thorn had been inside one, but she refused to bring Thistle.

They stood in the shadows and watched until, at last, she recognised one. He'd been there the night her parents died. He had a raspy laugh.

Exchanging nods, the pair dogged the vryko down a side street. As soon as the road was clear of other pedestrians, the air still, Thorn bolted, slamming the vryko against the wall. Thistle appeared beside them and pressed her gun into his temple. When she was focused, Thistle was the best backup in the world.

Thorn drew her knife and pressed it to his throat. 'Where's Veryn?' she sibilated.

The vryko sniggered contemptuously, reddish spittle flying out from between his lips. 'I'm not telling you.'

'You want to see what this knife can do? Tell me, or you're dead.'

He yanked his left arm free and made to swipe at Thorn's face, and Thistle fired on reflex. His body crumpled and blood began to pool on the road.

'Sorry!' cried Thistle. There was blood on her face and in her hair.

Similarly coated, Thorn wiped the sticky, copper-scented spatter from her face. 'No, you did good.' She summoned a reassuring smile. 'Better him dead than us. Come on.'

'I think that's about all I can handle tonight,' said Thistle. 'We've confirmed Veryn's alive and in the city. That's enough to go on.'

'We knew that already. I told Jinx that.'

'Then why don't we wait to hear from Jinx? We'll have better luck doing that than coming out here, picking them off one by one.'

Thorn wondered if Thistle didn't realise that she *liked* picking them off one by one. Humans had been hunted for years. It was time they hunted a little. The vrykos had it coming.

But she had a strange feeling that Thistle wouldn't understand. Not really. And the last thing Thorn wanted was for one more problem to chip away at the cracks she felt in their relationship.

Back at the mansion hours later, they bade each other goodnight and Thorn crawled into bed. Her skin smelled like sweat, smoke and copper. A reminder of the unfinished evening.

When at last she fell asleep, she dreamed vivid, colourful, sickening nightmares, and she awoke drenched in sweat and still exhausted.

Voices below her window distracted her from her fears, and it took her a second to realise Nithin and Kol were back from their trip. She sat up, rubbing sleep from her eyes.

It was only when she heard someone pause outside her door and then carry on that she got out of bed, feeling groggy but curious.

On the ground outside the door was a small box, a note stuck to the front.

She picked it up with a frown and unfolded the paper. It read: *I know there's no tape, but I hope you like them anyway.*

Perplexed, she closed the door and walked back to the bed. Sitting down on the edge, curling one of her legs beneath her, she opened the box.

Boots. Made of good leather, supple and well crafted.

She took them out and slipped them on over her socks. They went halfway up her calves and she was able to tuck a knife down the side. There was even a small loop to tuck the blade into so it wouldn't move.

Something else in the box caught her eye. A small thin parcel. She unrolled it and let it fall into her hand. On the inside of the paper was a single word: *Iron.*

She raised the dagger to the light. The blade was heavier than her father's and so sharp she had little doubt it could cut her skin with the softest swipe.

She stood and walked down the hall to Kol's room. She knocked twice.

The door opened to reveal a half-dressed, messy-haired, sleepy-eyed Kol. He leaned against the doorframe and nodded to her feet. 'They fit?'

'You know they do.'

He scratched the back of his head, barely able to suppress his smirk. 'Yeah, I asked Thistle your size.'

'Why?'

'Consider it an apology for the park. Besides, you'll be able to run even faster if your shoes work. I thought you'd appreciate that.'

A laugh left her lips without her permission and his grin eclipsed his whole face.

'I'm going to get breakfast,' she said, thumbing over her shoulder. 'I just wanted to say thank you.'

'You're welcome,' he replied. 'Give me ten minutes and we can go out. I'll show you the real gardens. No plaques, I promise. Just good old flowers and trees and a pond or two.'

'Don't you have work?'

'I just got back from work. I'm sick of work. Let me show you some place nice.'

She hesitated.

'Please,' he said cajolingly. 'Let me make up for the other day. Come on.'

She found herself agreeing before her mind caught up with her mouth. 'Can Thistle come?'

He wiggled his eyebrows. 'If you can convince her to leave Nith's bed, sure.'

'Gross.'

'I'm just telling it like it is.'

'I'm going to vomit on you.'

A low laugh resonated from his throat as he stepped back from the door. 'I'll be down in ten,' he said. 'Get a coat.'

Not remotely sure why she was even giving him a chance, Thorn retrieved her ratty coat from the bedroom she was using, slipped her gun into her jeans, and went to Nithin and Thistle's door. She knocked twice.

'What, Kol?' called Nithin.

'It's Thorn,' she said loudly.

A moment later, Thistle ducked out of the bedroom, a sheet around her torso. Her straight black hair was untidy, her eyes dancing with ease and good humour.

'Do you guys want to come to the gardens with us?' said Thorn. 'Please.'

'You and Kol?'

'Yeah.'

To her delight, Thistle nodded. 'Give me ten minutes,' she said before disappearing back into the bedroom.

Thorn meandered downstairs and shuffled aimlessly about the foyer until Kol came down. He was dressed in an expensive looking coat, hair brushed neatly, and she eyed him critically for a second. It was hard to tell if his taste was incongruous to his easy-going personality, or if it was the other way around.

'They coming?' he queried.

She nodded and stepped aside as he opened the door. A rush of air filled the room and she could smell dozens of types of flowers. 'You guys have a wicked garden,' she mused aloud. 'It's pretty.'

He cocked an eyebrow. 'Was that a compliment?'

'I was complimenting the garden. Calm down.'

'It's my garden.'

She snorted. 'Have you ever even set foot in it? Rich Suriias don't like dirt, I'm told.'

He stopped short, a curious expression on his face. 'Are you serious?'

'Wow, the rich really can't take a joke,' she said dryly.

'It's not that,' he said, rolling his eyes. 'Frai get their magic from nature. No one touches that garden but me.'

'Okay …'

'You really don't know anything about us, do you?' he noted, staring at her in such a way that it dissolved the angry retort that danced to her tongue at his words. There was nothing mocking in his tone. He sounded somewhat saddened.

She didn't know what to make of that.

A bashful look suddenly stole his frown, and he ran a hand through his hair, smiling crookedly. 'Do you want to get food on the drive or eat there? There's an outdoor café that's right on one of the lakes. It's nice.'

'Are there Suriias?'

'It's usually pretty deserted.'

'Sure.'

He gestured towards the coach and they headed across the driveway. It was a cool, breezy morning and she hugged her thin, threadbare coat around her torso. The move didn't go unnoticed.

'Didn't Nith get you new clothes?'

'I'm wearing them.'

'Not the coat?'

'I like my coat.'

'You're wearing my boots.'

'I like the boots.'

This response prompted a devilish grin. 'What if I get you a coat?'

'I may not like it.'

'Got the knife?'

'Yes.'

'Good.'

'Good?'

He bowed his head, suddenly more sombre than he'd been a second before. 'I knew the risks and the stories, but I didn't truly realise how bad it was until the other day. I'm sorry for that. I won't let anyone touch you, I mean that, but I feel better knowing you're armed.'

'Guess you weren't lying about the iron,' she said.

'I'd never lie about something like that. Iron is illegal for a reason. Don't wave it around unless you're in trouble. That'll get me in trouble, too.'

Before Thorn could reply, Thistle and Nithin stepped out of the manor and made their way over. Thistle's new attire was striking. Where Thorn still wore her same coat and jeans, Thistle was wearing an outfit that looked *costly*. That it was a dress, and paired impractical shoes to boot, left Thorn feeling strange. What if they needed to run?

Everyone clambered into the coach and Nithin drove onto the road which led out of town. When they went left at the fork in the main road, he raised the coach into the air, and they flew over the waters that separated the side of the island Nithin lived on from the side with Courtenz.

Thistle squeezed her hand and Thorn turned.

Are you okay? she signed.

Thorn nodded. *I'm fine.* As she lowered her hand, she caught Kol's eye in the mirror. He was watching her curiously.

'What?' she asked.

'Where'd you learn sign language?'

'It's not a language,' she said. 'We made it up.'

Kol twisted in his seat. 'Can you teach me?' he asked. 'I'm a fast learner.'

'Why would you want to learn a language that isn't even a language?'

'If it's used and understood, it's a language. Being used by two doesn't make it of less value. And besides, if I learn, that's *three.*'

After exchanging a look with Thistle, she nodded. 'What do you want to learn?'

'How do you sign "What's up?"'

Thorn rolled her eyes and showed him a few of the gestures she and Thistle had made up when they were children. Kol copied her perfectly. Amused, she taught him another, and then another. Somehow showing him didn't seem like betraying their childhood secret – the one that had saved them from so many Suriias when speaking would have killed them. Somehow it felt like letting him in on the secret. Like he was part of their tiny group.

A sudden, peculiar feeling took hold as Thorn found herself imagining what growing up would have been like with someone like Kol around. Thistle was her partner, her sister, her shadow and her guard; she was the same for Thistle. But she'd never been able to lower her guard. Not once. Idly, Thorn wondered what Kol would have been if he wasn't Suriia. If he was someone she could trust.

The thought made her sadder than almost any she'd had that week.

She finished teaching Kol how to sign 'Are you okay?' and returned her attention to the scenery beyond the window, heart heavy and jaw clenched.

Although the inner city was built up and overwhelming, with flying machines and neon lights and more technology than Thorn could begin to comprehend, the Suriias kept a clear division between the cities and the countryside. Drones combed the wilderness for signs of stray humans, but overall the air was quieter, the noise mostly wind or rustling grass, and the further they flew from magic and industry, the better Thorn felt.

Sooner than she expected, gates appeared with a sign over the entrance reading: ASHLAND GARDENS. Thorn snorted.

'The irony kills me too,' said Kol.

Nithin lowered the coach onto the road and drove slowly up the hill, letting them take in the view.

Thorn had never seen so many flowers in all her life. Some she recognised instantly, others she'd never seen before; most more fantastical than she could have ever envisioned.

The sun was tentatively shining out from behind the clouds when they stepped out of the coach. Thistle looped her arm through Thorn's, and they followed Nithin and Kol down the path towards the gorgeous arrangements. The park was so large it seemed more like its own ecosystem than a simple garden and everything smelled of petals and blossoms and sweet grasses.

As they made their way down the winding path, Kol began naming all the plants without even glancing at the descriptions and titles.

When he paused for a breath, Thistle asked, 'So why do frai like plants so much?'

Kol eyed Thorn for a second before turning his attention to Thistle. 'Our immortality is tied to the earth. We can only live so long as the world thrives. Without the earth, we're dead.'

'If it's any consolation, brother,' said Nithin drolly, 'I can't survive without sex. One of us will far outlast the other.'

'Why?' asked Thorn before she could stop herself.

Nithin regarded her for a moment, verdant eyes glinting in the sunlight. To her surprise, his reply came without sarcasm. 'On Salfar, every source of creation has an embodiment. Earth and air create, therefore frai; blood and soul create, therefore vrykos; death and flesh create, therefore ghuls; sex and desire create, therefore sbura.

'Back on Salfar, each group had its own tribe. Ruled themselves. At one point or other there was a king who united the tribes and the magicks all started mixing together: the pricos, who are descended from the vylkas and vrykos, formed their own race; the shapeshifters, born without race or gender, can be every form because they have no true form. And so on and so forth …'

'I never realised that,' said Thistle.

A smile spread across Nithin's face and he turned his head, capturing her in a kiss.

At some point, they branched off, not having stopped whispering into each other's ears and kissing every three seconds, leaving Thorn and Kol alone.

A flower-scented breeze picked up, sending chills down her spine, but then Kol took her hand, and she found that she was shaking for an entirely different reason. One she wasn't sure she was okay with or not. And when Kol stopped and showed her a plant which could cure migraines, his words danced into her mind, chasing away all doubts. Like magic.

She dropped his hand instantly.

He made no mention of it and they carried on. The park seemed almost endless and to her great relief, they ran into no one on their walk.

Around midday, Thistle and Nithin rejoined them, and Kol led the way to a café on the lake. The view of the gardens was spectacular and the table they sat at floated magically around the lake. A bridge appeared between it and the other islands whenever anyone placed their foot out. Like it could predict where someone wanted to go at any given moment.

Thorn was deeply unsettled by that, but trailed after Thistle anyway. Taking a seat at the table, she glared out across the water. Mist rose off the surface in places, and small creatures whose name she didn't know darted in and out of grasses on the other side of the bank. They were tiny beings, but far from helpless. She'd heard stories of the creatures creeping into human tents in the wilderness and biting their victims to death while they slept. Her mother called them Nibblers, but what their real name or purpose was, Thorn hadn't a clue.

'You look a million miles away,' said Thistle.

'It's the quiet.'

'You like the quiet.'

'Yeah,' said Thorn. 'But this sounds different. This is fake quiet.'

They gazed at each other until Kol and Nithin arrived a minute later with trays of coffee and sandwiches.

Fake was the best moniker Thorn could give the Suriia run world. Like an invasive species that had taken hold, killing everything in its path that didn't conform to the new way.

The next night, Thorn found herself exploring Courtenz alone. Again. The last conversation she and Thistle had about finding Veryn had ended with Thistle telling her to wait until Nithin and Kol went on their next business trip, but Thorn had a sinking feeling that Thistle simply didn't want to go. That she didn't need revenge like Thorn did.

Now that she had her bearings in the city, finding the vryko hangouts took no time at all and soon the pounding of the bass reached her ears. Covering her ears with her hair and keeping her mouth clamped shut to hide her human teeth, she stepped inside. There were enough humans inside – clearly not there by choice – that the vrykos wouldn't be automatically drawn by her smell. As long as she didn't look scared, she could move about.

Her eyes flicked from face to face as she searched for Veryn or any of his cronies. She could remember all their faces perfectly. Remember their accents, their smells. Even now, she remembered what Veryn and his gang smelled like.

Anger began to boil inside of her. Barely stamping it down, she walked over to the bar. 'Beer,' she grunted, not wanting to open her mouth and display her very obvious lack of fangs.

The barman slid a bottle across the counter, and she passed the fee card over the scanner on the bar. Nithin had given her and Thistle both one to pay for whatever they wanted. When the payment cleared, she took the beer and slipped back into the shadows. Watching. Waiting. She'd come here enough nights in a row to know it was her best chance of getting a lead.

The clock had ticked well past two in the morning when she finally spied someone she recognised. It wasn't Veryn, but it was one of the Soul Eaters.

To her relief, the vryko seemed to grow bored around four and left the bar with a few of his friends.

Thorn slipped out after him. The icy weather froze her lungs instantly and all her effort went into not coughing.

The vryko headed north and appeared to be going home until he wandered into another bar.

It took another two hours before the vryko was finally alone, and by that point dawn light had filled the sky and coaches were beginning to dot the air as the Suriias of daylight went about their routines.

The vryko stumbled drunkenly down a side street and Thorn seized her chance. Scaling a fire escape and sprinting across the rooftops until she was ahead of him, she waited until just the right moment and came down on top of him. She had the knife at his neck before he could react.

'Where is Veryn?' she asked, the blade nicking his skin and drawing beads of blood.

'I don't know.'

'Tell me!'

'I remember you,' he said, inhaling audibly and sighing in pleasure. 'Your mother tasted so sweet.'

Thorn raked the iron blade across his throat, sending blood everywhere. She stepped back and let him fall. Black veins spread from where the wound carved his neck open, the poison of the iron still spreading even as he died. Only when he stopped twitching did she bend down.

Yanking open his shirt, she took out her father's knife and inhaled deeply, readying herself.

For Veryn, she carved. Vrykos liked bloody calling cards after all.

Then, standing on shaky legs, Thorn turned and headed back in the direction of the mansion. By the time she was at the wall outside of Nithin's house, she was trembling badly and wretchedly nauseated. Climbing over the wall and into the bedroom took the last of her reserves of energy.

She collapsed onto the bed without bothering to change and drifted into the land of nightmarish memory.

When she finally dragged herself out of bed a few hours later, more nightmares presented themselves.

After twenty minutes in the shower, removing crusted vryko blood out from under her fingernails, she left her room and stopped dead at the top of the stairs. Thistle was there, staring down at the entrance hall, her body stiffer than a violin string.

Thorn tracked her gaze.

The hall was filled with Spotters. Each one wore the navy uniform that declared without introduction what they were and what they did. Stiff-backed and narrow-eyed, each was unappealing and unfriendly. They had terrifying guns at their sides.

'Another human?' said one. He looked *hungry* at the sight of her.

She couldn't move she was so scared. All feeling but fear left her.

'It's rare to see two humans together nowadays,' he continued. His eyes danced from Thistle to Thorn. 'So which of you belongs to Nithin?'

Belongs. Claim a human like a pet. The fiery, undoubtedly stupid retort almost left her when Nithin appeared. He sent Thorn a warning look before directing his attention to the Spotter. 'Thistle is my fiancée, Benjamin. Thorn's with Kol. Ladies, allow me to introduce Benjamin Cae, founder of the Unit of Prestigious Hunters.'

The urge to scoff was nearly overwhelming.

'And where did you find unclaimed humans, Summons? You never specified.'

Nithin remained remarkably nonchalant. 'They turned themselves into the Lathlak Corporation. A rising number of human refugees have, as my reports have indicated.'

Benjamin's eyes narrowed. He had the same cat-like eyes that Kol had, but Thorn found his gaze deeply disconcerting. 'You adopt such an air superiority, Summons, yet you've claimed humans just like the rest. You're not so much better.'

'I don't mistreat my fiancée, Benjamin.'

Benjamin's lip curled. 'And you, Sinn? You made such a fuss about leaving your father's company, yet here you are, a claimed human in your home.'

Kol, remarkably, appeared bored by the entire exchange. 'Don't make insinuations of our homelife. It's less than none of your concern.'

'The old rules will be overturned soon,' said Benjamin. 'With so few humans, allowing spares to be kept when caught is foolish. Soon enough all humans will be required to report to the camps.'

A blanket of dread wrapped around Thorn, threatening to suffocate her with fear; beside her, all the colour had drained from Thistle's face.

'Do not threaten my family again, Benjamin,' said Nithin coolly. After turning a disdainful sneer on Benjamin, he looked at Kol. 'Were you going to the temple or did you want to wait for me?'

'We'll go,' said Kol succinctly. 'I know Thistle's been wanting to see it before the wedding and they're closed for painting the rest of the week.'

Having the good sense not to act surprised, Thistle nodded.

Catching Thorn's gaze, Kol cocked his head towards the door.

The trio left without another word. Every step felt like the last step before a sprint. Only when they were in the coach and driving away from the house did Thorn's jaw unlock.

'I'm going to be sick,' she rasped.

'I know,' said Kol softly. 'I'm sorry.'

'No, I'm really going to be sick.'

He only just managed to stop the coach before Thorn raised the door and vomited onto the road.

Her arms began to shake, and her teeth chattered together painfully.

Thistle got out and pulled Thorn's hair back as she heaved. The bile stung her throat and tears burned her eyes. It felt like a ghul was clawing around inside her skull.

'You okay?' asked Kol, appearing on her other side.

'No,' she rasped. Hocking a wad of spit, she took several ragged gasps and wiped her mouth.

'I'm sorry,' he said. 'Really.'

Instead of looking at him, Thorn focused on a small red bug flitting across a moss-covered stump that was half rotted away, mushrooms growing around the sides. She knew that she might die trying to kill Veryn. She'd never cared. As long as they didn't take her alive, as long as they didn't get her, as long as Thistle was okay, then Thorn didn't care much either way. After all, what was there to look forward to but a life in hiding? Yet it was days like this where she remembered how fragile her life was. How it could end at any moment. Because there were figures in uniforms with more power, more might, and they hated her for existing. Did they even have a reason?

She watched the bug take flight, wishing she could get away so easily.

It was another while before she let Thistle help her back into the coach. Kol flew them into the city and they got out in a rooftop coach dock above one of the flying shopping centres. There was a garden that ran between all the shops and Kol brought them to an outdoor café. He walked between them and she noticed he didn't walk as casually as he had the first time he brought her into town. Now he seemed wary, and his hands twitched every time Suriias passed them, and she realised belatedly that it was only just occurring to him what life as a human was really like. How much they were despised. How many wanted them dead. It was something the Suriias could never understand. Yet Kol seemed to be trying.

In the café, Thorn sipped at her coffee and stared down at Courtenz. The heart of the city was unlike anything she had ever seen. She saw advertisements for wing brushes and talon sharpeners; watches that told the time, the air speed, your fortune, how many calories you burned walking, flying, or using magic, and so on; the sleekest new design in coaches, from ones that could transform for under water use, to ones that could change shape and tunnel into the earth. The mere thought made her shudder.

Kol suggested they walk around until Nithin gave them the all clear and Thistle jumped at the chance to be distracted. Thorn wandered along behind them, eyes raking over the Suriias who crowded the footpaths or flew above, wings pinned as they dove, or flapping gracefully as they rose high into the sky. She was so distracted she didn't realise the other two were shopping until Kol called her name. He was holding out a phone.

'What's that for?'

'You,' he said. 'You need one.'

Thorn stared at it, too surprised to react.

Kol opened the box and turned on the phone. He typed away before handing it back to her. 'I know you've been dying for my number.'

Thorn rolled her eyes, but she took the phone. The screen felt slick beneath the pads of her fingers.

'I'll give you mine, too,' said Thistle eagerly.

It was hard not to laugh. Something that should have been mundane was still novel to them.

An hour later, Nithin called to say that the Spotters had left, and the trio made their way back to the mansion. He looked tired and more dishevelled than normal, and Thistle went straight to his side and wrapped her arms around him.

'You okay?' she asked.

Thorn had to bite her tongue as indignation burned through her. Was *he* okay?

'I'm fine,' said Nithin, kissing her temple. 'You?'

'Better now,' said Thistle. 'But maybe we shouldn't have the party.'

Nithin pressed his lips to her forehead and inhaled deeply before replying. 'No,' he said firmly. 'We have nothing to hide.'

Thorn was truly starting to wonder if Thistle had hit her head at some point and lost all sense. 'A *party*? Seriously? For what?'

'We're getting married, Tor,' said Thistle.

'Are we?' Thorn winked at her. 'Darling, you haven't asked.'

Thistle laughed and whacked her affectionately. 'Nithin has plenty of friends who don't hate humans and who want to meet us. There won't be any dangers, any freaks, anything to worry about.'

Somehow Thorn very much doubted that was the case. If Suriias showed up and did nothing, it was likely out of fear of Nithin's wrath – whatever that was – as opposed to actually liking the humans being dangled in front of them. It was hardly a good incentive. Enforced morality meant nothing.

'I don't think so,' said Thorn. 'I don't feel like being bait.'

'Nothing's going to happen,' said Kol. 'We'll both be there.'

Thorn shook her head. 'You're not my guard dog, Charcoal.'

'But I'd be such a good one,' he bantered before looking at Nithin. 'We should invite Kassian. Tell him to bring Eva and Ivy.'

Nithin nodded thoughtfully.

'Who?' said Thorn.

'Nithin's cousin,' said Kol. 'Eva and Ivy are humans. They live with him. They're lovely.'

Thorn tried to overlook how the meaning behind that statement made her feel ill, and instead focused on the prospect of meeting more humans. Would they join Jinx's group?

'Yeah, I want to meet them,' she agreed.

Kol looked pleased with himself and nudged Nithin. 'Are the ladies coming to dinner with us?'

'Of course,' said Nithin, catching Thistle's eye and smiling. 'If you feel up to it after this morning?'

Thistle looked equally as stupid and they held each other's gazes for so long, Thorn turned away and wrinkled her nose at Kol.

'You're right,' she muttered. 'They are nauseating.'

Kol was still laughing as she followed him out of the house, leaving Nithin and Thistle behind. The shroud that had hung over the day since the Spotters' arrival felt like it was lifting, although she had little desire to go back out.

'I know you have doubts because of what he is,' Kol began abruptly, 'but Thistle's the only soul he's ever considered marrying.'

'So, there have been others?' Of *course* there would be.

Kol scratched the back of his head. 'Nith goes to the Speak Softlies to meet humans the same reason humans go there to meet Suriias who will protect them. I'm just saying that he's genuine. He loves her.'

Thorn leaned against the coach and crossed her arms. Distant clouds promised rain and a chill crept over her skin. 'Why do you care what I think of him?'

Kol brushed his hair back from his eyes before jamming his hands into his pockets. 'Because he's my best friend. Best friends are a reflection of who and what you are. I think highly of Thistle which means I think even more highly of you for having her as your best friend. I'd like you to think I'm decent. A decent frai who surrounds himself with decent friends.'

His admission left her slightly chagrined. 'Fine,' she relented, surprised that she wasn't saying it just to placate him. 'I'll give him a chance.'

Her words made him smile and he reached out, tucking a strand of hair behind her ear. 'Thank you, Rose.' His hand lingered on her face, just barely brushing her skin.

She was spared having to respond by the sound of the door.

CHAPTER FOUR
Girl at Odds

The night of the party was the furthest thing from Thorn's mind until Thistle brought it up one afternoon at lunch and suggested they get ready together. The prospect of spending time with Thistle was enough for Thorn to concede, and they whiled away several hours in Thistle and Nithin's room. Thistle insisted on Thorn trying on every outfit they had between them – which was three outfits for Thorn, and somewhere near seventy-five for Thistle, much to Thorn's utter incomprehension.

'Do you buy something every time he takes you out?'

'He likes buying me things.'

Thorn opened and closed her mouth several times. 'How are you planning on bringing all of this into the wild?'

Thistle shrugged. 'I'm not, I guess.'

'Kind of a waste, don't you think?'

'It's fun.'

Thorn had never felt more confused in her life, but she let the matter drop.

As the sun fell, Suriias began to arrive at the house, consuming the miniscule vestiges of calm Thorn had been clinging to. Each arrival sent a fresh chill down her spine and she desperately wished she could hide in her room. But then Thistle took her hand and tugged her down the stairs into a room filled to bursting with party-goers.

Nithin appeared almost instantly with a fellow sbura and, true to his word, two humans.

'Hi,' said the one with curly black hair. 'I'm Eva.'

'Ivy,' said the other.

Thorn and Thistle introduced themselves in turn.

'Are you guys liking Courtenz?' asked Eva. 'It's beautiful, isn't it?'

A very unsettling feeling welled in the pit of Thorn's stomach. 'Beautiful?' she echoed. 'There are signs for death camps on every corner.'

Ivy grimaced. 'Yeah, but that's normal at this point.'

Thorn gawked at her. Horrified. Sickened. How could something so repugnant just be accepted? Not only by the Suriias, but by the very humans they were hunting?

Thorn turned away, feeling like she needed a bucket to vomit in and a shower to wash the conversation off her skin.

In the corner of the room Kol stood with another Suriia. They seemed to be deep in conversation. Judging by the way the Suriia reached out and ran her fingers up Kol's arm, it was an intimate conversation at that.

Thorn rolled her eyes. 'This whole party needs help,' she muttered under her breath. Glancing back at Thistle, wanting to go, Thorn tried to catch her eye, but she was talking about regulations with Eva and Ivy, and didn't notice.

Now hurt and disgusted, Thorn made her way into the kitchen. She grabbed a glass and filled it with water from the tap.

She was barely finished swallowing when a hand ran over her shoulder, grazing her skin, and a feeling of desire coursed through her. She turned and found herself face to face with a sbura.

'And who might you be?' the sbura purred, moving closer. Pretty as she was, the thrall of her magic made her intoxicating. 'You're far too cute to be alone. So *much* energy. I can taste it.' The sbura leaned in, licking a stripe up her neck.

And then she was ripped away. The enchantment broke the second contact was and Thorn slumped against the sink, gasping and shaking so badly it was as if her skeleton was desperate to be rid of her skin.

Kol was standing between Thorn and the Suriia, eyes black with fury. 'Get out of my house, Gemini.'

The gleeful, proud laugh that slipped between Gemini's teeth sent a torrent of wrath through Thorn. Grabbing the glass, she lobbed it at Gemini's face. It hit her, hard, and cut her cheek and jaw. Gemini hissed and moved to retaliate, but Kol grabbed her wrist. Sapphire light glowed around his fist and his teeth sharpened to fangs.

'Get out before I throw you out.'

With a glower that conveyed future retaliation, Gemini yanked out of his grip and disappeared into the crowd.

Kol let out a steadying breath and his appearance slowly reverted to normal. 'Come on,' he said, turning to Thorn and holding out his hand. 'Let's disappear.'

'Won't your friend miss you?'

'Gemini?'

'No, the one you were in the corner with.'

'She's nobody.' He nodded to his hand. 'Come on.'

Still shaking, Thorn took his hand and followed him out of the kitchen, up the stairs, and into the sanctuary of his room. He locked the door behind them and gestured for her to sit.

'I thought only your friends were coming,' she said sharply.

'She's a friend of a friend with bad taste,' said Kol. 'And she's not welcome again.'

Thorn didn't respond.

'Should we watch something?' He picked up a small orb and waved his hand over it. The inanimate object floated into the air, glowing dark red and casting his room in a cosy glow. 'Pass the time until the idiots leave?'

She regarded the orb a second, wondering why it didn't bother her more, before taking the room in. There were dozens of books on his shelves and she plucked one up at random.

'Do you want me to leave you alone?'

'No,' she muttered.

'Then …'

Setting the book down and crossing her arms over her chest, she looked over at him. 'Aren't you going to be missed?'

'Nah.' He dropped onto the ground and gestured for her to take the bed. 'Nith's used to me bowing out early. He thinks I'm boring.'

Curling up on the bed, she pulled one of his pillows into her chest. 'How long have you been friends?'

Kol leaned back to catch her eye; he was remarkably handsome in the red glow. 'We've been best friends for two centuries. We moved here together.'

'Whoa.'

'Yeah.' He grinned. 'We met each other at school. He taught me how to fend off bullies.'

'Fancy Nithin with his suits can fight off a bully?'

'You'd be surprised.'

'Trust me, I am.' She eyed him curiously. 'Give me a "For instance …"'

Kol pursed his lips in thought for a moment. Then, 'I was an easy target for bullies when we were younger. I didn't like fighting and I was small.'

Thorn smiled at the description. She couldn't imagine him a scrawny little kid.

'An older boy had me on the ground and was forcing dirt in my mouth when I met Nithin. He's a few years older than me and was a lot bigger than me back then. He kicked the boy in the teeth, knocked two of them loose, and then walked me home.'

Slightly impressed, Thorn nodded in approval. 'I'm surprised there's not a super-secret frai way to magic dirt into fruit or something. Would've been handy.'

Kol looked at her for a second before bursting into laughter. 'Yeah,' he agreed. 'That would've been dead handy.' Still laughing, he reached out and picked up a bottle and two glasses off the bottom shelf of his bedside table. He poured dark liquid into both. 'Here,' he said, holding out a glass. 'Your first drink.'

Thorn took it and examined its contents. 'They say Suriia drinks are toxic to humans.'

'I would never give you something that would make you sick.'

'Or drugged?'

He took the glass he'd been holding out to her, made a show of drinking some, and then held it back out. 'I swear,' he said ardently. 'It'll only make you tipsy.'

'What's it made of?' she asked.

'Ilnethren nectar.'

She stared at him in bewilderment. 'What?'

'It's a flower,' he explained. 'Makes you drunk but tastes like sweet tea. Trust me.'

'No drugs?' she checked again. 'No magic?'

'Just fermented plants.'

She had no reason to believe him when she wouldn't have trusted a single other soul in the house aside from Thistle, but she was starting to think that when it came to Kol, she was a filthy hypocrite. And her earlier reservations had vanished.

She downed the whole thing in one go and gasped as it burned her throat.

'Whoa,' said Kol. 'Slow down.'

'Was I not supposed to do that?'

He pinched the bridge of his nose. 'You're adorable, Rose.'

'I don't know what all the fuss is about,' she muttered, glaring at the glass.

'Same.' He refilled their drinks and held his up. 'Here's to new experiences.'

'To enemies who act like friends.'

Kol clinked glasses with her. Thorn finished that glass, and then another, and when her limbs felt loose and noodlelike and her thoughts danced in a thrum of colour and fog, she looked over at him and nudged him with her foot. She was having trouble remembering why she didn't trust him.

'You know,' she mused drunkenly, 'you're the first Suriia I've ever found funny.'

A low chuckle resonated from his throat. It was a beautiful, deep sound. 'Well, you're the first human who's ever said that to me.'

She giggled, and then snorted, and then they both laughed harder.

At some point Kol stood and stretched out on the bed beside her, tucking his arm under his head so that they were face to face. Raising his other hand, he brushed a strand of hair behind her ear. 'You should smile more, Rose.'

'Why?'

His thumb traced over her cheek and then dropped. 'The world doesn't seem so bad when even you can smile.'

Silence descended again, and her eyelids grew heavy. Kol was warm and calming beside her and it had been days since she'd slept well, too used to Thistle beside her to get comfortable alone. She moved closer and rested her head in the crook of his shoulder.

'Do you want me to move?' he whispered.

'No,' she mumbled. 'Warm.'

His arm raised up and draped around her waist. 'Sweet dreams, Rose.'

'Sweet dreams, Charcoal.'

And then she was asleep, lulled by his steady breathing. She dreamed of a garden, and flowers filled with magic. Only the magic wasn't harsh and biting. It was colourful, sparkling, vibrant. The hum in the air was from determined insects and flapping birds, the gentle susurrus of the flowing grasses melding the sounds together in a beautiful orchestra.

Thorn reached a scarred hand out, but curious as she was, she couldn't bring herself to touch the tips of the petals.

'They won't bite,' said an amused voice, echo-y and singsong.

She turned and saw Kol. 'Some plants bite.'

'Only if you bite them first,' he teased.

She was still smiling at him when suddenly she was being dragged away. So, too, was Kol.

Teeth and nails tore into her flesh, but somehow the worst part wasn't the pain this time. It was seeing Kol grabbed by Suriias and disembowelled.

She woke with a jolt, shaking, head pounding, soaked in sweat. Kol was asleep beside her, eyes moving underneath their lids.

Still trembling, she rolled over, tucking her hands beneath her head, sick with fear for a reason she had never considered before.

Fear of what would happen to a Suriia who helped.

Thorn jerked awake hours later with a migraine and a mouth that tasted like cotton and evil. She opened one eye and saw a glass of water on the bedside table.

With a groan, she sat halfway up and gulped it down greedily. The second it hit her stomach, the urge to vomit quelled somewhat, but her skull still throbbed.

She dropped her head back, trying to soothe the pounding. The smell of the pillows filled her with comfort, and she closed her eyes again.

Her mind drifted back to the night before. When she remembered the sbura in the kitchen, anger came back full force.

Sitting up again, she pushed the pillow away and stood. It took a minute to propel her feet into motion and she stumbled out of his room and made her way downstairs, desperate for coffee. The threat of impending vomit kept rising in her chest, only to be forced down by several deep breaths.

Kol was nursing a cup of coffee in the kitchen when she walked in. He, too, looked like he'd just stumbled out of bed. His black hair was mussed, his eyes sleepy. Yet there was something quietly handsome about him.

'Hungover?'

'Oh yeah,' she grumbled. 'Coffee?'

He shook his head. 'Think you're up for shopping? Nith and Thistle are comatose and we're out of coffee.'

She raised an eyebrow at his mug.

He knocked it back and held up the now empty cup. 'See? All gone.'

Thorn tried not to laugh and failed. 'Sure,' she agreed. 'Whatever.'

'I love the enthusiasm,' he teased.

'My head hurts.'

'Knocking back nectar like it's water will do that.'

The day was blustery, but pleasant, and they headed to the coach and flew into Courtenz. Even after so many times having visited it now, she was still struck by its enormity. Buildings that went up, up, up and disappeared into the clouds above. Flying coaches and drones filling the air as much as the winged creatures who flitted from window to window without effort. Colourful bursts of magic that were as commonplace as the neon lights of the advertisements and signs.

Rain lashed down from the dark, ominous heavens as they landed on a coach dock and clambered out. Thorn was glad of it; sunshine would have been abhorrent with the headache she was experiencing. It helped that the coach park was emptier than it otherwise would have been.

As they walked into the shop, a light caught Thorn's eye and she paused. Jinx was on the other side of the road. There was a coin in his hand, and he was angling it in her direction, catching the light. When their eyes locked, he held up an envelope and then put it on the ground before disappearing around the corner.

Inside the shop, Thorn dallied anxiously, worried that someone else would find the envelope first. But she didn't want to tell Kol about Jinx. It broke every rule she had.

'I'm going to find coffee,' she told him. 'Meet you at the chocolate?'

'You sure?'

'I'm good.'

Kol nodded and looked back at the shelf in front of him where a wide array of pastries were on offer. 'Yell if you need me.'

'Will do.'

Thorn turned and disappeared around the corner. Ducking low, she bolted back outside, across the road, and snatched up the envelope. A quick glance around was enough to confirm that Jinx was gone. Somehow both disappointed and relieved, Thorn hurried back to the shop.

Her hair was slightly damp now, and she tied it back in a messy bun, hoping Kol wouldn't notice. Her eyes landed on the shelf with coffee. There were a variety of different flavours and strengths. Picking the one with the highest number, she was just rounding the corner when she found herself face to face with a ghul.

A sneering, frightening mockery of an expression twisted the features of his face, intention and ill wish contenders in his yellow eyes.

Before Thorn could react, an arm suddenly wrapped around her waist, and the smell of cinnamon and coconut wafted over her.

'There you are,' said Kol. He had a candy bar sticking out of the corner of his mouth and gave the ghul a nonchalant look.

The ghul rolled his eyes and kept walking. When he disappeared around the corner, Kol stepped away from her and held up the basket of items.

'Ready to go?' The falsely cheerful tone of his voice wasn't lost on her, and she could see renewed fury in his eyes as he finished eating the candy bar. He tossed the wrapper into the basket harder than necessary.

Thorn held up the bag of coffee. 'Yeah, let's go.'

Back outside, their bags in hand, they made their way to the coach in strained silence until she asked, curious, 'Did you ever notice it this much?'

'What?'

'How much they hate us.'

She wondered if he would lie to her and tell her that he had. But he shook his head, shame colouring his cheeks as he put his sunglasses on. 'No,' he muttered.

'Better late than never,' she offered, wanting to give him something for the show of honesty.

'Really?'

Thorn didn't have the heart to lie.

When they returned home, Thistle and Nithin were gone. Thorn told Kol she needed to use the bathroom, and went up to her room. The door locked, she opened the package Jinx had left. Inside was a note and a gun.

She unfolded the note. In untrained, unsteady strokes, he'd written,

Fancy an explosion?
Midnight.
J.

Heart hammering, she checked the barrel and saw that it was fully loaded. A smile spread across her face. Locking it, she placed the gun in the bedside drawer and headed back down the stairs.

Kol waved her in to join him in the game room. There was a table for a game called lielak, which was played on a large table where two opponents stood on either side. One stayed on the black carpet side of the table with half black balls, half dark red ones; the other player took the dark red carpeted side with a matching set of two-coloured balls. The aim was to get all your colours before the other side, while they knocked the wrong colours at you. It seemed entirely pointless, but spending an hour almost knocking each other unconscious with wooden balls was hilarious fun, and Thorn was in bright spirits by the time Thistle and Nithin came home.

'Did you have fun at the party?' said Thistle as she sat down beside her and took the coffee Thorn offered. 'You disappeared early.'

'I got sbura'd,' she said dully.

Oddly, while Thistle was clearly upset, Nithin's dark gaze turned even stormier. He claimed the vacated chair across from Thorn, his emerald eyes narrowed. 'What happened?'

'Callin brought Gemini,' said Kol tightly. 'I dealt with it.'

Thistle wrapped her arms around Thorn. 'You okay?'

'I'm fine,' she mumbled.

For his part, Nithin appeared furious. 'I apologise. I told Callin not to bring her. She's nothing but a backwards nuisance. Please know that she's not welcome in my home.'

Thorn might've thanked him if Gemini hadn't been in his house less than twelve hours ago, but she didn't bother saying as much. Ignoring him, she turned her attention to Thistle, who smiled.

'Want to spend the day doing nothing? We can watch movies and eat until we puke and not go anywhere.'

Thorn's heart leapt. 'That sounds amazing.'

An hour later, Nithin and Kol had departed, and Thorn and Thistle curled up on the sofa to watch more of Kol's vintage human film collection.

The day passed rather perfectly, and Thorn felt better than she had in a long time. The rest and relaxation cured her hangover and a little before midnight, she was pushing open her window and climbing out.

Manoeuvring down carefully, she dropped to the ground and then darted through the bushes towards the fence. Nithin had only two guards on at night and they were distracted by the blaring television. She rolled her eyes at their backs. Useless bastards.

She scaled the fence quickly, pulling herself up by the vines. When she dropped to the ground on the other side, Jinx was waiting for her.

He wore the same threadbare attire as the last time she'd seen him, but he looked like he'd managed to have a bath and some proper food.

'You good?' she asked.

'Found a new place to camp until we bounce,' he said, bobbing his head. 'The roof doesn't even leak.'

'Nice!' She'd been through more than a few winters with both leaking roofs and flooding floors.

He winked at her before cocking his head at the mansion. 'You were right,' he said. 'This place is ugly.'

'I know, right?'

'Anything worth stealing?'

'Only the food.'

Jinx let out a quiet bark of laughter. 'Nice night for a bit of sabotage,' he said with a wicked smile. 'You ready? We're going to Serantren.'

'Where's Jade?'

'I don't like bringing her on these trips,' he said as they set off. 'It's not safe. She's back at the place we're squatting in. Just us tonight, if that's okay?'

'That's okay with me.'

'Excellent.'

They slipped through the trees like ghosts. Well used to having to drag Thistle anywhere that wasn't a Speak Softly, having Jinx race eagerly beside her proved a welcome change. They matched each other stride for stride, only pausing when Jinx had to reorient himself.

When they reached the outer streets of the city, they went down into the tunnels where the public coaches picked up and dropped off passengers.

'How are we doing this?' she hissed.

'Hijinks,' he said, ducking under a barrier.

She followed him quickly. They darted through the shadows, past empty coach after empty coach. At a seemingly random one, Jinx stopped short and pulled a crude-looking tool out of his coat pocket. He picked the lock and raised the coach door.

Thorn crawled in after him. 'Where did you learn how to do that?'

'When it's pick a lock or get caught—'

'You pick the lock.'

'Exactly.' He turned the coach on and reversed out of the slot. He flew well and they drove out of the coach park and into the night's air traffic.

Jinx continued tapping buttons with remarkable know-how and a map appeared on the window in front of Thorn. He pointed from a moving red dot to a blue square. 'Give me directions to there.'

'Okay.'

Thorn kept her eyes locked on the map, directing him away from certain buildings and then out into the serene countryside.

In under an hour, the grim outline of the detention facility came into view. It was a notorious torture camp during the rebellion. Her father had told her stories of the horrors within, the experiments and torture methods. She knew too much about rape, dismemberment, waterboarding, exsanguination and eugenics to last a lifetime.

'I've asked a few of the others we've found if they know of a Veryn,' he said suddenly, the words pitched low, yet deep, as if confidence was a substance he brewed in his chest. 'Nothing yet, but everyone's keeping an ear out.'

The surge of gratitude hit her hard and fast. 'Thank you, Jinx.'

'Of course. Can't let the bastards get away with that.' His hands tightened around the steering wheel. 'I never got to kill my parents' killers. If I can help you with this, it'll be something.'

She reached out and squeezed his shoulder. 'We can find them, too.'

He shot her an appreciative look. 'I like that I believe you.'

'Didn't expect to?'

'Don't believe most.'

'I know the feeling.'

They shared smiles of understanding before refocusing their attention on the building which now loomed above them.

Jinx landed a short distance away and they walked through the waist-high grasses, taking in their surroundings with wide eyes, both breathing as quietly as possible.

'Cameras,' she said, nodding to the fence.

'You a good shot?'

Nodding, she took out her gun. 'This won't be quiet.'

'We better be fast, then.'

Thorn took in the locations of all five cameras and then shot them one by one. Sparks illuminated the night like angry fireworks. An alarm went off and they darted through the fence. Racing across the grounds, they went straight to the power centre. He handed her a pair of pliers and pointed to the wires she needed to cut as he disappeared around the corner. Thorn cut them quick and clean and stepped back just as Jinx reappeared.

He held out his hand and she took it, barely stifling a giggle. They sprinted away as the building went up in flames. Every sizzle and pop sent adrenaline pumping through Thorn's veins.

Smart enough not to linger, they clambered into the coach and Jinx flew off without delay.

'Whoa,' she said, giggling into her hand.

'That was amazing,' he said, gasping. 'You're amazing, Thorn.'

He was still grinning at her, breathing hard, when he looked away from the window, leaned in, and kissed her.

It was quick and she didn't have time to react before he was facing front again. His touch left her lips tingling and a funny, and not-entirely-pleasant feeling spread through the pit of her stomach. She'd never been kissed before and she hadn't wanted her first kiss to be taken.

'Shit,' said Jinx, pulling her from her misgivings. 'Coaches.'

Ahead, the bobbing headlights in the sky signalled the arrival of the Spotters.

'Can we turn off the lights?'

'We can,' he said. 'But they still have radar. Are you wearing a blocker?'

'Yeah.'

'Small mercies.' Jinx killed the lights in the coach and coasted lower and lower as the coaches drew near.

Neither of them breathed as the coaches passed above them, the collective sound like an active beehive.

Only when the lights had faded into the distance behind them did Jinx raise the coach and put the headlights back on.

'That was close.'

'Nah. That was fun.'

An hour later he let her out down the road from the mansion.

'Want to do this again?' he called softly.

'Definitely.'

He held up a hand. 'See you 'round, Thorn.'

'See you 'round, Jinx.'

With a final smile, she darted across the garden and back into her window.

CHAPTER FIVE
Unwell

The park was freezing, snow was falling, and the vrykos were within spitting distance. Thorn hardly dared to breathe. She had Kol's knife gripped tightly in hand. She brought her father's knife everywhere – she fully intended to carve Veryn's heart out with it – but the iron dagger made her feel better prepared than she used to. When one of them branched off, she followed, an armed shadow of vengeance.

The line of enquiry went as fruitlessly as ever. No Soul Eater was going to give up Veryn. But Thorn had an appreciation for picking them off one by one.

With a swipe of her blade, he crumpled, gurgling and choking. She kicked him over as red and black veins crisscrossed their way across his skin where she'd cut him.

'Thank you, Kol,' she whispered, slightly stunned by how effective it was.

Bending down, she opened the vryko's shirt and carved the blade across his chest with quick, jagged brutality.

For Veryn

She'd been leaving the words on corpses for days. It was crude and twisted, but Thorn hoped it would draw him out. Then, wiping the blood off the blade, Thorn tucked it into her boot and darted to the perimeter of the park. She hopped the gate and dropped down onto the cobblestone road.

Turning onto a side street, the sounds of raucous laughter filtered through the lashing rain, distorted and staccato as a result.

She stood on the street corner in the relentless, icy downpour, and watched the revellers in the night market. She saw vrykos dancing, vylkas playing a game and taking bets; she saw a sbura kiss a shapeshifter, who changed form every few seconds. She remained locked in place until she was frozen to the bone and shaking, her nose running.

It was nearly daybreak by the time she climbed the mansion's fence, stumbled through the garden, and heaved herself back into the bedroom window. A room that she still didn't think of as hers.

Thorn could barely keep her eyes open by the time she trudged down to the kitchen. Her cough had turned wet and painful, and she couldn't go more than a minute without wheezing and spluttering.

She managed to brew a pot of coffee, and then stared at it with wide eyes, feeling dazed. She didn't even realise she was swaying on her feet, completely zoned out, until Thistle all but shouted her name.

She jumped. 'Huh?'

'You okay?' asked Thistle, walking over to her with far more energy than Thorn had in supply.

'Fine,' said Thorn. 'Tired.'

Thistle felt her forehead and her expression instantly became alarmed. 'You have a fever, Tor. You need to lie down.'

'I'm fine.'

'You're not,' said Thistle sternly. Taking her hand, she tugged Thorn out of the kitchen.

Instead of going upstairs, Thistle brought Thorn to the sitting room and manoeuvred her onto the sofa. She then retrieved a blanket and draped it over Thorn's body.

'Now stay,' she ordered. 'I'll make you breakfast.'

As grateful as she was exhausted, Thorn stayed on the sofa while Thistle busied herself in the kitchen. When she returned with a plate of pastries and two cups of tea, Thorn lifted the blanket and Thistle snuggled in beside her.

'Tea, my dear?'

'Yes, please.'

Thorn cradled the mug between her hands, but instead of drinking it, she rested her head on Thistle's shoulder.

'Miss you,' she mumbled.

Thistle wrapped an arm around her. 'Miss you, too. Buttface.'

Thorn closed her eyes, exhaustion kicking in now that Thistle was beside her. She was just starting to nod off when Thistle cleared her throat.

'I'm heading in to Nithin's company today. Do you want me to get you anything for dinner?'

Thorn's good mood shattered. 'No,' she said hollowly. 'I'm fine.'

Thistle leaned back and caught her eye. 'You sure?'

'I'm sure.'

What had been so perfect a second ago now felt strained.

Thistle went to get dressed after a few minutes of uncomfortable silence. Thorn put the tea on the table and pulled one of the sofa pillows into her chest. Feeling sick was bad enough; feeling sick and sad was a thousand times more horrible.

Ten minutes later, Thistle stepped in to say goodbye, promising to bring Thorn soup for dinner, and then disappeared.

Thorn rubbed tears from her eyes as a wave of abandonment hit her full force. Coupled with her fatigue, she felt annoyingly emotional.

'I hear you're sick.'

She started. Kol was standing in the doorway, dressed in a suit, bag in hand. She wiped her face roughly. Stuffed as her nose was and as much as she'd been sneezing, she hoped the tears weren't obvious. 'Yeah,' she croaked.

'Do you need anything?'

She shook her head.

Kol raised an eyebrow, nodded disbelievingly, and then put his bag on the ground. He disappeared down the hall and returned with a box of tissues, a fresh cup of tea and a blanket over his arm. Setting the mug and the tissues on the floor in front of her, he spread the blanket over the one she'd been shivering beneath. The extra layer of warmth helped immensely.

'Get some sleep,' he said. 'Call me if you need anything.'

She grunted.

He left without another word and she heard the door shut and the coach start. Breathing through her nose, sounding remarkably like a rusty teakettle, she stared blindly at the flower bushes outside the window and wondered why it hadn't occurred to Thistle to stay.

Sick, tired and gloomy, Thorn drifted in and out of sleep, her fever worsening. She kept waking up soaked in sweat and shivering.

Sometime later, a soft voice pulled her from strange, nonsensical dreams.

She opened her eyes and saw Kol kneeling beside the sofa. He wasn't wearing his coat and his tie was gone.

'Hi, Sniffles,' he said with a sympathetic smile. 'I brought you meds.'

Thorn sat up and immediately regretted it as her head spun and her vision tilted. Everything hurt. Her mouth was dry, her lips cracked, her nose sore and raw.

'Here.' Kol held out two tablets and a glass of water.

She eyed the small red capsules with swirling powder; there was no hiding the magic inside them. 'I don't do drugs,' she said, taking the water and ignoring the tablets. What she meant was that she didn't do *Suriia* drugs, because as far as she knew, humans didn't have any anymore.

'Rose, you're soaked in sweat and shaking like a volcano about to erupt. I promise they're safe.'

'No.'

'It's medication.'

'No,' she said stubbornly. 'I can see the magic. No.'

Clearly a match in stubborn determination, Kol proved undeterred. 'If I take them, will you?'

'What?'

Kol held up the tablets, took one, and swallowed it. He then tipped another tablet out of a bottle and offered her two again. 'If you're poisoned, I'm poisoned. Take the medicine.'

Perhaps it was the result of being too sick to even make a fist, but Thorn found herself reaching out weakly and taking the tablets. She fumbled them into her mouth and choked them down.

Kol smiled at her when he took the now empty glass. 'Want to watch a movie?'

'I can barely keep my eyes open,' she mumbled.

'Well then, I'll watch a movie and you can get better.'

'Whatever.'

Clapping his hands together, Kol went over to the television, put a movie on, and sat in the chair adjacent to her. 'Let me know if you need anything.'

She blinked blearily at him. 'You're not going back to work?'

'Took the rest of the day off.'

'Why?'

'Being sick sucks,' he said with a shrug. 'And you shouldn't have to be sick alone. You need someone to get you soup and water and tissues – and a bucket in case you start projectile vomiting.'

Thorn eyed him for a minute, totally taken aback, before she dropped her head onto the pillow, too exhausted to protest.

She drifted off a few minutes later. But every time she jolted back to awareness, Kol was still there.

Night had eaten the day by the time she finally managed to sit upright and wipe the crust from her eyes.

Kol paused the movie – it didn't look like the one she'd fallen asleep to – and clambered out of the chair. 'How you feeling?'

'Groggy,' she grunted. 'And my mouth tastes wrong.'

He chuckled. 'Soup?'

'Uh … sure.'

Thorn sat dazedly on the sofa as he busied himself in the kitchen. He returned with two bowls in hand, a bottle of juice under either arm and a bag of crackers in his mouth. Thorn reached out and took one of the bowls.

'What're you watching?' she asked.

'I don't know,' he said with a laugh. 'I think the ice cream is evil.'

Thorn stared at him.

'I'm not even kidding.'

Still laughing, Kol un-paused the film. It took only a few minutes for Thorn to realise that no, he wasn't joking, it did seem to be a movie about evil ice cream. Humans fighting evil ice cream.

'This is amazing,' she said with a congested laugh.

Kol winked at her before blowing on the spoonful of soup he was holding. Thorn curled her legs into her chest and rested the bowl on her knees, letting the smell waft slowly up her nose. If she tried to breathe in, her ears would pop again.

The soup was filled with vegetables and tasted heavenly, and Thorn ate the entire bowl, half the bag of crackers, and drank the bottle of juice before drawing the blanket up to her shoulders.

Kol held out the small bottle of red, swirling tablets. After a moment's staring contest, Thorn nodded. He handed her two and sat back down in the chair.

She dozed off again and the next time she woke up she was back in the bedroom and morning light was streaming through the windows. There was a glass of water on the bedside table and a note.

Unfolding the note and angling it away from the blinding sunshine, she read it through squinted eyes.

> *I told you you'd feel better.*
> *Proof that I'm always right.*
> *Also, you sneeze in your sleep and it's adorable.*

Thorn rolled her eyes, a flutter in her chest. Being taken care of felt oddly wonderful and she didn't quite know how to process the strange joy.

But she was distracted from mulling it over by a sudden knock at the door.

'Yeah?' she called, shoving the note under the blanket.

'It's me,' came Kol's deep voice.

'Come in.'

The door opened and he stepped inside, closing the door gently behind him. He was dressed for work and, when he sat on the edge of her bed, she caught a faint smell of cinnamon and coconut, like always. 'Feeling better?'

'Much.'

'Good.' He held out a glass of juice and a plate with pastries. 'Take it easy today, okay?'

Thorn took the glass and plate from him. 'Thanks. You didn't have to.'

'I wanted to.'

'How'd I get upstairs?'

Kol rubbed the back of his neck sheepishly. 'Nithin's got a thing about germs and he wanted to clean the sitting room. We didn't want to wake you, so I carried you upstairs. Thistle was with me the whole time. I promise. She tucked you in.'

The small, unasked for assurance made her feel impossibly grateful. 'Thank you.'

He thumbed over his shoulder. 'We're heading to work now. Call me if you need anything? I can always duck out if you want someone to watch a movie with.'

She nodded.

Kol's grin broadened and he winked at her before disappearing out the door. It was only when she heard them outside that she realised Thistle had gone too.

Thorn stood on weak legs and hobbled to the window. She watched Kol, Nithin and Thistle get into the coach and fly off.

She stared at the horizon until her eyes burned.

CHAPTER SIX
The Suriia and the Dissenter

The mansion continued to reveal new rooms as the days ticked by and Thorn explored every nook and cranny in her boredom. The pool house she found proved by far the most surprising, but she didn't spare it much thought until one evening Thistle suggested they try swimming. Thorn almost agreed until Thistle said that Nithin and Kol would be joining them.

'No,' she said flatly, crossing her arms self-consciously. 'Absolutely not.'

Thistle frowned. 'Why not?'

Thorn pointed to her chest. 'Look at me.'

'You look fine, Tor. They're not going to care that you have a couple of scars.'

'A couple of scars' was a nice way of putting it, although it was woefully understating the truth. When Thorn was young, she'd been taken by a vylka. Jared. It took a sennight for her parents, and Clay, her father's brother, to get her back. Vylkas liked to claim humans. Bite them and enslave them, there was no fighting the magic. Once it happened, the only thing that freed Thorn was her father driving a knife through Jared's heart. It remained one of the worst weeks of Thorn's life.

'Look at *me*,' said Thistle, drawing her from her dark thoughts. She put a hand on either side of Thorn's face. 'You're beautiful. Your scars make you look unbeatable. You're the strongest person I've ever known. You wouldn't be you without being a little rough and a little scuffed. But that's part of your beauty. Okay?'

Thorn swallowed the lump in her throat. 'Thanks, Tiz.'

Thistle kissed her cheek before tugging her hand. 'You can wear one of my suits.'

To Thorn's utter relief, they were the first in the pool house. The room was dark with red and green lights in lanterns floating above them, suspended in the air by magic. The stone of the bathroom was black slate and expensive looking, and flowers and trees in large pots lined the walls.

While neither Thorn nor Thistle could swim, there was a separate hot tub at the other end of the pool, which was shallow enough to be able to stand in.

They sank into the steaming water and splashed about with giddy abandon until the other two walked in. Thorn tried not to notice how handsome Kol looked in a swimsuit and kept her eyes locked on the wall.

Kol and Nithin were talking about someone at work and Thorn tuned them out until Kol kicked her lightly with his foot and she glanced over at him.

'Sorry,' he said, 'we're being boring. No more work talk, I promise.'

Thorn shrugged, moving her hands in circles in the water and watching it churn. 'Talk about what you want.'

Kol gently splashed water at her. 'Do you not like swimming? This is the first time we've managed to get you in here.'

'We can't swim,' said Thistle, sparing her the trouble.

'Really?' said Nithin, surprised.

'Really.'

'I'll teach you.' Nithin wrapped his arm around her and brushed wet tendrils of hair back from her face. 'You should know how to swim.'

Thistle giggled. 'When did you learn how to swim?'

'When I was four,' he said. 'But I was born by water, so it was necessary.'

'Where were you born?'

'Elvery,' he said.

Thorn knew Thistle had no idea where that was, but she nodded like she did.

'And you?' Thistle asked Kol, leaning back against the wall and stretching her arms out.

'Zenegut,' he said. 'About an hour by coach from where Nithin was born. What about you?'

'The south side of the mountain,' said Thistle. 'Same as Thorn.'

Kol winked at Thorn. 'See, that just sounds so much cooler.'

Thorn wondered if he was being sarcastic. But he didn't seem to be. He seemed entirely genuine. As if being born in the woods was better than being born in a hospital with magic and medicine.

'How long have you two lived in Courtenz together?' Thistle prompted.

'Only a few years,' said Nithin. 'We moved here when we bought the Lathlak Corporation.'

Presuming this was their company, Thorn's curiosity got the better of her. 'What do you even do?'

'We're working to reform anti-human laws.'

Her eyebrows shot up. That sounded *much* too good to be true.

'He's already done so much,' said Kol with a smile. 'He's one of the reasons the law over half-Suriias was overturned.'

'The what?'

'Children of humans and Suriias,' he explained. 'Now they're allowed to integrate.'

'Let's not discuss legislation,' said Nithin, running a hand through his black hair and making a face. 'It's depressing.'

'I'm really proud of you,' said Thistle, smiling fondly at him. His eyes flashed green and he leaned in to kiss her.

Thorn turned away, mind whirling. Not that she believed it possible, but if such a thing were to happen …

'Ask something else,' said Kol, splashing water at Thistle and Nithin, who had resumed kissing. 'Save that for your bedroom.'

They broke apart and Thistle wiggled her eyebrows impishly at Nithin. 'First kiss?'

'Millicent,' said Nithin. 'When I was ten.'

'David. When I was six. Ha.'

The memory of little David, Clay's son, came back to Thorn and she wrinkled her nose. 'I can't believe you kissed David.'

Nithin, who was playing absently with Thistle's hair, smirked. 'Was David unappealing?'

'Yes,' said Thorn at the same time Thistle said, 'No!'

Everyone laughed.

'What about you, Kol?' asked Thistle. 'First kiss?'

'Winter,' he said, blushing slightly. 'When I was sixteen.'

'What was she?'

'A prico.' Rolling his eyes good naturedly, Kol looked over at Thorn. 'What about you, Rose? First kiss?'

'Tor's never been kissed.'

'You haven't?'

Three sets of eyes suddenly landed on Thorn and she hesitated. Did Jinx even count? Thorn didn't think so somehow. She hadn't wanted to kiss him. Her hesitation, however, did not go unnoticed by Thistle.

'You've been kissed?' She disentangled herself from Nithin, splashing water every which way. 'When? Who? Why don't I know about this? Is this recent?'

Behind her, Kol looked like he'd just swallowed tar.

'How could you not tell me?' Thistle pressed.

Thorn rubbed her forehead. 'Can we not turn this into a public debate?'

Thistle wasn't listening. 'When was this?'

Glaring at her, Thorn shot out of the hot tub and left without a word.

It was freezing in the main part of the house and she crossed her arms over her chest, shivering badly.

She was halfway up the stairs when someone cleared their throat behind her, and she whirled around to find herself face to face with Nithin.

He was dripping from the pool, his sable hair slicked back from his angular face. 'While I know you do not think much of us,' he said without preamble, 'please try to remember that we have feelings, too.'

Nonplussed, she said, 'Did I offend you?'

'Kol's my best friend. Please don't be cruel.'

'I haven't been.'

'No, but thoughtlessness can be accidentally cruel.' He bowed his head pointedly before turning and disappearing down the stairs.

Thorn carried on to her room. She had only just changed out of her suit and put on a shirt when Thistle stepped inside and closed the door. Her hair was wet and tied back from her face, but she had changed also.

'I'm sorry,' she said immediately. 'I didn't mean to upset you.'

'You didn't,' muttered Thorn. 'I just don't want to discuss my private life around them.'

Nodding understandingly, Thistle walked over to the bed. Dropping down with remarkable poise, she rested her chin on her hands, somehow adopting the stance of a figure in a painting. 'How come you didn't tell me you'd met someone?'

'I haven't. He kissed me randomly. That's why I wasn't saying anything. I don't even think it should count.'

Thistle's eyebrows shot up. 'Wait, who is this guy?'

'Guy from the roof. Jinx.'

'With the sister?'

'Yeah.'

'Since when are you hanging out with him?'

'He's looking for information on Veryn,' said Thorn. 'We've met up a couple of times.'

'Why didn't you tell me?'

'Didn't think you wanted to know.'

'Tor …'

'It's true, though.' Thorn held out her hands, frustration breaking through the seal she kept around her feelings. 'I know you can't sneak out of Nithin's bed all the time. Fair enough. But I miss you and Jinx is around.'

For half a breath, Thorn braced for a fight. Then, with a resolute nod, Thistle took her hand. 'Tell me everything now?'

Thorn grinned and decided to start from the beginning, eager to share everything. Yet when she was finished, Thistle's first words surprised her.

'He sounds a little off.' Catching sight of the look on Thorn's face, she held up her hand. 'Maybe I'm wrong. I'm totally willing to be wrong, Tor. It just … I don't know. I can't explain it.'

Thorn looked down at her fingers, picking the corners of her thumb nail. She had the same feeling, but she felt the need to justify him to Thistle. She didn't want Thistle to have one more reason to argue against when it was time to go.

'I'm sorry,' came the abrupt apology, prompting Thorn to glance back. 'Forget I said anything. I'd love to meet him.'

Her heart leapt. 'Yeah?'

'Definitely.'

Yet Thistle's words about Jinx stayed with Thorn as she crawled out of her window later that night, crept past the guard, scaled the fence, and headed down the road towards Courtenz. It took almost two hours to reach the city on foot, giving her plenty of time to think.

Perhaps there was something slightly strange about Jinx. Thorn didn't find it off-putting, though. If anything, it made sense. They were all slightly off. The result of a lifetime of being hunted, starved, threatened and assaulted. It hardly made for sanity and wise life decisions.

Unfortunately, the night yielded no new information, only two more dead vrykos, and she returned to the mansion just before the others woke.

Unable to sleep, Thorn went down to the kitchen and set about cooking breakfast.

Sunlight slowly crept its way into the kitchen as Thorn brewed coffee, made pastries from scratch, and cut up all the fruit she could find. She put the pieces into a large bowl and mixed them slowly together, careful not to bruise the fruit.

Kol walked in first. He quirked a dark eyebrow at the elaborate spread. 'What's the occasion?'

Thorn held out a cup of coffee. 'Couldn't sleep,' she said. And then, because she wasn't sure, she added, 'We good?'

He took the cup and sipped it before answering. 'Depends,' he said, humour dancing in his cat-eyes.

'On what?'

'You put chocolate in those muffins?'

She grinned. 'Of course.'

'Then we're good,' he teased. 'And the coffee is excellent. Thank you.'

Glad to have erased the odd feeling of guilt in her chest that had been festering since the previous day, Thorn turned back to finish washing the dishes.

'You have no reason to apologise to me,' he said, leaning against the adjacent counter. 'Nith told me what he said. He's a little over-protective. Please don't feel bad.'

'I—'

The sudden appearance of Thistle and Nithin kept Thorn from finishing her sentence and she sighed.

I'm sorry I hurt your feelings.
I didn't want to kiss him.
I really wish you hadn't found out.

'You cooked?' Nithin asked Kol, tugging Thorn out of her spiral. Dressed as ever in a suit, his black hair brushed back neatly, Nithin embodied his position far more authentically than Kol, who Thorn thought didn't suit a suit.

'Nope,' said Kol, tilting his coffee mug at Thorn.

Nithin glanced at Thorn, surprise morphing his usually stoic features. 'Oh. Thank you.'

She nodded and went back to washing the dishes.

'Smells good, baby,' said Thistle, coming up behind her and wrapping her arms around Thorn's waist. In a low voice, she added, 'Couldn't sleep?'

Thorn shook her head. 'Restless,' she mumbled.

About Jinx? signed Thistle, keeping her hand close to Thorn's torso, out of sight of the other two.

About everything, she signed back under the spray of the faucet before turning it off.

Thistle kissed her cheek and tugged her over to the table.

Kol left for work shortly after breakfast, while Thistle and Nithin went to sort out more arrangements for their wedding.

Thorn remained at the mansion, exercising or reading or staring off into space, lost in a million anxious thoughts. It was the delay, she reasoned. She'd lingered too long. They needed to kill Veryn and go.

By nightfall, after the others had gone to sleep, Thorn could hardly sit still.

She stared at her father's knife in her left hand and Kol's knife in her right for a long time, each so different, from the design to the weight to the stories they held. At last, with a sigh, she stood and went to the window. Tucking the blades into her boots, she doublechecked that her gun was locked and shimmied out the window.

Landing without a sound, she stole across the lawn and climbed over the wall. Jinx was there already, leaning against the wall, a lazy smile on his face.

'Ready for some fun?' he said.

'Always.'

As they made their way towards the draining factory, Jinx told her everything he knew about their latest target.

The corporations run by the Suriias were some of the most abhorrent creations she'd ever heard of. The factories, the laboratories, the research centres, the magical control groups, the death camps; every new Suric creation worried her more than the one before it.

'One of my friends on the north side, Sinjin, says he's heard of a Veryn,' said Jinx as they traversed a tricky incline. 'Thinks he's some rich bastard. Might be hard to get an exact address, but he's looking into it.'

A rush of such overwhelming gratitude filled her that she stopped short, unable to breathe without gasping. 'Thank you, Jinx.'

He reached out and brushed a finger over her lip. And then he crashed his mouth against hers.

Thorn tried to disentangle herself, but his hands came up to cradle her head and kept her from pulling away fully. Only when he drew back to catch his breath did she manage to extricate herself from his grip. She smiled tightly at him and gestured him on. A horrid, toxic fear that he'd be angry and refuse to let her and Thistle go with them to the mountains if she turned him down stilled her tongue.

It took almost three hours to reach the facility on the other side of the city. Thankfully once they reached the outskirts, company was a rare sight.

After hoping the facility's fence, they found a broken window and crawled in.

What greeted them was far worse than even Thorn had prepared herself for. The draining facility was as creepy as the name suggested.

'What do you think they did in here?' she wondered aloud.

'Aside from drain humans?'

A shiver went down her spine and her eyes fell upon a table where several brutal looking instruments remained. The serrated ones turned her insides to sludge. 'Those don't look like they drain blood or life force.'

'No,' he agreed grimly. 'Let's do this fast. I hate being here.'

Upon finding no humans – or Suriias – they set the explosives and crawled back out into the cold night. Their feet were barely on the ground when scuttling sounds reached their ears.

'Hide!' she hissed.

Jinx scaled the drainage pipe of the nearby shed and Thorn leapt on top of a coach.

Scuttlers rounded the corner seconds later, probing the area for signs of humans. Thorn's blocker kept her off their radar, but that was no guarantee of avoiding detection, and she wasn't sure if Jinx was wearing one. She hoped he was far enough out of the way that they wouldn't be able to track him.

The *tap-tap-tap* of the Scuttlers' metal feet upon the gravel prompted chills of fear to cascade through Thorn. Her grip on her knife and gun tightened.

Not a second later, the facility blew. The shock wave sent the Scuttlers flying into the trees.

'Now!' roared Jinx.

She jumped off the coach as he climbed back down the rail. They pelted as fast as they could away from the flames and ruin.

Dawn was colouring the sky pink and orange by the time they reached the mansion. Thorn turned to bid him goodnight when he kissed her again. This time the kiss grew in earnestness.

She pushed him away instinctively. Not sure how to tell him she didn't want him to kiss her without offending him, she said instead, 'Not here.'

Thankfully, he let the matter drop without issue. Cupping his hands, he gave her a boost up the side of the wall.

'Goodnight,' he called after her.

The night's events left her feeling off-kilter. She didn't know how to act around men, how to interpret their flirtations and expressions. If she did, she might be able to gauge how and when to turn him down. But with no compass of knowledge to guide her, all she knew was that Jinx made her uncomfortable and she wanted him to stop kissing her.

After a restless few hours of tossing and turning, unable to fall asleep, she stumbled downstairs to find everyone already out of the house. She made a cheese and avocado sandwich, but she was so dazed and filled with confusing thoughts that she didn't enjoy it much.

Once she'd eaten, she found herself growing antsy and couldn't stand being in the house a second longer. Thoughts of leaving with Jinx and Jade crashed into thoughts of Thistle and Kol. In an ideal world, she and Thistle would go without a hitch, but she wished Jinx wasn't the one in charge.

She left the property through the main gates. The guards didn't stop her, but she saw one lift his receiver. Beyond the gates, a light layer of frost coated the ground; winter was settling in and soon the icy rains would turn to snow and sleet.

A biting wind picked up as she moseyed along, blowing snow off the trees and sending shivers down her spine. The sun cast a bleak light upon the world, and she kicked at a rock, sending it into the brush on the side of the road.

The hum of an approaching coach made her jump, but she recognised the model and didn't bother to run.

Kol parked beside her and cocked his head to the passenger side door, which opened and lifted.

With a sigh, she got in. It was only as the heat enveloped her that she realised how badly she was shaking with cold. Like frost had infected the marrow of her bones and was threatening to freeze her from the inside. Knowing her lungs, she'd get sick again.

Kol took one look at her before tugging off his coat and offering it. 'Put this on. I'm not sure Nithin can handle more snot. He really has a thing about germs.'

Thorn tugged the coat on without a word, and drew her legs into her chest.

'Are you okay?' he asked, voice quieter.

'I don't know.'

'Something happen?'

'Lots on my mind.'

'Want a distraction?'

She glanced over at him, intrigued. 'Depends.'

With a grin of mischief, Kol raised the coach into the air and the miles fell away behind them.

'Where are we?' she asked when he'd landed and cut the engine. They were surrounded by trees of all shapes and sizes, each with leaves of different colours and curves. Some had spots, others had stripes; some were shaped like spades, others like hearts.

'The Wol Gardens,' he said as he stepped out. 'One of my favourite places in the world. It's protected, but untended and usually quiet. Less touristy than Ashland.'

Sure enough, as they wandered through the trails and orchards and gardens, Thorn caught sight of only two others, and no one came near them. She was able to properly appreciate the sights and smells. There were flowers growing up the trunks of the trees and a lake filled with fish of a dozen different colours.

'I love the wild,' she remarked contentedly as they walked. She felt so much better without buildings around her.

'Me too,' he concurred.

They carried on past a lake, over a footbridge, down a gently sloping path, and on into another part of the forest. Leaves fluttered down on wind which whistled gently through the branches and vines that stuck out around the trunks of the great trees.

'So, you really fly?' she wondered aloud as they meandered along.

He gazed at her for a second, apparently taken by surprise, before a low rumble of laughter resonated in his throat. He shook his head, a smile curving his lips crookedly. 'I know it's horrible, but I'm starting to like how little you know of frai.'

She scowled. 'Why?'

'If your first impression was awful, it would colour all the rest. As I can promise that all moments with me will always be awesome, the first impressions you'll get are going to knock your socks off.'

She laughed with genuinely affectionate exasperation. 'All right, Charcoal, let's see you fly.'

He hesitated, nudging a rock on the ground with his foot before scratching the back of his head. 'Nah. Maybe next time.'

'Why?'

'I don't want to scare you.'

Thorn didn't know what to say to that. Only that it was perhaps the kindest thing she had ever heard. Forcing a swallow around the sudden lump in her throat, she shook her head. 'I'm not afraid of you.'

'Yeah?' His gold-black eyes lit up with joy and he suddenly seemed far keener on the idea.

'Yeah. Let's see your wings. But no impaling yourself, Holey Koly.'

Cheeks reddening, Kol took his bag off and then, with a deep breath, removed his shirt. As she watched, wings slowly spread from his back. They could have been made of black velvet. Despite how truly otherworldly he looked, she could see his trepidation. She nodded reassuringly.

With a flap of his wings, he rose a few metres into the air. There was something beautifully graceful about the display.

He descended slowly moments later and in seconds he was back to his more human-looking visage and pulling on his shirt. 'What'd you think?' he asked nervously.

'I think you're easily the coolest Suriia I've ever encountered.'

'I'll take it,' he said, beaming.

Eyeing the clouds of breath coming out of him, she pointed to his coat, which she was still wearing. 'Want it back?'

'You look better in it,' he said, picking his bag up and slinging it over his shoulder. 'Do you want to get something to eat on the way home?'

'Okay.'

As they walked slowly back to the coach, Kol began telling her about frai magic and powers. And for once she didn't mind listening.

'Because we know the earth, we can track better than almost every other species. With few exceptions.'

'What exceptions?'

'Some Suriias exchange magic with others: for marriage, religion, power. When pricos marry, the enchantment they use forms a magical link. And few forms of magic are powerful enough to challenge that.'

'Why isn't it just a general spell?'

'Because it was created by the pricos and can only be used if you have vryko and vylka blood. It doesn't work otherwise.'

'But frai don't track with magic?'

'I mean, it's part of our magic – reading the earth. It's as easy as breathing for me.'

She pondered that for a moment, and then she thought about the Spotters, and her heart rate picked up uncomfortably.

'Can you cast spells?' Her father had always believed it possible, but she'd never heard a Suriia cast a spell.

'Once, I think. Not on Earth. Now spells are called "old magicks".'

'Why can't you cast them anymore?'

'The books were left on Salfar and while the Suriias were in hiding, long before the war, the old ways died out.'

'Huh.'

Rather than stopping at a restaurant on the way back, Kol flew to one of the largest grocery stores in the sky, bright with vibrant colours and flashing signs.

She raised an eyebrow. 'We're going shopping?'

'We're going to find everything you don't have to cook,' he said, wiggling his eyebrows. 'You game?'

'We don't have to eat here, do we?'

'I prefer the ground.'

'Me too.'

With a small grimace, Thorn followed him inside. It was instantly overwhelming. She'd never seen so much food, in so many packages and varieties, in all her life. Seeing Suriias nearby and not running was still a new concept for her. They tracked her with their eyes; some hungry, some with disdain. But when they caught sight of Kol, they looked away quickly.

Twenty minutes later, they finished shopping and Kol flew down from the shop and back to the ground below. He didn't seem to be following any signs, instead going off the roads and flying over the fields and lowlands. She could hear distant noises, animals and drones, but none close enough to see.

He landed after a while and drove them out into a field. Parking the coach, he got out. Bemused, Thorn followed him.

The night air nipped at her skin and sent chills down her neck and spine and then across her body.

He dropped his coat on the grass in front of the coach's headlights and motioned for her to sit down.

'Where are we now?' she asked, sitting on his coat and catching the box of cookies he tossed to her.

'Just a field in the middle of nowhere.' He sat down gracefully and drew one knee into his chest. 'I like places in the middle of nowhere.'

She smiled. 'Yeah, me too.'

'Tell me something I don't know,' he said as he opened a readymade sandwich.

'Like what?'

'Favourite animal?'

Thorn opened a box of cookies and picked out the one with the largest piece of chocolate. 'Dog. I always wanted one.'

'Well, maybe we should get one.'

She waved the suggestion off. 'Yours?'

'I like rabbits.'

There was something so utterly endearing about the way he said that she choked on the cookie and ended up coughing out half.

'What?' he said with a laugh.

A giggle left her entirely unbidden. 'Nothing.'

'Ask me something.'

It took her a minute to think of something. 'Would you rather go forward in time or back?'

'Forward,' he said, wiping sauce from the corner of his lip. 'I don't want to know what's going to happen. You?'

'Back,' she said. 'Guess we wouldn't be going together if we ever got the chance.'

The wind changed direction, tossing dark strands of hair over his face. He bent his head and for the briefest moment she watched him, struck by his handsomeness.

He opened a bag of fruit and offered her an apple slice. 'Well if you're there, I definitely won't know what's going to happen. So back with you is forward for me.'

It was impossible not to smile at him, and he grinned right back.

She ate the apple slice methodically and tried to think of another question. Before she could, a drone passed by overhead, and they tracked it with their eyes as it carried on.

Neither spoke.

It was well after dark when they got back to the house.

Slipping inside like shadows, they ascended the stairs side by side.

'Goodnight, Charcoal,' she said when they paused outside of her room.

He winked. 'Goodnight, Rose. Dream of me and chocolate.'

'Like side by side?'

'However you want,' he said, walking backwards toward his room and shrugging, an impish smirk playing on his lips.

Thorn rolled her eyes and stepped into the bedroom. It was only then, in the silence of her room, that she remembered Jinx's latest note.

She waited until no sounds came from the other rooms and then changed into her more durable running gear and slipped out the window.

Jinx was lurking on the other side of the road, cloaked in darkness. He kissed her in greeting before they set off through the forests.

The latest facility was only two hours away this time, nestled in the hills and they reached it without difficulty, although both were shivering from the damp chill in the air, their breaths leaving them in white clouds.

The building stretched out before Thorn and Jinx, a black mass against the sparkling midnight sky. Like a bad omen.

'What's in this one?' she asked grimly.

'No idea,' said Jinx. 'You hear rumours of places with stockpiles. Thought it might be worth a look.'

She appraised the building, trying to discern its full size. 'Are you sure it's safe?'

'It'll be fine. Come on.'

Thorn wasn't wholly convinced, but she wasn't about to protest if he was going. They moved through the trees as quietly as they could until they reached the deserted road that led up to the building. There was no sign of any guards or watchmen. If anything, the vicinity hadn't had visitors in years.

When they reached the front door, it took both of them to yank the rusty handle open. A damp, foul smell wafted from within and the air bit into her exposed skin.

'I don't know about this, Jinx,' she admitted as he began heaving the door ajar. Rust had long ago taken hold of the hinges and the frame had warped. 'There could be any number of things in there.'

'There won't be any Suriias. But it might have human records. It might have medicine. It might have weapons.'

The prospect was too tempting not to agree. 'Have you found more humans? For our group?'

'Yep. Found a pair of siblings the other day. Parin and Trinity. And a man, Pike.'

'How many is that?'

'Fourteen so far. We caught wind of a few more so we won't leave just yet.'

Her heart ached with how much she wanted to meet them all. 'You guys are amazing.'

He shot her a grin. 'You're coming, right? You and Thistle?'

'Definitely,' she said, although the gnawing in her gut about what Thistle would say upon leaving flared anew.

The door now open just enough to slip through, they crept inside and clicked on their torches. The air was heavy with humidity and Thorn began sweating almost immediately.

Like cats, the pair slinked through the hallways, searching the various rooms. There was a staircase that spiralled down several storeys into the darkest, dankest corridor she had ever set foot in. Every prison housed nightmares, but this one was decorated with bloodstains, grime and ash. In one room, unlike the others, there was something terribly disquieting.

There, in the middle of the room was a strange shimmer. It went floor to ceiling and was nearly invisible unless you looked straight at it. She could see through it to the other side of the room, but it was disconcerting, like she was opening her eyes underwater. It felt … magical.

Jinx stepped closer and she caught him by the arm. 'Don't,' she implored. 'I don't like it.'

'Why?'

'There's just something wrong with it,' she murmured, taking a step back. 'Come on, let's go.'

'It's just a room, Thorn.'

'Please.'

He acquiesced after another long pause. Then, shrugging, he cocked his head and carried on.

They made their way back down the corridor and Thorn was relieved to put as much space between them and the room as possible.

It took them an hour of searching but they found a good assortment of medicines and supplies before making their way back out.

'Are we going to blow it?' she asked as they closed the door.

'Not yet,' said Jinx.

'Why?'

'There's no reason to. It's not being used.'

Thorn looked back over her shoulder. No, there hadn't been anything obviously wrong in the room. But she couldn't shake the feeling that there was something *different* about the room.

'Do you want to come over? Jade is dying to see you and I'd love to spend some proper time with you when we're not running in the dark.'

'Sure,' she agreed instantly, eager to see Jade again.

Soon enough, Thorn and Jinx had ditched the coach and were making their way through the back alleys of the city like rats.

'Welcome to our apartment,' said Jade upon opening the door. They hugged and Thorn grinned at her. She hadn't seen Jade since the night they'd met, but Thorn found she missed her all the time.

'It's been condemned for ten years,' said Jinx, following her inside. He dropped onto the tattered sofa in the sitting room and spread his arms out. 'Took a bit of tidying up.'

'It was a nightmare,' amended Jade. 'But now it's almost homelike.'

Thorn heaved a contented sigh and looked around, taking it all in. The peeling wallpaper, the holes in the wall, the mould in the corners. 'It's lovely.' She meant every word.

Jade lit candles, giving the room an atmospheric quality and they turned off the lanterns as the various scents filled the room. 'Coffee?' she called over her shoulder as she disappeared into the kitchen.

Thorn heard a kettle switch on. 'Yeah, please,' she replied.

'Always, sis,' said Jinx. He waved Thorn over to the sofa. 'Come join me.'

'Milk?' called Jade.

'Yes!' said Jinx.

'I'm good!' said Thorn.

She'd only just sat down when Jinx leaned over and kissed her. When she made to pull back, his hand came up to cradle her face, keeping her there. His hands twisted in her hair as he deepened the kiss.

Unsure what to do or how to react, she let him carry on, wishing he would stop. Thankfully, he did soon enough, his eyes heavy-lidded, his mouth slack; he was looking at her in a way she deeply wished he wouldn't. And she was also distinctly aware of his breath.

She scooted away. Tucking her hair behind her ears, she tried to summon her courage. 'Jinx,' she began. 'I, ah … I've been thinking—'

'Me too,' he interrupted. 'I can't wait to introduce you to everyone. I've been telling them all about you. It's going to be amazing to leave this place behind.' He leaned in and kissed her again. 'With you.'

Thorn's rejection died in her throat. Heart-pounding and feeling strange, she smiled tightly, stood and walked into the kitchen.

Jade was almost finished making tea. 'I'm so glad you finally came by.'

Thorn nodded, but her stomach continued to twist like vines on a rose bush. Jade grabbed two cups, gestured for Thorn to grab the third, and disappeared into the sitting room.

Alone, Thorn wiped at her mouth and went to the sink. She washed her hands and her mouth; she swished water around and spat it back out. The sick feeling wouldn't abate, however, and she cursed herself for not plucking up the courage to tell him straight out.

'Thorn?'

'One second!'

Her heart didn't stop racing at a sickening speed until she was back over the wall of the mansion a few hours later. Closing the window carefully, she dropped onto the edge of the bed and stared tiredly at the wall.

The beep of her phone offered a welcome distraction and she pulled it out of her pocket.

Kol had written: *I can hear you sneaking out.*

There was a Suric symbol attached the end and she knew enough about the language to know it was the symbol for conspiratorial acts. It made her smile in wry amusement.

Wrong, she typed back. *I'm sneaking in.*

There was no reply for a few seconds, and she felt a wave of disappointment until she heard a creak down the hall. A moment later there was a knock on her door.

'Kol?'

The door opened and he slipped inside. He wore nothing but trousers. It was stupidly attractive. 'Where'd you sneak off to?'

'Dinner with friends,' she said, trying and failing not to admire him in the muted glow from the lamplight outside. She'd rarely come across anyone shirtless, let alone a Suriia.

He quirked an eyebrow. 'Didn't want Thistle to know?'

'Thistle has her own friends.' Then, realising how bitter she sounded, she added, 'Didn't mean to wake you.'

Kol waved off her apology and thumbed over his shoulder. 'Have a nightcap with me to make up for it?'

Suddenly the furthest thing from tired, Thorn kicked off her shoes and followed him.

Downstairs in the kitchen, she hoisted herself onto the counter and watched him make tea. He didn't say anything, and she was starting to wonder why he'd even asked her downstairs at all, when he handed her a cup of tea and cleared his throat.

There was a cautious yet oddly resolved look on his face. 'Why don't you want Thistle to know you have a boyfriend?'

Thorn's eyebrows shot up. 'I don't have a boyfriend.'

Kol leaned back against the stove and blew on the top of his tea. 'No one sneaks out at midnight for dinner, Rose.'

She looked at him pointedly. 'I do not have a boyfriend.'

It was clear he didn't believe her.

'I don't,' she reiterated. 'I've never even had sex.'

Her words made Kol still, the cup halfway to his mouth. He lowered it slowly. 'Never?'

Cheeks warm with embarrassment, she shrugged her shoulders, wishing she'd said nothing at all. 'You saw Tiz lose her mind because someone kissed me. I thought the fact that I'd never done anything was obvious.'

'Haven't you guys been going to Speak Softlies for years?'

'I take Thistle. I've never touched a Suriia.'

'There are humans there.'

She scowled at him. 'Then I guess no one's wanted to.'

He set his cup down and squeezed the bridge of his nose. 'No, I didn't—' He huffed. 'That's not what I meant at all. I'm just surprised.'

'Why?'

'Because I think you're beautiful.'

The air vanished from her lungs and for some unfathomable reason, her mouth went numb.

'And I would never judge you for not having sex,' he continued, voice quieter. 'I've never had sex.'

Her shock at this last admission finally enabled her to react. 'Bullshit.'

'Excuse me?'

'Your best friend is a sbura.'

'What, do you think sex rubs off or something?'

They both made faces at the accidental pun.

'I'm twenty,' she said. 'I'm guessing you're a lot older.'

'I am,' he affirmed. 'But what we do in our own time is no one's business but ours. My point is that you shouldn't be ashamed of how much you have or haven't done, not to make this a debate about my own prowess.' He put his palms on the countertop. 'Will you do one thing for me and I promise I won't enquire about your late-night buddy anymore?'

Her reply came out thick and halting. 'Depends. What?'

'Be sure.'

'Sure?'

'I'm not going to pry into your life, Rose, but … Just be sure.'

The way he said that took her breath away.

CHAPTER SEVEN
Hazy

Thorn spent the next few days mulling everything over. She tried to talk to Jinx twice more. The problem was that every time they met up, he'd bring up the future and hold her hand, and Thorn's stomach would twist at the thought of what offending him might lead to. He could leave without telling her. He could refuse to let her join. Heartbreak did different things to different people and rarely was it noble.

She longed to get Thistle's input, but Thistle felt more distant than ever, and her burgeoning friendship with Kol had a confusing, slightly heavy aura to it after their conversation in the kitchen. Every time they were alone, Thorn somehow ended up catching and holding his gaze. His smile proved infectious, no matter how preoccupied she was.

There were smaller moments too, like the day he came out as she was jogging around the mansion in the snow and gestured for her to stop. When she did, he put a hat on her head and then gave her gloves. Or the times she'd be watching a movie and he'd join her. At some point they developed a silent routine of him sitting down, pulling her feet into his lap, and stealing the bowl of whatever snacks she'd been eating. Neither moved nor spoke, but one movie often turned into two before they stumbled sleepily up to bed.

Late one evening, Thistle, Nithin and Kol returned from work to say that Kassian, Eva and Ivy were joining them for dinner. Without waiting for Thorn to agree, Thistle tugged her upstairs to change. Why they needed to change for dinner was a mystery lost on Thorn.

It was the first time in over a week that Thistle spent time in Thorn's bedroom, but she was filled with statistics and ideas for Nithin's company and Thorn lost interest quickly.

Kassian arrived when they were still upstairs, and Thistle shot to her feet and was already at the door when she turned back to Thorn.

'You coming?' she asked, too excited to notice that Thorn's mood could not have been more diametrically opposed to her own.

'I'll just be a minute,' said Thorn with a tight smile.

Her attention elsewhere, Thistle disappeared out the door.

Exhaling heavily, Thorn sank onto the bed and looked out the window at the cold, wintery night. The only good thing about living with Suriias was the view. Wide windows that could be stood in front of for hours with no fear of anyone reporting you, or memorising your face to hunt you down later, or simply coming at you without a second thought. She rubbed her eyes roughly, blurring her vision.

A soft knock made her start.

'Yeah?'

'Can I come in?' It was Kol.

She tried to ignore the sudden, unprompted shudder of giddy nervousness in her chest. 'Sure.'

He stepped inside and walked over to her. He'd changed out of his work attire and was in worn jeans and a shirt. It was far less off-putting than when he looked like he had power to wield.

'I'm sorry I didn't give you a heads-up about them coming over,' he said with an apologetic smile. 'It was last minute, and my phone was dead. I would have.'

She stared at him, completely dumbstruck. The silence dragged on and he rocked on the balls of his feet, jamming his hands into his trouser pockets.

'You okay?' he prompted after almost a minute without a response. 'You mad?'

'Thank you,' she whispered.

He did a doubletake. 'For what?'

'That,' she said, nodding to him. 'What you just said.'

A bashful smile curved his mouth and he thumbed over his shoulder. 'They're not so bad. Eva's active at Nithin's company even if he can't legally hire her; Ivy helps run a safechange. I think you'll like them if you don't mind the fact that they like Kassian.'

Rather entirely hypocritically, Thorn did mind. But she was too confused by the first part to bother with the second. 'A safechange?'

'One of the underground locations for humans on the run.'

She wasn't sure she'd heard him right. 'What?'

Her surprise was a match for Kol's.

'You didn't know about the safechanges?'

'No,' she said.

He nodded slowly. 'It's a death sentence for even Kassian if they're caught, but we give them money and they have contacts who try to sneak humans off the island.'

'To where?'

'The north of the continent. Less Suric presence due to the year-round cold and ice.'

'Suriias don't like ice?'

'There is no ice on Salfar.'

Thorn made a mental note to tell all of this to Jinx later. 'There's no north and south pole on Salfar?' she asked instead.

'I have no idea,' he admitted. 'I've never been. Like I said, I believe in levels.'

'I believe in reality.'

'Are they mutually exclusive?'

She rolled her eyes. 'I think you like arguing with me.'

'I *love* arguing with you.'

A heavy, hard to read stillness followed those words and Thorn's skin felt a little hot, as if something physical was growing between them.

She turned towards the window, not wanting him to read her.

'Do you want to come down?' he prompted. 'It's okay if you don't. I can bring you some dinner.'

The offer was tempting, but Thorn stood regardless. 'Tiz will make it a thing if I don't come down.'

'I promise it won't be that bad,' he assured her. 'And if you're desperate to leave, say you feel sick and I'll say I do, too. We can blame food poisoning.'

A small chuckle escaped her lips and his grin widened mischievously.

They left the bedroom then and wandered down the stairs. Nithin and Kassian were standing by the fire in the sitting room; on the sofa, Thistle was deep in conversation with Ivy and Eva. She waved Thorn over. To her relief, Kol followed her instead of going over to Nithin.

'How are you liking Courtenz?' asked Ivy, giving Thorn a smile. She was well dressed and spoke eloquently, but the scars on her face told the real story.

Thorn nodded. 'It's fine.'

'You should come with Thistle to the office sometime,' said Eva. 'We'd love your input.'

'Not really my thing.'

Ivy and Eva exchanged looks.

'You don't have to be on edge all the time,' said Ivy, almost patronisingly. 'Nothing's going to happen.'

'It could.'

Eva giggled. 'No, it can't. The guys would never let anything happen to us.'

'It's true,' said Ivy. 'Don't worry so much.'

Thorn's fist clenched in her lap.

'Rose, want a drink?'

Her eyes flicked to Kol, who had risen to his feet and was looking at her meaningfully. Glad of the out, Thorn stood and followed him out of the room.

In the kitchen, he poured her a glass of amber liquid and held it out to her. 'Got food poisoning yet?'

'Getting there,' she mumbled, taking the glass. The strong smell of brandy made her start.

'Want to go for a walk before dinner?'

'Tiz—'

'Is occupied. She and Eva have been chatting all day. It's going to be business talk. You showed your face, you grunted; you can ditch the small talk.'

That settled it. Thorn nodded and they went out the side door into the gardens. The sun had set, and the sky was darkening. A breeze swept across the garden, sending petals drifting into the wind like colourful snow. She meandered after him down the winding path towards the crest of the hill, and then slowly picked her way down to the creek. Sitting on the bench, she glared out into the dark night. In the distance, the lights of Courtenz twinkled, a million neon stars and rainbows. It didn't seem so bad from so far away.

'You know,' she mused aloud, 'I don't think there'd be any place for me in your better world.'

'Not everyone will be like those ladies.'

'No. But it's not my world.'

'It could be.'

'It can't. That's not me.'

'You can be whatever you want in whatever world you're in.'

'No,' she retorted. 'You really can't.'

'Maybe not easily. But you have to try.'

'Does that argument work for the ones who died before they had a chance?'

He held her gaze openly, a dark eyebrow arched. 'Arguments are arguments with or without luck,' he replied. 'Sometimes life is disgustingly unfair. It doesn't change the fact that you have to keep trying to live life as you want it to be. If we let the pain cripple us, there's no hope for anything.'

'I don't have any hope.'

'Of course you do.'

Her scowl deepened. 'You say that like you have the authority to say it.'

'I know you hope for humans to return,' he countered. 'I know you hope for a future for you and Thistle. I know you hope that, despite everything, you'll be proven wrong about us. And even if you don't want to believe that they do, you hope that good things still exist. If you didn't, you wouldn't fight to stay alive. I'm not saying any of this to mock you, Rose. I'm saying what I know about you. What you'd admit to Thistle but won't admit to me.'

Indeed, rather than admit he was entirely right about how much and how adamantly she hoped for all those things, she said instead, 'If you know already, it would just be redundant.'

'Yeah,' he muttered, scratching at his beard. 'But getting to know you would be nicer if it didn't feel like you have no interest in getting to know me.'

'I'm never going to be Thistle.'

'No one's asking you to be.'

Thorn pursed her lips. 'I feel like she wants me to change. To forget how we grew up and the things that were done to us.'

From the corner of her eye, she saw him reach out, and stayed still as he put his hand over hers. She held her breath, heart galloping in her chest.

'You shouldn't forget,' he said, tracing his thumb absently over hers. 'You should always remember. But shouldn't a genuine apology be a start?' Unmasked sorrow softened his features. 'I've never hurt anyone. I know it's a worthless statement when it's my side that's hurting yours, but not all my side thinks that's okay. I've made it my entire career to help humans. I want that to mean something. Even if it doesn't mean much.'

She blinked the tears from her eyes. 'Of course it means something. It sounds amazing. But words are easy, Kol. I've seen words become worthless after a day, and I've seen words become worthless after five years. Maybe if you succeed, somehow, the few humans left will believe that. And I really hope they do. But I've seen too much.'

'And I will keep proving you wrong,' he said adamantly.

His relentless determination made her chest burn with longing. 'I really wish you were human,' she whispered, choking on the want for it.

'I wish you didn't have to doubt me for not being human.'

'Yeah, me too.' Pulling her hand from his grasp, she drew her legs onto the bench and into her chest. 'Kol?'

'Yeah, Rose?'

'I don't have no interest in getting to know you.' She offered a small smile. 'I think you're a really good friend. And you're right, I'm hoping. I'm hoping you're not a lie.'

'I'm not.'

They lingered on the bench until Nithin's voice floated down from the house to inform them that dinner was ready. The food, despite its heavenly smell, held no appeal for Thorn and she was relieved when the evening came to a close.

After Kassian, Eva and Ivy finally left, Thistle announced she was exhausted and wanted to go to bed, only giving Thorn a small wave in parting.

Thorn spent the next hour taking her frustrations out on the dirty dishes before heading to the bedroom she was using and climbing out the window.

She darted across the lawn, past the guards, and climbed the wall. Dropping off the other side, she landed without a sound on the wet grass. Jinx was there already, leaning against a nearby tree.

'Evening, you.' He kissed her without warning. She jerked back, resisting the urge to wipe her face where she could feel the imprint of his lips.

'Hi.'

'You okay?' he asked, eyeing her curiously.

'Fine.' She stuffed her hands into her pockets. 'Just tired.'

'You sure?'

'Yeah.' She bobbed her head. 'How far is it to this place?'

'It's on the other side of the city.'

Thorn grinned in nervous, excited anticipation. They'd been planning this particular event for weeks now. It was one of the Suriia research facilities, where they grew humans in test tubes and kept them in cages. Thorn remembered Clay saying that once humans had done the same to animals, but she couldn't imagine it. She ate meat to survive but caging anything was cruel.

Two hours later, the pair reached the facility. Shaped like several triangles pushed together, its edges jutted up into the sky like sinister fingers.

'Want to explore?' Jinx proposed as they shimmied through a hole in the fence.

'No,' said Thorn, stomach twisting. 'This isn't a relic of history. It's a tomb of our ancestors.'

'A tomb of thousands.'

They exchanged sad, enraged grimaces before setting to work.

As Thorn cut the wires, Jinx disappeared to place the explosives. Abandoned as the building appeared, Thorn had no doubt there was a hidden security system and she didn't want to linger. He returned a few minutes later and they tore into the trees as the building went up behind them.

Only when they were far enough away to breathe did they turn around and watch their handiwork.

'We did it!' she cried, staring at the explosion. 'We fucking did it!'

Jinx pulled her close and claimed her in a kiss, his hands reeking of petrol and smoke. She broke away after a few seconds, not enjoying it at all. But when he tugged her close again and wrapped his arms around her, it was hard to pull back a second time. He was so excited; she didn't want to put a damper on the night. But she was relieved when he finally suggested they head back to the inner city.

'Want to come to mine for a celebratory drink?' he asked as they went.

She hesitated. 'Jade home?'

'Yep.'

The prospect of seeing Jade convinced her and she nodded.

'Awesome,' he said, taking her hand. 'Let's just chill out and you can not think for once.'

'Not thinking sounds nice. I just have to be back before they notice I'm missing.'

'Think they'd care?' Before she could reply, he answered his own question. 'I suppose they think of us as things they own. They won't want property getting away.'

Torn between agreeing and wanting *not* to agree, Thorn settled for a non-committal noise and followed him over the rooftops, through alleys, and down two drains before they came up in the street where he and Jade were squatting.

To Thorn's disappointment, Jade was sound asleep when they walked in and Jinx suggested leaving her be.

'She rarely sleeps well,' he whispered.

'I know the feeling,' said Thorn.

'Want something to drink?'

'What you got?'

'Tea? Something relaxing?'

'Sure.'

A couple of minutes later, he brought her a steaming mug that smelled strongly of ginger. She took a sip and warmth filled her chest.

Almost immediately, and quite unnervingly, her vision began to spin. 'Whoa,' she said, trying to focus on something. Anything.

She looked down at the mug in her hand. It moved in and out. 'What the fuck?'

'There's no magic in it,' he said, voice going in and out, in and out. 'Just Hazies.'

The words didn't compute straight away. It was like someone was swirling her brain around inside her skull.

'Hazies,' she grunted. The Suric party drug. 'You drugged me?'

'It'll chill you out, I promise.'

Seemingly oblivious to her outrage, Jinx reached out, took the mug and set it aside, and kissed her. His hands felt too hot on her skin, too rough; there was too much pressure.

'Wait,' she gasped, breaking away from him and taking ragged breaths. 'Wait, Jinx.'

She and Thistle had lived near the ocean once and Thorn had been swept into the tide and almost drowned. This feeling was not dissimilar. Drawing breath took great, ragged effort; her vision darkened and lightened, sharpened and then went hazy; the colours around her became brighter, sparkling, as if all the world were lit up with fifty different shades of neon starlight. She felt a strong inclination to get sick everywhere.

'It's okay,' he said, his voice still moving in and out, in and out. 'I took them, too. Just ride the wave, Thorn.'

'I don't want—'

But he silenced her with a kiss, and his legs moved between hers. His hand unzipped her trousers and slipped inside. She cried out, but he swallowed the sound.

'Jinx,' she said, louder, trying to source the strength to push him away. But she couldn't. Her arms felt as sturdy as jam and she couldn't get him off.

He put his other hand over her mouth as his lips moved down her neck.

'Jinx!' She tried to shout but his grip tightened, and it came out muffled. Fear turned to reaction and she slammed her knee into his side, unseating him enough to scramble away.

The second she was on her feet, her vision tilted, and she almost fell over as she refastened her jeans. Everything was too bright. Too loud. She felt like she was freefalling through a frozen rainbow made of glass.

'Thorn—'

She bolted.

Out the door, down the alley, and then back up the road. The cold rush of the night hit her hard and the drug's effects increased tenfold.

Halfway up the road, her legs threatened to give out beneath her, and she had to lean against a building to keep from keeling over.

She wanted Thistle. But before she had the chance to take out her phone, the sound of approaching sirens made her dart into the shadows. She barely got around the corner when the Spotter coaches appeared. They jumped out and began combing the area.

Thorn put a hand over her mouth, convinced her breathing was as loud as a scream, and blinked slowly, forcefully, trying not to collapse. She saw shapes in the corners of her eyes and the Spotters suddenly vanished.

She did a doubletake and stood, bewildered. And then she realised: Hazies made you see things that weren't there. Bad reactions could be nightmarish. Hallucinations that felt so real people had hurt themselves.

'I hate you so much, Jinx,' she cried as panicked, wheezing gasps tore their way out of her with astonishing violence. She almost fell onto her hands, only just managing to catch herself on the wall.

Taking her phone out of her pocket with immense difficulty, she somehow managed to dial Thistle's number. It went straight to voicemail.

She cursed shrilly, hysteria rising. The world around her was a neon, flexing fog and her mind was spinning inside her body, her blood dancing in a sickening, distorting way. If the Spotters really did show up, she was dead.

Putting a hand to her mouth, she clicked on Kol's name and tried to steady her breathing. Forming a coherent thought was next to impossible.

'Rose? It's three in the morning. Why didn't you just knock?'
The words swam in and out. In and out. In and out.

'Rose? Thorn?' She could hear him turning on his light and moving around. 'Where are you?'

'Can you come get me?' She was quivering so hard her head ached. Everything in front of her eyes suddenly went on fire and she jumped back with a yelp. 'Please, Kol.'

'Where are you?' His alarm was audible.

The wind whipping off the river – when had she reached the river? – was monstrously icy, biting with every slap, and she stared at the black depths, wondering just how cold the water was.

'Rose? You there?'

She blinked tears from her eyes and tried to focus. 'By—by a river. I don't know which one.'

'Okay,' he said with calm assurance. 'That's fine. I'll find you. I'm on my way.'

She wanted to cry with relief. 'Kol?' she croaked.

'Yeah, Rose?'

'How long do Hazies take to wear off?'

'How much did you take?'

'I didn't,' she whispered, clutching her skull and tilting slightly.

'You didn't?'

Her vision sharpened, and for some reason everything went purple. She blinked several times, her tongue feeling thick.

'Rose?'

'It was in the tea,' she said distantly, trying to figure out why her fingernails were green. 'He … he didn't tell me it was in the tea.'

'I'm coming, Rose.' She thought he sounded angry, but his words came out calm. 'I'll be there in less than five minutes.'

'Thank you.'

'Stay on the phone with me,' he said. 'Can you do that? You don't have to talk, just stay on the phone.'

'I can do that.'

'Are you alone?'

'Yeah.'

'Okay. I'll be there in a few minutes. Take deep breaths.'

'I feel dizzy.'

'I know. I'm coming. Just breathe.'

A sudden scuttling sound made her whole body go still.

'Fuck,' she cried. Though she could not have said why, she knew this time she wasn't seeing things. This time the danger was real.

'What?'

'Scuttlers.'

A series of remarkably foul expletives left Kol at that. 'Don't go anywhere,' he told her, and then the line went dead.

Despite how truly close she was to collapse, the thought of what the Spotters would do if they caught her pressed her feet into motion.

She darted into the reeds by the water's edge and ducked low. Water filled her boots and froze her to the bone, but even drugged, even terrified, Thorn didn't make a sound.

The other end of the call picked back up.

'Rose?'

She didn't answer.

'Rose, it's fine,' he said. 'I called Headquarters. They won't touch you. They know you're with me.'

A sob tore out of her and she put a hand over her mouth.

'Rose? Are you there?'

Fear had sealed her throat and responding proved impossible. Even breathing was difficult. Short, stilted wheezes cut out of her, hardly able to manifest around her hysteria.

'I'm almost there,' he said quietly. 'I promise.'

He kept up a calm string of words as she waited. She didn't process much of what he said, but she clung to the soothing sound of his voice.

After what seemed an age, lights shone in the air above. The coach landed without a sound and Kol jumped out. His long coat flapped in the wind and his boots crunched on the cold grass. She saw his eyes flash gold in the darkness, and he turned in her direction. In seconds he was at her side. Later, when she wasn't drugged out of her mind, she'd remember that the plants seemed to bend to his will, moving out of his way, out of hers, creating an open, unencumbered path between them. He reached her easily, not even getting wet, the ground no longer marshy, but solid and firm.

'Rose?' He put a hand on either side of her face and tilted her head up gently. 'Rose, you okay?'

Her teeth were chattering, and she was too cold and terrified to think clearly. 'N-not even a l-little,' she ground out.

He put his arm around her and steered her towards the coach. Her boots squelched with every step and shivers racked her body anew. Kol noticed and paused. Taking off his coat, he helped her into it. The coat was warm and smelled safe. Thorn couldn't think of another way to describe it. It just smelled safe.

'Rose,' he said softly. 'The hospital—'

'I don't need a doctor.'

'Please don't say that if you actually do,' he implored.

'I don't,' she assured him. 'He didn't get that far.'

The concern on his face quickly morphed into fury. Yet rather than pry, Kol opened the door to the coach. She climbed inside, feeling detached and robotic.

He jogged around the driver's side and started the engine. Then, to her surprise, he held out his hand without a word. Thorn put her hand in his and his thumb brushed absently over her skin, gentle and calm.

She didn't even register them arriving at the mansion until Kol got out. She couldn't propel her legs into motion and a second later her door was being opened. He helped her out and into the house. At the top of the staircase, he glanced at her, but she made no move to go towards her room, and after a few seconds he led her down the hall to his room.

Inside, everything smelled of cinnamon and clean laundry and the flowers which lined the windows, and the dust from the bookshelves. It was warm and cosy and felt like a sanctuary.

'You're soaked,' he said, grabbing a shirt and a pair of sleeping trousers. 'Put these on.'

She took them, but she was shaking too badly to be of any use.

'Do you want help?'

Thorn managed a nod.

Kol set the clothes down and helped her out of his coat, her wet coat, her boots, her jeans and shirt. She held her arms up as he pulled a shirt over her head and then she sat on his bed, warmer now, albeit shaking like ice in a blender. She crossed her legs and pulled one of his pillows into her chest. She felt the sudden, devastating urge to cry.

'Rose,' said Kol, sotto voce, sitting in his desk chair and watching her worriedly, 'what happened?'

She swallowed hard. It was like trying to force gravel down her throat. Her voice was raspy when she finally found it. 'I didn't know the tea had anything in it. He just … put Hazies in it without telling me.'

A furious expression distorted Kol's normally affable features. 'Did he hurt you?'

'I didn't want to,' she croaked, eyes and throat burning. 'I asked him to stop and he put a hand over my mouth …'

The tears broke through then. Seconds later, the bed dipped and Kol's arms were encircling her. She unfolded herself enough to curl into him. He held her until her sobs evened out and she was quietly sniffling.

'I need a shower,' she muttered.

'Do you want me to start one for you?'

Instead of answering, she stared at the wall, too shell shocked to be proactive. 'I should have told him weeks ago. I just didn't want to lose them …'

'Them?'

'People.'

And now she doubted Jinx would ever let her join them.

Tears ripped out of her anew and Kol drew her back into his arms, cradling her close and speaking soft and reassuring nonsense that brought calm to her soul.

At some point Thorn cried herself to sleep, and when she awoke to the sound of hammering rain the next morning, she was in Kol's bed and his arms were around her, and she realised she had slept without nightmares. He smelled like goodness and she closed her eyes and breathed as she gathered her courage.

After several more minutes, she sat up with stiff, pained slowness and looked down at him. He was awake and watching her. His dark hair, messy and tousled, fell into his cat-eyes, rendering him bashful. The concern etched on his handsome features filled her with gratitude and she managed a small smile.

''Morning.'

'Good morning,' he whispered. 'You okay?'

'My throat hurts.'

With slow, measured movements, giving her the chance to shy away, he reached out and traced the skin on her neck. 'Do you need anything?'

'A drink and a shower.'

He nodded and turned, picking up a glass on the bedside table. 'Here.'

The water helped soothe her aching throat somewhat and she managed a cough to dislodge the raspy, sick feeling.

'Who was it?' he asked when she'd finished the glass.

'It doesn't matter.'

'Rose,' he said, soft but firm, 'it does matter.'

Not wanting to answer him – not sure what she wanted to do about any of it – she climbed out of bed and began searching around for her coat and boots.

'He deserves to be punished.'

'He's been punished enough,' she replied, the story of Jinx and Jade's early years coming back to her. A lifetime of being hunted hardly made for good morals.

'Did you hurt him?'

She looked at him for a long moment before shaking her head and walking towards the door.

'Just because he's a human doesn't mean he gets a free pass to treat others like shit.'

'No,' she said, hand on the doorknob. 'But until I can think straight, what's to be done about him can fucking wait.'

With that, she left Kol's room, wondering why she felt both guilty and defensive about her words. She wanted Jinx to pay. She'd even be delighted to see Kol be the one to do it. But no matter how much she wanted to trust him, he wasn't human. There would never be a *we* between them. Only a *them*. And humans did not let Suriias into their business.

Thorn dropped down onto the bed and pulled the blanket around her body like a cocoon. It was confusing – feeling so much she felt nothing. She wanted to crumble to dust as much as she wanted to turn to ice and solidify. Mostly she wanted to cry, but couldn't seem to.

The sun was just starting to peek through the storm clouds when Thistle stepped into the room and crawled into the bed beside her. 'I'm so sorry I didn't answer. What happened?'

Not since their parents were murdered had Thorn broken down in Thistle's arms. She wanted Thistle to think of her as unbreakable. A force to always rely upon. Only now she wasn't. Now her skin was crawling, and she didn't know who was the friend and who was the enemy.

'Tor, what happened?'

Between gasps and hiccups, Thorn told her everything, in excruciating detail, and Thistle listened attentively, holding her hands the whole time.

'Fuck him, seriously,' said Thistle when she finished. Anger had twisted her amiable, kind features into something fierce. 'Promise me you won't go near him again.'

Thorn dragged in a rattling breath and leaned back against the wall. Her eyes ached and her throat was dry. 'He was my only chance at finding Veryn.'

'We'll find Veryn without him.'

'We?'

'I know I haven't been around much—'

'At all.'

'I can't sneak out without Nithin noticing. Do you know how on edge the Spotters are? They're noticing humans even more now. It's not safe to hunt Veryn right now. But we will soon. We just need to wait.'

Thorn didn't want to wait. She'd been dreaming of killing Veryn for years. It had been long enough. 'Have you talked to Nithin about Veryn?' she queried.

Thistle hesitated and Thorn's heart sank.

'I don't want to use him, Tor,' she whispered. 'I want to work with him. Do you know about how much he's done for humans already? He's working from the inside. He's going to do this the right way.'

'The Suriias won, Tiz. They won and we're dying out.'

'We're not gone yet. We can still come back.'

'We have to live first.'

'Yeah, we do.'

Thorn felt an odd sense of betrayal and she hated that feeling more than any other. 'We're supposed to be a team,' she admonished. 'There's not supposed to be Suriias on our team.'

'There are now.'

'Well, there shouldn't be.'

'You do realise Jinx attacked you last night and Kol brought you home? Think about that for a minute.'

'That's all I'm thinking about. Fuck you, Tiz.'

Thistle stood. 'I'm sorry this happened to you, Tor. I really am. But it's not Nithin's fault. You can't hate someone just for what they are. That's exactly the reason you hate Suriias! For how they hate us! This cyclical bullshit will see us all extinct!'

Thorn shot to her feet, infuriated. 'When I go around committing genocide, feel free to compare me to them. Until then, realise how stupid and ignorant you sound.'

'Maybe you should realise the same.'

'Oh, go back to your nymphomaniac.'

Thistle recoiled, completely offended, and promptly stormed out of the room.

'Fuck,' said Thorn, hands going to her head. Thistle might be acting naïve, but there was no reason to be a dick about it. Except that Thorn thought her point still held. In the twenty years they had been alive, they had met exactly two Suriias who hadn't attacked them. Two. And they had known Nithin and Kol mere weeks. There was no telling what the future held. There was no telling when Nithin and Kol would suddenly find new humans to entertain themselves with.

The thought left her more sad than angry, and she wanted to break everything in sight.

CHAPTER EIGHT
In the Shadows

When Thorn and Thistle were young, things hadn't been simple, but they had seemed *simpler*. Arguments brewed over silly things like playing alone, or not gathering the right size sticks to practise their sword fighting, or because one of them hadn't bothered to collect enough flowers to weave into crowns. They bickered like sisters, their fights forgotten about seconds after they began. Even after their parents died and they lived alone, for years differences between them dissipated before they began. Until Nithin came along.

The day of Thistle and Nithin's wedding dawned bright and sunny. It was hard to believe they'd been in Courtenz so long and Thorn was still marvelling at how fast it had all gone, at how little she'd achieved – and the fact that the wedding was actually happening – as she tugged on the dress Thistle had picked out for her earlier that week. It was a black dress, modest enough that Thorn didn't feel completely vulnerable. But she wasn't someone who had ever felt comfortable in a dress. Thistle wore them effortlessly, but Thorn felt unprotected and generally refused to.

She pulled her messy hair back into a loose knot, buckled her blade on the inside of her thigh, well hidden by the dress, and then slipped on her boots. She appraised herself in the mirror dubiously. It wasn't a convincing sight. She looked awkward, too thin, uncomfortable and deerlike.

Grabbing the coat Thistle had insisted she buy – it matched the dress, apparently – she left her room, closing the door behind her. Resting her head against the wall, she took a few deep breaths in a futile attempt at stemming her mounting insecurities.

Thistle's head suddenly poked out of her room. 'You look gorgeous!'

Thorn blushed.

'Come join me,' said Thistle, beckoning her over. 'I'm almost done.'

'Where's Nithin?' asked Thorn warily.

'Downstairs with Kol.'

Inside the large bedroom, clothes and cosmetics were strewn everywhere.

'Did a shop throw up in here?'

Thistle giggled. 'Sit down. I want to do your makeup.'

'Yeah, no. Not happening, Tiz.'

'Too bad,' said Thistle primly, pushing her onto the bed. 'Don't move.'

Never able to refuse her anything, Thorn sat down obediently, though she balled her fists as Thistle painted her face meticulously. The mascara and eyeliner made her eyes water and left her lids feeling unnaturally heavy. Like she was halfway through a head cold that was being held in place by paint.

Never one to risk a wrinkle, Thistle was only wearing undergarments and leggings, but her straight black hair was knotted beautifully, her skin highlighted by vibrant, shimmering makeup.

'You look beautiful, babe,' said Thorn softly.

Thistle beamed at her. 'Yeah?'

'You always do.'

They smiled at each other before Thistle began applying blush to Thorn's cheeks.

'Ever wonder what life would be like if humans were allowed to get married?' Thorn asked after a beat. 'To each other, I mean.'

'All the time,' said Thistle. 'But I love Nithin. Even if humans could marry, I'd still marry him.'

Thorn's chest twisted, but she said only, 'Is he nice to you?'

Thistle paused painting Thorn's eyelids and leaned back. 'Do you know what he told me?'

Thorn shook her head.

'He said he would kill any Suriia who came near me; he said he'd disappear with me before letting the death camps take me.'

'Nithin's not so bad,' Thorn allowed.

Thistle's smile broadened. 'You think?'

'Yeah. He's okay, I guess.'

They both giggled, and Thistle went back to Thorn's makeup.

'You look awesome,' she announced when she was done. 'Want to see?'

'No,' said Thorn. She had less than no desire to know what she looked like. She would see a million things wrong.

Instead, she sat on the bed and waited for Thistle to get dressed, not remotely sure how to feel about any of it. But Thistle's smile had never been so free, so easily given, and it was hard to be annoyed by that.

'Come on, then,' said Thistle when she was dressed.

The others were in the kitchen waiting for them. Kol looked up as they stepped into the kitchen. He started at the sight of them, and his eyes travelled over Thorn.

She glared at him defensively. 'Tiz made me. I know I look stupid.'

'That's not what I was going to say at all,' he replied. 'Thistle did a great job.'

Thistle jumped onto the counter, uncaring that she was in her wedding dress. 'I did, didn't I?'

As Kol appraised her, Thorn took in his attire. He was dressed in a form-fitting suit, his black hair brushed, his beard trimmed. He looked far better than Thorn felt.

Nithin too cut a handsome image. He was the definition of sleek and cool. He affected it so effortlessly it was simply impressive, rather than obnoxious. When his eyes landed on Thistle, they shimmered magically, and even Thorn couldn't stop her smile.

They headed out to the coach and Kol sat in the back beside her. He held up his hand, a slight blush spreading up his neck, and signed, *You look amazing.*

She bit the inside of her cheek to keep her smile in check and looked out the window, not sure what to do next.

The temple was on the other side of the city by the sea, grand and ornate. But it was the scenery more than the architecture Thorn appreciated. The sea hadn't changed much since the last time Thorn glimpsed it, but she felt a surge of something when she saw it. The building, on the other hand, was a monstrosity of gold and glass, blinding in the sunshine and nightmarish in the rain.

'Good grief,' said Thorn as they walked towards it. 'Why is it so ... sharp?'

Kol chuckled. 'It's meant to be an ode of might.'

'Ode to who?'

'Our ancestors. Suriias build everything in honour of those who came before. To remember all that was.'

'All that was, was gold and glass?'

'The most sought after of treasures; and how fragile we know it all to be.'

'Bit on the nose for a temple, no?'

'Well, a temple is where you sit and pray. Shouldn't that be reason enough for beauty?'

Thorn preferred sitting and praying outside, but didn't bother carrying the debate on.

As they walked into the temple, the true majesty of the building became overwhelming and the smell of burning candles was overpowering. Worse, the number of Suriias in the entrance hall was more than she'd ever had the misfortune to be around.

'It'll be fine,' said Thistle, sensing her unease.

'I'll keep you safe,' promised Kol.

But where Thorn wanted to hide, Thistle instantly greeted dozens who knew her by name.

In no mood to socialise with those who hated her, and wholly out of place beside her best friend, Thorn wandered away from the crowd and down a quiet corridor.

She walked slowly through the hall, taking in the odd statues and plaques and mosaics. Trailing her fingers over the backs of the chairs, she let her gaze flick around, taking note of the few available exits.

When she finally returned to the hall, more Suriias had arrived and the noise was deafening. There were vrykos, vylkas, frai, pricos, sbura and numerous others Thorn couldn't hope to identify as she knew only those she'd encountered personally. Introductions and chitchat were unbearable in small numbers. Large crowds were even worse. In the back of the chamber, Thorn caught sight of several vrykos. Her eyes darted over them, but she recognised none.

It wasn't long before a figure in uniform announced that everyone needed to take a seat.

Kol appeared at her side as everyone began moving to their seats. 'Sorry for disappearing on you. My father decided it was time for a lecture.'

She let her gaze travel over the crowd, but she couldn't pick any of them as obviously related to Kol. 'Did you listen?'

'I wouldn't be smiling if I had.'

She giggled. 'What's his problem?'

'Usual rhetoric about my failure to progress through life as promptly as he desires.'

'But you have a good job.'

'Not the job he wanted for me.'

They stopped talking as Nithin and Thistle kneeled before a frai in robes and silence fell. But Thorn almost verbally protested. Thistle was *kneeling* now?

'Want me to translate?' offered Kol as the frai in robes began to speak.

Thorn shook her head, but when a strange kind of light surrounded Thistle and Nithin's hands, she gripped the edges of her seat.

'It's okay,' said Kol quietly. 'It's just an oath of love.'

'It's magic.'

'She's safe.'

Thorn swallowed the bile that had risen in her throat, but did not relax.

When the ceremony finished, everyone dispersed into the adjacent chamber. Kol took her hand and steered her through the jostling bodies.

Just as they were leaving, her eyes moved over a balcony and she froze.

There, shrouded in the grainy, dust-speckled shadows of the alcove, Jinx stood watching.

Kol paused. 'You okay?'

'Yeah, give me a sec. Need to use the toilet.'

He nodded and carried on.

Thorn counted to ten before slipping through the crowds and up the staircase. Fury at Jinx's gumption mixed with the fear which always sprung unbidden at the thought of a human getting caught by the Suriias.

When she reached the top step, Jinx stepped out, hands in a pleading gesture.

'What the fuck are you doing here?' she hissed.

'I wanted to talk to you,' he said. 'I'm sorry about the other night. Things got out of hand.'

Thorn sneered at him, furious that he would shift the blame on to anything other than his selfish, reckless desire to get her undressed. 'You heard me say "stop".'

'I heard you moan,' he countered, shrugging his shoulders. 'I thought you were enjoying it.'

'I told you I didn't want to go that far, and you didn't listen.'

'Because I could tell how much you liked me! Because I really like you.' He moved towards her. 'Come on, Thorn. I'm sorry.'

'You used a fucking Suriia drug on me!' Her hands went to her head as the events of that night returned to swirl around her mind. 'They're our enemy, Jinx! What the fuck?'

He rolled his eyes. 'Everyone takes Hazies.'

The idea of other humans willingly partaking in Suriia party activities infuriated her. Did none of them care that it came from their oppressors? '*I* don't.'

'Well, you're unusual.'

'Go away,' said Thorn, backing up several steps and stilling at the top stair. 'And don't come back.'

'What about Veryn?'

Thorn wavered. 'Did you find something?'

'Yeah.' He nodded several times and held out a piece of paper. 'Last place he was seen. Don't think it's his home, though. But it's a start.'

She snatched the paper out of his hand, heart pounding. 'You're sure?'

'I'm sure. Listen, Thorn—'

'Rose?' Kol's voice trailed up from the corridor below.

'Go,' she mouthed to Jinx.

He didn't need to be told twice and he shimmied out of the window without delay. Thorn stared at the space he had been standing in for another second, stomach churning, before she turned and trotted down the steps, slipping the paper into her pocket.

'There you are,' said Kol when she reached him. 'You okay?'

'Got sick in the bathroom.' Sweaty as she was from nerves, it was believable.

Concern shadowed his features and he felt her forehead gently. 'We can leave, if you want?'

'I don't want to pull you away.'

'Nithin and Thistle are just glad you showed up. We can leave.'

His offer made her so grateful that she found herself shaking her head.

'You sure?'

'I'm sure.'

He held out his hand and she took it. When he spread his fingers, she interlaced hers without thinking.

They headed back into the hall, but instead of bringing her back towards the gaggle of well-wishers, he led her onto the dancefloor. 'Have I told you how beautiful you look tonight?'

'No,' she mumbled. 'You look nice, too.'

'So complimentary.'

She flushed, cheeks warming. 'I don't know how to compliment someone without sounding stupid.'

'Try.' He wiggled his eyebrows. 'Come on, how do I look?'

She hesitated.

'That bad, huh?'

With an exasperated – and somewhat embarrassed – smile, she said, 'I think ... I think in another life, in a world that's not so fucked up, seeing you tonight? I'd be the happiest woman in the world.'

He turned her in a circle that drew her into his arms. Leaning his head in, he pressed his lips close to her ear. 'This world *can* become that one, you know?'

She hated how badly she wanted to believe that.

Kol kept her close for several more dances, only stepping back to teach her a new move or spin her in a circle. But he seemed to like having her close, and every time his fingers traced over her skin, a jolt went through her body.

'Suriias often say humans have no grace,' he said a while later, 'but you are by far the most graceful dancer on this floor.'

Thorn snorted. 'I look like a duck on ice.'

'A very lovely duck.' He spun her in another circle and his hands came to rest on her hips. 'Very graceful and beautiful.'

She scoffed. 'I'd fall on my face if you weren't here.'

'Somehow I doubt that.'

'I'm only like this with you,' she muttered.

'What?'

'Close.'

'Close?' His lips brushed over her neck. 'How close?'

'Closer,' she whispered before she could stop herself.

He made a noise low in his throat before stepping back and holding out his hand. 'Drink?'

Skin tingling with excitement and arousal, Thorn let him steer her off the dance floor.

In another part of the chamber, Nithin and Thistle were surrounded, and Thorn could tell even from a distance that she looked happy. For the first time in Thistle's life, she was as social and popular as she'd always longed to be. Even if it wasn't real, even if it wouldn't happen without Nithin standing beside Thistle, Thorn couldn't help but smile at her friend's joy.

Kol gestured to a table and they commandeered two chairs close together. His hand, still warm from holding her own, came to rest lightly on her knee and he caught her eye. 'This okay?' he whispered.

She bit her lip, trying not to smile, and looked pointedly at her wine. His hand remained on her knee, his forefinger tracing circles on her skin. When he reached the blade she had strapped to her thigh, he raised an eyebrow. 'That cannot be comfortable.'

'The way you're acting, one would think you'd be glad I'm good at having something between my legs.'

He choked on his wine. Wiping his mouth, he looked over at her, eyes entirely black.

'There you are!'

Kol jumped and turned towards the Suriia who had just arrived. Thorn crossed her legs and picked up her glass of water, gulping it down. Her whole body felt flushed, and like she needed to be stretched in every direction.

'Adrian,' he greeted, standing and embracing the new arrival.

It was then she realised—

Adrian was a vryko.

Fear hit her like a brick, and she slipped into the shadows before Kol could even turn around. Ducking into the hall, she made her way outside. The night air was cold on her skin and she took several gasping breaths. She walked around, trying desperately to source calm. But she was remarkably poor at sourcing calm. That was Thistle's gift.

Under a minute later, her phone vibrated, and she took it out with shaking fingers.

The message was from Kol: *He's an old friend and he supports humans. But I sent him away. I won't make you meet him.*

She was about to stow it back in her pocket when it beeped again.

I'll meet you. You don't have to come back. Just tell me where you are.

She bit her lip, hesitating. It bothered her how much she liked that he cared, how much she liked *him*, when she hated and feared his fellows so greatly. There wasn't a lick of sense to it. It was hypocritical and ridiculous, and she almost threw her phone at the wall when it beeped again.

Please Rose.

She sighed and wrote back, *I'll be in the entrance hall. Can we go?*

His reply was instant. *Yes.*

Relieved, Thorn headed back into the temple. The distant sounds of revelry made her feel slightly bad for leaving Thistle, but the urge to be away from any and all vrykos was stronger.

She was halfway down the corridor when someone stepped into her path.

'Oh, my night keeps improving,' she groaned, glaring at the vylka. He was at least twice her size, muscular to the point of hulking.

He looked her up and down in a way that made her want to set him on fire. 'My night has just become memorable,' he crooned.

Thorn's knife was in her hand without missing a beat. 'Fuck off.'

'Been claimed before, girl?'

Thorn sneered at him. 'Yeah, and he's dead.'

'Then you're up for grabs.'

Before she could blink, the vylka had her against the wall, his hand around her throat. She slammed her knee into his crotch and sliced the knife across his face, sending him back enough to slip away.

It was at that precise moment that Nithin and Kol appeared.

Nithin was kneeling beside the vylka in the blink of an eye. He yanked him to his feet and slammed him against the wall as if he were a limp puppet. 'Bad dog,' he hissed, and then green light spread from his hands into the vylka's skin, eliciting a horrible scream.

It felt like a small eternity before Nithin released him and stepped back, glaring mercilessly. 'Get out,' he snarled, eyes flashing with more magic than Thorn wanted to see.

When he was gone, Kol turned to Thorn. 'Are you all right?'

'Fine,' she said, not fine at all.

'You two go,' said Nithin.

Kol nodded to Nithin before steering Thorn outside. The interaction had erased all thoughts of soul sucking vrykos from her mind and replaced them with memories of Jared. She had so many thoughts swirling around at once that she felt sick. It didn't help that she couldn't make sense of a single one. Every thought was disjointed, jagged. Filled with bright lights and harsh colours and so many different feelings she wanted to cry and scream and sleep all at the same time.

Kol pulled up in front of the house without her realising it. She did a doubletake before opening the door and stepping out.

The house seemed so much quieter with just the two of them. It was so large, and every sound was magnified. A bit like living in a fancy cave.

Inside, Thorn dropped onto the sofa and propped her feet up on the table. Her skin was crawling.

'Did he say anything else?' asked Kol.

'That I was up for grabs.'

Like a reflex, his eyes went solid black. 'Nithin will ensure he regrets that.'

She nodded, not sure if she believed him or not. But before she could dwell on vylkas and Suric justice, he took her hands and pulled her gently to her feet.

'Adrian interrupted us,' he said huskily.

'Interrupted what?'

He leaned in further, lips ghosting over hers. 'Do you want me to stop?' he breathed.

'No.'

'Are you sure?'

'Yes.'

And then he kissed her.

It was nothing like Jinx. Not rough, not sharp, not clanging.

She sank into him, her mind going blank, her focus reduced to bliss and want and *yes*. He tasted like chocolate and wine and heat. It was as if, by touch alone, Kol could erase everything inside of her that didn't feel good.

When he drew back, her lips tingled and her whole body felt like it was filled with a tsunami of bubbles and joy.

'Was that okay?' he whispered, face still close to hers.

She nodded. 'I think I'm going to count that as my first kiss.'

'Do,' he said, and then he kissed her again.

All thought fled her mind as he cradled her face with one hand, his other arm wrapping around her and bringing her in close.

At some point they ended up horizontal on the sofa.

Brushing her hair out of her eyes, he kissed her twice more before pulling back to smile down at her.

'I have to go out of town for a week,' he murmured. 'Will you be all right here alone?'

'I'll be fine.'

'Will you call me if you need anything?'

'Okay,' she said, surprised by how much she meant it.

He kissed her cheek. 'We should probably go to bed. It's late.'

'Probably.'

Neither made a move.

'I don't want to have sex tonight,' he prefaced, 'but would you want to stay in my room? It'll suck not seeing you for a week.'

She wanted to say yes, but habit prevented her from agreeing automatically.

'You can sleep with your knife under your pillow,' he added teasingly, and then kissed her neck just below her ear.

'Really?'

He bowed his head with complete seriousness. 'You can sleep by the window with your knife and gun if it'll help you sleep. I'm only looking for a spoon, I promise.'

The refusal fled fast and the giggle left her without her permission.

He raised an eyebrow. 'What do you say?'

'Okay.'

'Yeah?'

'Sure.'

Kol grinned broadly and got to his feet before pulling her upright. The stairs felt cold on her bare feet as she followed him. Inside his room it smelled like flowers from the open window, wafted up from the garden below, but the icy frost hadn't crept in.

'Do you want to grab your pyjamas?'

'Got a shirt?'

Kol handed her one of his shirts before turning around. The small display of respect made her chest shudder and she quickly changed out of the dress and into his shirt.

'All good,' she said.

He turned back around, and his eyes flicked over her. 'You make that shirt look *much* better than I do.'

A blush flared to life in her cheeks and she bit her lip to keep from saying something stupid.

As Kol changed out of his suit, Thorn walked over to his window and looked out into the garden. The flowers were forever in bloom, vibrant petals that never withered; even when they fell, the colours stayed strong. She knew it was because of Kol's magic and for once the thought of magic didn't make her heart race in fear.

'I think an obsession with flowers is the best Suric caveat I've come across,' she mused aloud.

She felt him behind her and then his arms were around her stomach.

'I can't say I don't have dreams about you in a pile of petals,' he said with a low, throaty chuckle.

She kissed him again before wandering over to the bed. Placing her knife on the windowsill, she stretched back on her elbows. Kol hadn't moved and was gazing at her with a smile she couldn't define. She cocked her head towards her blade.

'You sure you don't mind?' she asked.

'Do you feel safe?'

After a pause, she nodded.

'Then I don't mind.' He waved a hand at the lights as he walked over to join her in bed, turning them off magically. The absent-minded, habitual show of magic would once have bothered her profusely, but more and more she was finding that she didn't mind magic so long as the one wielding it was Kol. With him, it was almost endearing.

CHAPTER NINE
They Call Him the Duke of Courtenz

The night after the wedding ceremony, Thistle and Nithin departed for their honeymoon to the continent and Kol left to deal with a family obligation. It was the first time Thorn had ever been alone completely, and the prospect both terrified and delighted her. She had never had a house to herself before and it gave her time to think about her nights in the city and how little progress she'd made finding Veryn. Without having to worry about anyone hearing her or asking questions, she could move about freely and use Nithin's computer for research. Not that she knew where to begin. The Suriias had a strange computerised system of information that proved convoluted and bewildering to someone who had never been to school nor knew anything about how the country was run. She tried searching for Veryn's name in the open database, but it turned out to be a remarkably popular name, and she was wary that the search results would be monitored. Suriias didn't skimp on surveillance, after all.

The most fruitful piece of information she gleaned was the address Jinx had given her at the wedding. The night after everyone in the house left, she headed into the city, winding her way through the backstreets as she tried to track the house down. Two nights of searching finally brought her to the waterfront.

Wind slammed into her with every step and the smell of the nearby fisheries came harsh and overpowering. She wouldn't have pegged Veryn for someone who lived in squalor and judging how derelict and dodgy the area was, the house likely hadn't played host to Veryn and his Soul Eaters in years, but the prospect of clues pushed her inside regardless. Whatever she thought about Jinx on a personal level, she believed in his hatred of Suriias enough to trust the information.

She circled the building twice to make sure no one was hanging around before climbing in carefully through a downstairs window that had been broken long ago.

The putrid scent of decay assaulted her nose instantly. Decay and faeces and copper. Pulling her shirtsleeve down over her hand, she covered her mouth in a futile attempt to block out the smell, but the further she walked, the worse it became. Each step revealed more of the wretched scene.

Nothing could have prepared her for what she found in the sitting room: bodies. So many bodies. On the floor, in piles; several hung from ropes and chains.

Carved into the chest of the man hanging from the ceiling were three words:

FOR MY ADMIRER

It took multiple attempts to calm herself enough to move. She went to the man and cut him down as carefully as she could. He was heavy, stiff and frozen solid. Hands quivering, she closed his eyelids and whispered her apologies.

While the likelihood that he would have died by the vrykos' hands with or without her hunting spree was strong, it didn't erase her guilt. She hoped he was in a better place. A next life. One free of pain.

In the corner of the room, Thorn found a – suspiciously located – can of petrol, and she drenched the other bodies. The fumes gave her a sharp, throbbing headache and she gagged quite a lot. At last, tossing a lighter onto the petrol trail she'd made, she bolted out the window as the flames consumed the massacre.

Tears fell silently down her face the entire walk back to the mansion.

After she'd showered and crawled into bed, Thorn spent four hours dialling Thistle's number and erasing each subsequent message before she finally fell asleep, sobbing into her hands.

Horrible nightmares consumed her when sleep finally dragged her into darkness, and she could feel nails and teeth in her skin. She could smell blood, sweat, cologne.

She slept most of the day until a harsh beeping made her eyes snap open and she realised her phone had a new message. For the briefest second she thought it was Thistle. Somehow the fact that it was Kol wasn't disappointing.

Hope you're not going stir crazy, he'd written. *I know you must be missing me terribly.*

Thorn bit her lip as Kol's banter finally cracked through the shroud that had eaten at her since the warehouse. *I'm not missing you at all*, she wrote back. *It's such a nuisance having someone to talk to.*

In less than a minute, his reply appeared on the screen: *I'd rather be home with you, trust me. Everyone here is as dull as sand.*

Thorn sat up and pulled the blanket up to her chest, sufficiently distracted from her nightmares. *No master debaters?*

Not one master, trust me. One spent an hour discussing the design of his new office. I almost flung myself out the window just to escape.

This time she did laugh. *My heart breaks for you*, she wrote back. *Truly.*

Nith made these meetings bearable, he bemoaned. *Without him, I'm trapped in a sea of chitchat and luncheons.*

The idea of ever voluntarily wining and dining Suriias made Thorn's whole body constrict. If she were being honest, even if they'd been human, she still wouldn't have been inclined.

When you back? she asked.

I'm trying to get out of here early, he answered. *Miss me?*

Her fingers hesitated to reply honestly and instead she wrote, *I miss your chocolate. The cabinet's empty.*

There's more chocolate in my room, he wrote back. *Take as much as you want. Feel free to use the television, too. The movies are on my shelf.*

It suddenly sounded like the best idea in the world.

She crawled out of bed and wandered down the hall to Kol's bedroom. Inside she found the bookshelf of vintage movies and selected one. Sticking the disc into the machine on Kol's television, she searched around for sweets and saw, to her delight, a box of unopened chocolates on his desk.

She took out the phone. *The ones on your desk look expensive.*

Instead of messaging back, her phone suddenly trilled out a ringtone. 'I don't want to take them if they're fancy,' she answered.

'Eat as much as you want,' he said. 'You gonna watch a movie?'

'Might nap. Slept like shit.'

'You okay?' The audible concern in his voice made her smile.

'Fine,' she mumbled. 'Just bad dreams.'

'Want to talk about it?'

'Not really.'

'Not about me?'

'Not yet.'

He chuckled. 'I hope the chocolate helps you sleep, but let's be honest, it's going to be because you're in my bed.'

'I didn't say I was sleeping in your bed. I said I couldn't sleep.'

'I can hear my television, Rose.'

'You're hearing things.'

'Sure,' he teased. 'And don't forget my garden. The plants need attention.'

'They need attention?'

'Yes,' he said. 'They don't like to be forgotten about. It's not always watering and trimming. Plants like to get attention just like anything.'

'I'll go gossip to your flowers, Charcoal. Don't worry.'

'You're the best, Rose.'

Still grinning, Thorn ended the call and walked over to his bed. Drawing the blankets over her body, she opened the box of chocolates. She fell asleep halfway through the movie – and slept well.

Two days before Thistle and Nithin were due to return, Kol came back. Thorn was in the gym doing press-ups when he appeared.

'Hi,' he greeted in bemusement.

'Hi.'

'This is what you do for fun when everyone's away?'

'This is necessary.'

In what now seemed true to form, Kol didn't question, he just went along with what she was doing.

Taking off his shirt, he bent down across from her and joined in.

Only when her arms were burning and sweat glistened on her skin did Thorn stop and sit up, her blood thrumming through her extremities. Kol too, was covered in a light sheer of sweat and the corners of his hair were damp. It was impossible not to notice how nice he looked.

'How've you been?' he queried, leaning back on his hands.

'A bit restless,' she admitted.

'Anything I can do to help?'

She shook her head. She didn't know how to broach the subject of Veryn yet. She didn't even know if she could or would. What if that was the moment he started acting like the rest?

Something in her thoughts must have shown on her face because he frowned.

'What's wrong?'

'Nothing.'

'Come on, tell me.'

But how could she? You couldn't just recruit someone to kill. Even if you were killing murderers.

She eyed him for a long time before she stood and walked back into the house without another word. She spent the rest of the day in her room, pacing and meditating in alternating and frustrating measure.

It was well past nightfall when Kol knocked on her door.

'I made dinner,' he called. 'Come down. Stop being so awkward.'

Despite herself, Thorn smiled and left the room.

In the kitchen, Kol had set the table and laden it with food: roast chicken, green beans, baked potatoes, garlic bread with rosemary sprinkled on top; a small bowl of gravy was set beside the bread, steam wafting slowly off the surface.

'Smells good,' she complimented.

He grinned. 'Cheers.'

She sat across from him and pulled her leg into her chest as she picked up a roll. She didn't feel hungry, which was a strange feeling.

'What's on your mind?'

'Nothing.'

'Come on, Rose. I can tell something's bothering you.'

'I'm fine.'

'You are a woeful liar.'

Thorn continued to pick absently at the food on her plate, the memory of the dead bodies turning her stomach.

'Is it because of what happened before I left?' He suddenly sounded so very uncertain.

'No,' she assured him. Somehow kissing him was one of the few things she wasn't doubting. 'No, it's my own shit.'

'Can I help?'

'Maybe.'

His face lit up in surprise. 'Yeah?'

'I'm considering it.'

Kol didn't press the matter, but he couldn't stifle his smile. They ate in quiet company. Every once in a while he'd reach across the table to squeeze her hand and brush his fingers across hers. Like he couldn't get enough of her. But in a nice way.

They watched a movie after they'd done the dishes and Thorn fell asleep beside him on the sofa.

Sometimes around midnight, he nudged her awake and they stumbled upstairs. Outside her door, he paused. He took her hands slowly, interlacing their fingers. 'I really want to kiss you again,' he confided.

She didn't move, even as her insides suddenly felt like they were on the edge of a rushing waterfall; then, with a burst of courage, she stood on her toes and kissed him.

'Goodnight, Kol.'

'Sweet dreams, Rose.'

She paused, a hand on the doorknob. 'Do—'

'Yeah?'

'We could, um, do what we did last time. Just sleep. But, like, together.'

'Yeah?'

'Yeah.'

She felt sheepish and awkward, but her reaction only seemed to make Kol smile more, and they headed towards his bedroom hand in hand.

A strange sort of loveliness took hold in that brief stretch of alone time with Kol in the mansion. Life felt serene and kind in a way Thorn had never known firsthand.

'I wish you didn't have to go to work,' she told him the following morning as they lounged in bed, neither eager to greet the day. 'I'm so comfy.' Lifting her head from his chest, she caught his eye and smirked.

Kol held her gaze for the briefest of seconds. Then, picking up his phone, he tapped twice on the screen and put it to his ear. 'Ipo,' he said when someone answered on the other end. 'I'm sick. I won't be in today.'

Thorn giggled when he'd ended the call. 'You won't get into trouble?'

'I don't even care,' he said before crashing his lips against hers again. He kissed her like he wanted to make it last forever. She noticed, though, that he remained restrained. He wasn't entirely successful at hiding his arousal, but his self-discipline charmed her in a way few words could have.

Eventually their growling stomachs propelled them out of bed and down the stairs. Thorn made pancakes and fruit salad while Kol prepared coffee, eggs, baked beans and toast. When everything was ready, they put the dishes on a tray and brought it outside into Kol's garden.

After eating, they set about tending to the flowers and trees. He didn't pry about what she'd told him the previous day and things between them stayed mostly light-hearted, aided by the steady rhythmic work of gardening.

The sun was high in the sky by the time they finished and Kol suggested they swim. To her surprise, her previous insecurities about him seeing her scars had vanished, and she didn't hesitate this time.

Rather than change into Thistle's swimsuit, she jumped in wearing only her underwear. Following suit, Kol took off his shirt and jeans and dove in after her.

He resurfaced in front of her, his black hair slicked back from his face. 'Can I tell you a secret?'

She wrapped her arms around his neck. 'What?'

'I don't want them to come home,' he said with a small laugh. 'I want you all to myself.'

'Not sick of me yet?'

'Impossible.' He eyed her for a second before leaning in slowly, cautiously, giving her ample opportunity to pull away before his lips brushed hers. When her fingers curled in his hair and she kissed him back, his hesitation dissipated.

Only when both were desperate for air did they finally still, but Kol held her close to his body and she didn't pull away.

He opened his mouth as if to say something, but seemed to second guess himself. Then, holding her close with one arm, he swam to the side of the pool and hoisted her onto the edge. Remaining in the water, he stayed between her legs, still somehow taller than her.

'Am I the first human you've kissed?' she asked abruptly, not sure where the question had even come from.

'Yes,' he said, brushing wet tendrils of hair back from her shoulders.

'But you've never slept with anyone.'

'No.'

She eyed him, totally perplexed. 'Like … *how*?'

He hesitated, and when his answer came, she felt like she wasn't getting the whole story. 'I've been waiting.'

'For what?' she pressed.

His gold-black eyes bore into hers with an intensity that sent a jolt of longing through her. 'To be sure.'

She frowned, wondering if he was biding his time with her, too. 'When will you be sure?'

'I'll know,' he murmured.

The air felt suddenly thick, and she kissed him before she even processed the move. Just as eager and no more restrained, he wrapped her legs around his waist, their bodies pressing together like magnets.

It was another hour before they left the pool. They separated only to shower and change, and then spent the rest of the night watching movies. She fell asleep with her head on his chest and was woken hours later by the sound of a coach outside.

Thistle and Nithin came through the door the epitome of a loved-up couple. What was more striking – and for Thorn more alarming – was how Suric Thistle now appeared. From her clothes to her mannerisms to her demeanour. Even the slang she used when describing their trip was strange.

Thistle's tales of their trip around continent were somehow the most surreal part of the fact that she was now married to a Suriia. She spoke with an almost dreamy air, as if she had assimilated so thoroughly into Suriia society that its buildings and monuments were now worthy of praise and awe. Like their oppressors hadn't torn down human history and soaked the ground in blood to erect the monuments and statues; odes to genocide and slaughter.

Disgust coiled like a snake through Thorn's heart as she listened, and she tried to remind herself that Thistle was lovestruck, that she was being treated well by Nithin and it was distorting her view of things. But the more compliments Thistle gave the Suric sites and venues, the more Thorn lost her good humour.

She managed to bid Thistle goodnight shortly thereafter and locked herself in her room, too furious and hurt to do anything other than pace.

It was the sudden vibration of her phone that finally distracted her. She glared at the screen, not sure what to think. Jinx's name flashed in red letters.

Fear that something was wrong pushed her to answer despite her misgivings. 'What?'

'Thorn, help!' It wasn't Jinx, it was Jade.

Thorn was moving before she even knew what she was doing. 'Where are you?'

'The apartment!'

Yanking on her boots, she grabbed her knife and coat on her way out the window.

Halfway to the fence, she changed course and went to Nithin's coach. Running would take too long.

She unlocked the door and clambered in, glad she'd kept the keys in her coat pocket since he'd given them to her.

'Okay,' she said to herself as the engine purred to life. 'Okay, you can do this.'

Hands tight on the wheel, she steered towards the gates, which opened automatically. Driving was less daunting than flying, but she managed to raise the coach into the air without disaster as soon as she'd passed the barrier.

She reached the alley where Jade and Jinx lived quicker than she could have imagined possible. Landing, she shot out of the coach, eyes roving over the street for signs of backup.

There was a vryko in a coach parked outside and Thorn ducked down and crawled below the window. Taking a deep breath, she leapt up and buried the blade in the vryko's chest. She yanked it out, causing blood to spray across her face as he crumpled in on himself.

Thorn didn't even bother to wipe it off as she ran into the building. The smell of copper hit her first, and then the sounds.

Rounding the corner, she saw that the door had been smashed in. Jinx was on the ground of the sitting room, a vryko kneeling over him. He wasn't moving and she couldn't tell if he was alive. Jade was struggling to fend off another vryko in the corner.

Thorn threw her knife at the one bending over Jinx, catching him in the chest. He roared and whirled around just as she reached him. Kicking him in the teeth with all her might, she sent him stumbling backwards, momentarily distracting the one trying to rip Jade's arms off.

Jade seized the opportunity and snatched up the phone cord hanging off the desk beside her; she jumped onto the vryko's back and wrapped it around his neck. Scrawny and gaunt, Jade was still a ball of wiry muscle as she clung on as he teetered, choking and gurgling.

Thorn didn't have time to help Jade as the now injured vryko advanced on her, her blade in his hand. But it was the mark on his shoulder that caught her attention. A mark she would know anywhere.

'You're one of the Soul Eaters,' she gasped, heart slamming in her ears.

'Our reputation precedes us,' said the vryko. And then he leapt out of the window and into the alley below like a cat.

Thorn wavered a split second to take in the others' predicaments. Jade already had her vryko on his knees. Jinx was still on the ground, but breathing. That was all she needed to know.

Thorn scrambled out of the window and dropped down into the alleyway. The vryko wasn't far ahead, and she knew the streets better than the rats.

Cutting left, she tore through two side alleys before coming to a screeching halt paces in front of him.

'Tell me what I want to know, and I'll let you live,' she lied, raising her blade. The iron glinted in the lamplight above them.

'No human girl can best a vryko,' he replied snidely.

'Does Veryn still run with your group?'

It was clear he hadn't been expecting her to know the name. But he smirked, like he was proud to be in cahoots with a notorious murderer. 'The northside belongs to the duke, little girl. Everyone knows that.'

Duke. Northside.

Thorn had heard enough. She threw the blade with expert aim and struck him through the heart. The iron worked quickly and his skin began to blacken and burn. Racing forwards, she yanked it back out.

Kneeling on his chest, sufficiently soaking her jeans in his blood, she searched him quickly for any form of identification. She found none.

A clatter of metal on stone alerted her to company and a Scuttler appeared on the other side of the road just she darted up the fire escape.

Crouching low, she watched as the Scuttlers began to take stills of the scene and a beacon was blared into the sky, alerting the Spotters to their position.

With a grimace, she slipped into the shadows and darted to the adjacent roof, praying that Jade and Jinx had got out another way.

An hour passed before she was able to get back to the coach, but the flight back to the mansion passed uneventfully.

She was aching with exhaustion by the time she finally climbed back in through her window, and she dropped onto the bed without bothering to take off her coat or boots. In seconds, she was unconscious, two words swirling around her mind like fanged sheep.

Duke. Northside.
Duke. Northside.

Thorn was dragged from her fitful slumber by a sharp rap on the door hours later. Groggy and exhausted, she rolled over. She regretted it immediately. Her vision swam and the slamming in her head worsened by the second.

'What?' she groaned.

'Thorn?' Oddly, the call came from Nithin. 'May I come in?'

She sat up, pain reverberating around her skull. 'Why?' she called.

Before he gave her an answer, the door opened, and Thistle stepped in.

'Tor, there's blood in the—' Thistle stopped short at the sight of her. 'All over you. Why are you covered in blood?'

'What?' The question came from outside the room and before Thorn could say anything, Kol and Nithin were in the bedroom.

Kol darted to her side, checking her over frantically, fear alight in his black-gold eyes.

Thorn peered down at her mud- and blood-stained clothes. She had cuts on her hands from the fight (and she could feel the ones peppering her face), and there were tears in her jeans where glass and debris had torn fabric and cut into her flesh. It looked like she'd been the one thrown through the window.

'What happened?' demanded Thistle. 'Were you attacked?'

'Vrykos broke into a friend's apartment,' said Thorn hesitantly. 'We were defending ourselves.'

This half-confession drew three vastly different reactions.

'What friends?' said Thistle.

'Which vrykos?' said Nithin.

But Thorn couldn't look away from Kol. It was clear he knew she wasn't saying something. 'Are you okay?' he asked. 'Did anyone hurt you?'

Thorn ran her hands shakily over her face. 'No.'

'You have to stop this,' said Thistle quietly. 'You're going to get yourself killed.'

'Tiz!'

'I'm sorry.' Thistle crossed her arms. 'You told me you'd do this with a plan and you're just putting yourself in danger.'

Nithin and Kol looked between them, openly confused.

'What are we missing?' asked Nithin.

Thorn shot Thistle a warning look, but Thistle ignored her. 'She's trying to track down the vryko who murdered our parents.'

Horror cut across their faces.

'We'd been living on their property for a while,' continued Thistle, voice trembling. 'One night, they attacked our parents. Clay, Thorn's uncle, came to get us all out. He was attacked as we ran, and his son David died trying to save him. Thorn made me hide and went back. She saw what the vrykos did to them.'

Tears filled Thorn's eyes and she blinked rapidly, lowering her head so they wouldn't see.

'Tor—'

'Can you go, please?' she choked out, pressing the heels of her palms to her eyes.

She heard the door open and close, and finally let herself cry. The grief, heartache and exhaustion were all too much. More than anything else in the world, she wanted her parents back. She wanted her father to hold her and her mother to tell her everything was going to be okay. Learning more about Veryn hadn't helped, it had just brought the painful memories back to the surface to torture her once more.

She'd been sitting on the bed for almost an hour when there was a soft knock at the door.

'What?' she grunted.

'It's me,' called Kol. 'Can I come in?'

'Sure.'

He stepped inside, closing the door behind him. In his hand was a first aid kit. 'I was going to ask if you needed this, but it seems rhetorical since I can see that you do.'

Thorn moved to the edge of the bed. He walked over to her and drew up the desk chair. She put her foot on his thigh. Blood was dripping out of a gash where glass had gone in.

He held up a bottle. 'I know you're opposed to magical drugs, but will you use paste? It'll mean you can skip the scars and stitches.'

'Is there magic in it?'

'No.'

'Then what?'

'Just a lot of plants.'

'Promise?'

'I swear.'

'Do you know which plants?'

'I made it myself.'

'Okay, then.'

He put a large amount on the wound before wrapping it in a bandage; he did the same for the one on her ankle, her thigh, her hip, her shoulder and both of her upper arms. When he was finished patching her up, his eyes lingered on her myriad scars.

'I'm like a canvas of nightmares,' she joked.

'That's not funny,' he said seriously.

'No, it's not.' She crossed her arms over her chest. 'It's ugly.'

Kol reached out and took her hands. 'That's the stupidest thing you've ever said.'

Thorn snorted. 'Look at me.'

'I am.'

She put her foot back on his thigh and leaned back. Reclining on her elbows, she nodded to her foot. 'It hurts. Fucked it up jumping out the window.'

He let out a small huff and began to rub her foot. 'So, who were you meeting?' he asked. 'The humans.'

'Friends.'

Kol eyed her for a moment before a flush of anger passed over his face. 'You did not go to *him*. Tell me you didn't.'

'I went for his sister,' said Thorn. 'She hasn't done anything wrong.'

His eyes narrowed. 'Does she know?'

'Of course she doesn't know. I'm not going to take the only thing she has left in the world.'

'Thistle said his name is Jinx.'

Thorn froze. 'She told you about him?'

'She's concerned.'

'If she cared, she'd have been there.' Frustration renewed, Thorn pulled her hair back from her face and held it in a fist with her good hand.

'Do you know the vryko's name?' he asked quietly.

'Veryn.'

His lip curled in disgust. 'Yeah, Veryn Rigar's been needing to die for quite some time.'

It was like her entire world became Kol. And not for the reasons anyone's world should ever be so focused on another's. Intoxicating vengeance laced its way through her body, and she straightened up, heart slamming inside her chest.

'Rigar,' she echoed. 'That's his name?'

So many weeks of searching and Kol had known his name the whole time. She tried not to show her feelings, but she was almost shaking with anticipation.

Veryn Rigar. A duke, if the Soul Eater was to be believed.

When the others left for work shortly thereafter, Thorn went into Nithin's study. She turned on his computer and clicked into the search-engine. At least now she could narrow it down.

Hands trembling, she slowly typed out 'Veryn Rigar, duke'.

The headline of the first article she clicked read, 'FLYBYS SPONSOR DUKE OF COURTENZ TO HOST OPENING CEREMONY'. The Flybys were a weeklong racing competition that rich Suriias entered in the hopes of winning fortunes they didn't need and showing off their expensive coaches like wealth was something to be proud of.

Thorn scanned the contents of the page, lip curling at the photographs of Suriias posing beside their sleek coaches. But then, on the third picture, she stopped.

She recognised him instantly. A face to infect a thousand nightmares. 'Got you,' she whispered, writing down the address of the ceremony on a pad of paper, hand trembling slightly.

There was no hope of her waiting around. The Flybys lasted a week and it had already been three days.

Changing her clothes, she was out of the house in minutes and making over to the guards by the front gate.

'Hey,' she called when she reached them. 'I want a coach into the city.'

The nearest guard snorted. 'Then call for one yourself.'

'Do you want to help me, or do you want me to tell your boss that you were a dick?' she snapped back. She wasn't about to admit that she didn't have the first idea how to do it herself.

His scowl deepened, but he picked up the phone and called for a coach.

'Where are you going?' he asked her after a minute.

'The Viaduct,' she said. It wasn't far from the Flybys, but it wasn't near it, either. She'd seen it in the background of more than a few of the photographs.

He rolled his eyes pointedly and with all the weariness of an aged sloth. 'Which one?'

'The big one.'

'Kelethar,' he said into the phone. When he ended the call, he looked back at her. 'You going without the boss?'

'Is that your business?'

'It's your funeral.'

Resisting the urge to punch him, Thorn wandered back over to the gate to wait for the coach to arrive.

It appeared promptly enough, and she got into the backseat, a hand on her knife. Being alone with a Suriia she didn't know did nothing for her comfort levels, but the prospect of killing Veryn at last drowned out the other fears. The Suriia driver said nothing to her, however.

When they reached the Viaduct, Thorn got out and nodded to him. 'Charge it to the house,' she told him, and he bobbed his head and flew off without a word.

The Flybys drew a huge crowd and making her way through the streets became more and more difficult as she drew nearer to the main building where the sponsors were gathered.

She crept around the building until she found a propped open window that led into a storage room. Dropping quietly inside, she straightened up and glanced around to make sure there were no cameras, and then sprinted to the other side of the room where the door was.

A quick glance around the door revealed more cameras at either end and sensors on the walls.

Keeping her head down and checking her blocker, she stepped out. Blessedly, she reached the stairwell without hassle and began ascending the stairs.

The rumble of the crowds on every floor sounded increasingly ominous. Every time a door opened, she increased her pace, but she reached the top level. Beyond a cordoned-off area was a room filled with spectators and sponsors. Each one wore expensive, colourful clothing that would be woefully impractical for anything other than strutting.

Not wanting hundreds of Suriias staring at her, Thorn kept to the shadows, eyes darting over the milling crowd. It was a room of rich gamblers and aristocrats, all with money to burn and nothing productive to do with their time.

And then she saw him.

Long straw-coloured hair, scarlet eyes, and a mouth full of jagged, soul sucking teeth: Veryn Rigar looked like he had the night he murdered her parents. He was dressed in a suit that looked like it cost ten of Nithin's and wore jewellery that was simply obnoxious.

Her hands went to her gun and she flicked the safety off.

Out of nowhere, a hand grabbed her wrist and she whipped around.

Nithin looked ready to throttle her. His grip tightening on her arm, the expression on his face advising her not to protest, he tugged her back through the crowd.

Thorn glanced back to the balcony, but Veryn had vanished, absorbed into the sea of bodies. Out of reach.

Wishing Nithin would walk into a wall, she begrudgingly let him steer her back into the deserted hallway.

'What was that for?' she hissed. 'He was right there!'

Nithin rounded on her. 'Are you trying to get yourself killed?'

'I didn't know you'd be here.'

'That is so far removed from the point,' he retorted irritably. 'We're leaving.'

'I'm not going anywhere with you.'

The elevator pinged and a pair of Suriias stepped out. Nithin wrapped his arm succinctly around her waist.

The Suriias' presence kept Thorn from pushing Nithin away until they'd made it into the lift and the door closed. As to who moved away more quickly then, it was a tossup.

'It's bad enough that I have to worry about you and Thistle in locations I've *secured* for you,' he seethed under his breath, 'now you're showing up in places filled with those who support the death camps. You have a death wish, Thorn. That, or you're just remarkably stupid.'

'He killed my parents.'

Nithin held out his hand, utterly unmoved. 'And how is getting torn into tiny, insignificant chunks of meat going to avenge your parents?'

'Shut up.'

'Happily,' he snarled. 'Once you're home.'

'I'm not leaving.'

He pulled out his phone, almost like a threat. 'Fine. If I have to bring Thistle down here in the middle of the day to get you into my coach, I'll do it. Bear in mind that the second she steps through those doors, every vryko in here will catch a whiff of how good her blood smells, the way her soul hums just right.'

'That's low.'

'You're pissing me off.'

'So you'd risk your own wife? Why am I not surprised?'

'If you think Thistle's going to forgive me for letting you stay, you truly don't know the friend you claim to know better than anyone.'

The glares they both levelled at each other matched in their exasperation, anger and frustration, but Thorn nodded at last.

'Good,' he said, voice clipped. 'Let's go.'

To her annoyance, Nithin kept an arm hovering near her back as they left the building and made for the coach. The second they were both inside, however, neither paid the other any attention.

Nithin took out his phone and sent a message to someone as he flew, but said nothing to Thorn.

Only when the mansion came into view and she saw Thistle and Kol in the driveway did Thorn realise he'd contacted them.

'You're such a fucking narc,' she muttered.

Nithin said nothing until he'd landed and they were both out of the coach.

'Why are you two together?' asked Thistle. Her lengthening black hair was styled beautifully around her delicate features. Her dress, however, hugged her figure and exposed her arms, emphasising just how much muscle tone she'd lost.

Nithin shot Thorn a scowl as he walked over to Thistle's side. 'Yes, Thorn, why are we together?'

'Bite me.'

'What happened?' asked Kol.

Still furious, Thorn rolled her eyes and waved at Nithin. 'He's irritated that I crashed his party.'

'Wait, what?' Kol cut a questioning look at his friend. 'Weren't you at the Flybys?'

'Yes,' said Nithin. 'As was Thorn.'

Kol's eyes widened in dismay and his attention returned to Thorn. 'You went to the Flybys on your own? Do you have any idea how dangerous that is?'

Not in the mood to talk to any of them, not even Thistle, Thorn headed into the house and made her way up the stairs, Veryn's face playing in her mind's eye like a movie, the memory so vivid that her heart rate picked up with every replay. By the time she was in the bedroom, she was breathing heavily and shaking like a volcano about to erupt.

A knock at the door made her groan internally and she sank onto the bed without bothering to ask who it was. She wasn't in the mood for another lecture.

'Rose?'

She squeezed the bridge of her nose. 'What?'

The door opened and closed, and a second later Kol was sitting down beside her.

'Talk to me,' he urged, fixing her with an open, encouraging look that made her spill her secrets without thought or care.

'He was right there in front of me,' she growled. 'He was right there and Nithin dragged me away.'

'You would have died confronting him in public,' said Kol. 'What were you thinking?'

'I was thinking, *this bastard killed my family.*'

'And this was your big plan? Confronting him in front of a dozen or more agents? I thought you'd at least be smart enough to go to his mansion.'

Words like a war cry.

Her head snapped up. 'Do you know where he lives?'

Kol took in her sudden change in demeanour and shook his head several times, sending his hair into his eyes. 'I am not taking you to him.'

She took his hand. 'Please, Kol. I have to find him.'

'That's suicide. No.'

'Kol, please.'

'Don't ask that of me.'

'Please,' she begged. 'Help me.'

He stared at her and his eyes went wide with dismayed comprehension. 'It's you,' he concluded. 'The one killing the vrykos is you.'

'Are you actually surprised?'

'Rose, the—'

'He butchered my family! Thistle's family! He cut my father to pieces and raped my mother! He deserves to *burn*!'

Kol rubbed his face roughly. 'This is murder, too.'

'No,' she spat. 'This is justice.'

'Do you know what they'll do to you if they find out?'

'If he's dead, I don't care.'

'Don't say that.'

'It's true.'

'You don't care if you live?'

'I care that he dies. When Veryn's dead, I'll be done with it.'

They glared at each other for several long wretched seconds. Finally, with a weary, stilted sigh, he inclined his head. 'Okay. I'll get his address.'

Thorn froze, hardly daring to believe his words. 'You'll help me?'

'If you promise to stop.'

The mixture of emotions almost flattened her, tears of gratitude and relief burning her eyes. Without processing the move, she crushed her mouth against his with bruising force.

Kol's hands moved as if to push her away, but as they touched her back, he was suddenly pressing her into the contours of his body, and his hands set fire to her skin. Never in her life had someone only given, only asked, only supported the way Kol did.

He drew back, panting, eyes blown with desire. 'You hungry?'

A laugh tore out of her. 'What?'

'You haven't eaten and I'm starving,' he said, holding out his hand. 'If we stay here, I'm going to want to keep going, and I don't think that's the best idea right now.'

With a huff, Thorn took his hand and followed him across the room.

Before he opened the door, he paused and looked down at her. 'I'm not going to push you for anything you're not ready for,' he said, sotto voce, 'but I want you to be my girlfriend. So … I'm asking.'

He blushed as he said it, and she felt a flutter in her chest that she knew already was going to betray her.

Perhaps it couldn't be forever. Perhaps it could only be until they killed Veryn and she and Thistle escaped into the mountains.

But a smile spread across her face. A horrible, traitorous smile that was going to stab her in the back. 'Okay,' she said.

He grinned and leaned down to kiss her, something like love in the act.

It was, without question, the happiest she had felt since her parents were murdered.

CHAPTER TEN
You Don't Know a Lot About Frai, Do You?

'Fancy getting out of the city?'

The morning had been a quiet, slightly lonely one without Thistle. Thorn was halfway through her second cup of coffee, nose buried in a book on flowers. When she looked up at Kol, she saw that he was already dressed to leave, coat and boots on, sunglasses covering his eyes.

Ignoring the urge to stare at him and tell him how pretty he was, Thorn set her book aside. 'Depends.'

'I can promise chocolate,' he said mischievously. 'Chocolate and good views.'

'Yeah, okay.'

Outside, the sun was shining but crisp winter added a bite to the air. A lovely layer of snow coated the ground, crunching beneath their boots. The contrast of the world against the untarnished snow was striking.

A shiver ran down her spine and when Kol wrapped his arm around her. She snuggled into him, far less reticent about doing so these days.

'Where are we going?'

'It's a surprise.'

'I hate surprises.'

'Really?'

'Yes. I tend to react badly.'

They got into the coach and Kol started the engine. 'We're going to see my sister. She's been dying to meet you ever since I told her about you.'

'We've only been a couple for a couple of days.'

'Yes, and I told her yesterday.'

Thorn didn't know what to make of that, but there was something nice about being mentioned. Knowing Kol thought about her even when she wasn't around.

He continued, 'I liked you the day you arrived. Ayla, my sister, wanted to meet you straight away. I figured too many Suriias might be a bad idea, so I told her to chill. When she found out that we're a couple, she demanded. Don't worry,' he added with a wink. 'She likes humans.'

Thorn tapped her fingers on the windowsill. 'Awesome. I sound like a type of pet.'

'Her husband's human.' Kol raised the coach into the air and flew over the forest before glancing at her. He laughed at the look of astonishment on her face. 'Where do you think I got all my movies?'

'He's human?'

'Yep.'

Thorn instantly felt more excited about the afternoon, although she hoped he wasn't anything like Eva and Ivy. 'So we're going to their house? Do they live in town?'

'No, they have an estate in the countryside. It's safe. My parents own the neighbouring lands and it's well guarded.'

The sheer enormity of that took a moment to settle in.

'Are you rich like Nithin?'

'No. I make decent money, but his parents didn't take away his inheritance. He's, technically speaking, a lord.'

'I thought that was a joke.'

'Nope. Son of Lord Summons, heir to half the land up north.'

She whistled.

'His father loves him enough to not cut him out after learning about Thistle. My father cut me out when I left his company.'

'Were you a lord, too?' She'd meant it as a joke, but when he opened and closed his mouth and then grimaced, she did a doubletake. 'Really?'

He shrugged, looking bashfully embarrassed by the admission. 'It's not like I'm a lord now. I don't even have property to my name. Just a wicked film collection and a garden that costs perhaps a little more than is necessary for a frai. But I don't need much. Never have.'

Thorn was genuinely afraid to ask what his father did at his company, and Kol didn't seem inclined to tell her, so the matter dropped.

As they flew over the streets of the outskirts of the vibrant city, Thorn caught sight of the news bulletins. More humans were being rounded up and sent to the camps; there was fighting between the races of Suriias; and there was a great debate on the pros and cons of magic versus machine.

The further they drove from the city, the wilder and more beautiful the land became. The fields transformed into farmland and marshes, and then gave way to forests and mountains.

Kol stopped at one point and bought them burgers from a floating restaurant by the sea. The day was nice enough that they sat on the cliffside across from the restaurant to eat, gazing out across the water. Sunlight sparkled off the surface in a blinding, beautiful way and there was no one around to ruin the atmosphere.

'What do they tell Suriia children?' she wondered aloud. 'About humans? What was done to us?'

For a minute he said nothing, and she saw his jaw clenching. But he didn't change the subject. 'They tell us that for a time, there was peace. Suriias left Salfar and settled here and lived in harmony. And then one day the humans turned against us. Called us demon children. That they set our kind alight and cursed those who associated with us. That humans called us evil and soulless and wrong—it's true. But it's true too that we have done all the same ills we decry humans for. I think all kinds need to stop fighting. There's no need for it.'

Thorn scowled at her burger, the conversation turning her stomach. 'That's usually the ignorant call of someone who's never had to fight for anything.'

'Or the tired observations of one who has seen too much.'

She thought about that for a second. 'How old are you?'

'Two hundred and twenty. I was born after the Rising. Same as Nith.'

'The what?'

'The war.'

'We call that the Red Sky Rebellion.'

He frowned in thought, clearly not aware of the human name for the day the Suriias seized full control of Earth and humans were driven into hiding or taken into captivity. 'Because of the magic they used?'

'Because they slaughtered so many, the survivors thought it was raining blood.'

They gazed at each other for a long moment.

At length, she added, 'Good.'

'Good?'

'Yeah, good that you weren't born then.'

'Why's that?'

'If you'd been alive, it'd mean you participated. I'd never forgive you for that.'

Kol set his half eaten burger aside and took her hand. 'I've never killed a human, Rose. I've never taken without asking. I'm not denying that I've been extremely lucky, but being lucky isn't the same as being evil. And isn't realising my luck and trying to be better for it worth something?'

His words made her chest ache. 'Of course, it is. I'm sorry. I know you're nothing like that.'

He pressed his lips to her hand as if swearing some kind of oath. 'I will never be like them.'

She was really starting to believe him, too.

The sun had swallowed the clouds and cast the world in a golden hue by the time they reached Ayla's house. Kol set the coach down in front of a stone gate and opened it with a wave of his hand. A ward shimmered as they drove through, but Thorn was more struck by the odd beauty of the new location than about the magic used to guard it. The drive up to the house was entirely cloaked in hanging trees, flowers spilling from all sides, their petals brushing against the sides of the coach. The house at the end was nestled between trees, made of wood with a thatched roof. It was a home for one who loved nature and craved an abundance of it.

A frai home.

Kol parked and walked around to her side to open the door. 'It's going to be fine,' he assured her, taking her hand. 'Ayla's great.'

Despite his words, Thorn's legs shook with every step. Meeting new Suriias would never be easy.

Kol wrapped his arms around her comfortingly and kissed her cheek. 'When you meet Shadow, you'll feel better.'

'Shadow? Is that the human?'

'That's me.'

Thorn whirled around. Standing behind her was a man. A very normal looking man, one who didn't wear the clothes of Suric society. He was just … normal. He had shaggy brown hair and scars across his face and neck, just like her. There was nothing hazy or frightened in his eyes, and he looked healthy.

'You must be Thorn,' he said, extending his hand without delay. 'We've heard so much about you.'

She grasped his hand, unable to stop herself from beaming at him. 'It's nice to see a human.'

'Yeah,' he agreed. 'Want to come inside?'

'Okay.'

The interior of the house was as mesmerising as the exterior. There was an abundance of art and colour. Plants filled every bit of space not taken up by furniture and bookshelves. Everything smelled like flower blossoms and birds chirped merrily in an atrium that extended out from the sitting room. One of the walls was actually a fish tank, and large fish swam about, utterly at ease. The water let out at the bottom into a pond – a feat she guessed only possible with magic – and in the pond amongst the fish, turtles sat on rocks, bathing in the sunlight that streamed in through the opposite glass wall. Further scrutiny revealed snakes slithering across the floor while fluffy cats snoozed around them, unbothered. In the trees above, she saw tarsiers, lemurs and flying squirrels moving about at their own pace. A chubby sloth blinked at her.

'Do they all get along?' she queried, enraptured by the sight.

'Of course,' said Shadow. 'All of our animals cohabitate well. One of the cool things about frai magic. When everything's in harmony, there's no need for quarrels.'

'Are they charmed?'

'No. Not at all. Just at ease. The snakes keep to themselves; the cats know not to play with what isn't food.'

'We can't talk to animals,' Kol chimed in, 'but we can communicate in our own way. Work at it long enough and frai can communicate with everything that lives. There's a reason so many of us become zoologists and scientists.'

'How many animals live here?' Thorn couldn't look away. A dog she hadn't noticed trotted over and jumped up, scratching at her leg for attention.

'Most are outside,' said Shadow, nodding to the open door at the other end of the atrium. 'The whole property is protected, so we don't have to worry about anyone hunting them or any of them wandering off. The magic works as a fence, so there's no barbed wire or anything horrible like that. There are some kinkajous, too, but they're sleeping with the colugos right now.'

'I have no idea what those are and I'm so happy,' she told him, unable to stifle her grin. 'What else?'

'I'll show you the horses later.'

'Yes, please!'

'Have a seat,' said Shadow. 'Ayla will be down in a second.'

'I'll make coffee,' said Kol, clapping him on the back and disappearing into the kitchen.

'Where are you from?' asked Shadow as they sat down on adjacent sofas.

'The mountains. You?'

'I was born in a cage.'

'Fuck,' she cursed. 'I'm so sorry.'

'Ghuls,' he elaborated. 'A feeding farm.'

She tugged her shirt to the side, exposing her collarbone and scars. 'Vrykos and vylkas.'

'It's like a calling card at this point.'

'Was it the farm up by Surren?'

The question clearly took him by surprise. 'It is,' he said. 'Why?'

The memory from a few weeks beforehand, when she and Jinx had blown up the feeding farm in Surren, came back to her, and she shook her head, barely tamping down a grin.

A creaking of the floorboards caught her attention and Thorn turned to see a frai. One of the most beautiful she'd ever seen.

Ayla was simply breath-taking, and resembled her brother greatly. She had the same gold-black cat eyes, the same olive skin, the same casual countenance. Like Kol, she wore jeans and a loose shirt, unkempt and unassuming.

'Hi,' she said warmly. 'You must be Thorn.'

'Hi.' Thorn waved awkwardly. 'Nice to meet you.'

Ayla cocked her head towards the kitchen. 'Shall we have tea on the veranda? It's a lovely day and it looks over the water.'

Keen to see more of the place, Thorn followed Shadow and Ayla from the room. Kol joined them on the veranda moments later and everyone took a steaming mug of tea. He'd also brought a plate of scones and sandwiches.

'You're going to make us all fat,' said Shadow happily, seizing one of the scones.

'I delight in feeding people,' said Kol. 'It's a problem.'

'It's the best problem,' said Thorn, winking at him.

Kol grinned.

'How are you finding Courtenz?' asked Ayla, reclining in her chair and drawing one of her legs into her chest.

Thorn decided to be honest. 'I miss the mountains.'

'I know how you feel.' Ayla smiled at her before looking at Kol. 'Sick of the city yet?'

'Getting there,' he allowed. 'But it's close to work and I can't leave Nith.'

Thorn could understand that. 'How did you two meet?' she asked, glancing at Shadow.

'She saved me from a group of pricos.' He pointed to the scars on his cheek and neck.

'Did you ever consider marrying a Suriia?' Thorn couldn't help but ask Ayla. 'Doesn't seem to be that popular – picking one of us, I mean.'

'Only Shadow for me.' Nudging her brother, Ayla added, 'Seems to run in the family.'

'Isn't it fun being special?' said Shadow, wiggling his eyebrows at Thorn.

'Such fun,' she joked. 'How long have you two been together?'

'A century.'

She giggled, thinking it was a joke. It wasn't. 'What—how—*what?*'

Ayla and Shadow both laughed. To Thorn's surprise, Kol suddenly looked pensive and preoccupied, picking at a chocolate chip scone like it contained buried treasure.

'How much do you know about frai?' asked Ayla.

'You guys like plants.'

Kol failed to turn his laugh into a cough. 'I really think that should be our slogan.'

'Definitely,' said Ayla. 'But there's a lot more to it than that. The rules are stupidly archaic.'

'What do you mean?'

Clearly astounded by something Thorn hadn't yet been clued in on, Ayla glanced between them. 'He hasn't told you?'

Kol's brow knitted together. 'It hasn't come up,' he mumbled. 'And it doesn't need to come up now.'

'Sure, it does,' said Ayla. 'Thorn's interested. Aren't you, Thorn?'

'Ridiculously,' said Thorn. 'Please go on.'

Kol scowled at his sister, but she paid him no mind. If his reticence was anything to go by, there was something particularly important Thorn wasn't aware of.

'All Suriias have a different way of taking their partner. While humans married out of duty once, and then out of love, each race of Suriias has their own tradition. Vrykos fuck freely but they only turn the ones they want to spend eternity with. It's not many. They are linked to those they turn always. Vylkas tend to be free with their bodies until they pick a mate, and then they're together for life. Sbura feed off desire and energy, but if they marry and form a symbiotic relationship with someone, the person is then linked to their lifeforce. To the point of near-immortality.'

Thorn pondered if Thistle knew that. If she didn't, she really should; if she did, Thorn felt deeply bothered at once again being left out of the loop.

Beside her, Kol continued dissecting his scone with his utensils, creating a mound of crumbs on his plate.

'Frai are slightly cursed,' continued Ayla. 'The rest of the Suriias get to lust and fuck at will until they choose. We can't. The first person we sleep with is the only one we can ever be with.'

Thorn stared at her, trying to suss out what, exactly, she meant. 'Wait, *what?*'

Shadow nodded grimly and Ayla scrunched up her delicate features into a show of lifelong frustration with the rules of her magic. 'That was my reaction the first time my mother told me. It's fucking stupid. And it gets worse.'

Thorn was afraid to ask.

'We're immortal. So if our partner dies, we live on, forever alone.'

The rushing in her ears actually hurt. Tearing her attention from Ayla, she looked at Kol in bewilderment. All of his warnings about waiting and being sure suddenly made so much sense. 'Why would you *ever* pick a human?'

He simply looked at her with an indecipherable expression.

Still reeling, Thorn directed her next question at Ayla. 'How can a human *become* immortal?'

'It's not that simple,' said Kol.

'The Lady of the Tear,' said Ayla, ignoring her brother's discomfiture. 'Or the Lady of the River – she goes by both. She sometimes grants wishes for a price. But for frai she's kinder. She has a soft spot for love. Shadow didn't have to pay a price.'

'That's not true and you know it,' said Kol, voice clipped with warning.

Thorn ignored him. 'How does a rip between our world and your old one make a human immortal?'

'She's got more magic than anyone on Earth,' said Ayla. 'But we don't know how she got the gig or what her motives are. She's just there … guarding the Immortal River.'

'Enough, Ayla,' said Kol, voice so low it was almost a growl. 'Seriously.'

Thorn said nothing, mind filled with questions about the Tear, Suriias, magic, immortality and the human willing to embrace it all.

The conversation turned eventually and at last the tension dissipated. But it weighed heavily on Thorn's mind for the rest of the afternoon. And from the way he kept glancing at her, Kol knew exactly what was bothering her.

The sun had long set by the time he suggested they head back to the mansion. Ayla told him she had something for him, and the pair disappeared upstairs, leaving Thorn and Shadow alone.

She appraised him curiously, finding herself fascinated by him at every turn. 'How do you do it?' she asked.

He shook his head, clearly not guessing her train of thought.

'Love a Suriia after all they've done to us?'

'Anyone's mind can be poisoned at birth,' he said. 'That doesn't make their hatred innate.'

'I wish I could believe that.'

'Wouldn't things be better for you if you did?'

'Maybe,' she allowed. 'Or maybe I'd be the next human you know who dies.'

They were still regarding each other with heavy melancholy, both points valid, neither able to fully understand the other side but desperately wishing to, when Kol and Ayla returned.

Thorn bid Ayla farewell before walking out into the now rainy night. Kol followed her a few seconds later and they headed back to Courtenz in silence. In the distance, the moon and stars lit up the heavens.

Only when they got out of the coach at the mansion and Kol took her hand, did he speak.

'I'd never ask that of you, Rose,' he said abruptly. 'I told her not to bring it up. I'm sorry.'

'Were you going to tell me about the sex thing?'

Judging by his expression, he hadn't planned on it.

'Kol!' she cried, letting go of his hand and throwing her own into the air. 'That's something I have to be aware of!'

'I didn't want you to be,' he said bluntly. 'I want you to fall in love with me the same way I've fallen in love with you. I didn't want it to matter. It's on me. It does nothing to you.'

Thorn didn't hear half of what he said. She zeroed in on the middle and all the breath left her lungs.

Love. He was in *love* with her.

She knew right then that she could never sleep with him. She could never let it get that far. She had to kill Veryn and then leave before Kol gave up his entire life for her. The thought of him being unhappy forever made her want to punch a tree.

But that realisation also left her feeling hollowed out. Even in a world where things were different, she and Kol could never have a future. It wasn't fair on him. She was a human and could never give him the life Shadow had given Ayla. Their love story didn't end up well for at least one of them in any scenario.

'Rose, please say something.'

She cleared her throat. 'You love me?'

Kol shuffled his feet. Against the night sky, he looked made of shadows. 'I've not exactly been subtle about my feelings. I've been fairly clear from the start how I felt. I just didn't press anything on you because I knew how you felt about Suriias.'

'You love me.'

'Yes.'

She didn't know what to say, so she kissed him, because she couldn't say it back. Kissing Kol was like taking Hazies without the side effects. Her insides danced and she leaned into him, wanting to feel him against every part of her. With Jinx it had been a wet, weird feeling that left her wanting to shower; with Kol it felt like she wanted to wrap her body around him. Her arms lifted to wrap around his neck, her fingers curling in his hair. She wanted to inhale him.

A sharp squeal of delight cut through the moment and they broke apart, panting, lips swollen.

Thistle barrelled into her, tackling Thorn in a hug. 'I'm so happy!' she exclaimed. 'Took you two long enough!'

Thorn stared at her, trying to catch up. 'What?'

'Nithin called it weeks ago,' said Thistle happily, 'but I didn't believe him until now. I thought it was just Kol!'

Even Nithin looked pleased, the smile he offered Thorn perhaps the strangest part of the entire day.

She didn't know what to say or how to respond to their shared joy.

What did you do when the only one you'd ever liked could only exist with you in a fantasy, suspended from reality by nothing more than money and power? What happened the day the Spotters no longer honoured the Register? If it came down to humans versus Suriias, Thorn knew which side she stood on. As beautiful as his promises were, she didn't see Kol changing sides.

And she would never stand with them. True, maybe if she tried, Thorn really could have lived the fantasy. She could wake up every day next to Kol, work in an office alongside him and Thistle; she could walk through society with Kol's name to keep her safe and befriend the ones who didn't dream about eating her.

But she couldn't pretend. She couldn't forget. Their society didn't view her as equal and she had no desire to align herself with any of them. Why placate and befriend her oppressors? They owed *her* an apology. Humanity. And even then, even if they begged for her forgiveness, Thorn was hard pressed to forget what the Suriias had done them.

Murderers and facilitators did not deserve forgiveness.

CHAPTER ELEVEN
The Promises We Keep

A harmony took hold of the mansion in the ensuing days, as if Thorn and Kol's relationship signalled a change in the dynamic of the group. Thistle talked animatedly about places the four of them could go; Nithin made more attempts at conversation with Thorn than he previously had; Kol seemed like he was walking on clouds. It was as if everyone thought being with Kol could somehow change Thorn's perspective.

Kol's promise to help her find Veryn hadn't been brought up since and she was starting to wonder if he'd forgotten everything or simply didn't want to help.

And, then one afternoon, everything changed. She was in the midst of exercising, soaked in sweat, body hot and aching, when Kol came home from work. She heard the door open and looked up, perspiration falling into her eyes and making her squint.

'Isn't your boss going to be mad that you're missing so much work?' she asked, not pausing her workout.

'My boss is my roommate. I'm fine.'

She laughed.

He strolled over and sat on the ground beside her. In recent days, even his work attire seemed to have relaxed. Instead of a suit, he was wearing a scarlet jumper. Still immaculately put together, the changes were subtle, but she had a guess it was for her benefit.

'There's a dinner tomorrow night,' he relayed, fingers running absently over the grass. Inside the greenhouse, controlled by his magic, winter had not taken hold. 'Our company is hosting it. To raise awareness for humans.'

Thorn finished the set of press-ups and sat up. The offer was not unappreciated, but it was unappealing all the same.

'I'd love to bring you,' he continued, voice softer now, uncertain.

There were few scenarios she could imagine that sounded less abhorrent than sitting in a room all night with Suriias, begging for help. The death camps were no secret. The treatment of humans was not obscured. If they hadn't wanted to help humans before, they weren't going to now. And somehow others thinking she was in need of charity and pity was worse to Thorn than simple hatred. You shouldn't need a vote to decide not to eradicate a group.

'I think I'll pass,' she said, running her fingers over the grass. 'It's not really my thing.'

She heard him sigh and tried not to let it bother her, but it did. She looked back up at him. 'If you want to watch a movie or something after, I'll wait up.'

The offer felt measly, yet he nodded. 'Then I won't stay out too late,' he promised, his customary smile reappearing.

'I'll have the chocolate waiting.'

He got to his feet and held out his hands. 'Lunch?'

She let him pull her up. The change made her head rush, stars exploding across her vision. He kissed her slowly, cradling her face between his hands. 'You're so beautiful,' he murmured when they stilled. 'Come on. I'm making you lunch.'

They'd only just sat down to eat their sandwiches when Kol's phone rang. Whatever appeared on the screen made him frown and he stood abruptly. 'Give me a second,' he said before answering it and disappearing into the other room.

Thorn picked at her sandwich. The mozzarella, cucumber, sundried tomatoes and pesto spread all wrapped in toasted bread smelled delicious, but she was too preoccupied to eat.

When he reappeared, there was a grim set to his jaw and meaning in his eyes.

'Everything okay?' she asked cautiously.

'I have an address.'

'An address?'

He ran a hand through his dark hair and exhaled loudly. 'Veryn Rigar.'

She shot to her feet. 'Are you serious?'

'Yes.'

Seized by a sweeping, consuming gratitude, Thorn threw her arms around him.

'We can go tonight,' he said. 'And then you're done, right?'

'Then I'm done,' she agreed.

Kol held her, if possible, even closer. 'Please be careful tonight. I need you to come home with me. I need you to be okay.'

'He murdered my parents. He's the one dying tonight.'

The afternoon felt like it existed outside of time, painfully elongated, the air heavy with anticipation. She couldn't sit still and Kol didn't bother going back to work. Whether that was because he was equally as distracted or because he didn't trust her not to go after Veryn alone, she wasn't sure.

By dusk, not long before Nithin and Thistle were due to return, they got into the coach.

Neither of them said a word on the drive. Thorn loaded her guns and double-checked them as Kol drove.

They passed over tree after tree, leaving the city behind.

Kol slowed to a stop outside of a large building. It stood so high that it disappeared into the darkness of the sky. 'This it?'

'Yep.' Kol squinted up at it, eyes now entirely black as magic course through him. 'There's no way to get inside this place.'

'There's always a way,' said Thorn, thinking quickly. 'Are you good at climbing?'

'We have to get past his wards first.'

'Can you do that?' It didn't escape her notice that having a Suriia at her side was suddenly indispensable.

'If he's home, it won't take him long to notice.'

'We'll sneak in.'

'Well, sure, when you put it that way.' Kol let out a huff. 'We need a distraction.'

'Got anything in mind?'

His lip curled. 'If I shatter the wards and then fly up to the top, he'll probably notice that before noticing you. It'd draw everyone's attention.'

Thorn didn't like that idea much at all. 'You'd end up on the evening news if you're not shot first.'

'I'm fast.'

'Okay, in no way have I agreed to this.' She glared up at the house, trying to spy a way in.

'Don't think I can?'

'I think you've never broken into a building before.' When she looked over at him, there was a mischievous glint in his eyes.

'I'll distract them while you get in through a lower level. I won't get caught, and when they stop looking for me, I'll get in from upstairs.'

Thorn tried to come up with a better idea, couldn't, and relented. 'Fine. Be careful.'

Kol kissed her cheek, winked, and then darted out of the coach and up the road.

'Crap,' said Thorn.

A *thump*, like a pulse going off, went through the air, and she shot out of the coach and sprinted up to the house. Darting around one side, she found a window obscured by a large bush. Pushing the pane open, she crawled inside. She landed in what looked like the basement. A horrible, putrid stink wafted up her nose instantly. Worse, when she moved, a sucking sound.

She stopped short and looked down.

The basement was full of people. All dead.

Not just humans, she realised with shock. But Suriias, too.

If Thorn were ever to describe a nightmare to someone, the first place her mind went to was the night her parents were killed. The savage brutality the vrykos had shown them, how remorseless and cruel. The scene that greeted her in the basement now rivalled that.

The ground was so coated in blood, her boots stuck. The sound was wholly unsettling, like peeling plastic seal off a container. Every pulling, squelching noise cut through the basement's quiet in a raw, horrendous way. It took all her courage to press on up the stairs. Old wood creaked beneath her boots as she ascended with slow, trudging steps, each one threatening to expose her. On the last stair before the door, she stilled and checked her gun, her knife, and took a deep breath before turning the knob and pushing it open, ears straining to hear any sound in the hallway beyond.

But the hallway wasn't a hallway at all. She had stepped out in a large room. The décor was of a kind Thorn couldn't define even if she'd had a million years. Dark, garish furniture contrasted harshly with violent paintings on the wall that depicted, upon closer inspection, the mass murder of humans. She lingered longer than was wise, unable to break her gaze. Shivers scuttled across her skin, head to toe, and her stomach slithered into knots like her intestines were snakes, and the snakes were afraid.

Beyond the room was an open hall and a great staircase. She tip-toed to the railing and looked up. There seemed to be at least forty floors. There were also more floors below, going into the ground.

She barely had time to panic about how she would find Veryn when a shadow landed on the ground beside her. Where he'd come from, she didn't have time to guess.

Seeing Veryn from a distance at the flybys could not have prepared her for a face to face encounter. Her chest shuddered, her legs felt jellied, yet her hand was steady as she drew her father's blade.

'*My, my, my,*' he crooned. 'Who let the little birdie in?'

She swiped at his face with her blade.

Veryn caught her by the wrist before metal severed flesh and in a flash, he had her pinned to the opposite wall. His breath, wet and sickly sweet, brushed against her cheek as he leaned in. 'I do love getting dinner delivered.'

'I hope you enjoy eating your own heart then,' she snarled, slamming her knee into his ribs with as much might as she could muster from the awkward angle. The force of the kick loosened his grip enough that she wiggled free and scrambled away from him, readjusting her hold on her knife. She drew the iron blade, too.

He laughed.

The problem with being human against a vryko was that even as good at fighting as she was, even as strong and quick as she was, she couldn't move faster than sight, or fly, or survive being thrown several storeys.

He rushed her, tossing her over the railing like she was a limp puppet. She landed with a sickening thud on the marble floor below.

Thorn was still trying to remember how to breathe when Veryn landed beside her gracefully and lifted her up.

'I remember your father,' he crowed. 'He tasted so sweet. I wonder if you'll taste the same, little girl.'

Thorn could feel Kol's blade in her hand cutting into her palm. The iron only cutting, not poisoning.

Not daring to hesitate, she kicked out with her left leg. It distracted Veryn and she jammed the iron blade into his heart.

'Bleed,' she spat, twisting the knife before wrenching it back out again.

That was the thing about Suriias – they thought themselves so powerful they never allowed for the possibility that a human could best them.

Her victory was short lived, however. As her breathing evened and her adrenaline lessened, the shadows around her began to move.

A dozen Soul Eaters surrounded her.

She raised both blades, ready to kill them all. From the looks on their faces, they craved the same.

Suddenly, the ones in front of her were repelled by an inhuman force. As if the air had a mind of its own.

But it wasn't the air.

Kol landed lightly on the ground beside her, breathing hard. He seized her hand and they sprinted through the rooms as fast as they could, slipping on the marble and rugs. Somehow they managed to get outside without anyone stopping them.

The cold air of the night was a welcome bite against their faces, but they didn't stop until they reached the coach.

'Why aren't they following us?' she hissed.

'They know me,' he muttered. 'They're not stupid.'

She shot him a curious look, but left it alone. Part of her didn't want to ask.

'Are you okay?' he said as he started the coach and brought them into the air.

'I got him,' she croaked. 'I can't believe I got him.'

Kol reached out and took her hand, interlacing their bloodstained fingers together.

They held hands on the drive and Thorn tried not to cry with relief and exhaustion and disbelief. Part of her never actually thought she'd be able to find Veryn, let alone make it out alive. She'd always thought that Thistle would be at her side, too. Having Kol, a Suriia, holding her hand through the moment was a strange, surreal outcome. Her throat threatened to close every few minutes as surges of mixed emotions welled inside her and she said nothing as they drove back to the mansion.

Oddly, two coaches were parked out front when they drove through the gates.

'Oh, wonderful,' said Kol sarcastically as he turned the engine off. His eyes were fixed on a sleek silver coach parked just ahead.

'Who is it?' she wondered, dreading the answer.

'Our parents.'

'Oh.' Thorn grimaced. 'You expecting them?'

'No.'

Now looking thoroughly putout, Kol handed her a cloth to wipe off her hands before stepping out of the coach and walking around to her side. When she climbed out, he took her hand and they headed towards the door together.

'What do we say about our cuts?'

'We can say you were jumped, if you're okay with that?'

'Sure.' Better than saying they'd just committed murder on one of the city's dukes. 'Do they know about you and me?'

'Kind of. Ayla's told my mother.'

'How'd she take it?'

'My mother's been pressing me to get married for two centuries,' he murmured. 'Human or not, she's going to love you.'

'And your dad?'

'He … won't make a scene in front of my mother.'

Thorn gripped his hand tightly and followed him into the house.

'What do they think of Shadow?' she asked.

'It took some time,' said Kol honestly. 'But my other siblings have all married frai, so they have little reason to bitch.'

'But they do?'

'I was meant to be the heir.'

Thorn didn't feel remotely comforted by that. 'Okay, fuck – what does your father do?'

He shook his head and her heart sank. With frai running the death camps, she could fathom a guess.

In the sitting room, they found Nithin, Thistle and four unfamiliar Suriias. The two she recognised instantly as Kol's parents stared at her with open disapproval. Thistle and Nithin both looked like they wished they were elsewhere.

'Mother, Father,' said Kol, 'allow me to introduce my girlfriend, Thorn.'

Despite his words about his mother, the flicker in her gold-black eyes was not kind. His father's expression proved even less welcoming.

'It's a pleasure to meet you,' his mother said at length. 'Call me Iona. My husband, Lykar.'

Thorn crossed her arms.

His father snorted and Kol shifted closer to her.

'Problem?' she snapped.

'Of course not,' said Kol loudly, glaring at his father. 'Isn't that right?'

'No,' said his father.

Lord Summons, who seemed thoroughly bored by everyone, cleared his throat. 'We have important matters to discuss, Kol.'

Kol's eyes narrowed. 'Oh?'

Not wanting to remain near any of them, Thorn squeezed Kol's hand and exited the room. All her energy went into not sprinting.

In the hallway, she leaned against the wall, legs shaking so badly she could barely stand. It took several seconds for her to carry on to the kitchen. Talk about a long, eventful evening. All she wanted to do was tell Thistle Veryn was dead and then crash.

Craving a distraction, Thorn opened the fridge, stomach in too many knots to eat but needing to do something with her hands.

'You know,' said a voice behind her, making her jump, 'you're the first female my son has ever shown an interest in.'

Thorn peered around the fridge door at Lykar Sinn, a juberous feeling in her gut. 'I'm not sure if that's an insult or compliment.'

Lykar strolled into the kitchen. There was something panther-like about him. And not in a good way. 'It's neither.'

Not sure where he was going with this, Thorn pulled a packet of cheese from the fridge and withdrew a slice. She ate it methodically, waiting.

'Do you know what life you resign my son to if you follow this path?'

The cheese suddenly felt like sandpaper and she had to force a swallow. 'Yes,' she said, when at last she found her voice. 'Ayla told me.'

'And you would have him be nothing but a lonely shell?'

She regarded him expressionlessly. Even if she planned to leave, that was none of Lykar's concern. 'It's his life.'

'He's my son.'

'It's still his life.'

Lykar nodded slowly. 'And if I could grant you safety? Security? A good life as a human far from here?'

Thorn stared at him. 'How?'

'My son hasn't told you who I am, has he?'

'Father?' Kol appeared in the doorway. 'What's going on?'

Lykar clapped Thorn on the shoulder; it took all her willpower not to flinch. 'I was welcoming Thorn to the family.'

Kol cut a glance at Thorn, clearly disbelieving, and held out his hand.

When they returned to the sitting room, Thorn sat beside Kol. He didn't let go of her hand and the tension in his body left him stiff as stone. Despite his words of calm, Kol was anything but.

'Now that business is out of the way,' said Lord Summons, putting his hands together, 'let's catch up. Nithin, your mother tells me you're thinking of having children.'

Thorn's gasp of surprise turned into a hacking cough and Thistle patted her on the back, eyes wide, beseeching her not to make a scene.

'Yes,' said Nithin. 'But there is no news on that front to report.'

'Soon enough,' said Nithin's mother.

Restraint had never been Thorn's strong suit and she fixed her gaze on the window and stared out of it, tuning out the conversation until, after what felt like an eternity but was only twenty minutes, the four parents took their leave.

Thorn stood as the others left to walk them out and stayed by the window, glaring at their disappearing coach, heart hammering.

Kol rejoined her a few seconds later. 'Are you all right?'

'Your father,' she said quietly, 'how is he so powerful?'

He shook his head and rubbed a hand over his mouth, deliberating.

'What?'

'My father runs the unit.'

'The Spotters?' Thorn's whole body went cold. 'How is that even possible? Shadow—'

'Hypocrisy is something of a refined art form for my father. He sees humans as a commodity. As something to be used. But he also sees marriage as a contract – done for necessity. As half-Suriia children can still use magic, can still thrive in our society, he has no problem allowing Ayla to – in his woefully inaccurate opinion – use Shadow to reproduce and further the reach of his family.'

Thorn stared at him, wanting to puke. 'How can you even stand to be around him?'

'I can't. I don't work for the company and, if you've not noticed, I do not invite him around here.'

'Why is your mother even with him?'

'My mother wants everyone to get along. It's … taxing. She's as much a part of the problem as he is, but she has no personal hatred against humans.'

'How does Ayla put up with it?'

'She doesn't speak to them unless she has to. But my mother loves Shadow.' Kol leaned back against the wall and shrugged. 'As I said, hypocrisy runs deep in my family. He's "not like the others" apparently.'

'Ew.'

'Yeah.'

'I think humans have that problem, too,' she murmured. 'Bargaining with morality and being hypocritical.'

A smile spread across his face.

'What?'

'I like when you point out that we're not that different.'

Thorn's lips twitched, but she was too tense to smile. 'Why was he here?'

'He was offering me a job. Again.'

'And?'

'And nothing. I work for Nithin. I love you. I won't touch that company.'

'Why are you so sought after? Just because you're his son?'

'I took the exams years ago. They liked the results.'

She took a step back without meaning to. 'What exams?'

'See, I knew you would take that up wrong,' he muttered, running a hand through his hair and clenching at the roots. 'I don't want to lie to you, Rose. Stop making me feel like I should.'

'I'm not running. I'm asking. What exams?'

'All Spotters have to take exams to see how capable they are at tracking with magic. I did well. That's all. I did the exam to shut my parents up before moving here with Nithin. I never worked for the company. Not one day. I promise.'

After a beat, she nodded. 'Okay.'

'Okay?'

'Yeah, okay. I believe you.' She thumbed at the door. 'I'm going to take a shower. You should probably get some sleep. You've got that dinner tomorrow.'

He didn't move. 'Are we all right?'

'Yeah,' she said. 'We're fine.'

It was clear he didn't believe her, but he said nothing else as she walked out.

She'd barely had time to shower and change when a knock at the door made her jump, but the sight of Thistle brought a smile to her lips.

'Hey, you,' she called softly.

'Hey, you,' echoed Thistle, closing the door and joining her on the bed. 'Long night?'

'I killed Veryn.'

Thistle stared at her. And then tears filled her eyes. 'You did?' she choked out.

'I did.'

Thorn wrapped her arms around Thistle and pulled her close. 'Thank you.'

It was a long while before they broke apart.

'We'll be able to leave now,' she said, drawing back. The words, for the first time, did not sound staunch and unyielding. 'As soon as the others are ready. There's no reason to stay in Courtenz.'

'Tor ...'

'What?'

Thistle hesitated and Thorn's heart sank. Not in surprise, but disappointment.

'Tiz, come on. We agreed to this.'

'No,' said Thistle quietly. 'I never wanted to leave.'

'You promised me.'

'I like it here.'

Thorn stared at Thistle as something fundamental inside her *splintered*. 'You have to come. This was what we agreed to.'

'What about Kol?'

'What *about* Kol?'

'Don't you like him?'

'My feelings for Kol aren't going to override my common fucking sense, Tiz!'

It was clear, however, that Thistle had long since made up her mind. She slid off the bed, distancing herself from Thorn. 'I'm happy here. Nithin treats me well. He loves me. He's working towards securing a future for humans. Running off into the mountains isn't going to help anyone. It's certainly not going to help me.'

Thorn let out a scoff of disbelief. 'You can't be serious. For ten fucking years, this is all we've worked towards! A group of *people*.'

'Things change, Tor. Maybe you should.'

It was like being slapped. 'I used to be your family. You're picking a Suriia over *me*.'

'I'm picking my *husband*,' said Thistle angrily.

'What about me?'

The hesitation broke her heart. Somewhere along the way, she'd lost her sister.

Shaking her head in astonishment, Thorn turned on her heel and stormed off, so upset she knew if she didn't, she would say something she truly cruel. Or fall to her knees and beg Thistle not to leave her.

Her parents' warnings and last words went round and round her head, threatening to undo her.

Don't trust a Suriia.
Don't trust a Suriia.
Don't trust a Suriia.
I promise.
I promise.
I promise.

CHAPTER TWELVE
Friendships and Farewells

The storm had been Thorn's only company for most of the evening as she read beside the fire and ate bar after bar of chocolate. The others were out at the company dinner and the mansion was quiet save the crackling of the embers in the hearth.

A sudden, sharp knock on the window made Thorn jump to her feet. Setting the book aside, she drew out her knife and crept over. But it was only Jade, crouched low beneath the branches of the tree outside.

She waved happily at Thorn, who opened the window quickly.

'What are you doing here?'

Jade crawled inside. 'Haven't seen you in ages,' she said breathlessly, her curly black hair bouncing in front of her face. 'I wanted to see if you were okay.'

'Yeah,' said Thorn, grinning at her. 'It's just hard to get away unnoticed.'

'I get you.'

'How'd you know where the house was?'

'You told us,' said Jade with a laugh. 'Also, Jinx brought me. He had something to do tonight that's up this way.'

Thorn stiffened. 'Is he coming?'

'Said he wouldn't be able to,' said Jade. 'But he says "Hi".'

Relieved that he wasn't going to be joining them, Thorn waved around. 'Want a tour?'

'How long are the Suriias going to be gone?'

'At least until midnight.'

'Then yes!'

Jade took off her boots and coat and left them by the window. 'Oh!' she said, clapping her hands together. 'We're leaving in a week! We've found twenty!'

'People?'

Jade bobbed her head jubilantly. 'Jinx got wind of a couple others last week. You and Thistle are still coming, right?'

The confirmation that Jade still expected her to come made her feel weak with relief, only then realising how scared she was about Jinx changing his mind. 'Yes,' she said firmly.

Jade beamed at her.

Her enthusiasm proved infectious and Thorn brought her to the pool first. Jade let out a squeal of delight and they stripped out of their clothes and cannon-balled in. They splashed about for a few minutes before swimming over to the edge of the pool and hoisting themselves onto the wall.

'What do you think of these Suriias?' asked Jade, kicking the water idly.

'Sometimes it seems like Nithin really does love Tiz. It's hard to believe, even for me, but if he's lying, he's the best actor I've ever seen.'

'I hope he's not lying.'

'Me too.'

'And the other one? You said there were two, right?'

'His best friend, Kol.'

Jade nudged her. 'What's Kol like? You guys don't get along?'

'We do.' Thorn deliberated telling her, but then decided to go with her gut. Whatever Jinx's faults, Jade seemed an innately good person. 'Can you keep a secret?'

'Of course.'

'I like him. A lot. It's such a bad idea and goes against every instinct I have. I want to hate him. But I can't.'

'Is he nice?'

'Yeah.'

Jade pulled her legs into her chest, her wet hair a curtain around her shoulders and back. 'Maybe they're not all bad.'

Feeling melancholy about the whole thing, Thorn got to her feet. She retrieved two towels from the wall and held one out to Jade.

'Do you have any food here?' asked Jade, wrapping the towel around her too-thin torso.

The urge to take care of her came fast and hard, and Thorn seized her hand and steered her into the kitchen. She got out everything she could find that was high in protein, fibre, iron and vitamins and began cooking, letting Jade chat away animatedly.

'The new girl is so pretty,' she said as Thorn put vegetables into a slow-simmering stew before setting about making a banana and raspberry smoothie. 'Trinity.'

'Oh yeah?'

'She's really tall and she's got a scar here.' Jade pointed to the corner of her eye. 'I've sort of fallen in love with it. Is that weird?'

'It's not weird to me.' Thorn finished making the smoothie, poured them both glasses, and leaned against the sink. 'Tell me more.'

'She loves books, too,' said Jade dreamily. 'She's got a book of poems she found years ago. She can recite them off by heart.'

'Impressive.'

From the wistful cast to Jade's eyes, the poems Trinity could recite were more than impressive. Endearing didn't do it justice.

'Have you kissed her?'

Jade blushed furiously. 'I've only talked to her three times.'

'Then you'll just have to ask her if you can kiss her when you're in the mountains,' said Thorn, kicking her affectionately. 'But don't wait too long. If she's that pretty, someone else might ask her first.'

The sudden horrified look on Jade's face made Thorn want to slap herself.

'It's not gonna happen,' she added quickly. 'You're way too cute to turn down.'

Jade blushed six shades of pink. 'No, I'm not. I'm too short and never know the right things to say and I get tongue-tied every time she looks at me. She probably thinks I'm an idiot.'

Thorn set down her glass and held out her hand. 'Come on.'

'Where are we going?'

Rather than answer, Thorn led her out of the kitchen and into Nithin's library. 'Pick a few,' she said. 'Whatever you think she'd like. Write a small note so you don't get tongue-tied and give them to her next time you see her.'

Jade gaped at her. 'Seriously?'

'Seriously.'

Eyes wide as saucers, Jade scanned the shelves for a moment before shaking her head. 'I can't read,' she admitted. 'I wouldn't know what to pick.'

Thorn smiled. 'I can read. Just tell me what you think she'll like, and I'll tell you what the cover says. Then get her to be your teacher. It's perfect.'

Jade giggled, but she suddenly seemed keener on the idea and they perused the library for half an hour until Jade's constant growling stomach pressed them to return to the kitchen and Thorn set about finishing the stew. She also ransacked the closet for as much packaged food as she could fit into a bag and set it aside for Jade to bring home.

After they'd eaten, they curled up on the sofa to watch a movie. Like Thorn when she first arrived, Jade had never seen a film with human actors. She was as delighted as Thorn hoped Thistle would be, and they kept up a running commentary throughout the first half.

They'd only just passed the intermission when the sound of a coach outside made them both sit up.

Jade shot to her feet and grabbed her bag and the one Thorn had packed for her. 'I'll go.'

Thorn nodded. She could hear Kol, Nithin and Thistle outside. It seemed so wrong somehow, hiding someone from Thistle, but it also felt like instinct. Thorn didn't know what to make of that.

Jade hugged her quickly before darting to the window and scrambling out. 'Six nights starting tomorrow,' she hissed. 'Bottom of Tilo Street. Midnight.'

Thorn beckoned at her to run before she closed the window and drew the curtains. A second later, the front door opened, and she heard them enter.

Moving to the sofa, she grabbed the book she'd been reading before Jade arrived and pretended to be absorbed in it as they walked in. In the darkness, dressed in fine clothes, Thistle looked as Suriia as Kol and Nithin.

Thorn swallowed hard. 'How was the dinner?'

'Really good,' said Thistle. 'You should have come.'

'Not my thing.'

'Of course not.'

The jab made Thorn's eyes narrow. 'Guess some of us don't forget the ones who've hunted us.'

'We're going to bed,' said Thistle, rolling her eyes at Thorn and taking Nithin's hand. 'See you two in the morning.'

Thorn watched her leave, a hollow chasm growing in her stomach.

'Where's that chocolate I was promised?' Kol's teasing tone drew her from her thoughts and she looked over at him. His suit was far too expensive, and he smelled like too much money. It made her skin itch.

'Why don't you change, and I'll grab the chocolate?' she suggested, setting her book aside.

He chuckled. 'Sounds like a plan.'

By the time he returned to the sitting room, she'd sourced chocolate, sugared snacks, drinks, and put a movie on.

'Better?' he prompted. This time he wore loose black trousers and a rumbled t-shirt. He smelled like cinnamon, cloves and ginger.

'Much better,' she assured him, sitting on the sofa beside him. He raised his arm and she curled up against him.

He kissed the top of her head and a flutter went through her chest. 'You know,' he said as she opened the bar of chocolate, 'your friend didn't have to leave.'

Thorn sat up immediately, heart hammering.

He chuckled at her shock. 'The guards contacted Nithin the second she appeared on the property. He told them to leave her alone.'

Not sure what to say to that, Thorn broke off the edge of the chocolate bar and ate it without tasting it.

'I thought you'd appreciate that,' he added, sounding a little surprised.

'I don't like being watched,' she muttered.

'The guards aren't watching you. They saw someone break in the same way they've been watching you leave every other night.'

Thorn scoffed.

'You didn't think they didn't notice that, did you?' He looked slightly exasperated. 'Rose, the first night you left, you set off the alarm. We didn't want you feeling trapped, so we didn't say anything. You're not a prisoner. You can come and go whenever you want. You can have your friends over. It's your house, too. I only brought it up so you'd know it's not a secret and doesn't need to be. I'd love to meet your friend.'

Thorn got to her feet. 'I think I'm going to bed.'

'What? Why?' Kol stood and took her hand. 'I'm sorry I brought it up. I wanted to ask about your night and I didn't want to lie and pretend I didn't know. I'm sorry. Please don't go to bed. I've spent the whole night wishing I was home with you.'

She wavered. 'I don't like being spied on.'

'No one is spying on you,' he said. 'You've known about the guards on watch since the first night. We never hid them. They're here to protect us.'

More furious at herself than at him, Thorn let him tug her back to the sofa. She sat beside him stiffly until the movie was half over and at last her pride relented a little and she leaned into his side.

Midnight had come and gone by the time the movie finished. But she felt far from tired, mind racing with a thousand pending problems. Kol, on the other hand, yawned widely and suggested they turn in.

'Do you want to sleep in my room?' he proposed when they reached the upstairs landing. 'I'll behave.'

'Give me a second to change?'

Kol's grin broadened and he kissed her before disappearing down the hall.

Inside her room, Thorn took off her jeans and changed into a long-sleeved shirt and shorts. She eyed her knives on the bedside table for a second before leaving her room and turning off the light.

Kol was sitting on the edge of his bed when she entered. He had donned sleeping trousers and the pale light from outside the window cast him in a lovely glow that showed off his muscle tone.

'Where's your knife?' he queried.

'You helped me kill Veryn,' she whispered, moving to sit on his lap and putting her arms around his neck. 'I don't need my knife with you.'

His arms encircled her, drawing her in so close their bodies felt fused together. 'I love you,' he whispered.

Unable to say it back, Thorn kissed him, and tried to pretend it wasn't breaking her heart.

Thorn spent the rest of the week on edge and conflicted. Each day that brought her closer to meeting the other humans also reminded her that it would mean leaving Thistle and Kol behind forever. No amount of determination or necessity erased the ache of that knowledge.

The morning before she was due to leave, she suggested Kol take the day off work. He agreed without missing a beat.

'I was thinking,' he said as they had coffee in the garden. 'Do you want to do something fun?'

Thorn nodded. 'What did you have in mind?'

The twinkle in his eyes hinted at mischief. 'Get your coat.'

An hour later, Thorn was following Kol through a mountain trail. Water raged down a steep ravine to one side, thick forest obscured the world on the other.

'Do you prefer the mountains or the city?' she wondered, scanning the moss on the rocks as she went. Moss always grew towards water and it began appearing more and more often on the rocks as they went along.

'Oh, the mountains definitely,' he said without hesitation. 'Mountains and forests all the way.'

'Same.'

He glanced back, a smile lighting up his face. 'Well, we've got that in common.'

The higher they climbed, the colder and windier it became. One turn brought them to a steep ravine, another revealing a roaring river with a bridge across it.

Eventually the trees thinned out and the view opened. And suddenly Thorn found herself staring out over forests, mountains and valleys, the world spread out before her, beautiful and open.

An odd feeling gripped her. A kind of melancholy that had gnawed at her bones her entire life. Someday soon she would be in that wilderness, hidden from the world, where the loudest sounds were rushing waters. She wanted it so much she could taste it. But then Kol wrapped his arms around her waist and kissed her neck, and it was hard to be so certain.

'My mother used to tell me something to help me sleep,' she said abruptly, staring down at a great white bird with wings that contrasted beautifully with the dark foliage beneath it. 'She'd always whisper it, because you can't let noise travel in the dark. Noise travels faster in the dark. But even knowing why she had to be quiet, I always felt safe listening to her.

'She'd always start in the same place, too. "In the future," she'd say, smiling at me like it was going to happen. "In the future, there will be quiet nights. There will be no more hiding, no more running, no more fear. The future will be bright and open and free. Our bright tomorrows are waiting. We just have to get through the night."' Thorn exhaled quaveringly. 'But she'll never get to see tomorrow. She'll never know if tomorrow's bright or bloody.'

Kol tightened his hold around her, as if he could shield her from the horrors of the world. 'If it's the last thing I do,' he whispered, 'I'll make sure you see tomorrow. And every single one after that for as long as I live.'

A fresh wave of tears hit her, and she closed her eyes and leaned against him. She tried to believe him. She tried to set her doubts on fire. She tried to lock her memories away behind sealed doors inside her mind where not even the fiercest nightmares could spring them free. She tried *so hard.*

But sometimes horrendous acts could never be forgotten. Sometimes no amount of kindness or pledge of protection or oath of loyalty could ever fully erase the scars left by cruelty. Wishing for a change of heart was like trying to change history. And she couldn't do either.

When they returned to the mansion, Thorn made them hot chocolate and Kol prepared sandwiches, and they sat in the garden, hats and coats on, legs tangled together.

'Want to weed a bit?' she proposed when they finished eating. She wanted the day to last as long as possible.

He smiled bashfully. 'We don't have to. We can do something else.'

She reached out and took his hand, playing with the tips of his fingers. 'Do you know what I think about when I think about you?' she murmured.

'What?'

Trailing her fingers over his, she stood and pulled him to his feet. 'Coffee and chocolate and flowers.'

A deep, pleased sound resonated from his throat. Tucking her hair behind her ears, he cradled her face between his hands. 'And no nightmares?'

She swallowed hard. 'Not one.' It was true.

Kol's smile was brighter than sunlight on snow, and Thorn turned away.

She threw herself into gardening with him for the rest of the afternoon, marvelling at how odd it was that she wasn't spending her last day with Thistle.

'You're cute like this,' he said at one point when she'd wiped a line of dirt across her face scratching an itch. 'Dirt on your face, pollen all over your fingers.'

She threw a handful of leaves at him. 'And covered in sweat and smelling.'

'You smell like a garden.'

The words made her roll her eyes, but the joy came regardless.

'Come here,' he said, gesturing to the corner he'd been watering. 'I wanna show you something.'

Thorn brushed the dirt off her hands and went to his side. He pointed to a strange, beautiful plant. When his fingers brushed the petals, they quivered before changing from crimson to indigo to black.

'It's called *yosatha*,' he explained. 'A flower with a thousand colours, a thousand purposes. It stings those who try to weed it out, it gives fruit to those who water it, and no rain or boiling sun can ever make it wilt. It's always been my favourite.'

A laugh of delight left her lips and she reached out and touched the plant. The petals instantly turned green.

She rolled her eyes in fond amusement. 'Only you could make me think a Suric plant is prettier than a normal one.'

He replied with a kiss.

By the time Nithin and Thistle returned from work, the sun was setting and the cold had crept in, and Thorn's stomach was twisting painfully in anticipation.

She said nothing to anyone during dinner. She went mostly because she knew it would be the last time she saw Thistle or Kol, but she was too heartsick over leaving Kol, and too furious at Thistle for not coming, to do more than stab at her vegetables.

When dinner was done, the dishes cleared, leftovers in the fridge, Nithin bade them goodnight and left. Thistle paused in the doorway. She held Thorn's gaze for a long time. Neither of them said a word. After a stretch, Thistle hung her head and walked away, and Thorn knew that that was that.

'It'll be okay,' said Kol, wrapping his arms around her waist. 'Nith and I have fights, too. Things'll work out with you two.'

Thorn turned in his grip. She had too many things she wanted to say. Too much she still wanted to do with him. She wished more than anything that he was human. But then again perhaps not. Perhaps wishing humanity upon a Suriia was like wishing hardship and cruelty, and neither was something she wanted Kol to endure.

'I'm glad we came to Courtenz,' she said, hoping he'd remember her words later.

He tucked a strand of hair behind her ear. His hand lingered there, cupping her cheek. 'I'm glad you gave me a chance.'

Thorn kissed him then, until she couldn't stand it. Bidding him a quiet goodnight, she headed up to her room with burgeoning dread.

Locking the door behind her, she began to pack. She packed the clothes Thistle had picked out for her when they first arrived and the clothes she'd been given since. She tucked in packages of her favourite foods, a compass she'd had since she was six and her old, worn sleeping bag; atop these she placed the raincoat, gloves and hat Kol had given her. Finally, she added her journal with all the notes on the flowers and vines and leaves he'd taught her, all the fruits and vegetables and berries.

Her hands shook when she finally zipped her bag shut and put it by the window.

Running her hands through her hair to gather herself, she left the bedroom and crept downstairs.

In the garden, she used the blade Kol had given her to cut a stem off the rose bush. It was covered in thorns and in full bloom. One of her favourites.

Without a sound, she walked upstairs to Thistle and Nithin's room and slipped inside. The ease with which she did it sent a ripple of anxiety through her. If Thistle had been doing the same, Thorn would have woken. But Thistle always slept deeply.

Thorn bent down and kissed her forehead. Yet even as her heart broke, some deeper part of her thought maybe it was for the best. Sometimes lives diverged. And that was okay.

Taking out her father's blade, Thorn tucked it beneath Thistle's pillow. A parting gift. One that had seen her through so much.

In the hallway, her eyes went to Kol's door. Suddenly all she wanted to do was crawl into his bed, let him wrap his arms around her, and stay. But she couldn't.

On the inside of one of the chocolate bar wrappers, she scrawled one line: *Thank you for not being a lie.*

Wrapping it around the stem of the rose, she placed it in front of his door and returned to her room.

Then, with a last look around to make sure she hadn't left anything – and perhaps, just for a second, to remember the room that had never felt like *her* bedroom, but had at least been safe – she shouldered her bag and climbed out of the window for the last time.

CHAPTER THIRTEEN
The Scars That Unite Them

The midnight air was frigid and the sky glittered with a million stars, as if the heavens had aligned to light the way. Thorn stole across the garden, scaled the wall, and picked up a run as she headed into the city. The snow crunched loudly beneath her boots, but the few Scuttlers and drones she saw passed by without noticing her, and she reached the river without being stopped.

The scene that unfolded in the shadows of the abandoned building at the end of Tilo Street heartened her in a way few sights could. Other humans stood gathered already, all bearing arms.

Catching sight of Jade, Thorn darted over to her.

'Thorn, you made it!' Jade's whispered shout made her grin, and they hugged tightly. 'Where's Thistle?'

'She decided to stay,' said Thorn, chest clenching even as she said it. 'She wants to see if she can make a difference.'

Jade smiled bracingly. 'Maybe she can. Maybe she'll change everything, and we can come back someday.'

Thorn loved her a little bit more in that moment. 'Yeah.'

'Hi, Thorn.' Jinx appeared at Jade's side. Dressed in several layers, a gun holstered to his thigh and a blade sheathed around his waist, he looked ready to go hunting. Rather than give her comfort, the sight of him sent a shiver of disgust scuttling over her skin.

Thorn merely nodded to him before looking at the other humans. There were at least a dozen already. Distorted as they were in the neon lights of the city, each one took her breath away.

Not needing to be asked, Jade seized Thorn's hand and led her over to make introductions. 'This is Pine, Ajax, Cedar, Hash, Prosper, Trinity, Mile, Enzo, Genny, Grey, Parin and Pike.'

'Welcome to the group, Thorn,' said Grey, holding out a scarred and blistered hand. He was about Thorn's height with a head of curls and an infectious grin. 'Glad you could join us.'

She shook his hand eagerly. 'Glad to be here.'

'Where you coming from?' asked Trinity. She was as Jade described, with long blonde hair and a scar by her eye that only enhanced her features. Beside her stood Parin, who was clearly related.

'Only up the road,' said Thorn. 'You?'

'Evilian.'

Thorn's eyebrows shot up. The city was at the far north of the island and known to be one of the worst places for humans. The atrocities committed there during the rebellion had haunted her nightmares since Clay had told her the stories when she was seven.

'We sound much more impressive than we are,' said Parin with a conspiratorial wink.

'I don't know,' said Trinity, twirling a blade around her fingers. 'I feel impressive.'

Thorn laughed, liking them already. 'At this point staying alive is worthy of applause.'

'Then I declare a standing ovation,' said Grey, slinging an arm around her shoulders as if they were already best friends.

She found, to her surprise, that she *wanted* them to be best friends. She wanted to fill the space Thistle left that already felt like a rotting sore.

As they waited for the last of the group to arrive, she took in the appearances of her new companions, committing everything to memory. She couldn't help her fixation. Grey had black curls that stuck up in all directions, but was clean shaven with a wide, easy smile, and a scar from cheek to ear; Parin had such pale hair it was almost white, and three long scars across his face that disappeared beneath a trimmed beard; Trinity had messy blonde hair which tumbled every which way, and a bite mark on her neck that looked like it had almost been the end of her.

Thorn fell a little in love with each of them in those first seconds and from the looks on everyone's face, it was clear she wasn't the only one succumbing to giddy disbelief that they'd all been brought together.

'I like how scars are like human calling cards,' said Parin, unknowingly echoing Shadow's words from days ago. 'But I must say, we don them well, gents.'

Thorn grinned at him. 'Vylkas?'

'Ghuls. You?'

'A little from a lot.'

He winked at her. 'They only complete you, Thorny.'

Grey threw back his head in laughter.

The last of the group appeared shortly thereafter and Jinx waved everyone into a circle.

'Everyone pick a partner,' he instructed. 'And don't get separated. You're in charge of your partner.'

His arm still around her, Grey side-kicked Thorn. 'Wanna be with me?'

'Definitely.' She took her spare hand knife out of her bag and handed it to him. 'Here.'

Grey's jaw dropped and he took it delightedly. 'You're the best.'

'I object,' said Parin from his other side. 'I am the best partner ever. Don't steal my title.'

'You're not that great,' Trinity teased, ruffling his hair into his eyes.

Parin put his fist against his chest in mock-outrage. 'That hurts, little sister.'

Jinx's call that it was time to go quieted them and everyone began to move. The ragtag group hugged the riverbank as they made their way north through the outskirts of the city, keeping to the shadows, the tunnels, the underpasses.

When the last of the big buildings fell away, they cut through an empty park to the suburbs and then darted through the flower lined streets until at last they were on the road to the mountains, trees on all sides. The terrain grew only wilder and more untamed the further they got. Drones passed over every now and then, but none stopped. Jinx, it turned out, had equipped everyone with a blocker.

It was several hours before they dared stop for the night and set up camp. But the trees provided good cover and there were no sounds of magic or industry to give them much pause. After deciding on shifts for keeping watch, everyone settled in.

Thorn hunkered down between Grey and Parin, with Trinity on her brother's other side. The trio were cheerful and watchful, a combination Thorn admired.

'Thorn?' said Parin as they gazed up at the stars.

She tucked her arm behind her head to add cushion to her lumpy backpack pillow. 'Yeah?'

'You scared it's too good to be true?'

'I'm always scared.'

On her other side, Grey shifted. 'I've got your back, T.'

'And I've got this,' said Parin, raising his axe half-heartedly into the air, sleep already taking hold of him.

'I've got my guns,' said Thorn. 'And an iron blade.'

Parin whistled. 'Might sleep the night through, then.'

And, to Thorn's great surprise, she did just that.

The first week in the mountains were a remarkable mixture of exertion, anxiety and sheer, unharnessed joy. The group tackled untamed forestry, raging rapids that tore through ravines, hills that came apart beneath them, icy ponds and slippery moss. The rain came and went, but so too did the snow. Yet despite the weather and the wilderness providing a constant supply of obstacles, the mood stayed cheerful.

So far from the city, animals were less skittish and more frequent. Thorn hadn't seen so many foxes, rabbits, squirrels and pheasants in years. The snow, when it clung to the land and wasn't washed away by icy rain, was pure, unstained by the smoke and grime from city life. Even the rivers, where they weren't frozen solid, ran clear and glistening. And it was when they paused by the bank of one such river to refill their water bottles and catch their breath that the histories began to flow.

'Tell me your story,' said Grey, holding out his bottle.

She took it with a smile and drank a good bit before passing it back. 'I'll tell you mine if you tell me yours.'

He grinned and lit a cigarette. 'Fair enough.'

'I was born on the south side of the mountain,' she began, starting the full story she'd never told to anyone. She and Thistle had never talked about it in-depth, either. 'It was a pretty place to live, but the winters were hard and there was no food or medicine. A pack of vylkas owned a ranch at the bottom of the mountain and offered my parents a job. In exchange for working the fields, they could have the house and they'd be under the vylkas' protection.

'For years it seemed to work, too. Thistle and I grew up side by side. Happy, for a little while. My uncle Clay, his son David and his wife Amy, lived there also. We were happy. And then one day, the vylkas turned on us. Attacked us. Clay, David and Amy all died. I was claimed by one of them, but my uncle killed him. That's how he died.

'My parents and Thistle's went back into the mountains. But Thistle's mother was pregnant, and she got sick about a year later. When they went to find help, they found a vryko who agreed – if Thistle's father let them drink from him. Her dad didn't have much choice. When he brought them to his wife, the vrykos killed them both. And then mine. Thistle and I barely escaped …' She trailed off. Sometimes it seemed like she'd just seen her parents, talked to them. Heard them laugh. Other days they felt like a dream.

Grey reached out and took her hand. Clearing his throat, he said, 'I don't remember anything before about six years ago. I'm guessing my age. I think I'm from Dilevar because that's what my accent sounds like.' Tilting his head to the side, he pushed back the curly hair covering his neck. There was a jagged scar from his neck up to the centre of his skull. The scar tissue was pale and slightly bumpy.

'Ouch,' she said, grimacing in sympathy.

'Wouldn't know. Don't remember.'

'I wonder if that's better or worse than remembering.'

'Same.' He laughed humourlessly. 'I've been living in the sewers the last few years. It's safer than being above ground. Ran into Jinx one night scrounging for food.'

'I'm glad you're here now.'

'Same. You have no idea how grateful I am that he found me.'

She smiled sadly. Most days Thorn really hated Jinx. In moments like this, she didn't know what to do with her anger.

On they walked, listening to the birds and the dripping water of melting snow. The wilderness, for all its unknowns, was the most peaceful place in the world.

The trek into the mountains passed in a blur of early mornings, long days and cold nights. But every moment left Thorn marvelling at how wonderful it was to be around so many like her. Upbeat and optimistic, Parin made all of them laugh with his immature jokes and good-natured sarcasm; Grey resonated goodness, and calm, steady determination; Trinity was like a mother and asked five times a day if they were drinking enough water, needed to eat, or had cleaned their various cuts and scrapes.

The nights always ended up around a campfire, stories shared at random, each turn of conversation bringing new revelations. Some good, some terrible.

Pike had been across the channel to the mainland and horrified them with his secrets. On the continent, he told them, the situation was even worse. His tales of the dire situation humans faced abroad – experiments, monitoring, sterilisation, captivity – didn't mesh with the stories Thistle and Kol had told her, and Thorn wondered at how sanitised and divorced from reality that seemed.

Yet not every story they shared was grim. It was the stories of the others' small victories, their daring raids, their close calls, that she loved the most. To have come so far was lucky, to be sure, but it was hard won, and all of them felt like celebrating a little.

Still, every night when the conversation quelled, and everyone drifted off or stayed on watch, Thorn's mind drifted back to Thistle and Kol. And she never rested easy.

The first place they opted to linger longer than a night while the worst of the snow layered down upon the mountains, was a clearing nestled between trees and a rock face. The ground was uneven and covered in sticks and stones, but the secluded nature of the location more than made up for it.

Everyone quickly traded off roles and tasks without issue. Thorn and Grey volunteered to go hunting, and headed off into the rising snow with Ajax's crossbows while the others set up the tents and the campfire.

It took over an hour to find tracks, but soon they were on the trail of a fox. Hunting always left her uneasy. If she didn't need meat to survive, she wouldn't hunt at all. But the winter left them few choices.

When the tufty red creature stopped to nose at a patch of grass sticking up through the snow, they crouched down in unison.

A noise to her left made her start, and Thorn caught sight of a rabbit. Nodding to Grey, she left the fox to him and stalked the rabbit through the thicket.

She'd only just rounded an expansive tree with a trunk twice her width when she stopped dead.

Two humans stood in front of her. Well, *stood* wasn't the right word. Neither was completely upright. The pair wore hunger like a sickness and she quickly lowered her crossbow.

'Hi,' she said.

'Hi,' they echoed.

Walking over without delay, she offered her hand. 'Thorn.'

'Darren,' said one.

'Omar,' said the other.

'Are you guys living out here?'

Before they could answer, Grey darted out of the trees, foxless and crossbow in hand. But he lowered it immediately. 'Hi,' he said, as stunned as she.

'We're so glad we found people,' said Omar anxiously. 'Are there more of you?'

'A couple dozen,' said Grey. 'How long have you guys been out here?'

'Not long. We escaped a camp.'

Thorn's heart felt like it fell out of her chest as she realised then why they were in such awful shape. Both weren't far from developing frostbite. Their faces were sunken and their clothes, she realised, were part stolen Spotter uniform and part inmate attire.

'You're safe now,' she assured them. 'Let's get you to our camp so you can warm up.' Taking off her gloves, she helped Darren put them on, careful of his fingers, which were swollen and discoloured. She then wrapped her scarf around his neck, and gave him her hat. Grey copied her, offering his gloves, hat and scarf to Omar.

'Come with us,' he said when the pair were bundled up. 'It's okay.'

Back at the camp, everyone greeted Darren and Omar with open arms and unmasked empathy. But no one pressed them for answers. The pair didn't seem inclined to talk about what had happened to them, an experience everyone else knew only too well.

The mood around the campfire was subdued after that, and the night was quieter than any other since the first night they'd come together.

As the others tapered off after a sombre dinner, Thorn stayed awake, anxious and unsettled. She couldn't stop thinking about the death camp. About wanting to dismantle it with her bare hands and beat to death every torturer, every rapist, every killer.

Across the fire, Jinx laughed at something Enzo said and she sent him a death glare. He didn't notice.

'You don't like him.'

Thorn glanced at Parin. He'd said it quietly, and no one but Trinity was listening. Grey had already gone to sleep.

'No,' she murmured.

'You like Jade.'

'Yes.'

Parin's bright green eyes danced with an unassuming kind of cunning, one that was incongruous to his sarcastic, optimistic, extroverted demeanour. His next words only confirmed this, although he'd never been obvious about it. 'I don't like him, either.'

'No?'

'Just get a bad vibe is all.'

'Same.'

He moved to the empty place beside her and lowered his voice. 'If you ever feel uncomfortable, let me know, okay? Trin and I have dealt with more than a few rotten humans. Close proximity like this, sometimes dickheads try and take advantage.'

Thorn considered how he phrased that. 'Trinity?' she whispered.

'Not just Trinity.'

A sick feeling curled in her stomach like slow-burning poison. 'Same goes for you.'

'I appreciate that.'

'For the record?'

He cocked an eyebrow.

'Watch your drinks.'

'The Suriias drugged you?'

'Not just the Suriias.'

They held each other's gazes for a long while after this exchange.

It was Trinity who finally broke the silence. 'I'm going to bed,' she announced, getting to her feet and yawning widely. 'I need blankets.'

'Me too,' said Parin. 'You going to bed soon, T?'

'Yeah,' she muttered. 'Might wait until Grey wakes up for watch, though.'

Parin squeezed her shoulder before following Trinity over to their tent.

Snowflakes cascaded down and she readjusted her blanket around her shoulders. She tried to take comfort in Kol's words that Suriias didn't like snow, but it hadn't stopped any of the Spotters in Itannera before. If they kept going north, eventually they'd reach the top of the island. If they could find a way across the sea, they'd have far more land to disappear on. A whole continent stretched out to the east. More than enough room to—

Footsteps.

Thorn was on her feet in a flash, grabbing her gun and blade. She shook Grey, a hand over his mouth. When he realised what was happening, he was on his feet in a second. They split up and went into different tents.

Parin wasn't even out of his boots and he scrambled up when she leaned into their tent, a finger to her lips. One by one, they alerted the others.

Thorn had just grabbed Jade when a burst of magical green light suddenly, blindingly, illuminated the forest around them.

'SPOTTERS!' she screamed.

Everyone scattered.

Thorn raced through the trees without looking back, Jade and Grey on her heels. She could see Enzo and Pike further up and pelted after them.

But running in a forest in the middle of the night is far from easy. Ice slicked the mud, turned branches to spears, and leaves threatened to toss down snow in a blinding storm every time the wind shifted direction.

Jade and Grey kept pace with her as they shot down an incline and jumped across a creek bed.

'Halt!'

Thorn ran faster, sprinting around a tree just as bullets tore through the air. Wood blasted off the tree, sending a hail of splinters every which way and cutting her arm and cheek.

The forest was dense and made for good cover, but it also made running a trial. As she leapt up an embankment, the sight which greeted her made her heart stop. Jade and Grey skidded to a stop behind her.

Down the hill, Cedar, Hash, Enzo and Prosper were surrounded by a dozen blue-uniformed Spotters.

She glanced quickly at Grey and Jade. 'If I get their attention, can you get to the others?'

'I'll help you,' said Jade.

'Me too,' said Grey.

'I'm faster alone.' Thorn checked the barrel of her gun as quietly as she could. 'Just get them and get out of here. I'll meet you by the river.'

'Good luck.'

Thorn made her way around the Spotters as carefully as she could until she was on the opposite side of the clearing. Taking one of her stolen flashbangs out of her bag, she readied to throw it.

'Hey!' she yelled.

The Spotters whirled around, and she threw it as hard as she could. She dived down as it went off. The pulse burned her ear drums and snow went everywhere.

Ears ringing, Thorn bolted. She could hear the Spotters closing in around her. She ran faster and faster, on through the woods, slipping on patches of ice. Sounds came from all sides, but she didn't dare to slow.

She shot down a hill but skidded to a halt almost immediately. There was a Spotter coach up ahead.

A young girl – a *human* girl – beckoned frantically at her from the driver's seat. She couldn't have been more than fifteen or sixteen.

'Get in!'

With few choices available, Thorn hurried to the coach and opened the door, only to stop dead. The back seat had Suriias. Several of them. Not only that, but they were all dressed strangely. Their outfits looked three hundred years out of date.

A blast of magic rocked the forest behind Thorn. There wasn't time to question it or dally.

She leapt into the coach and the girl sped off. 'Who are you?'

'A friend,' said the girl.

'Why are you helping me?' she asked, looking in the rear-view mirror. The Spotters were already following them.

'I don't sleep much,' said the girl. 'I went walking around the neighbourhood and overheard some of them saying they'd found humans in the mountains. Came out here to look.'

Something flashed in the trees below them.

'Stop,' said Thorn.

'They're right behind us!'

'Stop!'

The girl slammed on the brakes and Thorn opened the door. 'Guys!'

Several figures hurried out of the trees and clambered into the backseat.

'Did anyone get snatched?' she asked frantically.

'I don't know,' said Grey. 'I lost track of the others.'

'Jinx?' asked Jade.

'I saw him disappear with Sinjin and Hash,' said Pike. 'They vanished into the trees.'

Jade let out a shaking breath of relief. 'Perhaps they got out,' she said. 'Perhaps they made it to another road.'

'Or perhaps they've been sent to the death camps,' said Pike.

Thorn punched the dashboard. 'How were we found?'

'They must have followed Omar and Darren,' said Grey.

'Figures.'

'Where should I go?' asked the girl, flying rather well through the gaps in the trees.

Jade sat forward. 'What's your name?'

'Ginny.'

'Kalid,' said the Suriia boy in the back. 'This is Shara.'

The youngest girl, Shara, was no older than eleven. She waved cheerfully at them. 'Don't worry,' she said. 'We're good at hiding from the law.'

Thorn had no idea how to respond to that and she returned her focus to the thin, scarred, mousy-haired girl in the driver's seat. She was clearly not from around Courtenz, but she had the ticks, the edge, of one who'd been fighting for a while.

Ginny didn't take her eyes off the forest flashing past around them. 'Where do I go?' she prompted again. 'I need a direction.'

With a sigh, Thorn pulled out her phone and turned it on. She hadn't used it since she'd left the mansion. There were no missed calls, but there was a missed message from Kol. Ignoring it, she dialled Thistle's number.

It took only a minute for her to answer: 'Thorn? What's wrong?'

'How do you know something's wrong?'

'You wouldn't have called otherwise.'

'The Spotters found us,' she relayed, glancing into the rear-view mirror as she said it. 'We may be, ah, rather fucked.'

'How many Spotters?'

'What's going on?' The question came from Kol somewhere near Thistle.

'We got picked up by a girl,' said Thorn, eyeing Ginny.

'Come to the house,' said Thistle. 'Nithin can keep you safe from the Spotters.'

Before Thorn could reply, Ginny slammed on the brakes and everyone collided with what was in front of them.

Thorn didn't have time to examine her bruises as the horror sank in.

On the road in front of them were several Spotters. Magic fizzled in the air around the blue-clad frai, and the coach was held fast. The engines turned themselves off.

'Fuck.'

'Tor? Tor, what's wrong?'

In front of the coach, the Spotters stood like haunted statues as they magically lowered the coach to the ground. Before the group had time to discuss what to do next, a loud growling, like a warning, sounded from somewhere to their right, and several figures suddenly filled the space between them and the Spotters.

Ginny let out a soft breath, her hands flexing around the wheel. 'Luk.'

'Luck?' said Grey. He'd moved onto the gearshift and was crouched between Ginny and Thorn.

'Lucien,' she clarified. 'It's Lucien.'

'Lower your weapons,' said the one in front, glaring at the Spotters. 'Now.'

Thorn presumed this was Lucien. He was wearing the same bizarre clothes as Ginny. A long brown overcoat, leather boots, a pistol at his side. There was a hat pulled low on his head and messy black hair escaped from beneath the brim. He had four deep scars across his face and his eyes were cerulean, inhumanly so.

'These humans are under arrest,' said one of the Spotters. 'We're taking them all in.'

'They're ours,' said Lucien, cocking his head to the side. Purple light coloured the air around him and the gun jumped into his hand; in a fluid motion, it was aimed at the Spotter's heart. As were the pistols his Suriia friends carried. He suddenly looked far more formidable. 'We were told we get to keep the ones we've claimed.'

Pike straightened up. 'What—'

Kalid clapped his hand over Pike's mouth. 'They can hear you,' he mouthed.

'You have claim only to your husband, Lightblood,' said one of the Spotters. 'Not to multiple renegade humans.'

'The humans belong to us all,' said a woman beside him. Like Lucien, she was covered in scars, thin and muscular, and heavily armed. The knives strapped to her chest made Thorn thoroughly envious; the pistol in her hand was a thing of beauty. 'We've been keeping them here. The cities aren't safe.'

'Precisely,' said Lucien. 'The air between him and the Spotters seemed to flare in warning. 'You are threatening my pack, Ivor.'

'Humans cannot be part of prico packs.'

'I beg to differ.'

There was a sudden flash of light and Kol appeared in the middle of the clearing. In all the months she'd known him, Thorn had never seen him look as furious and dangerous as he did in that moment. His eyes were solidly black, his teeth fanged. His wings beat menacingly. 'I will report you all to Lord Sinn if you don't leave immediately,' he threatened, sneering at the Spotters with more wrath than Thorn thought him capable of possessing. 'Now.'

The Spotters all exchanged looks. A few lowered their weapons. But no one moved.

'You have no authority here, Mister Sinn,' said one. 'This isn't your concern.'

Kol's hand closed in a fist and the Spotter dropped to his knees. He clawed at his neck, unable to breathe. 'Don't piss me off, Vikryn,' he said coldly. 'I can have your job for that little remark.'

'Are the humans yours or Lightblood's?' asked another Spotter, eyeing his fellows uncomfortably.

'They received permission from Lord Sinn to keep their humans here,' said Kol acidly. 'Mine along with them.' He relaxed his hand and looked over at the others. 'This little show of stupidity will be reported. And be aware that my father will hear of this.' Then, with a snap of his fingers, their identification badges flew off the lapels of their coats and into his hand. 'Now fuck off.'

Remarkably cowed, the Spotters got back into their coaches and drove off.

Ginny was first out of the coach, and she ran towards Lucien, flinging herself into his arms.

Still shaking like a pebble in a stampede, Thorn walked more slowly over to Kol. As she neared, he reverted back to his normal enough self with cat eyes and a crooked smile.

'Are you hurt?' he asked, reaching out as if to examine her myriad cuts and bruises.

'I'll live,' she muttered. 'No harm done.'

He opened his mouth as if he wanted to say more, but then he stepped back and let his hand fall to his side.

She didn't have time to dwell on it. Beside them, Lucien's loud, panicked question to Ginny, drew her attention.

'What does that mean?'

'He took the other coach,' said Ginny. 'With Eran. We split up when the group did. He went after some of the humans being chased.'

'We're leaving,' Lucien told his friends, eyes blazing with magic. 'Now.'

Thorn's feet moved instantly. 'I'm coming with you.' She didn't know who they were talking about or what they were planning, but she didn't care. The Spotters had Parin.

Lucien glanced at her. 'You sure, kid?'

'They have my friends, too.'

'I'm coming as well,' said Grey, checking the barrel of his gun and falling into step beside Thorn; Pike and Jade followed them.

'Rose, wait,' said Kol urgently. 'We can't go running to the death camps. We need a plan.'

'We're not waiting, frai-boy,' said Lucien acidly.

'You'll put everyone at risk if you run in headfirst!'

Lucien snorted and kept walking to the coach.

'Rose, don't,' implored Kol. 'It's a death sentence. Please. Let me find a way. Nithin can help.'

She shook her head. 'They have my friends.'

'You won't make it home from a death camp!'

'Neither will Parin,' she said helplessly before clambering into the coach after Lucien. The others got into the back. She closed the door and held Kol's gaze until the coach rose too high in the air.

'Do you have a plan?' she asked, peering over at Lucien, heart slamming in her chest. Now that she had the time to examine him, she realised that he didn't seem like any prico she'd encountered before. In fact, she was hard-pressed to think of any Suriia who was as *otherworldly* as Lucien. His eyes were solid blue, his teeth slightly pointed; the very air around him seemed to hum with magic.

'Rose, was it?'

'Thorn.'

'Thorn,' he echoed, nodding approvingly. 'I don't need a plan.'

'Are you powerful enough for this not to be a suicide mission?'

'Would that stop you?'

'No. I'm just curious.'

'No Suriia born on Earth is as powerful as me.'

'You're from Salfar, aren't you?'

'Yes.'

She wondered why that didn't frighten her more. Why this one Suriia who was as far from *earthly* as could be, gave her confidence when the others – including Kol – failed to.

'Why are you helping humans?'

'I help my pack.' He didn't elaborate.

Below them, the land flashed past in a white-brown blur and Thorn realised she didn't recognise any of the landmarks. They were headed to a part of the island she had never seen before.

'Are you sure we're going the right way?'

'Yes.'

'How?'

'I can track him.'

'You get Spotter training, too?'

'I'd rather eat dirt.'

'Then how?'

'He's my husband,' he answered, as if that clarified things.

It didn't.

'A little explanation goes a long way …'

'When pricos marry, they make magical imprints,' he said distractedly, fists clenching around the steering wheel.

'How?'

'He's had my blood. My blood has my magic.'

'So, you're tracking your own magic.'

'Yes.'

'And Kol said he was good at tracking.'

Lucien scoffed and turned slightly left, moving them away from a large lake and back over dense forests. 'Frai are useless trackers.'

She smirked. 'I'll tell him you think so.'

'If he doesn't know, he's also unintelligent.'

'He's not,' she argued, feeling a bit defensive of Kol's talents.

'I'm sure he's not,' said Lucien dismissively.

Mention of Kol prompted her to glance down at her phone. She clicked it back on and went into the messages. She opened the unanswered message, sent the morning after she'd left.

More than anything, he'd written, *I want you to be free.*

Suddenly finding it extremely hard to breathe, Thorn stowed the phone in her pocket and tried to ignore the burning of her eyes and the tightening of her throat.

Less than ten minutes later, Lucien suddenly descended, aiming for what appeared to be nothing but forest. But then she saw it – the camp. Even from the sky, the buildings had a cruel air about them, as if even the concrete resented its hosts.

The instant Lucien landed, everyone shot out. Thorn tried not to think about what had happened since she last saw Parin and Trinity. How much harm could have befallen them. Even in so short a span of time.

Lucien had far less concern than Nithin and Kol did about being subtle. Thorn watched, awed, as he walked straight at the front gates and blasted them open with a wave of his hand. His friends sent a secondary blast at the guards, knocking them flat with breath-taking ease.

The way clear, the group reached the building easily enough and Lucien blew the front doors off their hinges before leading the way inside. A long corridor brought them to a set of bolted doors. This time, Lucien paused. With a soft muttered spell, he unlocked this set of doors more gently. It was the first time Thorn had ever heard a spell – she'd only ever heard rumours –

and the language sounded smooth and guttural. But she didn't have time to think about enchantments.

The lights sprang to life automatically as they walked forward and the sickly sweet smell of chemicals hit her full on. But the smell was far from the worst thing about the room.

Dozens of humans were locked in cages. Some were too small to even stand in.

'What the fuck?' she breathed.

Lucien raised his hands and, with a pulse of magic like a sonic boom, the doors disintegrated in a blast of glass and metal.

'Nik!' he roared.

'Parin!' she yelled. 'Trinity!'

Their replies made her want to sob with relief. Racing forwards, she found Parin in the fifth cell. She darted to him and yanked him to his feet. He'd been savagely beaten, but he managed to stay upright.

'You're a fucking babe, Thorny,' he said, clapping her on the back.

They ran out of the cell to see Jade helping Trinity out of another cell further on. Grey had found Mile; Pike had Genny.

'Where're the others?' asked Parin.

'Jinx got a few away,' said Genny, voice distorted by the swelling of his bruised mouth and jaw. One of the Spotters had clearly tried to rearrange his features. 'Just us from the group.'

Thorn gestured toward the door. 'Let's go,' she said. 'The alarm's already gone up.'

When they reached the corridors, a blast of magic knocked everyone to the ground. As Thorn scrambled up, she saw the approaching Spotters.

Lucien appeared at her side. With a wave of his hand, he sent a blast of wind at the Spotters that sent them flying.

'Run!' he yelled at the others.

Everyone moved as he stepped between the humans and the Suriias. Shara appeared and took Parin's other arm.

'Come on.'

At Parin's enquiring look, Thorn nodded for him to go ahead. She watched them scurry off, drawing her gun.

'Better run, kid,' Lucien said to her.

'Fuck that,' she retorted. Taking the gun out of his pocket, she aimed both at the Spotters. When she fired, Lucien flicked his fingers. The bullets changed course mid-air and the Spotters were knocked to their knees, bullet holes in their throats.

Thorn and Lucien exchanged a nod before turning and sprinting after the others who had disappeared through the exit door.

Cold, wet air hit her in the face as soon as they opened the exit, and she slipped outside as quietly as she could. Lucien followed her soundlessly.

They stopped when they reached the side of the building and peered around. There was no one in sight.

'Where'd the others go?' she hissed.

'The forest,' said Lucien, nodding up ahead. 'I can hear them running.'

'All of them?'

'All of them.'

That was something at least.

'If we don't make sure this place is gone, they'll figure out it was us,' she said. 'It'll blow back on the others.'

'I wasn't aiming to leave this shithole standing.'

'What do you suggest?'

Like some kind of hero in a children's story, Lucien stepped forwards, drawing magic from the world around him.

As Thorn watched, the building's electrics began to crackle and fry, the wires snapped and fell, sending sparks cascading through the air. Fire quickly appeared inside the building, bursting through the windows and sending glass everywhere in a ruthless inferno.

'Whoa,' said Thorn, impressed.

He looked at her, sweat dripping down his face and smirked.

They were still grinning at each other when pain exploded through Thorn's chest. She looked down. Blood was spreading across her shirt at a remarkable rate.

Her legs gave out without warning and she pitched forward, but the impact didn't come. Lucien's arms were around her and he lowered her carefully to the cold, cold ground.

Darkness crept into her vision like an invasion of shadows, and the pounding in her ears muffled all sound.

'Hey! Hey! Don't!' Lucien clapped her cheek. 'Stay with me.'

Jarred back to awareness, she rolled open an eye.

'Hey,' he said again. 'Want to know a secret?'

She tried to focus on his face. It was almost impossible. Awareness was leaving her faster than blood.

'This is a nightmare world,' he told her. 'It's not meant to be. It's just a nightmare, okay? It isn't real.'

'Feels real.'

'It's a lie.'

A weak, gurgled laugh left her. 'Nightmares don't hurt.'

He wiped the blood from her lips and brushed the hair back from her face. 'Where I'm from, humans are in charge. Imagine that.'

A feeble smile twitched at the corners of her mouth and she felt herself slipping away. 'Now that sounds like a dream ...'

PART TWO
Heirs of Wrath

CHAPTER FOURTEEN
Dust and Blood

EARTH II
Seventy-eight years after the Suppression of Magic

The main street of Westend resembled most other ramshackle districts, though it had a few buildings left from before the war. Plaster over the old brick crumbled away in places, hinting at a time when there was money for this part of the world. But money had left Westend at the same time law and decency became myth and legend.

From the shadows of the alley, smoke billowing up from the underground steam vents that ran along the left side of the road, obscuring them from view, Lucien Lightblood could just barely make out the Enforcers up ahead, ransacking his shop. His fingers flexed around the wheel of his steamtruck and he clenched his teeth together hard enough that he heard a pop somewhere in his jaw. But he didn't budge. He didn't interfere.

'What time did Ally get everything moved?' Adair's voice floated over from his other side, pitched as low as possible.

Lucien didn't look away from the shop, though he tilted his head to the side to indicate he was paying attention.

'An hour ago,' said Naida from the backseat.

'That's not much time.' Adair shifted in his seat and the squeak of the leather made Lucien's hair stand on end. Suriias had far better hearing than humans, but he didn't like taking even the most minute of chances. Adair continued, 'Did he even have time for a second sweep?'

'No.'

Lucien scowled into the night, finding it difficult to make out the shapes even with the foggy streetlamp light, and watched the Enforcers toss their shelves, throw things around, breaking, ripping and standing on just about everything. The crass way they conducted themselves was perhaps the least abhorrent thing about them, but it still grated on Lucien's nerves. He'd been in prison, a war, prison again, and had spent the last decades living on the periphery of society, scrounging for scraps to survive, and he still managed to have manners. It wasn't difficult not to be destructive.

'They really are rude,' said Adair, clearly thinking the same thing.

'By all means go inform them of that,' said Naida.

No one moved. No one could. They would have, years ago. But the experience of the humans taking Eran for months after Adair punched one of the Keepers still haunted them all. When they finally got Eran back, the little boy was traumatised. That was over a decade ago and he still sometimes woke the house with his nightmares.

Another hour ticked by before the Enforcers finally tired of ransacking the little shop and departed, leaving the front door of the building wide open.

Lucien waited until their brake lights vanished around the corner and stepped out of his truck. The other two dogged his steps across the road. Past curfew, being out on the streets was a terrible idea. The Enforcers weren't always in the town, but the Keepers, their trained Suriia helpers – infamous for turning in their own kind – kept watch in their place. Unfortunately, if the pack returned in the morning, their shop would likely be empty. Crime in Westend was high and Suriias couldn't purchase insurance or use banks. They were always one emergency from homelessness.

Inside their shop, Lucien surveyed the damage with a furrowed brow, jaw locked so tight to keep from spewing expletives that his head started to pound.

'Fucking bastards,' said Adair, sparing him the trouble. 'One of these days …'

Lucien nodded, but said nothing.

Clean up proved tedious, and they had to do it in the dark and without making much noise. A difficult feat given the glass and pottery on the ground. The chairs were broken and in need of new legs or backs. One of the Enforcers had relieved himself on the floor and the smell was sickening. Lucien never missed his magic so much as when the humans reduced them to less worth than the animals they kept as pets. Thankfully, the pack had been through enough raids to have the system down, and they were heading back to the house before dawn.

The world around them was just waking up and dew clung to the tall, pale grasses. A light fog still lingered and with the windows down, the morning air filling the truck, the stain of the night ebbed somewhat.

A new day and all that, he told himself. Start fresh.

The turnoff to their property appeared and he drove onto the dirt road that suffered from potholes and puddles. It was impossible to keep it packed and flat no matter how many times they'd filled the holes. As Suriias weren't allowed to have gates on their properties, the pack had built their home far enough away from the road that they were at least afforded a sense of privacy. They'd planted trees over the years, which helped.

Lucien parked in front of the house and everyone climbed out, stretching stiffly and yawning. The house was a mix of old human architecture, age, and patchwork fixes the pack had made over the years. They'd claimed it when they were finally let out of the camps and allowed to commandeer the abandoned buildings the humans emptied during the war.

'Take the morning off,' he told the pair as they trudged up the steps.

'Are you going to the arena?' asked Naida.

'Not until tonight.'

Naida nodded, kissed his cheek, and then headed down the hall. Adair clapped him on the back before following her.

Lucien headed upstairs, every step taking all of his energy.

Paintings adorned the hallway walls and a statue of Lycaon, an ancient King of Salfar, guarded the entry to his study. Lucien had hated the statue, and all it represented, since Adair made the thing, but as a superstition – and yet another way to rebel against the humans – he left it alone.

Somehow too tired to sleep, Lucien went to his study and dropped down into his chair. His headache was now officially a migraine.

The photograph on his desk caught his eye and he gazed at it with mounting sadness. Taken the first year they got out of the electric fences, all of them looked sickly, gaunt and starved. Lucien's arm was around Geon's shoulders. Geon was staring at the ground, a far cry from his former self. The pose gave the impression that he was about to fall over, but he hadn't been. He'd been whispering nonsensical words over and over, like a mantra that either kept him sane or made it worse. Lucien had never figured out which. Adair, Naida and Jae stood behind them, each making the effort to smile, but none of them quite achieving it. The only one not facing the camera was Esme, who stood at an angle, her hand on her knife, the bloodstains on her clothes innumerable. She didn't trust photographs.

Lucien leaned back in his chair and exhaled slowly. He almost picked up the phone. Almost.

Dredging up the past was never good, but he missed his sister on nights like tonight. Esme would have never stayed in the truck, hiding like a coward. She'd tear them bone from sinew and paint a crude remark on the cobblestone path with their blood, something for the Enforcers to find. It was one of the reasons he'd kicked her out – and it was one of the things he missed most about her. His older sister had always been so much braver than him.

The ticking of the clock was the loudest sound in the house, but if he listened, he could hear the breathing of everyone still sleeping. It soothed him. Constant reminders that they were all alive. That his family were well.

Soft-footed pattering about in the kitchen reached his ears, signalling the start of another day and he got up, glad of the excuse to leave his study.

In his bedroom, he peeled off his wrinkled, smelly clothes and took a quick shower. The harsh heat of the water helped to wake him up and he re-entered his bedroom feeling somewhat more ready to face life. After donning a clean pair of trousers, a fresh shirt and a vest, he headed downstairs to the kitchen.

Eran, Adair and Naida's eldest son, and the only one of the children who remembered the camps, looked up from the stove where he was boiling water. He'd recently cut his hair and barely any remained on his head. It was a somewhat jarring change from the thick black mop he'd had for years, and somehow made him look younger.

''Morning,' he said.

'Good morning.' Lucien sat at the table and yawned widely. 'Can I get in on that?'

'Of course.' Eran poured the water into the coffee press and set it on the table. 'You look like crap, boss.'

'That's because that's exactly how I feel.'

With a laugh, Eran retrieved the morning's newspaper and sat down opposite him. He pulled out a few sheets of the paper and handed them to Lucien before settling back in his chair and reading studiously. Their morning routine had been going on for years even on nights without raids or complications. Lucien had suffered insomnia ever since Geon's death and it was getting no better. He usually passed the night hours in his study, thinking and brooding, or in the barn, working out his built frustration on the old, worn punching bag. Eran simply hated closing his eyes.

'More murders,' said Eran abruptly, setting the paper down so that the headline was visible. The front page was littered with stories of 'rogue Suriias' who'd found their way into the human districts without valid identification and papers and been shot on sight. The newspaper reported it as a good thing. *Those rabid Suriias stopped in their tracks.* Anyone with half a brain or an ear to the ground knew better. Humans killed Suriias simply because they could. But the news never told the truth.

Lucien sighed and peeled off the top page of the newspaper and balled it up before throwing it into the hearth. 'There,' he said, passing the paper back to Eran where the topmost story featured an article on the latest automata being designed in the city.

Eran smiled tightly at him before taking the paper back. 'Dad says if I'd grown up on Salfar, I would've had different complaints.'

Lucien chuckled ruefully. 'That's not untrue.'

'But I'd be able to walk down the street without a clip in my arm and a badge in my wallet that has to be renewed every six months just so I'm not arrested.'

'That's also not untrue,' said Lucien heavily. 'Which is why we need coffee.'

There was nothing to say that he, Adair and all the rest hadn't said a hundred times. And, just as he, Adair and all the rest had said, survival came first. They could fight back when there was an infinitesimal likelihood of survival. Such was not the current case.

The rest of the morning passed slowly and soon everyone was awake, heading off in this direction or that. Kalid and Shara both had lessons, and it was Isha's turn to teach them.

After much discussion, the pack had agreed to home-school the youngest members. It was safer – and Lucien didn't trust anyone in the district enough to let the children wander off alone. The Suriias were all in the same district, but it hardly meant they were all friends.

By mid-afternoon Lucien was back in his office, trying to sort through the mountain of paperwork he was never quite able to get through in a day, thus ensuring that every subsequent day had piles of receipts and orders and reports that needed looking over, signing off here and there.

A sharp rap on the door made him look up. 'Yes?'

The door opened and Shim stepped inside.

One look at her stormy expression informed him his day was about to get worse. 'What's wrong?'

'Trenton's not going to show up.'

'Why?'

'Because Arlyn just told me to take the matter to Henna.'

Lucien growled under his breath. 'Trenton's supposed to be meeting me tonight.'

'Ten chips he won't show.'

It wasn't a bet Lucien was in the mood to take. Trenton owed them a large sum of money, but more and more it was apparent that he wasn't going to pay. And since the money was owed on off-the-market contraband, it was doubtful even Henna, the magister, would step in. Henna would tell them to eat the losses and move on. Trenton wasn't the first to play turncoat and would hardly be the last. Still, it was money the pack had been counting on. The new damages accrued by the Enforcers' raid on the shop would be costly. And Lucien quite liked being able to put food on the table.

'I'll deal with it,' he said.

'Want backup tonight?'

'No, you need to go on the delivery. I'll be fine.'

'What if there's trouble?'

'There usually is.'

Shim laughed in agreement and left him to the epic pile of paperwork that awaited him.

He spent the rest of the afternoon going over the reports and expense receipts, setting up a new schedule for the businesses and sorting payment for the pack and their employees. Before he knew it, the evening had rolled around and he was on his way to Westend Circle.

Deciding to walk instead of drive, Lucien headed into the chilly evening, declining Adair's offer to join. If Trenton was there, Lucien had a few words for him that would be far more effective without backup; if he wasn't there, it was a useless trip, and Lucien believed none of his pack should have to be at the arena for longer than necessary. It was dangerous, even for him.

The wind turned and a faint scent made his nose tingle: fumes from the factories that were located at the other end of the district. The humans didn't have to breathe in waste like the Suriias did. It turned their air to smog, their water to murky clouds; their lungs became wheezy, their noses runny. Sickness was a constant foe for Suriias of the district, but there was no leaving the island, and there was no fighting back. The last time they'd tried, a third of them were executed.

The noises of the arena reached him before he'd even left the trail and a wary, unenthusiastic feeling set into his bones. He took a deep breath, mentally preparing himself for what awaited him inside.

Westend Circle was, as far as arenas went, not overly large or particularly off-putting from the outside. Built in one of the old districts of the former shanty town that had once been their prison, it was comprised of crumbling stone, tarp and thatch roofs covering places where the old structure had come down; it was never insulated, and in contrast to the drafts and damp that came in with the wind, sounds and screams filtered out.

The arena was subjected to raids from Keepers and Enforcers alike, but it always came back in some form: a black market; a foul tempered creation in the aftermath of unforgiveable violence; a dark corner that was still somehow the safest place for the most hated in society.

Past the large entry way made of metal and twisted wire, the hodgepodge collection of walls that divided the shops were stained in blood; a variety of shades of paint and graffiti only worsened the effect, and holes from the number of times flesh met stone were interspersed with gouges from when metal met stone instead. The ground was of a mud so hard and compacted that it felt like solid stone. Everything smelled strongly of dirt, metal and blood. Sulphur and the smoke from sizzling meats of a questionable and undoubtedly unappetising origin hung in the air like incense. The light was dim and cast everything in slanted shadows.

In the human arenas in the city, there were fancy seats and fine dining and the fights were between automata, for humans would never sully their hands with such displays.

Here in the Suriia arena, blood was currency. And it was the arena which drew in the most money. The most sport. The long abandoned seats that surrounded the fighting ring were cracked, stained and bare. In clusters and pairs, the gambling onlookers shouted, bargained, fought, all trying to get a piece of profit out of the evening.

'Our next fighter is old!' shouted the announcer in the centre of the ring. He was an unctuous man, with slicked-back hair and yellowed teeth. 'Old, yes, but he fights like a snake and flies like a wraith! Please welcome, Raguel!'

Lucien let his gaze flick over the spectators. Trenton was not amongst them. A quick look around showed no sign of his pack, either.

Disinterested in the psychotic, yet strangely childlike antics of Raguel, Lucien turned away, flipped his hat back onto his head, and gave the arena a wide berth on his way to the exit.

The announcer's voice reached him just as the cold night air kissed his face.

'The prize for this fight – offered up by our very own Clarence Ashby – is a human!'

Lucien glanced hesitantly at the gates where one of Ashby's lackeys was dragging in the human. Ashby stood off to the side, a cruel look on his face. He was one of those irredeemable souls who enjoyed inflicting pain simply because he found it funny. If killing him would not have placed an immediate target on his pack, Lucien would have done it years ago. But when all you had were enemies, it was a question of weighing which ones you could endure the longest.

It wasn't uncommon for humans to be bought and sold in the arena. Most were older, mid-twenties or mid-thirties; nobodies who would not be missed or noticed by the Enforcers. This human, what little Lucien could see of him, was thin and clearly abused. There were scars all over his bare arms and torso.

A sick feeling swelled inside Lucien's throat. He had no desire to watch. He knew what would become of the man. The last girl who had been won lasted no more than three days. The newspapers reported that she had been beaten to death and that her killer was still at large. Lucien knew better, but as much as it disgusted him the human wasn't worth the fallout. Even still, he watched Ashby pull the hood off the human's head.

The rushing in his ears turned all other noise to a low hum; he was quite certain pain shot through his entire being and set his insides aflame.

The human was the spitting image of Geon. Geon, who had been dead for twelve years. Geon, who most definitely did not have any children.

But there was no mistaking the resemblance, nor the familiar smell of blood. Even with so many others in the area, even from so far away, Lucien could smell the blood in the cuts on the man's face and neck and knew it like he knew his own smell.

It was *the stupidest* thing he could have done, but Lucien stepped up to the side of the arena. His hands and feet moved without his permission. He took off his hat, coat, and shirt before walking onto the packed dirt of the arena.

A roar went up and Raguel turned to see who his opponent was. Their eyes locked and hunger sprang to life in Raguel's irises. He'd hated Lucien for years. One of those souls who always interpreted insult where there wasn't any.

The ringmaster waved Lucien over. He was beaming. Things in Westend Circle had suddenly become interesting. 'My friends!' he crowed. 'We have our opponent! Lucien Lightblood of the Blackwood Pack verses Raguel Fuente of the Chester Pack. The winner gets a walk to the front door without being accosted and the human to do with as he sees fit!'

Lucien's hands balled as rage coursed through him.

'Begin!'

Raguel lunged, rising off the ground in a move that would make any bird of prey envious. They collided with a sound like bottled thunder.

Raguel's serrated teeth tore into the nape of his neck, and his nails ripped the skin on Lucien's back so deeply that he could feel the blood dripping down his spine and soaking into his jeans.

Grabbing a handful of Raguel's thick black hair, Lucien jerked him around, kicked him hard in the back, and sent him flying into the wall. Catlike in his grace, Raguel landed on the tips of his fingers and flew back at Lucien in a rage.

One of the many reasons Lucien abhorred fighting vrykos was the fact that they were dirty fighters. Untrustworthy outside of the arena and known for looking out for themselves and virtually no one else, vrykos were amongst many of the Suriias Lucien steered clear of just to keep himself from accidentally angering one – or being so annoyed he killed one to shut it up. In the arena, it was even worse.

Raguel came at him like a bat, landing an innumerable amount of punches, swipes and jabs that jarred Lucien to the bone – and he only saw about a third of them coming.

'You should have known better,' said Raguel, laughing in his ear, effectively pinning both of his arms behind his back. 'There are no equals to me in the arena. But I may let you watch as I collect my prize. I'm sure it'll be a good show.'

An anger Lucien had not known for many years burst out of him and, his fingers elongating into claws so sharp he could slice through bone, crunched two of Raguel's ribs in half.

Yanking his bloodied hand out of Raguel's chest, Lucien left him to crumple. 'Do you concede?' he hissed contemptuously.

Raguel sneered at him, displaying his mouth of jagged teeth. Teeth used for sucking the lifeforce from victims. 'Take him, then. See how high and mighty you are when you return to your pack with a human by your side.'

Lucien sent one last furious kick at Raguel's head. The force of it sent Raguel flying back against the wall, and this time, he did not rise to his feet. Vrykos had always siphoned blood and souls, but they had been different on Salfar. On Salfar, they had formed symbiotic relationships amongst their own kind, giving and taking in turn. Something about Earth had twisted their cravings, distorted the old ways.

Breathing heavily and angrier than he cared to be around so many enemies, Lucien went over to the ringmaster. He knew a few of his bones were cracked, if not broken, and he was going to be sore until he healed, but with how poor the pack had been eating recently, it would take much longer than it should. He remembered being able to heal bones magically on Salfar, but the clip made it impossible.

Clarence Ashby was standing beside the slave in question, amused and thrilled by the fight that had taken place over his prize. If there was one thing Ashby liked best, it was a show. The human was watching Lucien with narrowed eyes.

'I didn't think you were looking for a slave,' said Ashby.

'I'm not.'

Eavesdropping, the ringmaster stepped up beside them. 'There are only two ways a human can leave the arena, Lightblood.'

'I know.'

It was clear Ashby had not expected that. He raised a bushy eyebrow. 'I thought you had your eye on Shim? That was the rumour in these parts.'

'I'm surprised I'm worth idle gossip.'

'After your attack last month on the Greenwell leader, you've become quite the celebrity.'

'Fantastic,' said Lucien sardonically. 'Just what I've always wanted.'

Ashby appraised him for a moment, clearly inclined to ask more questions, but he seemed to sense Lucien's volatile mood, and gestured for his lackey – Lucien thought his name was

Briggs or Figgs or something similar – to bring the human over. If it was at all possible, the human looked even more terrified than before. Lucien could not fault him that. Outside, humans ruled them all, but in Westend, a human was as exposed as a gazelle in a lion's den.

'Someone fetch the cunning woman,' said the ringmaster, his eyes alight with interest. 'We have a spell to spin.'

With every Suriia implanted with a clip, a human-made implant that somehow – none of them knew *how* – kept their magic on lockdown, very few could perform spells anymore. Those who survived the war had been clipped by the Enforcers. Those born after the war were clipped at birth. Only outliers, those who had managed to stay hidden, escaped suppression. The cunning woman was an old vylka who had long been casting enchantments in the arena (for the right price).

Lucien wiped his scarlet stained hands on his dirty trousers – he had a feeling so much blood would only give the human cause to distrust him – before he finally worked up the courage to appraise him properly.

The human's resemblance to Geon left Lucien feeling like bees had burrowed into his chest, and although he had a million questions to ask, he managed to contain them. Instead, he asked the young man his name.

'Nik,' came the quiet, belated answer. His accent had a lilt, and it was clear he wasn't from around Westend Circle. Perhaps not even from London, the human city outside the Suriia districts.

'Lucien.'

Nik stared at him for a long moment. And then he spat, hitting Lucien on the neck and cheek. 'Fancied a slave, Lucien?' he snarled. Laughter and hollers went off around the edges of the arena.

Lucien wiped his cheek and sighed. Amongst the whispers were words of hunger and wicked pledges, and Lucien knew that he couldn't let things escalate. Stepping closer to the man, he pitched his voice low and hissed, 'Do you want to know what your choices are? Me, or death by teeth.'

If there had been any colour in Nik's cheeks before, there wasn't anymore.

'I can spare you that,' he continued, wishing more than anything that he could have a private conversation and all too aware of how impossible that was. 'I can walk you through the front door and no one will touch you if you work with me.'

'What will it do to me?'

'Nothing,' said Lucien firmly. 'You're not a prico. You just have to drink my blood.'

Nik did not look remotely inclined. Not that Lucien could blame him. He wouldn't have touched a stranger's blood if he'd had a choice, but there were some moments in life where the options weren't 'good versus bad' but 'I hate this option slightly less than that option'.

'If it does nothing to me, what's the point?' asked Nik.

'It carries a death sentence in the human world for a human to join our ranks. It brings you down to our level.'

'Why do you even care?'

'Because it felt like the night to be altruistic,' he growled, fear of someone overhearing their conversation mounting. Nik wasn't exactly quiet. 'Take it or leave it. Your other option is Raguel. And I won't eat you.'

On the other side of the arena, Raguel stood beside the rest of his pack, shouting obscenities most likely aimed at Lucien.

The distrust and hatred didn't leave Nik's brown eyes, but he nodded belatedly.

'You sure?'

'Whatever.'

It wasn't ringing endorsement, but the cunning woman arrived a few seconds later, and Lucien gave his consent to the enchantment; Nik echoed him after a beat, though it was nearly inaudible.

As matches were not something often seen in the Westend Suriia arena, it was no surprise that dozens of onlookers gathered around to watch shamelessly as Lucien cut open a small gash on his arm and held it out for Nik to drink.

Nik looked ill as he stared at Lucien's arm but, in the end, he proved tougher than Lucien had given him credit for as he managed to drink a fair amount without puking. Lucien then offered a blade to Nik, nodding for him to do the same.

With all of the joy of a man on the way to the gallows, Nik cut a line across his arm and held it out as blood drizzled down his skin.

Lucien felt awful. 'Are you sure?'

Nik shrugged. 'You're better than death.'

The heady smell of his blood filled Lucien with a hunger he never let himself acknowledge, and he lowered his head, fangs sharpening as he did so.

The cunning woman said her words in the old language of Salfar, and a thick coil of what appeared to be black veins slithered through Nik's skin, from his mouth to his arms. Thick, bloody letters inked themselves around his wrists, and Nik winced in pain.

It took only a few minutes but by the time it was finished, Nik was even paler, a fresh sheen of sweat had appeared on his brow, and he looked ready to faint. Lucien himself barely kept his footing after it was done to him.

'All done,' said the cunning woman.

Mute with anxiety, Lucien donned his shirt and coat, nodded to Ashby and placed a hand on Nik's back.

Regardless of the looks sent their way, no one bothered them as they left, and soon the cool air of Westend filled Lucien's lungs, and the sounds of death and the smell of decay faded away as the smells of fire and wood overcame them. The distant smell of fumes from the industrial factories tainted the air, but after so many years it was almost comforting.

He'd only taken a step when Nik spun around and punched him in the jaw. Half-expecting it, Lucien didn't fight back; nor did he bother trying to stop Nik from seizing his knife and pressing the tip into his neck.

'Do it,' he said calmly. 'If you think you can make it more than ten steps.'

'I'm not going back in a cage,' Nik snarled, drawing enough blood that Lucien could smell it.

'I was going to offer you a bed, but there's a perfectly good bench outside, if you'd prefer?'

'I'm not sleeping with you.'

Those words, raw and uncomfortable and unwanted as they were, confirmed a few horrible guesses and Lucien wanted to offer something conciliatory, but no good words came to him. No answers. The starved, bruised, abused human in front of him was never going to find him comforting and whatever else they could have been had died a fast death the instant Lucien bought him. There was no getting around that.

Nik stepped back after a few beats, still gripping Lucien's knife like a snake poised to strike.

Blood dripped down Lucien's throat and into his collar, and he wiped at it with a grimace. He was trying to formulate something to say that might ease the tension when the sound of voices filtered over, the volume rising with every step that brought them nearer.

Lucien snatched the knife out of Nik's hand with a quick move; he slid it back into its holster and had his arm around Nik just as the Suriias came into view.

They paused at the sight of Nik, their eyes raking over him with either hatred or hunger, and Lucien growled low in his throat. To his relief, they carried on towards their automobile without issue.

'We should go,' he said when they drove off, letting his arm drop. Gesturing for Nik to follow him, he turned left at the bottom of the hill and set off down the winding sideroad to home. He heard Nik follow slowly and kept going, resisting the urge to turn around.

The streets were mostly empty. Those who weren't betting were lying low; the Keepers already come and gone.

Halfway down the road, the sound of chattering teeth made him stop short. Taking off his coat, he turned back, holding it out. 'Before you freeze to death.'

'What do you care?'

Lucien offered it again. 'Will you please take the coat?'

Clearly wishing him nothing but ill, Nik snatched the coat out of his hand and donned it. Lucien sighed and carried on.

Each step was both a blessing and a curse. He was glad to put the arena behind him and he was desperate for a shower and a change of clothes, but the prospect of explaining the night's events to his pack made his stomach twist with trepidation. They had all vowed a long time ago that they would never participate in the gruesome, twisted, perverse activities that many of their fellows revelled in. All the Blackwood Pack had had their fill of vileness and dark rituals. Not to mention it felt fundamentally wrong to treat the humans as the humans treated them. But what other option was there?

They walked on in silence, the light of the moon illuminating the roads and casting Westend in a far more likeable light than it deserved. The city, while more rural than urban, with trees and farms for the packs, boasted seedy inner streets and alleys and was known for trading the vilest of substances, the most depraved contraband. It certainly wasn't a kind place to grow up, yet it had long been his home and he had come to love its shortcomings. There was a melody to the madness, a charm to the chaos.

They were more than halfway there, tense silence thick in the air between them, when exhaustion and fear finally overcame Nik. He asked Lucien to pause and he slid down against the trunk of a tree, body trembling from fear and fatigue. He was also dangerously underweight, badly bruised, and likely ill.

'Do you have water?' he rasped.

'At the house,' said Lucien. 'It's not far.'

The distance, however, didn't matter. Nik took several choking, gasping breaths, and then passed out.

Lucien lifted him easily into his arms and carried on. Without Nik's slow gait to contend with, he reached the manor quickly.

It took only ten seconds for most of the pack to crowd onto the front porch. They stared in shock as Lucien carried Nik up to the door and into the manor.

Adair stepped towards him. 'What—'

'Just fetch the med kit.'

The heady smell of dinner and the warmth of the roaring fire in the drawing room greeted him upon entrance. Those who were home trailed in behind him as he brought Nik upstairs to his room.

Adair and Mi appeared a minute later. There was a medical kit in Mi's hand.

'Want me to mend him?' she asked, eyebrow raised. 'Although it might be quicker simply to buy a new one.'

Adair, who had been appraising Nik, looked up in bewilderment. 'Is he—'

'Yeah.'

Lucien gestured for Mi to tend to Nik's wounds. She was the closest thing they had to a doctor.

He then went to the bathroom. His clothes reeked of the arena's pungent odour and he wanted any remnants of the night off his body. Stepping into the shower, he set the water on its hottest temperature and watched with sick fascination as the blood was erased from his body.

He could hear Adair and Mi speaking in his bedroom, evaluating Nik's injuries and poor health. Trusting Adair more than himself to take care of Nik, Lucien didn't hurry. The wounds on his back stung as the water sluiced over them, and he punched the wall as the soap bit into the claw-marks on his back, marks that he was sure were more than fingernail deep.

When at last the water ran clear, he got out of the shower, wrapped a towel around his waist, and appraised himself in the mirror. There was a dark new bruise forming around his eyebrow and temple, and his lip was cut. The bridge of his nose was bleeding slowly, and one of his eyes was purple, blood mixing with the steely blue they normally were. It gave him an almost haunted appearance.

Reaching a hand up, he ran his fingers over the scars on his face. They still ached when touched. If he blinked, he could see them the night they'd been slashed.

He dropped his hand and left the bathroom. There was no sign of Adair, but Lucien could hear him downstairs with Naida.

Dressing quickly in a simple shirt and some comfortable trousers – and fashioning a brace from cloth for his bone-bruised wrist – Lucien moved to Mi's side to watch critically as she tended to Nik's injuries.

'I want you to find Jae,' he said when she finished.

Mi inclined her head. 'What should I say?'

'Tell him we have a serious matter to discuss,' said Lucien. His stomach knotted unpleasantly. 'Tell him he has a nephew.'

'Yes sir.'

Leaving her to it, Lucien headed downstairs to the kitchen. Isha was at the table mending the clockwork wolf they usually kept by the front door. Made of metal but enchanted with a zane charm, it trilled out its howls when the Enforcers were near the perimeter of the property.

After everyone had eaten, Mi and Isha prepared themselves for the trek to track down Jae, and Naida got the children ready for bed, while Shim and Adair began cleaning up the kitchen.

Lucien watched them all for a moment, an intense feeling of pride swelling in his chest, before heading outside.

The night had grown even colder, threatening a midnight frost and the barn door swung open with a creak that sounded like a furious feline. Flicking on the light switch, he stepped inside and shut the door to block off the night's chill. With a crackling sound, the gas in the lanterns caught and the hanging lights illuminated the drab training room. There were weights in one corner below a wall of weapons. On the opposite wall, a mat stretched from end to end. There was a worn, patchy punching bag hanging in the left-hand corner.

For the next hour, Lucien lost himself in the repetitive rhythm of punching and dodging, punching and dodging, and was sufficiently soaked in sweat, his blood thrumming, when he heard someone enter behind him.

He looked over his shoulder. Adair was leaning against the doorframe, arms crossed, brow furrowed. 'Geon's son?' he noted. 'I didn't see that one coming.'

Lucien wiped sweat from his forehead and rotated his arms and shoulders. 'Neither did I.'

'Geon wasn't seeing anyone. Not once since we got to Earth.'

'No. Not as far as I'm aware.'

'He didn't leave the house, either.'

'No.'

Adair scowled in thought. 'Well, that's one question we need answers for. That, and how Nik ended up with Ashby.'

'Ashby probably snatched him from the city. Or paid someone to. They're always picking up homeless humans.'

Adair ran a hand through his long, curly black hair and scowled. 'The only reason we've not been raided in years is because we don't court trouble. That's gone now.'

'I couldn't leave him there.'

'I know,' said Adair understandingly. 'I would've done the same. But now we have a bull's eye on us. A *human* bull's eye.'

'I won't let anything happen.'

'We can't guarantee that without magic.' Adair raised his arm where the clip was implanted. 'I used to be able to level a forest and now I can't even protect my family without trickery and deceit, working with scum I would sooner see in prison. I'm useless now.'

Adair's fury with their constraints was something he'd brought up daily since their magic had been locked down. What was once second nature to him was now inaccessible.

Lucien held out his hands, in complete agreement and clueless as to how to fix it. 'What do you want me to do? I buried Geon. Don't ask me to bury the only piece of him left.'

It felt like a blessing of some kind. Like the universe had decided he'd been through enough and directed him to Nik. A man they'd never known existed.

'We should find Ezzie,' said Adair with audible resignation. 'That's what we should do.'

Lucien almost laughed at the awful suggestion. 'Because you and Naida don't have enough marital problems?'

'Because she's the only one who can help us. And don't bring my marital problems into this.'

'I don't have to,' said Lucien. 'She will.'

'That was a long time ago.'

'Esme can't stand to lose.'

'Which is exactly why we need her.' Adair's earnest pointedness was obvious in his stance and voice. 'She's the only one powerful enough – and crazy enough – to help.'

'Esme doesn't come without blood. I'm tired of blood.'

'I'm tired of burying friends,' said Adair. 'And I will not bury my children. I will burn this island to the ground before I let that happen.'

Lucien looked down, taking the opportunity to rewrap his hands, using the pretence to give himself time to swallow the lump in his throat. When he raised his head, his old friend was studying him with a sombre expression. These days, Adair was somehow his best friend, his mentor, his brother and father all in one. Lucien's move from following Geon's lead to being their leader had been more reactionary than anything, but in the years since, he'd run every decision by Adair. Until tonight.

'Did you ever think it would get this bad?'

'No,' said Adair dispiritedly, the grief in his tone an echo to Lucien's. He brushed black hair back from his forehead, fisting the roots agitatedly. For an immortal Suriia, he looked bone-weary and his eyes were older than their years. Which said a lot, since Adair was pushing four hundred. He added, 'But I fell for the serenity. Two quiet centuries. Two almost perfect centuries.'

The wind picked up outside the barn and sent howling shrieks through the rafters. A chill snaked down Lucien's spine and he had to work to resist the urge to shiver. 'Sometimes I wonder if I didn't dream all of this,' he muttered, the words barely louder than the wind, almost swallowed whole. 'If I'm not still locked in the Tower.'

Adair had no trouble discerning Lucien's words. 'It's real,' he said. 'None of it was a dream.'

'If it's not real, Geon is alive.'

'Geon is dead, Lucien. The last three hundred years were real. This nightmare is real, and our family is all we have left. Esme is part of that family. And I'd trust her insanity over any other form of protection. I need that level of insanity, Lucien. I can't lose my children.'

Regardless of his misgivings, Lucien had to concede that Esme was the best equipped of any of them to handle a growing threat. 'I'll think about it,' he said begrudgingly. 'I'm not saying yes.'

Adair nodded. 'Better than nothing. And get some sleep. You look like shit.'

Lucien flicked his fingers at Adair before turning back to the punching bag. But no matter how many times fist met fabric, he couldn't drive the human from his thoughts.

CHAPTER FIFTEEN
The New Additions

Lucien was in the midst of trying – and utterly failing – to get some of the expense receipts sorted out for the accountant when he heard a sharp cry from down the hall. He was out of his office like a bullet, pulse thrumming, heart in his throat. There was no sound from the wards, which were designed to trill out when anyone neared the perimeter; the sounds came from his bedroom.

Hesitating only a second, he slipped into his room and strode over to the bed. Tossing and turning, tangled in blankets, Nik was crying out in his sleep. His fists were balled in the blankets and his veins stuck out starkly against his pale skin. Somehow the strain of anguish made him look even thinner, even more fragile.

Lucien put a hand on his shoulder, firm but gentle; Nik's skin was cold, but his skin was glistening with sweat.

'Nik!' he barked. 'Nik, wake up.'

Nik's eyes snapped open.

'Sorry.' Lucien withdrew his hand quickly. 'You were having a nightmare.' He turned and was halfway to the door when Nik said quietly, 'Wait.'

Lucien paused.

'I …' Nik seemed to be fighting himself. He looked away from Lucien. 'Can you just sit for a second?'

Not sure what to say, Lucien walked over to the chair by the window and sat down.

Shrouded in shadows cast by the curtains around the fourposter, Nik sat up and drew his legs into his chest. Propping his elbows on his knees, he pressed his hands to his forehead. His raven coloured hair was slick against his bloodless face, and the hollows of his cheeks were even more pronounced.

He looked, Lucien realised, not like one of the humans who hated him, but like one of the Suriias who stood at his side. Like half of Nik was locked away inside himself where he'd be safe. A place where it was entirely possible to get lost and never find a way out.

Lucien sat in silence, uncomfortable, concerned, and feeling utterly useless. He watched Nik take in his surroundings, eyes narrowed, straining to see in the pitch-black room. For Lucien, the lack of light was nothing his eyes could not handle, but he realised belatedly that it was likely disorienting for Nik.

'Want me to turn a light on?' he offered.

'Yeah. Lights are good.' Nik sounded a little disconnected from reality. 'Not too bright, though. My head's pounding.'

Lucien stood and walked to the corner of the room. Turning on one of the lamps, which cast his bedroom in eerie shadow, he then returned to the bed, handed Nik an extra blanket, and sat down at the end.

'What was it about?' he prompted. 'Your dream.'

'Bunny rabbits and rainbows,' said Nik quietly, staring at the back wall.

Lucien did not call him out on his lie. He'd probably regret it even if he managed to get the truth. 'Are you hungry? I can get you something from the kitchen. I doubt you've had much in the way of sustenance with Ashby, and the food here is brilliant for as broke as we are. Naida is an excellent cook.'

At the mention of Ashby, Nik flinched. But his next question was different still. 'Why me?' he queried, picking at a hangnail, lips turned down in a moue of distaste. 'Didn't see anyone else to buy?'

Lucien took a breath before replying. 'I went there looking for a man who didn't show and I was leaving. I had no interest in fighting Raguel. I never have.'

'Then why did you?'

'Because I know your face.'

'What does that mean?'

'It means your father was my best friend.'

Nik's head snapped up. The anger vanished from his face, leaving only shock, amazement. 'You know who my father is?'

That simple query confirmed a few of Lucien's own questions, although it raised a dozen others. The last decade flashed through his mind, and he suddenly questioned where Nik might have been at each moment. Where was he when the sickness hit five years ago? Where was he when the riots happened? Had he been near the human neighbourhood that a dissident group of Suriias bombed?

'His name was Geon,' he said, memories of his best friend hitting him like a steamroller.

'Geon?'

'Just Geon, really. We don't have surnames on Salfar. Others called him Kal Geon, if you want to know. "Kal" was a term used to denote your place in society there. Think of it like calling someone Lord or Prince, only it was insulting. It meant "peasant". But he wore it like a badge of honour.' Lucien wasn't sure why he was rambling, but it had been a long time since he'd talked about Geon to someone who didn't remember the end. How did you describe someone who vanished before your eyes?

'He was poor?'

'Beyond poor,' said Lucien, his old frustration with the caste system setting his teeth on edge. 'He was living in the forest when I met him. Unlike most, however, he didn't change his name as he increased his standing. Even when he was walking in and out of the castle like a lord, he was still using Kal. He used to introduce himself to other lords with that title. Their expressions were priceless.'

Nik nodded thoughtfully, a hard to read look on his face. 'Was he a lord?'

'For a little while.'

'How'd he become a lord if he was dirt poor?'

'He was good at making friends.'

'That sounds manipulative.'

The thought of Geon manipulating anyone made Lucien almost snort. 'No, he was charming. So much more so than me. Everyone liked him.'

'You talk about him like he's dead.'

'He is.'

The way Nik's expression shattered was painful to witness. 'He's dead?'

Remembering Geon's last days hurt. Worse than he could ever say to Geon's son. Lucien felt like someone had taken a shovel and dug out his intestines – and was still doing it years later. 'He died twelve years ago.'

'How'd he die?'

'He killed himself.'

'How?'

'No,' said Lucien sharply, picking at the edge of his fingernail and making blood bead on his skin. 'His son doesn't need to know how he died and no one in this house will tell you. Don't ask.'

Nik sat forward, wincing, and Lucien could hear the wheeze in his lungs from a bad beating. The sound made his heart race, but not nearly as much as Nik's next words. 'Okay, I won't ask how. *Why* did he kill himself?'

'I, ah ... I don't ...' He wasn't giving Nik much, which wasn't fair, but he didn't even discuss Geon's last day with Adair, who knew him best. That day belonged to the back cage of Lucien's soul where it couldn't break loose and destroy him.

The silence dragged on so long that Nik looked away, out the window across the room, a distant, melancholy cast to a face that was malnourished, scarred and weary.

Wanting to give him something, Lucien forced the next words out of his mouth, which felt dryer than a rock in the sun. 'His mind was gone. I think it became too much. He wasn't Geon for a long time.'

'Was it like post-traumatic stress? From the war?'

'No, it was magic.'

'Magic?' Nik blinked several times, absorbing this with obvious disbelief. 'I thought all Suriias wore clips.'

'He removed his.'

'Aren't they implanted in your arm?'

'Yeah. He removed it himself. With a knife.' Unable to bear anymore, Lucien redirected the conversation. 'Who's your mother?'

'Her name was Alice,' said Nik hesitantly. 'I was born in Whitestone.'

The town was familiar enough to Lucien. Whitestone was two cities over, in ordinary territory. It had a smattering of prewar architecture and was now a burgeoning metropolis. He wondered how Geon had even crossed paths with the woman.

'She never told me who my father was, only that her pregnancy embarrassed her family.'

That brought a sneer to Lucien's face. 'Only humans would cast out one of their own for bearing a child. At least Suriias cherish their young.'

Nik was silent for a time before he said, 'My mother died a year ago, street sickness. I got sick, too. Ashby picked me up when I was half-conscious. I woke up in his basement.'

Lucien entertained a brief daydream of removing Ashby's arms and waving them back at him. But Nik's next question proved enough to divert him.

'You never knew about my mother?'

'No,' said Lucien. 'And before you ask, Geon knew nothing about you. Had he known, you would've grown up here with us.'

'Are you in charge?'

'Yes.' After a moment, Lucien added, 'Can I ask you something?'

'Sure.'

'How old are you?'

'Twenty.'

It gave a date for Geon's whereabouts, but it still left Lucien with numerous questions.

Nik ran a hand through his oily hair and sat back. 'I think I'm going to go back to sleep, if that's all right?'

'Sure,' said Lucien, getting to his feet. 'I'll go.'

He was halfway to the door when Nik's next question made him pause.

'Is this your room?'

'Yes.'

'Didn't mean to kick you out of your own room.'

'You didn't.'

Lucien left it at that. He spent the rest of the night's hours on the sofa in his study, glaring out the window, falling in and out of a daze that could hardly be considered restorative.

When sunlight blazed in through the windows, he gave up the pretence of trying to rest and sat up, cracking his neck. His clothes were sticking to him and he felt gross and clammy, but he knew his discomfort was for more reasons than wanting a bath and a fresh change of clothes.

He meandered down the corridor, trying to come up with something to say to Nik that wouldn't be either awkward or depressing. By the time he was outside his bedroom, he still hadn't come up with anything.

After a moment, he heard pages turning and raised a hand to knock twice.

'Yeah?' called Nik.

'It's Lucien. Can I come in?'

'Sure.'

Nik was sitting crossed legged on the bed, a blanket around his shoulders, his nose in one of Lucien's novels. ''Morning,' he greeted.

'Good morning.' Lucien eyed the blanket. Nik was so skinny, it was a wonder there was any meat on his bones at all. Without a word, he went to his closet and retrieved one of his smaller coats from the back. Bringing it over to Nik, he held it out. 'Up long?'

'Not too long,' said Nik, taking the coat from him. 'Thanks.'

'Yeah.' Scratching his chin, Lucien gestured to the door. 'You hungry? I can already smell the coffee.'

Nik nodded and set his book aside. There was a slightly more animated air to him now, as if he was starting to relax a little, and it made something loosen in Lucien's chest. 'Starving, actually,' he replied. 'Last thing I ate was half a rat that crawled into my cage.'

Lucien's fist balled involuntarily, his mind flashing back to how poor their food options had been during the war. He'd eaten worse than rats, but Nik didn't need to know that. 'I'm really going to have to do something about Ashby,' he muttered.

Nik ran a hand through his messy black hair, attempting to slick it back and failing utterly. 'Something?'

'Justice.'

'What does prico justice look like?'

'Intentional.'

Nik pursed his lips and drew the coat tight around his thin body.

'Does that frighten you?'

'I want him dead.'

Lucien was tempted to offer Nik Ashby's head, but he worried that wouldn't go down well all things considered.

Now that he was no longer limping quite so badly, Lucien could see that Nik had Geon's easy stride, that his legs were slightly bowlegged, and he stood stiffly on habit, rather than on edge. He had Geon's same pale skin and straight black hair that fell in front of his face no matter how many times Nik swept it back. The effect was in equal parts handsome and endearing, but Lucien forced himself not to look, a guilty feeling brewing in his chest.

Only Naida, Adair and Shim sat around the breakfast table. Side by side, they formed a portrait of weariness. Shim, scars on her face and arms, her hair in desperate need of a cut, was a match to Adair's bushy beard and greying hair. The deep bags under Naida's eyes gave her otherwise wholesome appearance a hooded, distressed edge.

The glorious smells of breakfast offset the sorry sight, however. Naida had made pancakes and fruit salad, and there was a pot of tea which smelled tantalisingly good. Music trilled out of the phonograph on the table by the window, filling the room with as much life as the sunlight that filtered in through the windows.

'Good morning, gents,' said Adair as they took their seats. Adair, always polite and welcoming, smiled at Nik and handed him a plate of toast and a jar of honey.

Nik raised an eyebrow at the honey.

'Trust me,' added Adair conspiratorially, 'you won't regret it.'

With a dubious expression, Nik spread honey over the toast and took a bite. He nodded to Adair after a moment. 'Yeah,' he agreed. 'It's good.'

'Told you,' said Adair. 'You'll soon learn that I am always right.'

'Thanks.'

'Is that Lucien's coat?' asked Naida. 'It looks a bit large.'

'That's because Lucien isn't small,' said Shim, smirking. She threw a piece of bread at him and winked. 'We'll find you some proper clothes after breakfast, Nik. I think there's some in your size.'

'Eran might have some,' said Naida. 'He's grown rather rapidly, so I'm sure there's something for you. I was sorting through them last night.'

Nik nodded diffidently. 'Thank you.'

'When you're up for a proper tour, let me know,' she added. 'Kalid and Shara are dying to show you around.'

'Sure.'

The meal continued without event, no one broaching personal or wary topics, and when they finished, the others took Nik to go find some clothes, and Lucien stayed to help Adair clean up.

'He does remind me of Geon,' said Adair, as he washed one of the plates. 'Especially his hands. Geon was always twitchy.'

'I'm glad I'm not the only one who noticed,' said Lucien, taking the proffered plate to dry. Where the humans in the cities had great steam-powered devices to wash their dishes, none of the Suriias could afford them. But Lucien wasn't sure he'd get one even if they found the money one day. There was something calming about washing dishes. And he *loathed* automata.

Adair chuckled. 'Do you remember when he bent all of the spoons in half out of sheer boredom and because none of us would tell my mother who was responsible, we all had to unbend them, and then polish the lot until they shined?'

'We made him pay for it later, didn't we?'

'Yeah, we did,' agreed Adair. 'I'd never seen him blush before that. A truly priceless moment. Ezzie could be so cruel.'

A sudden laugh slipped out of him. The pranks they used to play on each other brought joy to his heart.

When the kitchen was spotless, he headed up the stairs, following the sounds of voices. He found the others in his bedroom fussing over Nik. Clothes of all shapes, sizes and colours were strewn across his bed and the window seat, others had been flung over the standing mirror.

Lucien cleared his throat. 'I assume this is all going to find its way into a wardrobe somewhere?'

Entirely unbothered by the mess, Shim waved airily. 'We found all the clothes around the house that looked like they might fit Nik and—'

'Puked them on my bed?'

'We've been meaning to put them in storage, and this gives us the perfect opportunity! Everything he doesn't like, we'll box up. Deal?'

Lucien rolled his eyes. 'Fine.'

A now familiar scent, like honeysuckle and musk, reached Lucien's nose, and he turned around. Nik was standing in the doorway, wet from a shower. He was holding up the wrap that Mi had put around his torso. His scars were more obvious as he trembled, his skin pale as ice.

'I can't do it,' he said awkwardly.

Lucien raised a hand with slow hesitation. 'Do you want me to?'

'Do you mind?'

'No, not at all.' Lucien went to his side. 'Tell the ladies which pieces of clothing you will and won't wear while I do it.'

Nik's eyes widened at the assortment. He didn't seem to know what to make of the pack any more than they knew what to make of him. But he managed a small, slightly bewildered smile. 'That is a *lot* of clothes.'

'We keep everything that isn't torn up or full of holes,' Naida explained, holding up a pair of trousers that Nik nodded to. 'It means that some items are worn by three or four people before they go. Recycling and all that.'

'Industrious.'

Lucien bent down beside Nik, wrapping the bandage around his stomach. He could think of seven or eight potions from Salfar that would heal Nik instantly, but he had access to nothing but cheap bandages.

'Where should we put his things?' asked Shim, folding the shirts with knowing, purposeful hands, not even bothering to look as she picked up each item and folded without thought.

'In my wardrobe,' said Lucien. 'The spare one. Everything else can go into storage.'

They began putting the clothes away, and Naida went to fetch some boxes from the cellar.

Nik re-emerged from the bathroom a minute later, dressed in a dark red shirt that was once Adair's, one of Isha's brown jumpers, and Eran's trousers. He added a waistcoat that had once been Lucien's before tugging on his shoes. The clothes gave him a much healthier appearance. There was a renewed confidence to him, too. Being put together could often do that.

'Better?' prompted Lucien.

'Yeah,' said Nik. 'So ... what now?'

Lucien had dozens of things to do, but most of it would have to wait until the next day. His thoughts were too scattered to be of any use and he had a few visits to make before he could do anything. 'Your uncle's on his way. I thought perhaps we could all talk and try to work some things out. Then ... whatever you want, I suppose.'

Nik bounced on the balls of his feet and tapped the fingers of each hand against his thumbs in a continuous sequence that spoke to his bubbling anxiety. 'Jae, right?'

Lucien inclined his head. 'You'll like him. He's, well, he's rather different from Geon, but he's great when he's sober.'

'He drinks?'

'We all did, for a time. Jae just drinks more than most.' Considering everything they'd been through, Lucien thought Jae was handling the situation rather well.

Nik's brow furrowed deeply. 'You know, you act like a soldier.'

'I am a soldier.'

'You are?'

'I fought in the war.'

'What'd you do?'

'Broadly, or do you want specifics?'

'Specifics.'

Lucien held his gaze with an open, honest one of his own. 'I was one of the signatories on the wall.'

Nik's eyebrows shot up. 'You were?'

The *109 Signatures* was a now infamous letter signed by Suriia leaders throughout the island who had promised war if another Suriia was targeted by a human without provocation. The human chancellor at the time responded by leaving the bodies of ten Suriia dissenters in the town square, stripped naked, religious symbols carved into their chests to ward off what the humans believed were unholy spirits. Lucien was among the group who retaliated the following morning; Geon, Jae, Adair and Naida beside him. It was there that they'd met Shim and Isha.

The humans called that fight the Main Street Massacre. Everyone else called it the Suriia Uprising. Two days later, the humans spread poison throughout the water systems of the island, killing or severely weakening every Suriia who got thirsty.

The sound of the door opening downstairs snapped Lucien out of his reverie. He gave Nik a small nod. 'Wait here,' he said, and turned on his heel.

The sight of Jae was hard to take. His old friend was a husk of his former self. Taking him by the arm, Lucien led Jae to one of the bathrooms on the ground floor and pushed him into the shower stall.

'You smell like carcasses and mould,' he rebuked. 'Clean yourself up, drink some tea, and then I will let you meet your nephew.'

Jae, who was clumsily pulling off his clothing, blinked brown eyes that, once so vibrant, were now dull and dead from years of grief and turmoil. 'Is it true?'

'It's true,' said Lucien. He stepped out of the way of the water and took in the extent of the damage Jae had done to himself. 'And he's not going anywhere, so take your time cleaning up. You smell like the bottom of my boots. I'll fetch you something to wear. Meet us in the kitchen when you're not going to embarrass yourself.'

'Lucien …'

'Don't apologise. Just be sober.'

Lucien left then and returned to his bedroom.

Nik was once again reading, this time curled up on the window seat. A gentle rain kissed the window but beyond the pane, the wet day had left the grass vibrantly green. The day's pale sunlight cast his slim, sharp body in shadow. It was a strange contrast to the sight of him the night before, so bloodied and numb.

'Do you like reading, or do you just have nothing else to do?' asked Lucien, wandering over.

Nik closed the book, keeping his finger inside to hold his place. 'I like reading. We could never really afford to buy books, so I had to make do with whatever we found on the streets. I found some, ah, interesting stories that way.'

'Penny dreadfuls?'

'Badly written cheap romances.'

'Ouch.'

Nik laughed.

'You're welcome to read whatever you like that's here,' said Lucien. 'And there's a bookshop in town that I can take you to. You can go whenever you want. The owner owes me a few favours, so he'll let you have anything that sparks your interest.'

Surprise glinted in Nik's chestnut eyes. 'You don't have to do that.'

'True. But won't it make you happy?'

Nik looked out the window at the fields and forests that surrounded them, at the mountain in the distance. 'Why do you care if I'm happy?'

The question stung. 'I take no pleasure in another's suffering. No matter what you might think of me.'

Nik did not turn away from the window, and Lucien wondered what he was thinking about.

Unable to come up with something else on the subject to say, Lucien turned his attention to the book in Nik's hand.

'What're you reading?'

Nik raised the book without looking at him and Lucien's eyebrows shot up as he realised which book it was. 'You speak French?'

'It was one of the few books on the shelf I could reach,' said Nik ruefully. 'I didn't want to climb on your bookcase trying to get to the ones in English.'

'There is something highly amusing about that mental image,' mused Lucien. 'As long as you don't knock all the books down, I don't care. Climb as much as you want. So, French?'

'Yeah.'

The tension between them seemed to have come back with a vengeance, and Lucien had no idea as to how to diffuse it. Instead, he stood and thumbed over his shoulder. 'How about meeting your uncle, then? I know he wants to see you.'

Nik put the book down and stood. 'All right.'

'Great,' said Lucien, not feeling positive in the least. 'Come on.'

Jae was in the kitchen when they entered; his face was shadowed with stubble, his eyes still ghostly, though more alert than Lucien had seen them in many years. Jae gave off an aura of such insurmountable sorrow that he could have walked with the ghosts of men from wars generations past and fit right in.

Lucien sat down at the head of the table and gestured for Nik to sit across from Jae. 'Jae, this is Nik, your nephew; Nik, this is Jae, your uncle.'

Neither Nik nor Jae held out their hands. They were both too busy staring at each other; with fear, in Nik's case, or fascination tinged with regret, in Jae's.

'Hi,' said Nik at length.

'Hello,' said Jae, still staring at him.

Lucien wanted the ground to open up and eat him whole.

Thankfully, Naida had left a pot of tea on the table and he busied himself pouring them all cups. Tea seemed to be the one thing everyone in the house could agree upon to drink.

Jae's voice was raspy from disuse when at last he spoke. 'You look like him.'

'Lucien said that.'

'Isha told me you met at the arena,' Jae noted, glancing at Lucien who nodded confirmation. 'Baxel?'

'Ashby.'

'How is that possible?' said Jae. 'The Keepers raid pack houses.'

Somehow that question hadn't occurred to Lucien and he looked sharply at Nik, wondering what other horrible information he didn't have.

'He has a secret door in the basement,' said Nik. 'I wasn't the only one there, either. I had a friend. Ginny. I don't even know if she's still alive.'

Lucien abruptly left the kitchen. In the front room, he found Naida, Adair and Shim. They got to their feet when they saw the look on his face.

'Shim,' he said. 'Don't let Nik out of your sight.'

She nodded and disappeared into the kitchen. He could hear Nik asking her where he was going.

'We're going to Ashby's,' he said to Adair and Naida, barely pausing to grab his coat as he led the way out the door.

It was drizzling slightly outside, dark clouds filling the skies. They clambered into his steamtruck and headed towards the north side of town. A train filled with coal chugged past as they drove through the fields, heading for the Suriia mine.

'What's the plan, boss?' asked Naida.

'I don't have one,' he admitted, eyes fixed on the road. 'Nik said they still have a human.'

'That's not news. At least four houses at any time have a human captive.'

'Yes, and now I know which one does.'

'They'll attack us in retaliation.'

'Then let's send a strong message.'

With a put upon sigh, Adair checked the barrel of his pistol.

It took them all of twenty minutes to reach Ashby's. The pack's house was made of metal and chrome, steam billowing from an iron chimney. Lucien hated the house, right down to its door knocker. The loud grating sound of industry made his head pound and he wanted to leave before he was even out of the truck.

Kicking down the door easily, he strode in, Adair and Naida at his side. They found Ashby, Keller and Yastos in the sitting room.

'What is this, Lightblood?' said Ashby, already on his feet.

Lucien seized him as Naida and Adair pinned the other two to the floor.

'Not happy with your purchase?'

Lucien's dagger was buried in Ashby's throat before he could speak. He didn't even register the action until Ashby fell to the floor and he stepped back, blood on his hands.

Adair had Keller pinned to the ground; Naida had Yastos against the wall.

'Where's the girl?' Lucien looked between them.

'Eat me,' said Keller.

Adair punched him in the ribs. 'Manners.'

'Behind the shelf,' said Yastos, nodding to a shelf with a variety of items on every level.

There was no way to discern a door was behind the shelf just from looking at it. Lucien wrenched the shelf forward, effectively sending the items everywhere, and found himself at the top of a set of stairs. He descended quickly. Everything smelled rank and mouldy, the air heavy with stink.

At the base of the steps, a room revealed itself. The type of sordid creation that belonged in a ghost story and had no place in civilised society. A room of cages and tables and hooks. And, in one of the cages against the far wall, crouched a girl. She was a frail little thing, bruised and covered in grime and wearing rags.

Lucien walked over and bent down. Breaking the cage's lock easily, he tossed the pieces of metal aside and opened the door. 'Are you Ginny?' he asked, careful to keep his voice kind as she scrambled to the back of the cage. 'Nik sent me.'

A sob slipped from between her lips and a second later Ginny took his hand and let him pull her out of the cage. Removing his coat, he helped her into it. The fabric hung down past her calves, making her seem even more delicate. A feather in a tornado.

'Can you walk?'

She nodded.

'Come on.'

Lucien kept a gentle, steadying arm around her shoulders as they ascended the stairs.

As he walked past Keller, Lucien paused. Taking his pistol out, he cocked the trigger and pressed it into Keller's neck. 'Touch another human and I'll be back. Ashby's death will look like a painting.'

Keller hawked a wad of bloody mucus at him. 'You broke the law, Lightblood!'

'Tell a Keeper then. We both know you'd be in more trouble for having a human.'

Adair smashed his fist into Keller's face. Naida shoved Yastos away from her and wiped her hands on her trousers, disgust twisting her face.

'That wasn't a good idea,' said Adair as they made their way to the truck.

'No,' said Lucien. 'It wasn't.'

They clambered into the truck and Lucien took the fast route to the old boutique that served as the local clinic.

In human cities, Suriias weren't allowed to have insurance and were rarely seen to on the off chance they were brought in.

Sear Gong, the local doctor, was greedy only to a point, and loyalty to his own kind won out over reporting to the Keepers.

There were several patients in the shabby waiting room already. After giving the receptionist money, they were waved through to the backroom. There was a bed and Ginny sat down gingerly, tense and twitchy. Naida plunked herself into the adjacent chair.

'We need a female doctor,' he said to Sear.

'She's busy.'

'We'll wait.'

Thirty minutes passed before Sear returned with a frai nurse. Ginny looked much less frightened by her than she had by Sear, and Lucien stepped into the hall leaving Naida inside with Ginny and the nurse.

'The girl makes two, Lightblood,' said Sear, voice deep with warning.

Jamming his hands into his pockets, Lucien leaned against the wall. 'Word travels fast.'

'This is foolish.'

'He's my husband.'

Sear waved at the door. 'And the girl?'

'The girl is also under my protection.'

'As what? Your slave?'

'Shim's wife,' he lied quickly.

The smirk Adair sent him was clue enough as to how much Shim was going to kill him for that later. But Sear relaxed somewhat.

'No more humans, Lightblood.'

'Of course not.'

With a snort of exasperation, Sear left them alone.

Shortly thereafter, the nurse opened the door and announced that they were set to go.

Lucien approached Ginny carefully. The nurse had given her a change of clothes, at least. 'Do you need me to contact anyone?'

She shook her head. 'There's no one to contact.'

'Do you want a place to stay? Nik's with us.'

The hope and relief on her face made something inside his chest constrict. 'So, he's okay?'

'He is.'

'Thank God,' she breathed.

'Do you want to come back with us, then?'

'Yes.'

The drive home passed in the silence that often comes after an emotional and life altering event, especially when the consequences were yet to be determined.

Lucien was still trying to figure out how he was going to break the news of another human to his pack when he walked through the door and Nik shouted in delight.

He shot to Ginny's side faster than an arrow and they threw their arms around each other.

The rest of the pack appeared in the hallway behind them, stunned at the sight. Lucien rubbed the back of his neck and wished – for the tenth time that week – someone else was in charge. 'Shara, can you take Ginny up to one of the spare rooms and help her settle in?'

'Sure.'

When Ginny and Shara departed, Lucien waved a hand after them, attention shifting from one bewildered face to another. 'She was in a cage in Ashby's basement. What was I supposed to do?'

'Well, when you put it that way,' said Jae.

Adair clapped Lucien on the back. 'Oh, Shim? You're her wife. In case anyone asks.'

Shim gawped at him. 'I'm sorry, what?'

'Don't blame me. Blame Luka.' Adair smirked at Lucien before taking Naida's hand and disappearing through the door into the kitchen.

Lucien wanted to throttle him.

'I'm married, Lucien?' Shim crossed her arms. 'Really?'

'I was out of ideas,' he said helplessly. 'Perhaps Eran will marry her in ten years and we can tell everyone you broke up.'

Shim walked over and smacked him upside the head. 'You're the worst.'

'You adore me.' Winking at her, he finally turned to Nik. 'Do you want to get out of here? Talk a bit?'

'Yeah?'

'Yeah. Come on.'

Outside, the cool air helped waft away the tension in his body. Lucien had always breathed easier in the forest and he dragged in several breaths of respite as they moved towards the trail. The only disturbance came from a rabbit darting across the green and disappearing into the thicket, clearly in no mood to pause and inspect them.

'You know what humans don't tell us?' said Nik quietly.

'What?'

'How beautiful it is here. They say it's just a shithole. Leftover ruins from the camps. But it's not. It's poor, but it's beautiful.'

Lucien had no idea what to say to that. Gesturing for Nik to follow him, he led the way into the forest.

'I'm sorry about your mother,' he said after a beat.

'My mother?'

'You said she died. I'm sorry.'

'Oh … Thank you.'

Lucien wanted to reach out and take his hand but settled for pointing to a break in the trees up ahead. 'This is one of my favourite spots.'

On the other side of a dense cluster of trees, the sunlight, even half-hidden by the clouds, glinted off the water of a beautiful lake. The water ran clear, fish visible as they bobbed and swam. Everything inside this grove was always so calm, so serene. A place for the anxious and the meditative alike.

'I want to stay,' said Nik abruptly.

'You don't—'

'I don't have a home anymore.' Nik tilted his head, mahogany eyes catching the light and seeming even more ethereal. 'I never did. Not really. But this seems like a nice one.'

'We try.'

Perhaps something in his tone came out wrong, as Nik still looked uncertain. 'Is that all right?' he asked, shifting on the balls of his feet.

Lucien nodded, much more readily this time. 'It's all right with me.'

They appraised each other for a moment; Nik scrutinising his face for answers. 'And you don't want anything from me?'

'No,' said Lucien.

'Thanks.'

'Shouldn't thank someone for basic decency.'

Nik rubbed at the stubble shadowing his face. 'Still … A week ago, I thought I'd die in a cage. Now I've got food and clothes and … friends. It's hard not to feel stupidly grateful.'

'If you want to go, tell me,' said Lucien, wanting there to be no confusion on the matter, no misinterpretations. 'This isn't a prison. But if you leave, you can't come back. It'll bring the Enforcers down on top of us. And there are children here.'

'I wouldn't turn you in.'

'I appreciate that.'

'But I can stay?'

'Yeah. You can stay.'

A breeze picked up, gusting over them and across the water, sending the surface into a frenzy of ripples and waves. It was hard for Lucien not to think about all the times he had stood here with Geon. But where the last hundred years of Geon's life had been a torrent of madness, Nik's presence quieted Lucien's mind for the first time in centuries.

CHAPTER SIXTEEN
The Blackwood Pack

Dawn skulked into the skies grey and grim, like the night was angry it had to yield to the sun. Lucien had managed only minor amounts of sleep before giving up and leaving his study. He went for a run, took his frustration out on his punching bag, made coffee, and was just passing by his room on the way to his study when Nik opened the door.

Messy-haired from sleep, his clothes wrinkled, Nik was the picture of a well-adjusted man. There was no tension in his stance anymore, no fear. Listening carefully, Lucien discerned that his heart was beating steadily, too. The way one's heart only ever does in a peaceful home.

Lucien smiled at him, pleased that he was finally settling in. 'Sorry. Did I wake you?'

'Not at all.'

'Good. Might grab some stuff, actually?'

'Of course.' Nik stepped aside and waved him in. 'Where have you been sleeping?'

'My study.'

'That doesn't sound comfortable.'

'It's fine,' said Lucien.

He grabbed himself a change of clothes from the wardrobe and went into his bathroom to dress and brush his teeth.

'What does a Suriia actually *do*?'

The question filtered over the sound of spraying tap water and Lucien leaned out of the bathroom, the toothbrush still in his mouth. 'What do you mean?'

'Do you work?'

Lucien finished brushing his teeth, his mouth cold from mint, and walked back into the bedroom. 'Suriias aren't allowed to hold the same positions as humans,' he explained. 'So, we work around it; do this and that.'

Nik pursed his lips together in thought, his brow scrunched up rather adorably. 'But you don't, like, look Suric? Not all of you, anyways. The ghuls and vrykos, sure. But not you. Not the vylkas. Not the sbura. How do humans even know?'

Lucien crossed his arms. 'I can. Claws and fangs like any monster in your human books.'

'Even with the implant?'

'It prevents us casting spells. It doesn't prevent us changing.'

'Why bother looking like humans?'

'Why does a porcupine relax its quills? Suriias have always had multiple forms. My brother used to say it was a gift. Leftover talents from our last life. A form for fighting, power; a form for gentler moments, for loving.' Lucien shrugged. 'But the Suriias born on Earth are different. They're not … they're different.'

'How do you mean?'

'You know how vrykos drink human blood and steal their souls?'

Nik nodded.

'They don't on Salfar.'

'What changed?'

'I don't know,' said Lucien honestly. 'Vrykos on Salfar use blood magic, but they don't need blood to survive or be immortal like they do here. None of us have ever been able to figure out why. Honestly, I don't think any Suriia was meant to be born on Earth. Our bodies are for Salfar.'

Nik leaned back against the bedpost and folded his bony arms across his chest, absorbing this information. 'You never did answer my question.'

'What do I do? We own a few of the businesses in town and run the weed trade within Westend.' Cannabis was legal in the human cities, but it was banned for all Suriias.

'Which businesses?'

'A hardware shop, an outdoor shop, two gyms and a weekend spot at the farmer's market.'

Nik chuckled. 'Wait, really?'

'Have you seen how many of us live here? The weed and guns keep the roof over our heads; the legitimate businesses cover everything else.'

'How do other packs get their money? Outside the districts no one really knows much about you guys. Just rumour and bullshit.'

'Like what?'

'Like you're all cannibals.'

Lucien wasn't sure whether to feel insulted or not. 'The humans keep us on the ground, but it's across the ground that we spread. We're in every shop, every street, every town. Every pack has a legitimate source of income that's supplemented by something else. It's the only way we can live with how the humans tax us. The Chester Pack sell other drugs; things I won't let in my house. The Kinzi Pack deals in exotic pets and bootleg moonshine. Oh, and fancy automata.'

Nik absorbed this information with the air of an academic analysing history. Sometimes removing emotion made difficult subjects easier to absorb. But only sometimes.

'Did my dad ever kill anyone?'

'When it was necessary. He never killed for fun.'

'Good. That's good.'

They left it at that and headed down to the kitchen. The whistling of the kettle greeted them upon entry, the smell of tea strong in the air. Shim and Jae were the only ones there, a plate with a variety of biscuits on the wooden table between them.

'Pour the tea,' said Shim.

Rolling his eyes, Lucien went over to the stove and poured tea for everyone before joining the others. 'Lazy,' he said as she picked up one of the cups.

'Strategic, boss. I'm strategic.'

Lucien tossed a biscuit at her.

'Thanks, Luka,' said Jae. Like Nik, he seemed lightyears better than Lucien could have thought possible. There was no way to erase the lines of strain the years had etched into his face, but overall it was almost like the world had gone back in time and they were young again, untarnished by the war and all that followed after.

'We've to be in town in an hour,' said Shim. 'Ally called. Deliveries are ready.'

'Let me have coffee and we'll go.' Lucien glanced at Nik. 'Do you want to come?'

'Where you going?'

'Business.'

Nik looked surprised. 'Really? I can come?'

'If you want. Might be good to learn the ins and outs.'

'Yeah, okay.'

'Want company?' asked Jae, and there was no missing the cautious note to the question. 'I'm a bit rusty but I know the trade.'

Lucien eyed him for a second. 'You good?'

'I'm good, brother.'

'All right, then.'

Jae's shoulders sagged in relief.

There was a sudden loud knock at the backdoor. Instantly on alert, Lucien stood and moved to the door.

But it was only Henna Olen, the magister. Dressed in fine clothes, their parasol tapped on the ground with every step. The rustle of their skirts sounded like a warning; some kind of gathering swarm.

'Good morning, magister.' Lucien was not good at being warm, nor was he good at being welcoming, but there were certain boots to lick to keep his family safe. Henna was the least objectionable. And they adored him.

'My dear Mister Lightblood, you have been causing a stir.'

'Anything particularly galling to you?' he asked with a smile. There was a chance they would let him away with a warning. If he was charming enough, they let him away with a great deal.

'You didn't invite me to your enchanting,' said Henna tartly. 'I expected to be in the front row, and I wasn't even invited. I'm hurt.'

Lucien swept off his hat and bowed low. 'It was a matter of ill-timing. We were in Westend Circle.'

'Ah! So, the story is true. Come, tell me everything, my sweet. You know I hate being the last to know.'

'My dear magister, you are the first outside my family.' Lucien gestured to Nik. 'Henna Olen, this is Nik.'

'No surname?'

'Lightblood,' he supplied. In truth, Lucien didn't particularly care about Nik taking his name or not, but outside of not actually knowing Nik's surname, the Suriias would be far less inclined to attack a human with a Suriia name. And his was well known in Westend.

Henna appraised Nik with a shrewd eye. 'Come here, human,' they said, holding out a hand. 'Let me look at the latest addition to our hellish little hamlet.'

Remarkably calm, Nik walked around the table and offered Henna his hand.

'I never thought you of all creatures would take a human,' they mused aloud, looking back at Lucien. 'Then again, the Blackwood Pack is famed for its devotion to each other. And he does look like young Geon.' Their brow furrowed, considering. 'Surely, then, you were bewitched? Out of your mind?'

Lucien bowed his head. 'Surely, magister,' he said dourly. He added, 'I learned that Ashby had him as a slave for two years. Not only him, magister. Another.'

'Another?'

'A girl,' he said. 'They can both testify to Ashby's torment. Such abuse will see the Enforcers rain shit down upon us all.'

Henna nodded in thought. 'Fetch the girl.'

Shim disappeared succinctly. When she returned, Ginny was at her side. Her light brown hair was pulled away from her face which he could see was covered in freckles. She was much too thin, and her eyes darted around, but when she saw Lucien, she relaxed and walked over to stand beside him, straight-backed and defiant.

At Henna's prompting, Ginny and Nik relayed the depths of Ashby's torment.

'We were his favourites,' Ginny finished, voice thick with contempt. 'He only sold Nik because he owed someone money.'

'I think this is a simple enough matter,' said Henna, clapping their hands together, and Lucien almost sagged in relief. 'I will tell the Penziks that they'll simply have to get over it. None of us are sorry to see the last of Ashby, Lucien, but do try to avoid stabbing anyone else.'

Lucien bowed his head. 'I will try, magister. Would you care for some tea?'

'I must go, dear boy.' Henna beamed at him. 'More to see.'

'Then have something for the road,' said Naida, who had appeared behind Ginny with a basket of pastries. They couldn't really spare the food, but keeping Henna happy was more important.

Henna took the basket. 'A pleasure as always, Blackwoods.'

When Henna was gone, Lucien nodded to Nik and Ginny. 'Anyone who comes near you now will have Henna to contend with as well as the rest of us. And if any Suriia asks, use my name. It's safer.'

Ginny picked the corner of her fingernail with an anxious air. 'What's your name?'

'Lightblood.'

'I like that,' she agreed. 'Ginny Lightblood. I sound so cool.'

Lucien ruffled her hair. 'Did you get coffee?'

'Nope.'

'Get coffee and then find shoes. We're leaving for town soon. You can come if you want.'

'I'm going,' Nik added. This, it seemed, was more than enough for Ginny.

After breakfast, Lucien spent a few minutes with the pack sorting out everyone's plans for the day while Nik and Ginny dressed for the city. They reappeared twenty minutes later wearing worn but fitted trousers, boots, heavy coats and hats, knives and a pistol each sheathed to both their waists. Lucien couldn't help but grin at the sight. Human styles were sleeker, expensive, tailored; Suriias wore clothes that were hand-me-downs, homemade, cheap, salvaged or discarded. And where the silk and lace of human fashions were easily damaged, most of what Suriias wore was made of leather, cotton or wool. Dressed as they were, Nik and Ginny looked like members of the pack. Even a Suriia would mistake them for a fellow outcast if they weren't paying close attention.

'Do you even know how to use a pistol?' he asked Nik, eyeing the gun cautiously.

'Point away from self and shoot, yes?'

'More or less.'

'We'll teach them how to fight later,' said Shim with a shrug. 'They're mostly just for show. Neither gun has any bullets.'

Relieved, Lucien led the way out of the manor. It was still raining, and they all got wet as they crossed the grounds to where his steamtruck was parked. The truck had been Geon's once upon a time, and Lucien had never had the heart to get rid of it. He called it Smokestain and spent more time repairing it than not, much to his pack's amusement, but he loved his truck.

He drove first to Rolling Woods. About twenty minutes' drive out of Westend into the hillside, the ocean sinking into the horizon, Rolling Woods was a nearby farm that the pack owned and operated. Hidden in the hills, to the naked eye it was a normal shooting range and designated hunting ground. Most of the locals used it to go running or bring their dogs. But in the far backwoods, the Blackwood Pack had acres upon acres of cannabis fields.

Isha unlocked the gate when they arrived and after going over the routine checks, Lucien and Shim heaved the bags Isha and Mi had spent the morning packing into the truck. Jae taught Ginny how to take stock and enter the reports whilst Nik accompanied Lucien as he spoke to Aidan and Ally, his growers. The pair had been homeless and living on the streets when Lucien found them. His offer of work and shelter had gained him lifelong loyalty from both. Now they had green thumbs and full bellies.

'Should make bank with this load,' said Ally.

Lucien clapped him on the back. 'That's what I like to hear.'

'Going to the shop next?'

'I think Naida wanted the afternoon off,' said Shim.

'Why?'

'It's their anniversary.'

Lucien winced. 'Shit, I forgot. Yeah, tell them to take the day. There's extra chips in the stash if they want.'

Isha's eyebrows shot up. 'Yeah?'

'Yeah,' said Lucien. 'Anniversary present.'

'You old softie,' said Shim, slinging an arm around his shoulders.

In town, he made for Westley's, an automata front shop that dealt under the counter, to drop everything off. Only twenty-five, Westley was one of the few dealers Lucien hadn't had to worry about. He was honest and liked things hassle free, just like Lucien.

Across from Westley's was the local bookshop, nestled between a chemist and a barber's. Every time Lucien glanced over at Nik, he was watching the library with the sort of hungry for knowledge edge that his father had displayed.

'Hang on,' said Luke, leaving Westley with Shim and jogging over to Nik and Ginny. 'Come on,' he beckoned.

'Where are we going?'

'You guys can grab some books while I finish up here.'

Neither hesitated to race after him. From the outside, the shop wasn't much to look at. But inside it was another matter entirely. The interior was razor thin and went up, up, up, with mechanical conveyor belts that would bring the books to the ground where a mechanised arm stacked them neatly to await the reader at the bottom. Books covered every surface and were stacked floor to ceiling in places where there was no furniture for them to be put on or under.

Ekva, the owner, peered over a large tome to see who had entered her shop. Too old to be anything other than unflappable, she barely reacted to the arrival of two humans. 'Shit weather today.'

'I couldn't agree more,' said Lucien. He gestured to Nik and Ginny. 'They're with me.'

Ekva didn't press the matter and she returned to reading the book in front of her. Nik and Ginny disappeared into the stacks and Lucien sat on one of the chairs by the window.

The bell over the door dinged, signalling Jae's arrival. 'All done at Westley's,' he said. 'Shim's in the truck.'

'Good. Thanks.'

Jae nodded. 'I'm sticking around, you know?' he added, nudging Lucien with his boot. 'I won't let you down this time.'

'Don't make me a promise I'll want to rely on if you can't keep it.'

'Geon would want me to look after his son. To be at your side in his place. It's time to come home.'

'Good. It's been quiet without you.'

'If you need to go take care of business, I can stay here and watch them. I won't let anything happen.'

For a second, Lucien hesitated. The thought of leaving either alone in Westend wasn't appealing, but Jae was capable when sober, and Lucien had more than enough to do.

Thanking him, Lucien stood and wandered through the maze of books to find Nik and Ginny. They were both in the far corner, each with growing piles of books around them.

Promising them he'd return in a couple of hours, Lucien left the duo safe amongst the stacks and headed out to finish his errands with Shim. He tried not to worry about Nik and Ginny and focus instead on work, but the pair wouldn't leave his thoughts for even a second. The worry for them was wholly new and he didn't know how to process any of it.

By late afternoon they were back on main street, the day's work having gone curiously smoothly despite how distracted he'd been.

Pulling up in front of the bookshop, Lucien honked. Moments later, Nik, Ginny and Jae were clambering into the backseat.

'Find much?' he asked, eyeing their bulging bags in bemusement. 'I always thought the manor needed a fourth library.'

'Loads,' said Nik, not far from giddy. 'Mostly folklore, philosophy and history.'

Lucien nodded in approval and glanced back at Ginny. 'And you?'

'Books on meditation. And a few mysteries.'

'Excellent choices.'

Twilight was just starting to creep in when they reached the house.

Leaving the others, Lucien headed straight into his study to telephone the Blackfeather Pack to express his irritation at Trenton's failure to show up at the arena. Inevitably, what he hoped would be a two minute phone call lasted half an hour.

After rearranging the meeting at a new location for later in the week, his head now pounding with frustration, Lucien hung up. He rubbed his temples, mentally drained.

A soft knock at the door preceded Nik sticking his head inside. 'Adair says dinner's ready.'

'I'll go down in a minute.' Waving at Nik to sit down, Lucien reclined in his chair, resting his ankle on the adjacent knee. 'So, what do you think of everything we do? Get your answers?'

'It's so … normal.' Nik held out a hand. 'Yeah … normal.'

'We're as much a part of this world as humans even if they like to pretend otherwise.'

'It's nice, though.'

'What? Shady business deals?'

'No, the set up. The way you run everything. It's like a family.'

'We are a family.'

'It's nice,' Nik reiterated.

The sincerity in his claim hit Lucien harder than he could have expected. For the first time in a long time, he felt like he'd done something right. Something good.

The kitchen was bustling with energy and chatter when they came down minutes later. Heavenly smells wafted up from the bowls of food that the children were placing in the centre of the table. A potato and spinach bake laden with seasoning and cheese sat beside a bowl of tofu and vegetables mixed together with the egg noodles Eran and Kalid had spent all morning making. It was topped off with a rich brown sauce. Naida had also baked a fresh loaf of sourdough bread and the sight of it, white and fluffy, a stick of butter in the dish alongside, made Lucien's stomach growl.

There was also the wine that Isha had traded for at the market; for Shara and Kalid, she poured her special roselle juice. The greenhouse at the back of the property was Isha's domain and no one dared touch it for fear of losing the precious collection of herbs, berries and flowers she'd collected over the years from traders in the underground market.

'We need to talk to Vane in the morning,' said Adair, taking a seat. 'The accounts are wrecking my head. I hate numbers.' He grimaced at the papers in front of him, spreading out several dizzying spreadsheets between the bowls and plates. 'Something's not adding up. We're poor, but we're poorer than we should be.'

'By how much?'

'Thousands.'

'Seriously?' grunted Lucien.

'Afraid so.'

Nik picked up one of the papers curiously. 'Can I?'

Lucien waved him on. 'Go for it.'

Kalid, Shara and Adair brought over the last of the food while Mi retrieved several bottles of beer and ginger ale from the icebox in the corner.

The instant everyone was seated, the food began to disappear. To Lucien's relief, both Nik and Ginny ate heartily. They might have been underfed and scrawny, but their appetites hadn't deserted them.

'Anyone see the headlines?' Adair's thick eyebrows were drawn together pensively. 'The proposed referendum for integrating the universities was rejected.'

None of them were surprised, but disappointment darkened all their faces. It was rare for a Suriia to go to university but with strong recommendations and a great deal of bribery, the humans occasionally allowed it. With the right acquaintances, a Suriia could assimilate and live a quiet life with access to food and healthcare, and no raids by the Enforcers in the middle of the night. Getting enough money for bribery was all but impossible, however, so they tried to go about Eran's applications the right way. Now there wouldn't be another chance for years.

Lucien skimmed the article before tossing it aside and returning to his food. Bigotry and blind hatred knew no bounds, whether on Earth or Salfar.

'I didn't want to go anyway,' said Eran. Upbeat as he sounded, Lucien knew he was upset.

'Things will get better,' said Adair, squeezing his son's shoulder bracingly.

'When?' asked Shara.

None of them thought fast enough to lie. None of them, that was, except Mi.

She whipped three bars of chocolate from her coat pocket and held them out to the children. 'Nothing's permanent,' she said with a confidence so smooth that Lucien almost believed her. 'Not even when it seems so bad that it'll never get right again – it will. One day.'

Shara's eyes were now saucers of hope and yearning. 'Promise?'

'I promise.'

When Lucien caught Mi's eye, he gave her a grateful nod. What little childhood the kids could find, Lucien wanted them to have.

'You're being robbed,' said Nik abruptly, drawing everyone's attention. He was holding one of the documents and eating with his other hand. 'It's not a calculation error. It's fraud.'

'What?' said Mi, taking the paper he'd been examining. 'What makes you say that?'

Nik pointed at various entries. 'See? A good chunk of what you're bringing in isn't actually coming into *you*.'

'How do you know about this?' asked Lucien.

'Numbers are easy for me. Makes sense if you know what to watch out for.'

'And you know?'

Nik set the papers down. 'I helped my mum survive the streets. I know more than you think.'

Lucien didn't doubt it. 'I don't know how we missed that,' he mused, frowning. 'Vane should have caught it.'

'Vane's probably the one stealing from you.'

It wasn't the first time they'd been screwed over in their legitimate earnings, but it was a hassle Lucien was in no way in the mood for. 'Adair,' he said heavily, 'Shim. Do you two want to come sort it out with me tomorrow?'

They both nodded.

After dinner, everyone splintered off in different directions. Lucien and Nik wandered upstairs in silence. But it was thankfully a companionable silence, not a strained one. In the upstairs hallway, they stilled outside the bedroom door.

'Are you coming in?' asked Nik.

'I have some reading to do,' said Lucien. 'Things for tomorrow.'

'Want to do it in the bedroom?'

'You don't mind?'

'I've never liked my own company.'

Lucien almost laughed. Not because it was funny, but because he sounded like Geon. 'Sure,' he said at length. He then gestured to his study. 'Let me just get my things.'

Nik nodded and disappeared into the room. Lucien gathered what he needed from his office and returned to the bedroom. Nik was curled up on the window seat once more.

Claiming his favourite chair, Lucien began sorting through the receipt books. He was going to have to review everything to ascertain how utterly Vane had screwed them over. The human tax authority loved sending Suriias to prison for even the most minor of mistakes in their paperwork.

'Lucien?'

He didn't look up, too distracted by a transaction he couldn't remember making. 'Everything all right?'

'I was just wondering about something.'

'What is it?'

'Was I the first human in this house? Before Ginny, I mean.'

Lucien raised his head, taking in the curious creases in Nik's face. 'Yes.'

'Is it weird?'

'No.' But there was clearly something weighing on his mind. 'Are you worried?'

'Not about you or anyone else here.' Nik rubbed at his jaw, stretching the cut on his lip and tearing it open. The scent of his blood made Lucien tense automatically, but Nik didn't notice. 'The Enforcers, yes. The Keepers. The other packs.'

'No one's going to touch you.'

'That's kind of hard to believe.'

'My pack is the only one in Westend whose members have not been beaten or imprisoned or assaulted by the Enforcers. And that's not because we're lucky. I have more than a few tricks up my sleeve, clip or no clip. So long as you listen to me, you're safe.'

'I'm glad you won over Raguel.'

'I'm glad you're safe now.'

Nik's lips curved in the most minor of smiles. 'You know, I can hardly remember what it's like to have a family.'

'You have one,' Lucien assured him. 'And I won't let anything happen to you.'

'Because I'm Geon's son or because of the spell?'

Lucien felt suddenly made of glass and feared speaking would shatter his poor attempt at maintaining control of the situation. Could he tell Nik that he thought him handsome? Could he tell him that he wanted him? That it had nothing to do with the enchantment but was entirely down to the fact that he'd never liked someone quite so much before?

No. He couldn't say any of those things. Because Nik was traumatised. Because Nik was human and Lucien was a thousand times more powerful. Because on the off chance that Nik ever even liked him back, Lucien knew he'd never be able to touch him. Because he'd *won* Nik. Like a trophy. And the mere fact of that made bile lap at the back of his throat, like his insides were rejecting the truth.

After a terribly long pause, something that wasn't the right truth, but was a truth all the same, fell from his lips like a confession. 'My brother used to say that when you save someone, they become your responsibility. And that's true. But for me, at least, I know what it's like to be bought and sold. I know what it's like to have no hope left. At the end of my world, your father appeared and saved my life. It's why I have hope at all. No one should ever have to close their eyes and wonder who will come for them when they're frightened and in trouble. I had your father. Now I have my pack. I can't give you much, but I can give you that. Whatever the future holds, from now on, you have a family who will always protect you. Come for you. You will never be forgotten.'

Nik stared at Lucien for a long time after he trailed off, immobile, hazel eyes fixed with astonishment. And even from across the room, Lucien could hear Nik's heartbeat.

How loudly it was racing.

CHAPTER SEVENTEEN
Try, Try Again

From the outside, the accounting office attempted to exude respectability, although how greatly it achieved its aims was left to the eye of the beholder. The gardens leading up to the front door teamed with well-manicured flowers that weren't native to the island, and statues made of shiny metal or sleek marble that were too expensive for both the building and the street stuck up at random between the flowers, as if the landscaper hadn't the faintest idea of where to set them. The brick building had also recently been painted a harsh white, ensuring that the office stood out against the neighbouring wooden and haphazard shops that were barely making rent. To top it off, the fancy lettering over the entrance was embossed in tacky gold. But the colour matched Vane's interior design insofar as the inside was equally as showy. Really, Vane's desire to flaunt how much money he'd acquired ought to have been a clue as to how underhanded he was.

The conversation, predictably, did not go well.

'You stole from us,' Lucien repeated for the third time. 'That's not something we can just let go of.'

Vane, no longer pretending to be innocent of the charges, sneered at him. 'You can't prove it.'

'We can, actually,' said Adair.

'And who are you going to report to?' Vane's words dripped with knowing confidence. 'No one is going to take your word seriously in a court of law. No court would even entertain your presence unless you're in handcuffs. Your businesses are half off the books and one word from me will land you in prison for life. If they don't hang you.'

The brutal fact of the matter was: Vane wasn't wrong. No one in the human world, and no Suriia with standing, would ever defend them. Henna liked Lucien and thus helped him wiggle out of trouble here and there, but Henna was a rare exception to the rule. Lucien's name was dirt in every office of law in the country. There was nothing he could do aside from walk away.

Giving the accountant a disgusted look, he put his hat back on and stood. 'I hope you get what you deserve,' he called over his shoulder as he walked out, Adair and Shim flanking him.

'Fucking dick,' said Shim under her breath as they headed for the truck.

The roads were blessedly deserted on the drive back to the house. Grey skies and heavy humidity in the air hinted at a lacklustre afternoon to follow the wretched morning.

'We'll have to find a new accountant,' he said belatedly.

'Why?' Shim propped her boots on the dashboard. 'We can do it ourselves.'

'I am rotten with numbers. You're worse. And take your filthy boots off my truck. I just cleaned her.'

'Yeah,' she said with a rueful laugh. 'But your husband's clearly good with them. Let's make him our new accountant.'

Lucien tensed. 'Don't call him that.'

'That's what he is.'

'The enchantment was necessary to save his life. But we're not together.'

Shim wisely noted the tone of his voice and let the matter drop with an apologetic nod.

'May as well give him something to do,' said Adair, far less afeared of Lucien's bad moods. 'He'll lose his mind sitting around the house all day.'

'He's reading like it's a dying artform.'

'You'd read all the time too if you'd been locked in a cage.'

'It's not the worst idea, boss,' added Shim. 'Gives him a job and keeps him out of the other unsavoury businesses we've got.'

'You should have led with that,' said Lucien. The idea of keeping Nik out of town and thus out of harm instantly lessened the tension tightening his gut.

Exiting the thoroughfare onto their winding country road, Lucien rolled down his window and let the fresh smells of wet grass fill the truck.

Half the house was outside when he pulled up. Shara and Kalid were in the midst of a sparring session, Mi and Isha were on the porch mending old boots, and Nik was curled up on the porch swing with Ginny, both absorbed in their books.

As Lucien neared, he set his book aside and waved. 'How was the meeting?'

'Fruitless. How'd you like to be our new accountant?'

'Really?' Nik beamed at him. 'I'd love to.'

How anyone could love numbers baffled Lucien, but he'd take joy where he found it. 'Then the job's yours. Adair can show you everything,' he added. 'Not my skillset.'

'What is your skillset?'

'Not finishing his assignments,' said Adair, opening the door and waving them inside.

'You guys went to school together?' Nik's eyes were saucers of copper curiosity as he followed them.

Adair burst into laughter. 'No,' he said cheerily. 'I was his teacher.'

'Seriously?'

Lucien nodded. 'Tutored your father, too.'

Nik straightened up at this bit of information, looking eagerly from Lucien to Adair. 'You did?'

'I tried,' said Adair. 'Geon didn't like to listen.'

'He read everything,' said Jae, appearing from the kitchen. 'He just hated being told to read anything.'

'I started telling him not to read things just to get him to,' said Adair wickedly.

Nik grinned. 'Did it work?'

'Until he figured it out.'

As the conversation drifted to everyone's opinion on formalised education, Lucien found himself regarding Nik, whose whole demeanour seemed to have brightened at the mention of his father. Twelve years without his best friend and he still felt like he'd been robbed. How must Nik feel?

After lunch, Lucien headed back out with Mi, Isha and Shim to check in on the vandalised shop, leaving Nik and Ginny with Adair and Jae. Nik and Ginny both pestered him about coming along, but his suggestion that they stay at home and redecorate one of the back rooms to be Nik's office proved a smart decision as there were Enforcers in the centre of the town when he parked outside the hardware shop an hour later.

'We could just go home,' said Isha unhappily.

'No,' said Shim. 'We have too much to do.'

'We have no reason to hide,' said Lucien. But saying it and feeling like it was true was a difficult task even for himself.

Huffing at himself, he got out. An Enforcer a few paces away came over immediately to check the plates and registration on his truck; they looked almost disappointed when the machine beeped that everything was dated correctly.

Ignoring him, Lucien unlocked the door to the shop and led Isha, Mi and Shim inside.

Two Enforcers followed them into the shop. The silent pair checked the shelves without a word, as if Lucien and his pack didn't exist; when they went behind the counter and began rifling through the shelves, Shim clenched her jaw. Lucien shook his head. The last thing they needed was a citation for a rude remark. The wrong word could get them a prison sentence, too.

Finding no contraband, the Enforcers left the shop like disgruntled hyenas.

'I hate this world,' said Shim when the door closed.

Lucien couldn't honestly disagree or agree. Salfar hadn't been great, either.

The rest of the day blessedly passed without incident and they had enough customers to make it less than a total waste, but by the time they left Westend Circle and headed back to the house, Lucien was more than ready to be done.

He didn't say much during dinner – which was a mouth-watering stew with a side of potatoes, homemade bread and grilled vegetables. He couldn't handle all of his mounting problems at once, but he also couldn't figure out which ought to take precedence over the rest.

His plate barely touched, he excused himself without explanation halfway through the meal and spent the rest of the night in the barn taking his feelings out on the old punching bag, bruising his knuckles a little more with each swing.

It was well past midnight by the time he returned to the house. Everyone was asleep, soft, snuffling snores reaching his ears even downstairs. But one member of the house wasn't sleeping soundly.

Nik's sharp cry cut through the serenity of the shuttered house and Lucien shot up the stairs. Slipping inside his bedroom, he went to Nik's side and shook him awake. He'd been thrashing, badly, and the blankets were half pulled off the mattress.

Nik started, almost pulling away from him. When he realised it was Lucien, he relaxed and dropped his head back on the pillows. 'Sorry,' he muttered. 'Was I loud?'

'No.' Lucien appraised him, worry dancing in his chest like marionettes on a string. 'What were you dreaming about?'

'Nothing good.'

'Is there anything I can do?'

'Can you stay?'

Lucien hesitated. 'I'm not sure that's—'

'Please. I hate sleeping alone and the nightmares are making it bloody impossible.'

Lucien acquiesced after several tense seconds. 'Sure.' What else was he supposed to say to that request?

Joining Nik on the bed without taking off his boots or coat, he sat stiffly in the corner, not quite sure what to do next. He hadn't slept next to someone in years.

Without a word, Nik rolled over and turned out the lights. Remarkably, he fell asleep mere minutes later and soon the whole room was filled with the gentle susurrus of his breathing. But if Lucien listened carefully, he could hear Nik's heart, which sounded like a rabbit, trapped in his chest.

Part of Lucien increasingly wanted to press Nik to talk about what he'd been through. He tried to remind himself that letting Nik tell him how to help was probably a wiser course of action than telling Nik to talk about it when he wasn't ready. *Tried* being the operative word. Memories of Geon's suicide couldn't be reasoned away and all Lucien did as the hours slid by was obsess over Nik's mental health.

Distracted as he was, Lucien got no sleep and he was wideawake when light returned to the skies hours later.

Nik didn't wake up slowly. When fingers of light snuck between the curtains and coaxed him to consciousness, his eyes snapped open, his heart rate rocketed, and he went stiffer than a board. Yet it took only a moment for him to calm back down.

'You okay?' asked Lucien carefully.

'Fine,' said Nik.

'Want to talk about it?'

'Talk about my stunning case of PTSD? No, I'm good.' Nik sat up, brushing matted hair out of his eyes.

Lucien nodded understandingly. It wasn't like he was keen to relive his own trauma. 'Can I get you anything?'

'Coffee?'

Grateful to have something to do other than gawp like an idiot, Lucien left the bedroom and trotted down the stairs to the kitchen. Coffee was already gurgling in the pot on the stove, the heady smell calming in a familiar way.

Jae sat alone at the table, nose buried in a book. He glanced up when Lucien walked in. 'Good morning.'

''Morning,' Lucien mumbled. He filled two cups with coffee and, remembering how Nik liked his, added two sugar cubes and a dash of milk to one. 'More coffee?'

'Yes, please.'

'When was the last time you slept?'

'It's been a while,' said Jae. 'You?'

'Yep.' Lucien cocked his head at the door by way of a farewell and headed back upstairs.

Nik was up and dressed when he stepped into the bedroom and he took the cup gratefully.

'Breakfast?' Lucien didn't feel particularly hungry himself, but Nik seemed like he needed a distraction from his own mind. 'Or we could go for a run?'

Nik eyed him critically. 'A run?'

'Yeah,' said Lucien. 'You know, the speed faster than walking.'

'Sure,' agreed Nik. 'Let's go for a run.'

Minutes later they were heading out into the brisk morning. Mist still clung to the ground and the air was damp.

The path was a well-worn dirt trail that had been trampled upon by the pack so many times it had become a compacted road. They ran without speaking and the calm sounds of the forest provided a soothing soundtrack that filled the silence blossoming between them. Nik easily kept up with him, although Lucien checked himself a few times automatically, not wanting to exhaust him.

By the time they reached the end of the trail, the house once again in view, Lucien slowed to a walk and Nik copied him. They parted in the entrance hall, exchanging nods and smiles that Lucien didn't know how to interpret.

He spent most of the day in his study, combing through his files. It was a tedious, thankless job, but mindless paperwork was a blessed alternative to how chaotic things had once been. Nowadays, he didn't mind a little monotony.

Just as his head started to spin from staring at numbers for hours, there was a knock on his office door, and he looked up.

It was Ginny.

'Are you busy?' she asked, hands twisting and untwisting. Her mousy brown hair fell messily out of her ponytail, only adding to her nervous air. For one so fierce, she sometimes seemed so small.

Lucien waved her inside. 'Everything all right?'

'I was ... I was wondering ...' Rather than sit down, she leaned against the bookshelf and picked up a small bronze globe that he had acquired at a flea market some years ago. She rolled it around her hands, not looking at him. 'Everyone here knows how to fight.'

'We never got much say in the matter.'

'I want to know how to fight.' She held his gaze with unchecked determination. 'If I can fight, maybe I'll be able to sleep.'

Lucien watched her for a moment. 'Anyone you want to teach you?'

'You.'

Surprised, he sat back in his chair. 'I don't teach anymore.'

'Why?'

'I'm not nice.'

'You win.'

That was debateable, but he found it increasingly difficult to refuse her. After another minute, he rolled his eyes, relenting. 'Be downstairs at six tomorrow morning.'

'Really?'

'Really. But I warn you, I'm not a good teacher. I'm gruff and mean and don't have much patience.'

She put the globe down and clapped her hands together. 'I just need to not fear the shadows.'

'Shadows are just dark things we imagine to be nefarious. But things that are intangible aren't worthy of fear. The real things, those are what to fear.'

'Well, it's a good thing I've got such a good teacher, isn't it?'

Such a simple thing to say and yet it astonished and delighted him in equal measure. Acceptance from the offspring of one of their oppressors wasn't something he ever thought he would receive, yet Ginny offered it offhandedly, as if it weren't even a question up for debate. He knew he shouldn't care, but Lucien craved acceptance the way kings craved power.

The rest of the day passed uneventfully, although he found himself tuning out the work as the voices of the others downstairs distracted him. Nik's laugh filtered up from the kitchen and left him feeling strange.

Forcing himself to focus, he smoked in agitation, desperately trying to clear his head, until he gave up altogether and went for another, faster run on his own. When he wasn't holding back for Nik's benefit, he was faster than a wolf.

The Blackwood grounds went up through the forest and backfields, stopping at the lake to the southeast. Here he lingered. Everything smelled like earth and wood, pine and blossoms. But in the distance, smoke billowed up from the factories like an omen. He used to stand on the bank and glare across the water, watching, wondering, waiting for the next war. The next slice of violence.

Now, as he stood there, letting the cool night air kiss his skin, he thought of something different. A week ago, he thought of life only in terms of existing. Of surviving. One foot in front of the other. And then he met Nik, and Ginny, and now he thought of the future. For the first time in a long time, when he looked into the future, he *had* a future to look forward to.

It had been centuries since he'd been truly powerful, but the thrumming of his blood was familiar. A call to arms he had tried to bury was making itself known once more. The question was: did he cling to the safety of the cage they'd allowed themselves to thrive in – or did he tear it apart and start over? Again.

Only when it was well after midnight did he head back to the house.

He found Nik in his bedroom reading, but he set his book aside when Lucien closed the door.

'Didn't think you'd ever come in.'

'Were you waiting for me?' Removing his coat, Lucien hung it on the back of the door. He kicked off his boots and unfastened the buttons on his shirt cuffs. Being alone with Nik felt oddly domestic, but he knew that things between them weren't that friendly.

'Not much a fan of the dark at the minute.'

Lucien winced. 'I'm sorry. I would have come in sooner. I wanted to give you space.'

'I don't need space from you.'

'Are you sure?'

'Aren't we friends?'

Not expecting that, it took Lucien a moment to nod. 'Yes, I suppose we are.'

'Friends keep each other safe, right? I'd sleep with Ginny, but she kicks.'

'She does look like a kicker.'

'Hogs the blankets, too.'

Lucien couldn't help his grin. 'I can't say I'm not glad to know you prefer my bed – if only because I don't kick.' The admission left him unintended and he caught Nik's eye, not sure how he would take it.

To his surprise, a wry smile spread across Nik's face and he patted the space beside him. 'Unless I smell bad?'

Lucien walked over and sat on the corner of the bed. 'Trust me,' he grunted, 'you do not smell bad.'

'Think I smell good?'

Lucien held his gaze, considering. He had been in love once, but it was so long ago he barely remembered the feeling. Talo was a blacksmith from the city. Like so many in those days, Talo died much too young. Executed without cause or trial. After that, Lucien's marriage to Astril was arranged and he wasn't allowed to look at anyone else without risking his father's wrath. In the centuries since, he hadn't looked twice at anyone. It hurt too much. Now, everything felt like it was changing. Speeding up without his permission. Therefore, while a dozen suggestive quips sprang to mind in response to Nik's question, he swallowed them all. If there was one thing Lucien knew all too well, it was the disgust of unsolicited propositioning.

So he said nothing.

CHAPTER EIGHTEEN
Luk and Gin

Ginny was already waiting at the bottom of the stairs when Lucien came down early the next morning. She was dressed in Shim's old clothes and she flashed a bright, chipper smile at him, far more energetic than he.

'Ready?'

'Ready,' she said gamely.

It was hard not to find her utterly endearing.

The world was mostly asleep when they stepped outside. A thick, cold fog still hung heavy in the air, obscuring anything more than two paces away. Only a few creatures of the night remained awake to greet them: the fireflies, who bobbed about sluggishly, and the owls, who hooted in the surrounding forest, signalling their presence and warning all to stay away.

Lucien led Ginny across the dark grounds towards the old barn. Opening the doors, he turned the gaslights on one by one. The pale light took a while to illuminate the full breadth of the training room, but when it did, he heard her squeak in surprise.

'Approve?' he asked, almost worried that she wouldn't.

'It's wicked.' She pointed to a vicious throwing blade. 'I want to know how to use that.'

'One step at a time.'

'So, what first?'

It had been years since he'd trained anyone. Shim and Adair tended to run most of the drills for the pack, and he kept to himself. But as he put Ginny through a series of basic beginner steps, he realised how much he missed it. Geon's death had kept him from ever wanting to bring anyone new into the fold, but there was something inspirational about Ginny. He felt the need to try harder simply because she was. No matter how many drills he set up, how many times he told her to start again, to adjust this stance or that, she never backed down or asked for a break. Ginny was skinny, but determined, and had natural talent to make up for her small size. She was quick and wiry, and every time she fell, she rolled her eyes, laughed, and stood up again.

When they returned to the house two hours later, both were soaked in sweat and neither could stop grinning.

Mi, Isha, Adair and Shim were seated at the kitchen table when they trudged in. The wonderful smells of eggs, butter scones and hot coffee wafted up Lucien's nose upon entry and his stomach growled.

Adair raised an eyebrow at their appearance. 'Training?'

'Yep.' Lucien dropped into one of the chairs. Picking up a napkin, he wiped the sweat off his face. 'Anything new?'

'Henna wants you to drop by.'

'Should be fun.'

'Can I come?' said Ginny, brushing matted hair back from her face.

Lucien shook his head. 'If we're seen with a human, we'd be shot on sight. The marriage loophole only works inside the district. Henna lives beyond the gates.'

'Do the Keepers report to the Enforcers about humans living in here?'

Shim passed Ginny the jug of juice. 'Sometimes. Not often, but if they're feeling greedy or stupid or cruel, yes. It's why we're keeping a low profile.'

Ginny made a face. 'The rules are so stupid. They act like you don't have thoughts and feelings.'

'To them we're not people,' said Adair matter-of-factly. 'We're monsters.'

'As far as I'm aware, kidnapping and rape happen on both sides of the districts,' said Ginny. 'It's not the Suriias ruling over the humans; it's not the Suriias ordering registers and bans and segregations and executions. You didn't start this. The ones in charge did.'

Lucien was still mulling over her words when Nik appeared in the doorway, diverting his attention. 'Good morning,' he greeted. 'Sleep well?'

Brushing mussed hair out of his eyes, Nik nodded. 'Where'd you get off to?'

'Gin wanted to train.'

Nik and Ginny shared a look. 'Finally got him to cave?' he surmised.

'Told you I could.'

The idea of them talking about him made Lucien's interest pique. 'Talking about me?'

'Of course,' said Ginny. 'You're like our hero.'

'Is that so?'

'Maybe.' Nik held his gaze for a moment, a smile playing on his lips, before he sat down beside Lucien.

'Aw, boss,' crowed Isha. 'You old softie.'

Lucien threw a chunk of scone at her. She ducked and crumbs went everywhere.

'You're cleaning that up,' said Mi.

Everyone laughed.

When breakfast was finished, Lucien bade the others farewell and headed out to his truck. But he was barely out the door when it opened behind him and Nik darted out.

'I know human cities. I should come.'

'If I'm seen bringing you back into Westend, they'll shoot me on sight.'

'Even if I tell them I'm not a slave?'

'Even if.'

'But—'

'No.' Lucien stopped at his truck, his hand gripping the handle as his anxiety mounted. 'Give me this one.'

'Will you be careful?'

'I'm always careful.'

'Promise?'

Lucien wasn't prepared for the sudden surge of ... something inside his chest. For reasons he didn't want to dwell on, he still didn't expect Nik to care about him. 'I promise.'

Reluctant, Nik stepped back. But it was a reluctance they shared, and Lucien held his gaze in the rear view mirror as he drove away. Each second that passed increased the off-kilter feeling. He'd always fretted about leaving the pack alone, but with Nik around, the sense of unease had morphed into a chronic, gnawing swill in the pit of his stomach.

The gate out of Westend was several miles down the thoroughfare and there were no other automobiles on the road that morning to concern himself with. Still, he hated going near the checkpoints even when he had nothing to hide.

Luckily, there were no Enforcers lingering about that morning. Lucien bowed his head to the Keepers as he drove past. Jacques and Damien nodded back; children of the Blackfeather Pack, both had gone to school amongst the humans and spent enough years in the system to be given the job of Keeper. They were snitches, but he couldn't really fault them for it.

As he drove past the fields, the world seemed to move forward in time with every passing minute. The human cities were always a strange experience. Unlike the Suriia towns, which hadn't changed much over the years – where, because of regulations and restrictions, progress had been stalled for decades – the human cities were sprawling and vast. Their steam engines flew, their food was in excess, and their products were cheap, sourced from the minimum wage labour given to Suriias with no other choice.

Henna lived in one of the few neighbourhoods which allowed Suriia magisters residency, provided they agree to invasive examinations and testing, and had to report and verify their whereabouts and acquaintances whenever asked. Yet life amongst the humans was as affluent as any Suriia could get, and Lucien felt wholly out of place as he stepped out of the truck in front of Henna's house.

Jogging up the path, aware that his every move was being tracked by nosy, bigoted neighbours, he knocked twice on the door, bouncing on the balls of his feet.

An Enforcer in uniform paused on the footpath, one hand on his weapon, just waiting for an excuse to shoot.

To Lucien's relief, Henna appeared instantly and ushered him inside.

'Thank you for coming, my dear,' they said once the door was shut.

'Of course.'

After a few minutes of ritual chitchat over cups of tea, they pushed a file across the table towards him. 'I found your girl.'

'My girl?' Lucien opened the folder. Ginny's picture stared back at him.

'That, dear boy, is a very big problem.'

He turned the page, reading the scribbled report quickly and feeling sicker by the second. 'Does anyone else know about this?'

'Only me.'

Lucien closed the file with a snap. 'I'd be most appreciative if it could remain that way,' he said calmly.

Henna's smile turned conspiratorial. 'Of course, dear boy. You know I love my secrets. Almost as much as I love my garden.'

Without missing a beat, Lucien produced the bulbs he'd brought. They were from Salfar, and the flowers and fruits they created were widely sought after and could bring in vast quantities of wealth. A few were growing behind their cannabis fields, but he had saved these for when he knew he'd need them.

Henna waved a hand over them and the air glittered with magic. 'Oh! Lucien! They're perfect!'

He let them drop into Henna's hand. 'All I want is my pack safe, magister. You know me. I don't want trouble.'

Henna nodded several times, not taking their eyes off the bribe. 'Consider yourself my first port of call on all matters regarding your humans.'

'Always a pleasure,' he said, bowing his head before taking his leave.

When Lucien returned home, he found Ginny in her room, doing press-ups on the floor. He paused in the doorway and watched her thoughtfully. Without a long-sleeve shirt, he could see the damage which paraded itself across her skin. There were more scars than he could count, and most looked to have been brutal once. She was sixteen years old. She was more innocent than most of them. It shouldn't matter where she came from. He'd never cared that Geon and Jae had come from nothing, or that his introduction to Shim was pulling her father's knife out of his stomach.

Catching sight of him, Ginny paused mid-press-up and stood, dusting off her hands. 'Hi! How'd it go in town?'

Lucien closed the door and walked over to her, holding out the file. With a frown, Ginny opened it.

'Why didn't you tell me?' There was no anger in the words, which he found strange. If anyone else had lied to him about something so important, he would have lost his temper.

Ginny closed the file. 'This is my home,' she said simply. 'You said so.'

They appraised each other, both wondering what the other was thinking. But he could no sooner tell her to leave than he could tell Shim or Adair to go.

'No one else can know,' he said, taking the file back. 'I mean it. Not anyone. Not even Nik.'

'I won't say anything,' she promised. 'I'm not stupid. I didn't want to be kidnapped but I don't want to go back.'

'It says your fiancé is searching for you.'

'My parents told me I had to marry him when I was twelve. I hate him.'

Twelve.

Lucien wanted to track her parents down and make his feelings known and it took a concerted effort to stay calm. 'He does look obnoxious.'

'He's vile.' Ginny rubbed the corner of her eye. 'He wanted children with me when I was thirteen. I ran away from home and that's how I got snatched.'

Lucien raised a hand, hesitated, then put it gently on her shoulder. 'You're safe here. Just don't lie about things that could get us all killed.'

'I won't.'

'Okay.'

'Lucien?'

'Yeah, kid?'

'You're really not going to make me leave?'

'No,' he assured her. 'My father arranged my marriage once, too.'

'Did you have to go through with it?'

'Yes.'

Empathy pooled in her brown eyes. 'What happened?'

'My best friend came and helped me escape.'

'Friends are good.'

'Friends are everything,' he murmured. 'Friends are family.'

'Can humans be family?'

'Anyone can be family.'

She threw her arms around him. 'I won't let you down,' she said. 'I'll be useful. I promise.'

Lucien found that he didn't doubt that in the slightest.

'Also,' she said when she drew back. 'I thought of a nickname for you.'

'I don't do nicknames.'

'Tough.' She stuck her tongue out. 'I'm going to call you Luk.'

He scoffed. 'That's awful.'

'Nope. Luk and Gin. How cool is that?'

'We sound like a beverage.'

'A beverage of death.'

It was a horrible joke and he was still laughing when he left her room. In his study, a low fire crackled in the chimney as usual and he walked over to it, the file in hand. The heat from the hearth instantly prompted sweat to bead on his forehead, but he didn't back away. Kneeling down, he dropped the file onto the coals.

He didn't move until the flames consumed every single page, all trace of who Ginny was reduced to ash. Others would be looking for her in the human districts, but as far as the Suriias were concerned, she was a nobody. Just another unfortunate soul to wander across their path.

CHAPTER NINETEEN
The Iron Blade

Like clockwork, Jimmy the delivery boy brought the morning newspaper a little after dawn each day. A century before, Suriias published daily papers. The war brought out a slew of them. The number of journalists arrested during those years, disappearing without a trace, still kept Lucien awake at night. Now papers were censored and the only Suriia contributors were Keepers or magisters. But still the paper came, and still he read the headlines.

Lucien caught the paper before it hit the ground and flicked back a chip. Jimmy caught the chip with all the deftness of a sports star. A young vryko, he was a quiet, calm lad and a good friend of Eran's.

'Thank you, Mister Lightblood!' he called, waving energetically.

Tapping the brim of his hat, Lucien wandered back towards the house, unrolling the ink-heavy pages. The front page had all the usual nonsense humans concerned themselves with: materialistic grievances that Lucien couldn't have cared about in a million years. But on the back page was an announcement that caught his eye. The travelling expo had come to Westend for its yearly show and would be open all weekend.

The others were gathered around the table drinking coffee, most still wearing their pyjamas, when he walked in. Claiming the empty chair beside Nik, Lucien passed the paper to Adair before pouring himself a cup of coffee.

'Want to go?' asked Adair, clearly finding the expo advertisement first.

As much as he did, Lucien shook his head. 'We should probably keep a low profile. There'll be Keepers there.'

Nik tilted his head, black hair falling in front of his eyes. 'Where?'

'The expo.'

'Expo?'

'It's honestly nothing,' said Lucien. 'I have enough to be getting on with. I don't need a day of mindless distraction.'

'Everyone does,' said Shim. 'Go with Adair. We'll be fine.'

'We will,' agreed Nik. 'You need a break from reports before numbers tattoo themselves on your eyeballs. Go.'

After a few more half-hearted protests, Lucien agreed to go with Adair and, snatching up a few buttered scones to eat on the drive, the pair clambered into the truck.

The morning was cool and beautiful, the air scented with cut grass and morning dew, the sun hidden behind a line of thick clouds that resembled smoky candy floss. A good number of motorcars and trucks packed the roads already, along with the odd carriage or buggy. Not everyone in Westend could afford an automotive, after all.

Past the curved, unpaved road out of the centre of town, was a rickety metal bridge that led to the small isle where the expo was held. Away from Westend Circle, away from the poverty of the districts and the prying eyes of the human towns, the isle was a breath of fresh air.

At the entrance to the exposition centre, Henna stood with several Keepers and the heads of a few packs. They nodded to

Lucien as he drove through and he waved his hand. He didn't miss the scowl on the faces of some of the others, but he paid them no heed. Picking at a wound that was festering was ill-advised, to say the least.

Parking in the first empty space he found, Lucien and Adair got out and joined the jostling crowd making its way into the building. Inside, the chaos and joy of sellers and buyers brought a fresh atmosphere to Westend. A kind they rarely got. While the buyers were all Suriia, many of the sellers and innovators were human. Humans, after all, weren't barred from anywhere. The prices were always higher than they were for the human buyers in the cities but it was also one of the only ways to get decent wares, supplies, tools, automata and other such items inside the district.

Letting Adair take the lead, Lucien followed him through the rows of pop-up shops and kiosks, his eyes flicking over the displays. He didn't have money to burn, but he made a mental note of things to make at home for cheaper.

Adair stopped at a table with used books and began perusing. Remembering the genres Nik and Ginny had mentioned liking, Lucien bought them each a couple of books, plus a few for Eran and Shara, and then carried on as Adair remained behind, enraptured by an enormous tome Lucien couldn't make out the title of. He wandered on to a smithy who had blades and weapons on display. It wasn't legal to sell them, but no one would say anything.

A particularly lethal-looking blade immediately caught his eye. It was the finest craftsmanship he'd seen in a while. The curved blade was engraved with intricate designs, the handle made of bone. The price tag was far more than he should rightly spend, but he couldn't draw himself away.

Adair appeared at his side and whistled. 'She's a beauty.'

Lucien picked the blade up. It was light, easy to wield. He flipped it, testing the weight. He glanced at the prico trader, curious. 'You don't feel uncomfortable carrying this around in your truck?'

'I'm good at dodging stray blades,' said the prico with a shrill laugh. 'You'd be surprised how many would pay a fair chip for such a weapon. Not all Suriias are friends, you know?'

'That's true.' Before he could talk himself out of it, Lucien pulled out a bundle of chips and handed them over. 'Toss in the holster.'

The trader smiled wickedly and passed over a leather holster before quickly pocketing the chips, his tongue flicking out to wet his lips.

Lucien stowed the blade and holster in his bag, where none of the Keepers would see it, and fell into step beside Adair.

'You have a holster,' said Adair.

'I know.'

Adair grinned wolfishly. 'Marriage has made you nice, Lucien.'

'I'm not married.'

'You kind of are.'

'Shut up.'

'I mean it. Not just the married part. You're different. Happier. It's been a while since you've been so animated.'

Lucien held out a hand. 'It's been a while since anything's changed.'

'Have you thought more about what I said?'

'Yes.'

'We could leave Westend,' murmured Adair. 'For good. Go to the continent and start over somewhere there aren't any humans. There must be safe places. And if Esme's got magic, she can help us get rid of the clips.'

'Trying to leave Westend would get us all killed,' said Lucien in a low voice, stomach tightening in knots at the mere thought. 'They have nets in the ocean. Ships patrol the waters. Anyone caught escaping is sent to the factories or prison.'

'That doesn't leave us with a lot of options.'

'I know.'

They stopped at another half dozen shops before calling it a day. The foot traffic was only increasing and every new arrival grated at Lucien's fragile grasp on patience.

'First we get wards,' he said once they'd reached the main road and there was no danger of being overheard, 'then we make a move. One way or another, this isn't going to be up in the air for long.'

'The continent could be just what we need.'

'We'd have to get there first.'

'I'm working on that.'

'Oh?'

Adair nodded, but didn't elaborate.

At the house, Lucien parked the truck, but neither got out straight away.

'One way or another,' said Adair quietly, 'I'm not ending this year how we started it.'

Lucien nodded grimly. 'It's only a matter of time before there's a sweep. Before someone says something about Nik and Ginny.'

'Then let's not be here when there's a sweep,' said Adair, opening his door and stepping out. Lucien followed him.

The cheerful sounds of the others cooking in the kitchen greeted them upon arrival, but Lucien didn't go in to join them. Taking the stairs two at a time, he knocked on the door to his room and waited for Nik's call to open it.

'Come in.'

Nik was curled up in the window seat as usual, a pile of books on the floor beside him. Three of them were open and turned over.

'You're going to learn the secrets of the universe this way,' said Lucien by way of greeting.

'That's the plan.' Nik raised his head, a half-smile curving his lips. 'So how was the expo? Manage to relax?'

'I don't really relax.'

'That doesn't surprise me.'

'I got you something, actually.'

'You did?'

Slightly nervous now, Lucien walked over and held out the holstered blade on top of the books he'd picked out.

Nik set the books aside before unsheathing the blade. 'You're giving me a knife?'

'Do you know anything about Salfar?'

'No.'

Lucien took a deep, steadying breath, and tried to formulate what he wanted to say into something that wouldn't frighten or overwhelm Nik. 'I'm not asking for anything,' he prefaced quickly. 'But, ah, after the enchantment—well, it's actually a three-step process. A gift, a pledge, a spell. We've already done the spell and I've sworn to protect you, and I know we're only friends, but I wanted you to have something to protect yourself with and I'd like it to come from me. If that's all right? I don't know how to not at least offer. Oh! And it's iron. It'll poison any Suriia it cuts.' He was officially rambling. Perhaps taping his mouth shut would help.

Nik seemed to be trying not to laugh at how flustered Lucien was. 'A three-step process to what?'

Bracing for the inevitable argument or accusation, Lucien said, 'To … marriage.'

Nik's eyebrows shot up and he almost dropped the blade. 'That enchantment's used in marriage?'

It required all of Lucien's courage to admit the next part. 'On Salfar, that's only what it's used for. Here they use it for binding enchantments, too. But on Salfar that would never happen.'

Astonishment narrowed Nik's eyes to slits, but he didn't look angry. 'Then why do it?'

'To save your life.'

'How long does the enchantment last?'

'Forever.'

Nik set the blade aside and put his hands together. 'I can't believe you did that for me. I mean … if you think about it, that's just really nice.'

Lucien snorted.

Far from laughing it off, Nik leaned closer and put a hand on Lucien's forearm. 'I'm serious. You said it does nothing to me. Only you.'

'Winning someone is not nice.'

'Offering to be with someone you don't want to be with just to keep them safe is nice,' said Nik adamantly. 'There's no other way to spin that.'

Lucien could think of myriad ways to spin it, but he chose not to. Despite how much he didn't agree, he liked that Nik thought he was nice.

'What does it do? To a prico?'

'We can only cast the enchantment once and it ties us directly to the one we're making the pledge to.' He hadn't had to perform the enchantment at his first marriage by mere chance; Astril had been a vryko. Had she been prico, he'd never have been able to escape.

Nik cocked an eyebrow. 'Say what now?'

'If you die or are harmed, it affects me.'

'How?'

'Well, if you die, it kills my magic.' A strained, humourless laugh escaped him. 'So, you know, try not to die.'

This was clearly not what Nik had been expecting. 'What would that do to you?'

'It leaves me a phantom.'

A strange expression on his face, Nik returned his attention to the dagger, the bones in his hand almost as defined as the edges of the blade in his grip. 'It's beautiful.'

'I'm glad you think so.'

'You'd really let me keep this?'

'I'd prefer you kept it on you at all times,' said Lucien bluntly. 'Even at home.'

'You don't trust the pack?'

'I do,' said Lucien. 'That's not the point. You're weaker than everyone in this house aside from Ginny. I don't like that. I don't like knowing that you're vulnerable. I want you to have a way to be on equal footing. This is a start.'

Nik sheathed the blade and sat forwards, wrapping his arms around Lucien's neck. 'Thank you.'

'For what?'

'Always surprising me.' When Nik leaned back, he did so slowly, and then, to Lucien's utter astonishment, he kissed his cheek. The sensation went straight through Lucien, leaving his skin tingling and raw.

Resisting the urge to kiss him properly, Lucien thumbed at the door. 'Do you want to go for a walk?'

Nik stretched languidly and cracked his neck before glancing out the window. 'You do know it's raining?'

'I like the rain,' said Lucien. 'But we don't—'

'No, let's go.' Nik smiled at him. 'I like the rain, too.'

Reaching down, Lucien picked up the belt and knife and held them out to Nik. 'Put it on.'

A bemused look crossed Nik's face, like he hadn't thought Lucien was serious, but he put the belt on without protest.

'I like it,' he said softly.

'What?'

'That you take care of me. No one ever has.'

Those words broke Lucien's heart.

Outside, the rain quickly stained their coats. The chilly breeze enhanced the thunderstorm's fury, tossing the leaves of the trees this way and that. Spiderwebs in the branches glistened with fat drops of water but stuck determinedly, much stronger than they appeared.

'Eran's really nice,' said Nik as they wandered down the path, their boots making quiet squelching noises in the mud. 'He had lunch with me.'

'He's a good kid. I wish his prospects were better. He could be a doctor if they'd let him.'

'Do you ever regret it?'

'What?'

'Leaving Salfar.'

Lucien rubbed his beard, barely stamping down the resentment he held towards his home world. 'I doubt you'll believe me, but this life is actually less of a prison than my last.'

'I can't imagine that.'

'I wouldn't want you to.'

'Well, that's probably the saddest thing I've ever heard.'

Side-stepping a puddle, Lucien turned down the path to the lake. Berry bushes spilled onto the trail from the weed strewn foliage that densely packed the small area creating a bushy, makeshift – but rather helpful – fence.

'So,' said Nik, clearing his throat. 'How did Suriias get to Earth in the first place?' In the pale light of the stormy day, the circles under Nik's eyes were a deep purple, but there was notable improvement in his pallor. The decent meals he'd had since arriving seemed to be doing him good. He held himself with less fear than the night they'd met. Telling him more didn't seem as unwise as it first had.

'The Tear,' said Lucien.

'The what?'

'Geon cut a hole in the universe. I wouldn't advise it.'

'The universe?'

'Where did you think Suriias were from?'

'Dunno. Afterlife?'

'We're not demons,' he said with a small laugh. 'Though I suppose I can't blame humans for thinking we're omens of death.'

'An alternate universe?' asked Nik. 'Parallel? Same or different reality?'

Lucien shook his head. 'I don't know. I only know there's more than one. More than mine, more than yours. I don't think Geon was aiming for Earth, really. The spell he cast just cut a hole to the nearest habitable place. Which turned out to be Earth.'

They were by the river now and they stilled on the edge of the bank, watching the water. The rain was causing the surface to ripple and roil, somehow creating calm chaos.

'And that's what drove him crazy? Using so much magic?'

'He had to steal magic to do it and the spell ate him alive.' How terribly simple it was, Lucien mused, to summarise horror with a single sentence.

'Why'd he do it?'

'To save my life.'

Nik's eyes widened, and it was clear he wanted to ask more, but to Lucien's unending gratitude, he let the topic rest for now. They stood by the lake and watched the rain in comfortable silence. And then, to Lucien's amazement, Nik reached out and took his hand, gently interlacing their fingers. His skin felt warm, in a perfect sort of way. One Lucien could honestly say he'd never experienced with anyone else. Geon and Adair had held his hand in comfort or fear or solidarity, but no one had ever held his hand gently, as if enjoying the sensation, idly tracing a finger over his skin.

The rain steadily worsened, but neither made a move to turn back to the house until they were both officially soaked to the bone and trembling with cold.

'You said you had more than one library here,' said Nik once they were inside, kicking off their wet shoes and hanging up their coats on the coatrack.

Lucien arched an eyebrow, slightly stunned. 'Didn't get enough books at the shop?'

'Almost finished with them.'

'There are more in my study,' he offered, too bemused to point out that he'd just bought Nik more books to read.

'Come on, then,' said Nik, tugging him up the stairs.

As Lucien went over the workbooks, Nik browsed the shelves with steady dedication, plucking books off the shelf at random to peruse for a few minutes before either setting aside or returning them to the shelves. He reminded Lucien of Geon, and he found himself watching Nik and smiling wistfully. Geon had never been satisfied with the amount of knowledge he had.

'There's not enough time to read everything!' had been his unending cry of woe. Every time they found a new bookshop on Salfar, Geon came away with another dozen. Before they'd left everything behind, Geon's house had more closely resembled a library than a cottage.

But then, his thirst for knowledge had been what saved them in the end. What saved Lucien.

He swallowed hard and looked away from Nik. Unfortunately, the income forms for the shops in town weren't distracting enough and pain constricted his chest.

'Are you okay?'

'Fine,' he grunted.

'You're a bad liar.'

'But I'm an excellent shot.'

'What's that got to do with anything?'

Lucien threw a coaster at him. It hit Nik in the centre of the chest. 'See.'

'Mature.'

'I try.'

Nik walked over and dropped down into the chair across from him. 'You seem gloomy.'

'That's a common accusation from the pack.'

'It's true.'

Lucien shrugged. 'Live through a few wars and you'll be perpetually gloomy, too.'

'The humans all have different stories for what started the Suppression.'

'I'm sure they do.'

'What happened?'

With a heavy sigh, Lucien leaned back in his chair and crossed his arms. 'There were only five of us who came through – or so we thought. At the time, this island was called England. It was, as they termed it, *the year of our Lord, 1806.*'

'Their Lord?'

'God.'

'I wonder why they don't still call it that,' said Nik thoughtfully. 'It's been "after the Suppression of Magic" for years.'

'I don't think the current leaders have much care for the historical ones. Don't they view them as weak for letting the Suriias onto Earth at all?'

Nik nodded.

'Humans like to call Salfar "The Underworld". It's under nothing. It's a land of ever-trees and ever-light, filled with magic and machinery the likes of which you could only dream about here. Sometimes the houses change position based on what kind of mood they're in. Sometimes the forests decide they want more water and move a thousand leagues away and leave nothing but a plot of empty land behind. Sometimes the rain gets temperamental and the temperatures change by the hour. For Suriias, Earth was the afterlife. We couldn't *die*, per se. The magic keeps us continuous in some sense. But we could be killed. And the fear for so many was to be killed; for death on Salfar meant birth on Earth. Rebirth into something so fragile, so breakable, you could never endure. And the greatest fear for a Suriia is what comes next. Because if you're fragile as a human, surely the next incarnation is even more delicate. Until we're nothing but wind and whispers …

'I think of it another way: we are reborn until we become the magic we started out with. And someday, those whispers become beings, and those beings are reborn. There is no end. Just a new adventure of unknowns. But more than half the universe fear the unknown.' Lucien rocked his head slowly, finding himself calmed by the words. It was something Geon used to tell him. It was how the book had worked at all; the souls trapped within had been stolen by an ancient Suriia. And those whispers, for all the ill they had wrought to Geon's sanity, had wisdom to share.

Nik nodded thoughtfully. 'Why leave? Why risk it?'

'Because sometimes simpler is better,' said Lucien softly. 'But we were wrong about that, too. For a time, we lived quietly. Jae, bless him, couldn't relax. He feared too greatly the fallout of what we'd left behind and dedicated himself to ensuring that the humans knew nothing of magic. Knew nothing of our world. But when Geon's mind began to fail, he lost control.'

Confusion darkened Nik's face. 'What do you mean?'

Lucien rubbed his jaw roughly, the memories of Geon cutting deep. 'We were forced to use magic to subdue him one night and we were seen. The human ran and told the priest, and the witch-hunts began.

'It was then that we discovered others had come through the Tear after us. Hundreds of them. Some kept hidden, seeking sanctuary like us. Others kept a low profile. Until the burnings started. Fighting broke out everywhere. And that's when the war began.

'At some point the humans discovered a disease that crippled us. Made from wolfsbane. When enough of us had died, and the rest were too weak to fight back, they rounded us up and put us in death camps. For years we were kept inside them until legislations were passed to allow us the most minor of freedoms. We could work, but only within the camps. When it became obvious that we were the cheapest source of labour they had, they traded freedoms for agreements, and so the hierarchy built itself.' Finished, Lucien lit a cigar and stood, walking over to the window. He stared out across the fields, a decades-old melancholy gnawing at him.

By the time they were finally released from the camps, none of them had been whole. Geon least of all. Lucien had tended to Geon daily, but his friend made little sense and often exploded in fits of rage or fear. He still had scars on his back and chest from how hard Geon fought him, so blind was he to the magic that had consumed him.

And yet, the last memory he had of his best friend, his brother, was impossibly perfect.

He'd found Geon by the river, gazing across the glistening waters, a smile on his face. For years, every interaction with him had to be approached cautiously, but Lucien sat beside him and Geon didn't react poorly or twitch. He seemed at peace.

'It was worth it,' he'd said, voice soft.

Lucien remembered almost falling over in shock at how normal he sounded. 'What was?' he'd asked, careful to keep his tone calm and even.

'Coming here,' said Geon. 'Leaving Salfar.'

'Was it?' Lucien shook his head. 'Sometimes I wonder.'

'It was.'

And then Geon had given him this *look*. This loving, knowing, assured look; one that Lucien hadn't seen on him since they'd been on Salfar.

'I couldn't save my parents,' said Geon. 'I couldn't save my sisters. But I saved you. I saved Jae. It was worth it.'

Lucien had hoped that day was a turning point. And, in a way, it was: the next morning he woke up to find Geon's body.

He'd killed himself in the night.

The letter Geon left for Lucien said that he was all right, that he knew what he was doing, that dying would return the souls, the impossible magic, to the book where they belonged. After all, only the Cold King, whose blood was tied to Salfar, could have mastered them and kept control of his sanity. But like most things in his life, Geon had just done it. A reaction to Lucien's imprisonment.

'I've heard stories of the camps.' The tone of Nik's voice was darker than Lucien had ever heard it. 'The things they did …'

Lucien let out a shaking, stilted breath, his mind jumping from one series of memories to another.

'It fixes nothing, but I'm sorry.'

'You didn't do anything.'

'I'm sorry.' Nik fixed Lucien with a hard look. He then raised his arms and wrapped them around Lucien's neck, drawing him in. 'I'm so, so sorry.'

It took several seconds for Lucien to return the gesture, but as he did so, three words danced to the tip of his tongue, daring to be uttered. Had things been different, he would have said them in an instant.

CHAPTER TWENTY
Night of Crimes

The Blackfeather Pack lived in the middle of Westend Circle in one of the newer houses. Links to the Keepers meant that they had a nicer place than most of the other packs. The pavement in the driveway was unmarked by automobile oil or rain, the paint on the walls fresh, the roof re-shingled. Built after the district was established, the houses held no history, their walls no memories. But they were erected on land that had once been a graveyard, and Lucien didn't know how they slept without hearing spectres. Perhaps finery was enough for some.

Parking his truck, Lucien got out, and Shim fell into step beside him as they made their way to the front door.

Lucien knocked sharply twice.

It opened and they found themselves face to face with Kairi, Trenton's eldest son.

'My father's not home,' he said, not opening the door fully.

'Where is he?'

'Out.'

Lucien resisted the urge to bark at Kairi. 'He was supposed to meet me. He never showed. Your father owes me a rather large sum of money.'

Kairi shrugged. 'Prove it.'

Lucien put his hand on the door threateningly. 'Do you really want to burn bridges with me? It'd be a mistake.'

The sound of footfalls preceded the arrival of Lark, Trenton's wife. 'He'll be at the arena tonight,' she said, tone biting. 'At seven. Now please get off our property.'

Lucien tipped his hat to her before turning and trotting down the steps. Shim shadowed him, her annoyance almost a third party behind her.

They stopped at the fields next and spent another two hours helping Ali fix a plumbing problem that had resulted in a flooded field. The work was messy, smelly and exhausting, but with all three of them divvying up the work, they fixed the pump without having to buy any new parts. If Lucien had been able to use magic, he'd have bent the metal to his will, forcing it into shape.

Once upon a time, he could melt iron with a whispered enchantment and a flash of light. That was something, too, that the Suriias born on Earth had never known. Too many years in hiding followed by hunting and then genocide and then war, meant there was little time to pass down old traditions. Only those who'd come from Salfar itself could still remember the enchantments of their old world.

The sun baked down upon the land with relentless gusto all throughout the morning and sweat was dripping from Lucien's brow by the time he got into his truck and made the drive back to the manor, this time alone.

He headed straight for his study and went to work combing over his reports from his dealings with the Blackfeather Pack. None of it could ever be shown to the authorities, although Henna had listened to more than a few monetary disputes in the area. But if he wanted to keep Henna on his side for other favours, he couldn't pester them with this one. And he had a feeling he'd need their help with Nik and Ginny sooner rather than later.

If Trenton refused, there wasn't much Lucien could actually do about it. But he would remember it. Trenton's pack would never get another favour from him again.

At twilight, Lucien readied himself for the Circle. But getting ready for the Circle was like going to the surgeon-dentist for a tooth extraction. Which, in the district, was rarely done with anything to dull the pain. They couldn't afford proper drugs, after all. But at least Dr Ellicott and his pliers weren't purposefully trying to maim you. Not like those who frequented the Circle.

It was a still, breezy night and the air smelled of lush grass and fragrant flowers from the garden. Lucien, Shim and Jae climbed into the truck and set off to the Circle in silence.

The arena's nightlife was already in full swing by the time they arrived, the dilapidated walls filled to bursting with the gamblers, traders, thieves, dealers, grifters and other various characters of differing levels of nefariousness.

They found Trenton in the canteen with a beer in front of him, pack members on all sides.

Lucien and Shim sat down opposite him. Jae remained off to the side, a hand on his pistol, watching the scene unfold with a critical eye.

'Two humans, Lucien?' drawled Trenton. 'That's either impressive or downright stupid.'

'I like to keep things interesting.'

'Reckless,' said Trenton. 'The Blackfeather Pack doesn't do reckless.'

Lucien took off his hat and brushed his hair back from his face, taking the time to gather his thoughts. It was clear several other patrons were eavesdropping. Lighting a cigar, he tried to tamper down his frustration. He couldn't afford to ignite the anger of another pack, but he ached to bash Trenton's teeth in. 'You agreed to meet me.'

'I like being entertained.' Trenton shrugged obnoxiously. 'But I won't trade with you.'

Lucien blinked at him, trying not to showcase his frustration. 'Why?'

'Humans are messy. Your new husband is going to get us all killed.'

'I did nothing a dozen others haven't before me.'

'Four others, Lightblood. And you'll notice they never lasted very long with their new pets. Humans don't belong inside our walls.'

Lucien scoffed. 'Ah yes, how could I forget the hierarchy of a *cage*.'

'A cage it may be, but at least we run ourselves.'

'Do we?'

Trenton sneered at him. 'I don't deal with humans, Lightblood. Come back to me when you're two humans short and we can talk trade.'

They glared at each other for several seconds before Lucien stood. Shim and Jae followed him through the throngs of Suriias milling about.

'Arrange a fight,' he said to Shim as they walked. 'Tonight. We'll use the winnings to buy wards and sort out the packs next week. One fucking problem at a time.'

Jae rubbed his jaw. 'Who are you going to fight to win that much?'

'Raguel will jump at the chance of a rematch,' he said. 'He's been itching to tear me apart.'

Shim darted off, slipping through the bodies like a minnow. Lucien and Jae found an empty enough corner of the arena and sat down on a stack of discarded boxes that had been there long enough to acquire a layer of dust.

Thankfully, they didn't have to wait too long. Less than twenty minutes had ticked by before Shim reappeared and flicked a coin at Lucien. The coin was given to the ringmaster before a fight.

'One hour,' she said. 'Raguel.'

'Excellent.'

Jae grimaced uncomfortably. 'You sure about this, boss? There are better ways to get chips for wards.'

'We don't have the luxury of time,' said Lucien. 'And seeing as how our accountant just stole most of our emergency funds, I don't think we have much choice.'

'He's got a point,' said Shim grimly.

Jae's lip curled unhappily.

The minutes leading up to a fight always dragged, and Lucien was on edge and irritable when at last they made their way over.

The arena was already packed to the rafters by the time they reached the fighting ring. Onlookers crowded around the metal fences, shouting and drinking, feeding off the energy of the group and devolving into a nearly manic state of voyeurism.

'Anything goes wrong, you know what to do,' Lucien told Jae before stepping into the arena. Shim followed him, shedding her coat as she walked and tossing it back to Jae, who caught it deftly.

Raguel and Jalal entered from the other side to raucous applause.

'Do we want to give them a chance?' she asked mockingly. 'It's been a while since we've had some fun.'

'Let's get the money and go.'

'But we can play first, right?'

Lucien couldn't stifle his grin at her eagerness to show off. The difference between his friendship with Shim and his friendship with Geon still made him marvel somewhat. Geon taught him how to make a fist, how to be daring, how to fight back. But he always followed Geon's lead. Until Geon lost his mind. Then, with no choice but to take the lead, Lucien somehow found that he had enough in him to catch more than just himself. By the time Shim came along, it was Lucien teaching her how to fight.

Over the years, Lucien and Shim had fought more than a few arena matches. Usually done out of necessity, Lucien secretly enjoyed them. He enjoyed knowing how powerful he was. How little he had to cower and beg. He knew he could win. He knew the odds were in his favour.

Without the fear of protecting Nik, fighting Raguel this time was more of a game than a mission. They traded blows with the sort of skill that comes after spending a century hating each other but having to exist in the same fishbowl. Raguel was a good fighter, catlike and cruel, but Lucien was far older – and had far more to lose.

Both he and Shim were covered in bruises, breathing heavily and soaked in sweat when they stepped out of the ring half an hour later, much richer than they'd entered it. Good thing, too, as their clothes and boots were ruined.

Lucien handed the bag of chips to Shim. 'Go buy us wards. And make sure they're Jakob's best.'

Wiping blood from her eyebrow, Shim pocketed the bag and disappeared into the dispersing crowd. There might be another fight that night, but the crowd never did wait around.

'Come on,' said Lucien, tugging on Jae's sleeve. 'I don't want to be here a second longer than we have to.'

'Agreed.'

The night air was a relief to both of them, and they dragged in audible breaths as they made their way over to the truck.

'You know, Nik thinks you don't like him much,' said Jae, blowing out a funnel of smoke from a cigar he'd just lit.

Lucien's head snapped around to him, incredulous. 'Did he say that?'

Jae nodded.

'When? Why?'

'He told me the other day that he feels awful because he knows you don't like him, but you're stuck with him because he's Geon's son.'

Those words stole the air from Lucien's lungs, and he couldn't respond straight away as he stifled a cough. 'Jae,' he rasped, 'if I liked him anymore, I would lose my mind.'

'Then why not tell him that?'

'I *won* him.' The admission made Lucien heave and he put his fist to his mouth.

'You're not forcing anything on him. He's a grown man.'

'If any part of him fears what I'd say if he turned me down, it's not on.'

Jae looked at him in astonishment. 'You're *not* Astril.'

Lucien's scowl only deepened.

'You're not.'

'I won't ever put that in question,' said Lucien. 'Ever.'

'So, you're going to be married to a man you never touch? What's the point?'

'The point is that he's no longer Ashby's plaything,' he snapped. 'The point is that he's safe. This isn't about me.'

'It can be about you a little.'

'No,' he said sharply. 'I won't say it again.'

Jae sighed, but let the matter drop. Now feeling ill as well as wracked with guilt, Lucien plucked the cigar from Jae's fingers and smoked agitatedly, hand shaking and sending ash all over his coat. The sounds from the arena that were carried over to them on the wind turned his stomach and he glared into the night, wishing Geon was there.

'Do you ever imagine it?' he murmured. 'What would have happened if Faren hadn't died?'

A hand was suddenly gripping his shoulder and he looked over at Jae. 'Don't,' he said. 'That wasn't your fault.'

'No one else believed that.'

'Faren would have.'

The lump in Lucien's throat only grew and he smoked until the cigar was gone and he ground it into the dirt with the heel of his boot.

'Boss!'

Lucien's head snapped up. Shim had appeared in the entryway, chest heaving. She'd clearly run across the arena to find them.

'Nik's here,' she gasped. 'He followed us.'

Lucien and Jae bolted in unison.

If his magic hadn't been clipped, Lucien would be able to track Nik with his eyes closed. But he didn't need to have his magic to be able to cut through the din and identify the jeers of a rowdy crowd.

Nik was pinned to the ground by one of the zane traders, Eno.

A fury Lucien didn't like to acknowledge brewed in his veins and he had to force himself not to react impulsively. He would have, once. Before the war. But he'd long learned that patience brought more victory.

He took out his pistol, finger hovering beside the trigger. 'Eno,' he snarled, attention pinned on the spot where the trader's fingernails dug into Nik's flesh. Soft as his voice was, the call was enough to draw everyone's attention even with the din of the crowd. 'I am giving you less than three seconds to let go of my husband before you discover how badly you fucked up.'

Winston Vasil, one of the other traders, nudged Eno and sent him an imploring look. After a beat, Eno's grip on Nik relinquished.

Nik scrambled to his feet and limped over to Lucien, wincing with every step. He was badly bruised and bleeding from more than one cut, dust and dirt coating his clothes and the side of his face.

Lucien's urge to commit a multiple murder was now almost at a tipping point. He glared at the onlookers. 'Unless anyone here harbours a death wish, I sincerely suggest you go.'

'Now!' barked Jae.

The traders dispersed, muttering furiously amongst themselves.

Tempted as he was to cause a real scene, Lucien left without another word.

'Lucien—'

'No,' he growled. 'Not a word.'

The four of them got into the steamtruck. He didn't speak on the drive back to the manor, nor did he get out. He waved Shim and Jae inside, but remained in the front seat while Nik stayed in the passenger seat. The engine grumbled, steam coughing out of the exhaust pipe and dancing like a ghost into the night.

'I can't do this,' he said abruptly.

'What?'

Putting the truck in gear, Lucien drove away from the manor. He took the safe route, the one Isha and Mi had found a long time ago. Few knew of it and the pack kept it that way.

The thick trees lining the road enveloped them, casting everything into total darkness. The human cities with their gas lighting and great buildings and flying machines could be seen and heard from far, far away. There was no softness to human might, no quietude. Everything was noise and metal and machine. But quiet places felt on the precipice of turmoil as a result and he was aware of every sound.

Lucien tightened his grip on the steering wheel. He didn't know who or what was to blame for his current situation, but he felt like screaming at Geon.

'Lucien—'

'No.'

For an hour, there was nothing but forest and field on either side, and then the gate loomed in the distance. Only here it was dark and unmonitored.

Lucien parked a short distance away and got out. He walked over to the fence and waited for Nik to join him. The night air bit painfully into his skin and only served to further sour his mood.

Nik trailed after him uncertainly. 'What is this?'

Lucien reached out and drew back the loose metal fencing. 'Humanity.'

He could recall so well, pelting across that same field after an incoherent, rambling Geon. He'd been fighting with the voices in his head again. His monologue then turned to screaming, hands on his head, the world around him bending unconsciously to the overwhelming magic always close to bursting out of him. It took Lucien, Jae and Esme to get him home. But then, Geon belonged with them; in the world as it was, by his very existence, Nik would never be able to.

Nik looked from the gate to Lucien and back again several times. 'I don't understand.'

'Go,' said Lucien. 'Go through the fence, keep walking straight, and in an hour, you hit the bridge. Go to the Enforcers, tell them about Ashby. Don't mention Geon. They'll find you a place to stay. All kidnapped humans are given new lives.'

Nik didn't move. 'Are you kicking me out?'

'I'm giving you humanity. Go.'

'Because I messed up? I'm sorry! Don't kick me out.'

The hysteria in Nik's voice made Lucien's whole body constrict and his fingers tightened around the metal of the fence. 'You should go,' he ground out, the words hissing between his teeth, not wanting to be uttered. 'It's the best thing, Nik.'

'Why?'

'Because you belong with your own kind. In a safe place.' Lucien looked fixedly at the gate as he said this and didn't move, still holding back the wire, half-wishing it was electric.

'What if I don't want to?'

In the distance, owls hooted in the forest and Lucien could hear predators slinking around. Yet somehow, he felt like he was at the end of the world and all was deathly quiet, waiting to hear his bones crumbling to dust.

Lucien tried to remember how to get air into his lungs, but it proved challenging. He didn't want Nik to go. Far from it. Still, he forced himself to say, 'You don't want to be here. You don't want to belong here.'

'Yes, I do.' Nik reached out and put his hand over Lucien's where it gripped the fence. He tugged once and Lucien let go of the wire with fingers that didn't feel capable of bending.

'I don't want to go,' said Nik softly, stepping closer.

'Letting you go is the right thing to do.'

'And staying or going is up to me, isn't it?'

Lucien swallowed hard. His legs felt made of metal, his joints of cogs, his heart a bloodless hole. 'If you stay, your life will always be in danger. Your future will always be uncertain. I don't want that for you.'

'Luka, stop. I'm sorry.' Closing the small space between them, Nik reached out, resting his hands on Lucien's hips. His fingers felt cool, but wonderful. 'I'm sorry I scared you and I'm sorry I was reckless. I'm not used to thinking about anyone but myself.'

'How do you think I feel?' Lucien stared at him beseechingly. 'You think this is easy for me? Do you have any idea how much I hate this? I want someone I can't have.'

'You do?'

Lucien glowered at him. 'Don't act coy. It's annoying.'

'Fine,' said Nik bluntly. 'Then you should know you're totally unsubtle about watching me every time I take my shirt off.'

'It's good to know you're trying to get a reaction.'

'I've been trying to get a reaction for weeks. I *like* you.' Raising his hand, Nik cupped Lucien's cheek and pressed gently until Lucien gave in and turned. They stared at each other for a brief, almost painful second, and then Nik kissed him.

Lucien pulled back automatically, ragged breaths tearing out of him. 'Nothing about our situation is okay,' he said thickly. 'It started wrong. It's always going to be wrong.'

Nik shook his head in clear disagreement. 'I don't care that you're Suriia. I never have. I care that you saved me. I care that you've been kind and polite and you've protected me. I care about you. Stop telling me I don't have a choice when I'm choosing you right now.'

'You didn't choose me. I won you.'

'You offered to let me go and now you've driven me here, out of bounds, to try and make me go. It's my choice to stay, isn't it?'

Not sure what to say that wouldn't be unfair to Nik or alarm him, or just be downright cringe-inducing, Lucien settled instead for grinding his teeth together.

'Isn't it?'

The shaking, tremulous gust of air that left Lucien filled the silence, but he managed a nod after several excruciating seconds of fighting with his own morals. Bad as he felt about everything, he had no right to tell Nik how to feel.

As if their history wasn't as brief and as twisted as it was, Nik kissed Lucien like he'd done it a thousand times before. Like this was something easy, something that wasn't terrifying Lucien to his core. Never in his life had kissing anyone been this easy and he knew right then that he'd made a horrible mistake. That he should have simply slaughtered everyone in the arena that night and saved Nik. He wished more than anything that the enchantment had never happened, and they met on even footing, and Nik was kissing him because *he came back*, not because he *had to stay*.

Keeping his hands at his sides took such a concerted effort that Lucien left welts in his palms from how hard he was clenching his fists. Nik, on the other hand, seemed to have no reservations and deepened the kiss with unguarded desire. But he stilled abruptly, not missing Lucien's stiffness.

'Do you want me to stop?'

'No.'

'Then act like you want to kiss me.'

The request was a difficult one to comply with, albeit not for the reasons Nik would think if Lucien voiced them. What he *wanted* was to grab Nik, bend him over the front of his truck and do everything with him that came to mind; what he *did* was rest his hands lightly on Nik's waist, a noticeable distance between their bodies, and kiss him with painfully maintained restraint, desperately wishing the entire time that they hadn't met the way they had. Because no matter what Nik said, *Lucien* wasn't okay with it.

Regardless of his mounting reservations, Lucien still felt lighter than air and high on Nik's proximity when he got into the driver's seat a while later and started the truck. Nik put his hand over Lucien's on the gearshift.

The smile came unbidden. The day had been remarkably wretched, but he now felt oddly content. Like time was slowing down, giving him a peripheral view of him and Nik.

Something loosened in his chest.

But halfway up the road, perhaps because the night wasn't interesting enough, the engine sputtered and then died. Smoke began seeping out the sides of the bonnet as Lucien managed to coast it to the side of the road before cutting the engine and putting the parking brake in place.

'Great,' he muttered, concern for his truck rising at the same time he mentally calculated how much the repairs were going to cost.

'Can you fix it?' asked Nik, sitting forward in his seat and peering down at the bonnet.

Lucien shrugged and opened the door. He'd have to fix it, or they were leaving his truck. Being on the side of a main road in the middle of the night with a human was a death sentence. They couldn't stay long.

'What do we do?'

'Fix it. Quickly.'

He popped the bonnet and a billow of steam escaped.

'Fuck,' said Nik.

'It's happened before.' Lucien waved away the steam and squinted, examining the damage.

'What is it?'

Lucien glanced at Nik, who looked thoroughly baffled. 'Do you know anything about steam engines?'

'No.'

'Do you know what a radiator is?'

'Nope.'

'It keeps everything from overheating.'

'Hence the steam.'

Lucien nodded, trying not to laugh. He glanced back down. The steam had cleared, and he could now fully inspect the damage. 'The pressure seal is fucked.'

'That definitely doesn't sound good.'

'No.'

Before Lucien could do anything, a sound further down the road reached his ears. So far from the district, at this hour, there were only two things it could be. Ice swept through him and he turned around.

In the distance, and coming closer by the second, were headlights.

Nik followed his gaze and Lucien could hear his heartrate pick up. 'What happens if it's the Keepers?'

'What happens if it's the Enforcers?' he countered, already knowing the answer.

The precariousness of their situation was thankfully not lost on Nik. 'What's the fastest way back to the house?' he asked, already stepping away.

'You can't—'

'I'm going to have to. Which way?'

By this point, the car was almost upon them.

Lucien pointed left. 'But you'll pass by the Penziks—'

Nik was already running into the trees. He vanished like a ghost. For a human, sometimes Nik seemed so much like a Suriia.

'Fuck,' said Lucien, turning slowly towards the car behind him, which had just grumbled to a stop. He could hear Nik's footfalls tapering off, and he prayed Nik was leaving, not lingering in the trees to see what happened. But he didn't have time to check.

Three Enforcers stepped out of the vehicle and made their way over at a pointedly slow pace.

'What seems to be the trouble, friend?' asked the one on the right.

'Engine trouble,' said Lucien politely.

They exchanged dogged looks that made his hair stand on end. The last time one of the pack got stopped, Adair ended up with three broken ribs and Eran was beaten so badly he couldn't see out of his left eye for a sennight.

'Let's see if we can't get you on your way,' said the one in the middle.

'Identification,' said the third.

As he handed the Enforcer his identification card, the other two moved behind him. He didn't have to turn around to know the screeching sound was from them doing deliberate damage to his truck.

The urge to show them how he really felt built dangerously and he clamped his jaw shut so hard his head ached. He couldn't afford to get angry. He had a pack, a family, relying on him.

'You're out of bounds after curfew, Lightblood,' said the one in front of him, handing him the card back. 'That's a fineable offence.'

Lucien said nothing.

The Enforcers crowded around him.

'What do you reckon, boys?' asked one. 'Two hundred?'

'Oh, five hundred,' said the second. 'He's making us late for check-in.'

'Five hundred,' said the third. 'Or we'll bring you back with us.'

Lucien pulled out five hundred-chip notes and stood motionless as the Enforcers got back into their car and left.

He let out a shaking sigh and turned back to his truck. The bastards had cut one of the main wires. It wasn't a hard fix, but it was an expensive one.

A series of exceptionally foul words left his mouth and he was tempted to kick his truck, but the poor thing had been through enough that night.

With nothing else to do, Lucien pushed his truck as far off the road as possible, obscured it with branches and vines, and then set off at a run back towards Westend Circle.

CHAPTER TWENTY-ONE
A Brief Reprieve

The house finally came into view well after daybreak, but the sun hid behind the clouds, banished by the grey softness of the rainy day. A lifetime of rainy days was par for the course for those who lived on the island, but it had never bothered Lucien. He quite liked the calmness of the mist and wind. It was snow he hated.

But today, everything was annoying. Insects bobbed low in the humid morning air, eager to feast on his sweat-covered skin. The wind was filled with water droplets and every gust left him a little more uncomfortable. The marshy countryside to the east was less than no fun to traipse through and his boots were filled with muck, rocks, twigs and an unknowable amount of water. Rank smells wafted off his skin. He was poorer than he'd planned on being, exhausted, dirty, and in an exceptionally foul mood. To top it off, he'd also lost his hat.

Shim greeted him on the porch in her pyjamas, holster slung low on her bony hips. Her eyes flicked over him. 'Good night?' she asked, a teasing tone to her voice. One she wouldn't have had if anything else was amiss.

'Bite me. Nik home?'

She waved over her shoulder. 'He's still cleaning up, I think. Came home covered in mud and told us what happened.'

Dropping heavily into the rocking chair, Lucien began unlacing his manure encrusted boots and yanked them off, pebbles and grass and muck falling all over the porch. It looked like he'd brought half the bog back with him.

'Lovely,' she remarked.

'Tell me about it.'

'Where's the truck?'

'Gelnekath Road,' he said, setting the boots aside to air out and taking his keys out of his pocket. He tossed them to her. 'Send whichever lazy shit didn't do their chores last night.'

'That would be Isha.'

'Perfect.' He peeled off his soiled socks and spread them over the railing to dry. Nodding to Shim, he trudged upstairs wearily. Each step felt like it took ten times the effort it should, and his muscles ached from exhaustion.

Inside his bedroom, Nik was just out of the bathroom. Steam rose from his skin and the smell of shampoo filled the air. His stopped short at the sight of Lucien, eyebrows disappearing under his damp hair. 'What happened to you?'

'Nothing,' said Lucien. 'Why were you covered in mud?'

'I fell into a swamp.'

The thought of Nik falling into a swamp greatly improved his mood. 'Seriously?'

A flush crept into Nik's cheeks. 'It was dark.'

'Graceful.' Though he laughed, he continued to appraise Nik for any possible sign of damage. 'But you're all right?'

'I'm fine.'

He nodded, letting the assurance wash over him. 'I'm going to clean up. I'll meet you downstairs.'

To Lucien's surprise, Nik sauntered over and took his hand. The fact that he was half-naked really, really did not help Lucien's determined detachment, and he found himself leaning in when Nik kissed him.

'Making sure you didn't change your mind,' said Nik, the words brushing against Lucien's skin, uttered like a wish.

'I didn't,' said Lucien, voice thick and hoarse.

'Good.' Nik winked at him before heading over to the dresser and pulling out a black shirt. A tattoo on his shoulder caught Lucien's notice. Three lines, all connected on one side.

Curious as he was, Lucien had a policy about prying and decided not to ask.

'I'll meet you in the kitchen,' said Nik. 'Want anything?'

'Coffee, please.'

Twenty minutes later, showered and in dry clothes, the sounds of the others downstairs in the kitchen drifting up through the floorboards, Lucien left his room, more than ready to put the night behind him. Pausing in his study to jot down a list of things he needed to pick up to mend his truck, he almost didn't notice what was different.

It was as he walked by the sealed cabinet that he realised the wood of the door was slightly bent. The patch job was so good most would not have seen it. But Lucien knew his office right down to the cracks.

Unlocking the heavy metal lock and setting it aside carefully, he opened his cabinet, eyes raking over the items one by one. His guns, all accounted for; the registration files for the pack, all neatly compiled, not one name missing; photographs from over the years that were now too painful to look at but would never, ever be thrown out were piled neatly. All the spellbooks he'd rescued from the war's wrath and kept over the years, waiting for the moment he might be able to remove the clip and use magic again to its full potential were there; bottles of poison and homemade explosives that were always kept out of reach of the others; and in the back corner by his daggers …

'No,' he breathed. Then, 'ADAIR!'

Adair was at his side in mere seconds, faster than an arrow when he needed to be.

'It's gone,' said Luke, horrified beyond recall. 'Someone broke in.'

Adair's hands went to his mouth. 'But the wards—'

'Weren't replaced until this morning when Shim brought them home.' Lucien's fingers gripped the cabinet door so tightly the blood left them. 'Someone has the bloody book.'

'We can't tell anyone,' said Adair, pitching his voice so low that even Lucien had to strain to hear him. 'They won't know what this means and it'll just cause panic.'

'This is worth panicking over.'

'Not until we know more. Perhaps—perhaps it was misplaced.'

'Or perhaps Raguel broke in and stole it thinking it was worth something. Or maybe a blasted Keeper wanting to trade it to the Enforcers and really seal our fate.'

'The Enforcers have no use for a book like that. Odds are they can't even read it.' Adair squeezed his shoulder reassuringly. 'You're the only one who was supposed to be able to use it. Geon used bloodmagic to jailbreak the forsaken thing. No one else would know how. Not on this world.'

Lucien relaxed a fraction. That was true. No one but him would actually be able to use the Book of Ten Thousand Souls. Anyone who tried would end up like Geon. He let out a trembling wheeze. 'Right. But we need to find it. Fast.'

'Agreed.'

Most of the others were already seated around the table or standing around cradling mugs of steaming coffee when they entered. Kalid and Shara both had cups of hot chocolate, judging by the sweet smell that mixed in with the familiar scent of coffee and tea leaves.

'All good?' Nik eyed him worriedly. 'You shouted.'

'I thought the wards were broken,' said Lucien, drowning the lie in a mouthful of hot coffee from the cup Mi proffered.

'Are they broken?' Shim blanched. 'I—'

'The wards are fine,' Adair assured her soothingly. 'Lucien's just exhausted.'

It didn't feel right, lying to the pack, but Lucien also didn't know how to begin explaining any of it to them. Only Adair, Naida, Jae and Esme knew about the book's existence. Knew what its power could bring to the very fabric of reality.

Lucien had barely finished breakfast when Naida waltzed in and dropped a pile of chips in front of him. She flashed a proud smile and plunked down in the adjacent chair.

He picked up a chip and whistled. 'Did you rob a bank?'

'Good hand of poker,' she crowed, kicking off her boots wearily while Adair fixed her a cup of tea. 'I thought we could all go buy new clothes and restock the kitchen. Will you let me shop for you? You're looking dire, boss.'

Adair choked on the piece of toast he'd been devouring. Naida often pestered Lucien about his wardrobe. She pestered them all, in truth. Naida held to the idea that the better you looked, the better you felt, therefore the better you would do. Lucien didn't believe it, but it had been a long time since he'd seen her so happy and he couldn't bring himself to contest. She was also having Eran, Kalid and Shara wash his truck, so he felt agreeable.

'All right,' he grumbled. 'Within reason.'

Naida squealed and threw her arms around him. 'Nik, you're coming, too.'

From the other side of the table, bathed in sunlight from the open window, Nik looked up from the report Adair had given him to double check. A pen stuck out of his mouth, ink smudges on his fingers and cheeks. 'Heh?'

Lucien had never seen someone who could look both devastatingly handsome and bashfully adorable at the same time. He swallowed with difficulty and tried not to let his mind go where it so desperately wanted to.

'Can I come?' asked Mi.

'No,' said Lucien, voice gruffer than he intended. 'This is not a pack outing. Naida and Nik can go.'

'We could make it one!' Naida looked positively delighted by the prospect. 'Oh, come on, Luke. We could do with some fun.'

'Shopping is not fun,' he countered.

'Agreed,' said Shim disdainfully.

'If I'm going, Lucien has to go,' said Nik, looking back down at the stack of receipts and reports.

Lucien shook his head. 'Yeah, no.'

'Come on, boss,' said Ginny. 'You need new clothes and you have to try them on.'

'I do not.'

'You do,' everyone chorused around the table.

He scowled at the lot of them. 'I'll happily disown you all.'

Undeterred, Mi threw a piece of toast at him. 'It won't kill you not to have three holes in every outfit.'

'Shopping may kill me.'

'What if we make Nik try things on without a shirt?' asked Ginny, green eyes glittering with mischief.

Nik's head snapped up, cheeks flaming red. 'No!'

Lucien grinned. 'I'll come if I can see that.'

'No,' said Nik.

'Guess I don't need new clothes.' Lucien held Nik's gaze, forcing himself not to smile and finding it increasingly difficult not to.

'Come on,' said Shara from the other side of the table. 'Please, Nik!'

'Only if I can pick out something for you,' said Nik, eyes still locked with Lucien's. 'Whatever I want.'

Everyone turned to Lucien.

He heaved a sigh, but it was more out of resignation than disdain. Their gaiety proved infectious and he wanted his pack to smile for once. 'Fine. We can all go.'

Naida cheered and went to tell the others.

After they'd checked in on the fields, the pack headed to the shops. Lucien, Shim and Ginny spent the first hour avoiding all clothes and shoes and instead opted to go to the arsenal to look at pistols.

Seklor's Arsenal was one of Lucien's favourite shops. In addition to its ordnances, camp equipment, tools, instruments and appurtenances, it had antiques, relics, and other types of metalwork.

The chaotic cheerfulness of the shop had an oddly calming effect. A rhythm to the crowds, a banter in the bargain. Inside the shops, bazaars and fairs, Suriia culture had flourished into life of its own. Something different from Suriia society on Salfar, but noticeably, blessedly different from the constraints of human society.

In the years since the walls came up, dividing Suriia from human, built around the rundown, war-torn buildings left barely standing after too many battles, ingenuity, repurposing and upcycling had all formed important cornerstones of district life. There was plenty to be found so long as you didn't ask too many questions or cared how many had owned the item before you.

After an hour's perusal of the wares and trinkets, bits and bobs, the trio finally dragged themselves to the clothes' shop where the others were gathered, trying on this and that.

They entered just as Nik stepped out of the changing room. He'd donned a pair of dark brown trousers and a fitted white shirt with a high collar. 'Do I look all right?'

Slightly stunned, Lucien reached out and hooked a finger in the waistline of his trousers. Pretending he cared about what Nik wore even a little was difficult. He was entirely certain that Nik would be handsome wearing only a potato sack and socks, but there was something ravishing about the sight of him dressed like one of them. In fitted clothes made in the district, upscaled from donations or pieces cut from this garment or that, Nik looked like he was embracing their life. And Lucien felt slightly dizzied by the notion of it. Like teasing the edges of a dream he couldn't quite reach just yet.

'You look good,' he grunted quietly, the gruff words no doubt causing poets everywhere to roll over in their graves, groaning at his incurable lack of romance.

Even still, Nik's eyes dazzled with pride. 'Yeah?'

Lucien pressed his lips to Nik's cheek. 'Yes.'

Nik beamed at him.

Ginny and Shim appeared from a room further down and Lucien couldn't stop himself from rolling his eyes in amusement. Shim had clearly outfitted Ginny; she was wearing tall brown boots, black trousers, and a long leather coat over a dark red waistcoat. Somehow both comfortable and practical.

They returned to the house an hour later and everyone hurried inside to unpack the bags of shopping. Leaving them to it, Lucien caught Nik's eye and cocked his head to the door.

'Where are we going?'

'Target practise.'

They wandered around the barn and down a dirt path that disappeared into a thick cluster of trees. At the bottom of the hill, Lucien pulled a few bottles out of the box they filled and cracked the caps open on the corner of a post. Handing one to

Nik, Lucien began lining up empty bottles in a row along the table he and Adair had made.

'So, who taught you how to shoot?' asked Nik.

'A gun? Taught myself. Fighting? Mostly learned with Adair through trial and error.'

'Impressive.'

'Sometimes you have to teach yourself when your life's on the line and there's no one around to ask.'

'I know the feeling.'

The way Nik was regarding him told Lucien there was something he wasn't saying, but as there was a good deal he was withholding, too, he felt no urge to press boundaries.

'Let's try again,' he said, gesturing towards the target and forcing his questions and secrets out of his mind.

'Have you shot anything else?'

'Weapon or target?'

'Weapon.'

Lucien nodded. 'We had arrows on Salfar. The knights had these gold-tipped arrows that could pierce through armour. The ones fighting back had to come up with new things. Enchanted arrows became the citizen secret. If you could control them with your magic while fighting, you had a good chance of escaping the guards. But keeping your focus while you're fighting and running is difficult.'

'Was it ever a good place? Before things got bad?'

'Yes,' said Lucien honestly. 'I had a lovely childhood.'

Nik smiled. 'Yeah?'

'I spent most of my time in the forests with my brother,' he said, suddenly feeling wistful. 'It was when the king turned against the land and its people that things changed.'

'Why'd he change?'

'Because sometimes that's what happens.' Lucien shrugged. 'Sometimes those who need answers are satisfied with working for them. Sometimes they aren't and cheat. And sometimes cheating leads to darkness.'

Nik eyed him for a moment before raising the gun and firing at the target. Lucien watched, astonished, as the bottle shattered. Glass burst into the air, catching the sunlight before vanishing into the grass.

'I used to have a sling-shot,' said Nik with a grin. 'I've got a good eye.'

Lucien chuckled. He couldn't deny that there was something alluring about seeing Nik handle a weapon. He watched Nik shoot another ten bottles, each time finding himself ever more enamoured with him. There was a sleek sort of grace to Nik, a strength that was as captivating as it was impressive.

The sun was low in the sky by the time they returned to the house. Music trilled from the phonograph in the kitchen and delicious smells wafted out of the open door.

'How long until dinner?' he called.

'Soon,' said Naida, not turning around. She was stirring what smelled like vegetable and noodle soup.

'Excellent.' Lucien eyed the pot longingly. Her food was truly one of the highlights of his life.

An upbeat song suddenly picked up and Adair, who appeared in remarkably high spirits, pulled Naida close and then spun her in a circle. Both giggled foolishly, the way they had when they first got together, all those years ago on Salfar.

Lucien whistled loudly. The first time he saw them dance was on Salfar. Adair was trying to make Esme jealous. It worked. When Esme confronted them in the corridor, Naida told them they deserved each other and left, head held high. It had taken Adair all of ten seconds to follow her and beg her forgiveness. She flatly refused. For over a year, he wrote her letters until, at last, she returned to the same dance the following winter. They'd been together ever since.

Three centuries of marriage and they still danced in the kitchen like newlyweds.

When they paused, breathless, Naida returned to the stove and Adair chugged a glass of water.

'You both are amazing,' said Nik, clearly stunned. 'Where'd you learn to do that?'

Naida tossed her head back dramatically and raised her arms in a mockery of a pose. 'That's what years of dance lessons will do.' She laughed gaily. 'You should see Lucien, though. He puts us all to shame.'

Lucien scowled. 'Thanks for that.'

'It's true!'

'You can dance?' Nik didn't seem to know how to process this information.

'I can hold my own,' he allowed.

'Show me.'

'Not likely.'

'Please?'

Half certain Nik could talk him into anything, Lucien took his hand begrudgingly.

The cheery music continued to play on the phonograph, and everyone danced around the kitchen.

It was one of those brief, fleeting moments of joy that could be recalled later, in darker days, when memory was the only light to see by.

CHAPTER TWENTY-TWO
Ladies Lost

The whereabouts of the book was not revealed in the days that followed no matter how many places Lucien and Adair searched. They canvased every one of their properties and dug through every nook and cranny in the house, but found nothing. Someone had come into Lucien's office, known exactly where to look, and fixed the cabinet door without any of them noticing. The details of it left Lucien feeling oddly violated on top of his mounting concerns about the implications. Someone had been in his *home*.

Unfortunately, the missing book and what that meant wasn't the only issue to rear its head after the confrontation at the arena. Danger came one morning with the paper, too.

Jimmy tossed the paper to Lucien as he always did, barely pausing as he peddled by in his tatty brown suit, splashing water every which way as he cycled through the roadside puddles. His coat was half-darkened from rain drops and he seemed to be gripping the pedals and handles with all his might to keep from slipping off.

Lucien caught the paper before it hit the ground and stepped back under the cover of the porch to unroll it.

Beneath a large black and white photograph of Ginny was a headline that made Lucien's heart still.

NOAH GREEN SEARCHES FOR MISSING DAUGHTER

The ongoing search for Genevieve Green, the youngest daughter of Noah Green, Head of Her Majesty's Enforcement Squad, continued this week with new evidence pointing to a kidnapping. Eye-witness reports place a Suriia at the scene.

'Our first concern is to determine if this is a case of retaliation or a random act of malice,' said the Speaker for the Enforcers. 'The weight of the DES response will be determined in due course.'

The next step of the investigation will be a search of the districts, led by Judoc Fairfax, Genevieve's fiancé and heir to Fairfax Industries, the largest silver, brass and chrome provider in the country. Fairfax was unavailable for comment, but a spokesperson for the company emphasised the likelihood that Genevieve was being held for ransom and would be returned, and that Fairfax had no intention of ending the engagement until a body is found.

(continued on page 13)

Lucien folded the crisp paper in half and hissed out a curse. The only minor upside was that the Ginny in the picture looked almost nothing like the Ginny in his house. She looked polished, unscarred and emotionless. More doll-like than girl. And immensely disconcerting as a result. Ginny wasn't demure and soft, she wasn't prim and proper. There was evidently a good deal that he didn't know about Ginny, but the girl in the picture looked dead inside.

He went back into the house and took the stairs two at a time. Rapping on Ginny's door, he stepped inside the second she called out.

'Ginny,' he said in a quiet voice, closing the door behind him. 'Your fiancé is in the district.' He held out the paper and let her read over it before adding, 'I want you to stay out of sight.'

'Okay.'

'They find you, we're dead.'

'I know.'

Lucien nodded and took the paper back.

'Why can't we pick our family?' she asked, voice small and raspy.

'We can,' he said. 'We have.' He held up the paper. 'This is external. It's no bearing on your importance to the pack.'

Her eyes filled with tears. 'I can't go back, Luk.'

'You won't.'

If there was one thing Lucien had learned from Geon over the years, it was how to take care of their broken family when someone outside of the group was trying to tear them apart. You didn't wait for the problems to find you.

After giving Shim, Jae and Adair strict orders not to let Nik and Ginny out of their sights, Lucien headed into the town.

Parking across from the hardware shop, he'd only just stepped out when he saw the meticulously shined, expensively designed steamtrucks of the Enforcers.

Off to the side of the main square, a man in an expertly tailored suit stood with a top Enforcer, his rank made clear by his black uniform, as opposed to the dark blue the others wore.

Noah Green.

Another man, dressed in expensive attire, stood to the left. Lucien presumed this was Judoc, Ginny's fiancé. The one she hated.

It bothered him immensely to see the age difference up close.

There was nothing Lucien wanted more than to cross the street and let the men know his exact feelings on the matter of Ginny's betrothal, but he was powerless. All he could do for Ginny was hide her out of sight.

Lucien felt sick as he went into work, grinding his teeth until his head pounded.

Around midday, Naida came in to say that everything was fine at the house.

'There's a new meeting,' she informed him, sitting down on the stool behind the till. 'Henna's called it. Westend Circle tonight. Everyone's expected.'

'Everyone?'

Naida nodded slowly. 'Everyone. Henna expressed that pretty clearly.'

'How many are going?'

'All the packs. Apparently it's important.'

'Just when I didn't think today could get worse.'

'Got to keep us on our toes.'

'At this point my toes are bleeding,' he muttered darkly. 'Where's Ally? Tell him to come mind the shop. I want to go home.'

Naida picked up the telephone and rotated the dial.

Thirty minutes later, they were back at the house. It was a relief to see both Nik and Ginny safe and sound. But every second felt like they were pressing their luck a little bit more.

Adair looked close to murder and didn't stop pacing, his agitation mounting; Isha cracked ever-worsening jokes that made only the children laugh; and Lucien obsessively cleaned and recleaned his weapons until it was time to go.

Evening brought howling winds and lashing rains, and humidity made the night hang heavy. Regardless, everyone got ready to head into Westend Circle. Even the children.

At the door, Lucien paused and caught Nik's arm, fear's iron grip around his lungs, choking every breath. 'Do not leave my side,' he implored. 'Do not say a word unless Henna asks you a direct question. Do not be an idiot.'

Nik rolled his eyes. 'I'm not.'

Lucien raised his eyebrows pointedly.

'I'm not going to say or do anything, Luka. I promise.'

The pack clambered into their two trucks and drove into the centre of town. Dozens of automobiles and steamtrucks were parked in the lot already.

As one, the pack got out of the trucks and headed inside. Lucien in front, Adair at the back. Without being told, Shim kept her hand on Ginny's back protectively, and any Suriias who might've looked twice, didn't once they saw the glare on Shim's face. Somehow it was more fearsome than the weapons at her side.

Adair walked on Nik's other side, a hand resting on the pistol in his holster. It reminded Lucien of years back when they'd lived vastly different lives.

The packs all trailed into the arena, the only space large enough for everyone in the district to gather. It wasn't usual for them all to crowd together and Lucien couldn't help but look around to see if there was anyone with magic they shouldn't have. Anyone who might have stolen the book. If they wore a clip, they wouldn't even be able to open the book in the first place, but what if someone had learned how to remove a clip?

His spiralling anxiety was only stilled by the hushing of the crowd as Henna stepped up onto the podium. Dressed in pastel colours with sequins and jewellery, they cut a striking figure.

'We have a new threat,' said Henna without preamble. 'The humans have created a way to, as they put it, remove Suric traces.'

'What does that mean exactly?' called Raguel.

'It means we're fucked,' said Trenton. 'Doesn't it?'

'It means they want to make us human,' said Henna.

'That's not possible,' said Adair loudly.

Henna nodded to him. 'Apparently it has a low success rate. A low success rate and a high mortality rate.'

A ripple went through the crowd.

'We should do something,' said one of the frai across the room. 'Strike before they do.'

'Strike how?' called a prico.

'We should start by getting rid of the humans,' said Raguel, looking directly at Nik as he said this.

Lucien scowled at him. 'Do not threaten my pack again, Raguel. You barely walked away from me on an off day. Imagine what I'll do to you if you come at me when I've eaten all my breakfast.'

'The humans amongst us are not the concern,' said Henna forcefully. 'They're as doomed as the rest of us. The threat are the humans outside the districts. We must come up with a plan. I want the leaders of the packs to convene here at the end of the week with ideas.'

As the crowds dispersed, a shiver went down Lucien's spine and the weight of someone's gaze made him linger.

It was then he saw her. Standing at the far back of the room, a glint in her eyes to match the weapons strapped to her waist and chest. His sister looked no worse for the wear.

She grinned wolfishly when he caught her eye. And then, as suddenly as she'd appeared, she vanished into the milling bodies leaving the arena.

Lucien kept a hand around Nik's waist as they moved through the crowd.

Halfway through Westend Circle, Raguel and his lackeys stepped out of the shadows and blocked their way. They looked like tarot card characters come to life.

'She matches the photographs,' said Raguel, stepping up, gloved hands clasped together. 'Your little human's wanted by the Enforcers.'

'Keep your delusions to yourself, fang-boy.'

Raguel inched closer. 'Not even Henna's going to save you when they find out what you're hiding.'

'That's enough Raguel,' said a voice behind Lucien. Henna had arrived and they didn't look amused at having to intervene in pack squabbles.

'He's endangering all of us, magister,' said Raguel. 'The girl can't stay.'

'The girl is part of my pack,' said Lucien, all but growling. 'You want to back off, Raguel.'

'What do you think the others will say when they find out?'

Lucien moved without thinking, seizing him by the lapels and slamming him against the wall.

'Enough,' said Henna. 'Let him go, Lightblood. Take your pack home.'

Tempted as he was to ignore them, Lucien slackened his grip and shoved Raguel away from him, sending him gracelessly into Matías.

No one said another word until they were back in their trucks and driving home.

'I'm sorry,' said Ginny, her voice thick with anxiety. 'Do I have to go?'

Lucien shook his head as he drove out of the carpark. 'No, of course not.'

'But Raguel—'

'I told you that you were part of this pack,' said Lucien. 'I meant it. Raguel will be dealt with.'

'Are you sure?'

'I'm sure, kid.'

Night had well and truly set in by the time they returned to the house. Everyone trudged to their rooms, no one in the mood to talk. Lucien followed Nik into his bedroom. They got ready for bed, but all Lucien could think about was Henna's warning, and Raguel's threat.

'You okay?' asked Nik after several minutes of silence.

'I'm fine.'

'Liar.'

Lucien didn't reply.

When at last Nik fell asleep, Lucien slipped out of the room and tiptoed to his study. Sitting at his desk, he lifted the phone out of its cradle.

He set it down after a few seconds and put his head in his hands. Cursing, he picked it up again. Turning the dial to the first two numbers, he hedged, and put it back down. Finally, with a sigh and a burst of determination, he dialled the old familiar number.

'Ezzie,' he said when a low voice answered the phone. 'I need your help …'

A throaty laugh. 'Do you?'

'Please, Ezzie.'

Her sigh exuded satisfaction, like a cat with a mouse caught helplessly in its paws, but her next words sounded sincere. 'Help with what?'

'My pack isn't safe. The humans are getting suspicions. And someone's stolen the bloody book.'

There was a painful pause.

'I'll be there first thing tomorrow.'

He sagged in relief. 'Thank you.'

Crazy as his sister was, he wanted her there. After all, sometimes crazy was the best way to handle an insane situation.

Esme arrived just after breakfast the next day, clothes soaked from the journey, boots and trousers caked with muck. She had as many tattoos as scars, and even more scratches than bruises. One of the few who travelled alone, she came onto the property with no warning, striding out of the morning fog like an omen in a dream.

Lucien, having sensed her presence later than he'd care to admit, jogged down the porch to greet her halfway. 'Hello, Ezzie.'

As if it hadn't been twelve years since last they'd really seen each other, she kissed his cheek. 'Looking well, big brother.'

As slight and wiry as ever, Esme had more muscle these days, more scars, too. The effect was fearsome, something Esme seemed to have in spades.

When she caught sight of Adair and Naida on the porch, Esme's smirk turned wicked. 'You two look well,' she drawled. 'Married life has given you grey hair.'

'You need a bath,' said Adair bitingly. Naida crossed her arms, scowl deepening.

'Want to give me one?'

Lucien grabbed her arm. 'Enough.'

'Spoil sport.'

'We're going upstairs,' he told the others, steering Esme up the steps and away from them. Naida and Adair tracked Esme with their eyes, but neither spoke.

'Do you have to start a fight?' he growled under his breath as they ascended the stairs.

She shrugged unapologetically. 'I was having a laugh.'

'They didn't find it funny.'

Ever acting the part of the most put upon soul in the universe, Esme huffed loudly. 'That's because they have the combined humour of beige teacups.'

Rolling his eyes, Lucien said nothing else until they were in his study and the door was closed.

'Forget Adair and Naida,' he said, taking his seat behind his desk. 'We have more pressing problems.'

'You really lost the book?'

He nodded grimly.

'Any idea where it's gone?'

'None.'

'But no one can open it here.'

'We hope.'

'Maybe it doesn't matter. My informant told me something interesting.' She crossed her legs and leaned back, lounging languidly. Esme always lounged. She would have been at ease on a battlefield. She had been.

'What's that?'

'District 6.'

She always had a story to spin, but this was a new angle of crazy. 'District 6 was blown up during the war.'

'Apparently not.' She folded her fingers together. 'Apparently the district whispers.'

'It ... whispers?'

'Yes.'

'I have no idea what that means.'

Esme waved her hand, a smirk quirking her lips, sparkling aether crackling tauntingly between her fingers. The magical fabric of the universe hadn't been accessible to Lucien in years and he ached for it. 'Come now, Lucien, you know the rumours just as I do. The humans are sourcing the magic for their clips from somewhere.'

'We don't know if there *is* magic in the clips.'

'Yes. We do.' Her eyes narrowed. 'There's more, too. I may have found a solution.'

'A solution for what?'

'Everything. But I need your help. I want your help.'

Lucien weighed these words, a bad feeling brewing in his gut. Trusting Esme was like trusting wildfire. 'You don't need help.'

She snorted in disappointment. 'How did we end up switching places, brother? It used to be you who protected me.'

The implication made his lip curl. 'You don't need protecting on Earth.'

'If you had stayed with me, that would be true.'

'My pack needed me.'

'I needed you.'

Frustration building, Lucien squeezed the bridge of his nose. Memories flooded his mind and all he could think about was Geon. 'I never wanted a war,' he muttered. 'I wanted nothing to do with that life. I've never lied about that. I just wanted to be left alone.'

She rolled her steely blue eyes. 'You can't change who you're meant to be, Lucien.'

'No,' he said with great finality. 'I left that life with Geon, Jae, Adair and Naida. And we're not going back.'

She threw up her hands. 'How is this life better?'

'There's less bloodshed.'

'Bullshit!'

'The humans started this,' he retorted. 'Not us. We lived here for two centuries in peace. They were the ones who grew fearful. Who believed us witches.'

Esme's mouth twisted into a smirk. 'I always liked that accusation.'

'You didn't seem to find being burned at the stake so funny.'

'Yes, well, they singed my favourite dress. Do you have any idea how long it took me to start liking dresses? And then they go and set me on fire. It was so rude.' Esme's magic kept her from being burned and she stepped off the pyre, naked, soot-covered, and annoyed enough to kill the entire village.

With a sigh, Lucien stood and walked over to the table in the corner and poured them both cups of coffee.

'I hear you're married,' she said abruptly. 'Congratulations.'

He handed her a cup and sat back down. 'Thank you.'

'Do I get a name?'

'His name is Nik. He's Geon's half-human son, apparently.'

The cup froze halfway to her lips. 'Geon fucked a human?'

'Ezzie …' he said warningly.

'Don't tell me you're not surprised, too,' she retorted. 'Geon hated humans.'

'Geon hated everyone who put his family in harm's way. Human or Suriia.'

She shook her head. 'He never looked twice at a human except to hurt them.'

The implication made him bristle. 'Geon did not hurt Nik's mother.'

'How do you know?' she challenged. 'None of us know what he was capable of by the end. Perhaps he ra—'

'No.'

'The magic ate his mind, Luka. He attacked you once.'

'He didn't know it was me,' said Lucien defensively. 'He was blind to it. He apologised after we got through to him. He never forgave himself.'

She held out a hand as if that proved her point.

He wanted to protest her insinuation, but the truth was that they *didn't* know. All they knew was that Nik was half-human and Geon lost his mind. How it went down was a mystery. But the thought of Geon as a rapist made Lucien's bones feel hollow.

'I'm tired of this life,' she muttered. 'We came here to be free of our oppressors, not to bow before new ones.'

'I know.'

'Then help me,' she pressed. 'What happens if it's found out that you've got a human here? They'll send you to prison. Nik will be executed if he's not used first. It's a bitter end for everyone. But if we can get rid of your clips, we can fight back, and then perhaps we can be free.' She reached out and put her hand over his. 'You and me, brother. Isn't that how we got this far?'

'Our friends are how we got this far.'

'Then let's keep our friends alive.'

He held her gaze for a long time, not sure what to say.

But she knew him, and she knew why he hesitated. 'What Lektor and Astril did to us will look like child's play if your enemies get their hands on your human husband.'

Bile rose in his throat, and he found himself nodding.

'I can back you up and I can keep your human safe. All we need is magic. And there's magic in District 6. But I want to come home, Lucien. I miss my family.'

'You can't be reckless this time,' he said. 'Not with them.'

'I won't,' she promised.

Resigned, Lucien nodded. 'Okay. You can come home.'

She left a few minutes later to gather her things and make final arrangements, and Lucien headed into the kitchen after watching her vanish into the trees like a ghost.

'What did Ezzie want?' asked Jae.

Taking the seat adjacent to Nik, Lucien glanced at the stack of papers in front of him with a small smile before looking around the group. 'She had a proposition for the pack.'

'Don't leave us in suspense,' said Ginny.

'She thinks the humans are getting the magic for the clips from a hole to Salfar in District 6.'

Jae frowned. 'That's near where we came in, isn't it?'

'Dead on.'

They all exchanged weighted looks.

'It's a risky excursion,' he continued. 'And I want us all to agree before we go. If we're caught, it could mean never coming back here. But if there is magic, and we're rid of the clips …'

'Then maybe we can be free,' Adair concluded.

Lucien held out a hand. 'We came to Earth to be safe, not to be enslaved.'

'Who would need to come?'

'The children should stay home,' said Naida.

Mi countered, 'Better to bring everyone.'

Eran inclined his head. 'I don't want to be left out. And besides, if you get seen and are forced to run, they'll come for us next.'

Lucien hadn't thought about that. He nodded in agreement. 'If we're going, we should all go together.'

'It'll make for a better alibi,' said Isha. 'We can say we're heading into District 4 for re-registration if we're stopped on the way.'

'Districts 5 and 7 are wildly out of bounds,' said Mi pointedly, crossing her arms and straightening up.

Shim leaned forward on her elbows. 'We'll have to walk it.'

'And we'll have to be fast,' said Naida.

Isha held up a hand. 'What do we say about the humans?'

Lucien looked over at Nik and Ginny. The pair of them had changed so much in the weeks since they'd moved in, but neither was combat ready. Both needed months of training before it would even be a laughable idea. As it stood, it was signing civilians up for a combat zone.

But Ginny, filled to bursting with bravado, showed no fear for all the dangers that lay waiting for them. She tucked her hair behind her ears and straightened up in her chair, bold as can be. 'I have a really, really bad idea.'

Lucien wanted to tell her there wasn't a chance. He wanted to tell her she wasn't allowed. He wanted to tell her that she was too green – no pun intended – too young, too much of a liability to bring into a fight, at least for several years to come. But the words never quite formed. In the face of her enviable optimism, determination and conviction, Lucien's good sense was soundly defeated by his admiration, and he found himself waving at her to join in. 'This is a wretched idea. Toss yours in.'

'Well,' she said slowly, clearly thinking through her plan as she went, 'the districts are weirdly laid out. There's no consistency to them. Some are random shapes, one's entirely square and three are circular. I think one looks like a pear actually. Like a jagged, fucked up pear.

'There's twenty-three districts on this island alone, with only five that allow Suriias free travel and another four that allow it with special permissions. You guys are going to have a fuck of a time just getting there in a group. Add in check points, random searches and potential problems, travelling with us two is stupid. But you also can't get into District 6 without going through 7 or 8. And 7 is forbidden to Suriias.'

The others looked flabbergasted by the depths of her knowledge on the system, but growing up the daughter of the top Enforcer would mean she went to the best schools, knew the ins and outs of the system, of the districts and the divides.

Lucien mulled all this over. 'What do you suggest?'

'The river,' said Ginny. 'Drive us as far into the districts as we can get, we'll swim the rest of the way. It's the only way to avoid the checks. Nik and I can meet you in 8. We can find a way into 6 from there.'

'If that's the case, we can all swim together.'

'The kids can't swim that far,' said Ginny bluntly. 'Nik and I can.'

'That's miles of ocean.'

'We've had to do worse.'

She wasn't *wrong*, but Lucien still found himself wholeheartedly disinclined to the idea. Unfortunately, no better options manifested in his mind, and judging by the expressions on everyone's faces, no one else could think of a better idea, either.

CHAPTER TWENTY-THREE
Various Theories of Matters Uncertain

Rain fell most of the following day, leaving the air smelling sharp and crisp. A little after breakfast, Esme returned. Lucien met her on the porch, and they embraced. Even after so many years, even after so much bloodshed, he was grateful to have his sister with him. At his side.

'You ready?' she asked after kissing him on the cheek.

'No,' he said bluntly. 'But I need a change.'

'I'm not going to let anything happen to you,' she assured him. 'You're my big brother.'

'I'm not worried about me.'

She leaned in and caught his gaze. 'I will *disembowel* the first one to touch your husband.'

Strange were the days those words sounded normal in, but the gratitude came hard and fast. 'Thank you, Ezzie.'

'Come on,' she said, linking arms with him and steering him off the porch. 'It's going to be fine. We're going to get everyone magic and we're going to get away from this ridiculous island and we're going to be free.'

'Promise?' he asked quietly, glad the others weren't in earshot.

'I promise,' she said.

The group joined them shortly thereafter and everyone clambered into Lucien and Adair's trucks, and the pack set off down the road. It was impossible not to feel the shared sense of trepidation that became not unlike heartburn to them all.

Lucien drove past the marshlands, taking a roundabout route around Westend. They lived in District 18, which was not close to District 5 or 7 in the least. The roads weren't packed, but that meant nothing. There were always Keepers at the checkpoints. Nik and Ginny were hiding in the leg area of the backseat, crammed between the others. If the Keepers demanded a search, there would be no hiding them.

As they neared the first checkpoint, Lucien's adrenaline picked up.

'It'll be fine,' said Esme. 'Just don't say a word.'

'This had better work.'

'It will.'

A Keeper stepped out of the booth and waved at Lucien to stop. He did so with mounting tension. Everyone in the truck also seemed to be holding their breath.

The Keeper reached Lucien's side of the truck and took out his notebook. 'ID.'

Before Lucien could speak, Esme leaned over, a wicked smirk on her face. She put her hand on the Keeper's arm and whispered the spell under her breath.

A dreamy look overcame the Keeper and he smiled dazedly, nodded, and stepped back.

Lucien drove ahead slowly into District 15. When they had driven far enough up the road that the checkpoint couldn't even be seen in the rear-view mirror, the group let out a collective sigh.

'I miss magic,' said Adair, the raw, unmasked ache in his tone going straight to Lucien's gut.

'Why haven't we done that before?' hissed Nik.

Lucien caught Adair's glance in the mirror, but didn't reply. Esme's penchant for bloodshed and brutality was what got her kicked out in the first place. Adair hadn't wanted her around his children.

Steam and smog filled the air of this district. The ground was gritty and littered with discarded bits and bobs. Lucien's eyes passed over the wires, cogs, and metalwork that littered the ground outside of an abandoned factory.

District 15 was known for its automata factories. It was the district that created not only self-operating machines, but everything from toys to weapons. The same company which made little wooden toys that clapped their hands together also made the clocks that chimed every time a Suriia was executed in the prison. The company also assembled the robots that had adapted technology to round up and detain Suriias.

Jae's question finally pulled Lucien's attention from the scene. 'Remember the hybas?'

The flying contraptions they'd used on Salfar were a far cry from the steamtrucks and hot air balloons and trains that the humans had created.

'Vividly.'

'Miss them?'

He shook his head. 'I do miss the unicorns. Remember Hark?'

'Hark!' Jae laughed at the memory of the ornery chestnut unicorn who liked to chase them around the paddock. 'He was fantastic.'

Eran jerked around in his seat, bug-eyed. 'Hang on, there are *actually* unicorns on Salfar?'

Ginny and Shara, too, looked positively delighted.

'Dragons, too,' said Jae darkly. 'Don't get too excited.'

'Unicorns, though?' Eran was beside himself and as they carried on, he hounded the adults with questions about what else he didn't know, more animated than he'd been in months.

When they'd passed as far into District 15 as they could get, the pack parked on the edges of the bank and everyone got out.

The world felt much too quiet. Like their every breath echoed across the island to alert the Enforcers to their location.

'I don't like this,' he said gruffly.

Nik gave him a sly grin. 'I'm a good swimmer.'

'That's not my greatest concern.'

'I'll be fine, Luka.' He pressed his forehead against Lucien's.

'These humans aren't going to let you down,' said Ginny with enviable bravado.

Shim ruffled her hair affectionately.

'It'll be fine,' Nik reiterated. He stepped back, winked, and then dove into the murky, brownish water.

Ginny followed suit a second later.

'Ew,' whispered Shara.

'We should move,' said Esme, appearing at Lucien's side.

Lucien forced himself to look away from the water. If he'd had his magic, he'd be able to at least feel Nik somewhere out there. But he couldn't even do that. Where the magic should have been, the clip dulled all sense.

None of them talked as they continued on to the next checkpoint.

This checkpoint, too, proved uneventful. But halfway through the district, Enforcer vehicles surrounded them.

Lucien pulled over, heart hammering.

'I can handle them,' said Esme, eyes dancing with unhindered magic.

'No,' said Adair.

'You used to be fun,' she retorted, exasperation laced into the complaint. 'I remember when we—'

'No one cares, Ezzie,' he snapped.

Naida glanced between them, but said nothing.

Not in the mood for dramatics, Lucien glanced at Esme and shot her a warning look. She held up a hand, conceding it for the time being.

The Enforcers converged on the truck and Lucien rolled down his window.

'Where are you headed?' asked the Enforcer.

'The Registrar's Headquarters,' said Lucien. 'To get our six month permits.'

'Papers.'

Shim passed Lucien the folder and he handed it to the Enforcer. The Enforcers checked each photograph with each Suriia in the truck, but after twenty minutes of pointless interrogation, they were allowed to carry on.

The dirty, rubbish covered banks of District 9 slowly came into view and they got out. Lucien wrinkled his nose at the water. Swimming with the kids was going to be stressful at best, but doing so in what looked like a biohazard zone made Lucien queasy.

'Gross,' said Mi loudly.

'Yep,' he grunted.

'I'm going to need more shots,' said Adair, disgust in every word.

'Medical or alcohol?'

'Either.'

'Same.'

With grim looks exchanged, the group waded into the murky water and began the long swim to District 6. The smell of the water was worse than the feeling, though both left Lucien wanting to bathe for the next decade. The air was thick with the smell of chemicals and sickly sweet fragrances; the water felt oily and gritty at the same time. More than once, his feet touched off something metal in the depths below him. Likely a sunken tank or fallen aeroplane from during the war.

'There aren't bodies in here, right?' called Mi.

Adair cursed. 'I hate you for even mentioning that right now.'

'Agreed,' said Lucien.

'We're all thinking it,' said Mi darkly. 'I think I just felt hair.'

Adair gagged loudly.

It took every ounce of concentration for Lucien to continue on without getting sick. But swimming in his own vomit was a level he wasn't going to let himself sink to.

Foul moods were universal by the time they reached the banks and stumbled ashore, everyone grumbling and whispering. He felt Nik's presence before he saw him. But there he was. Sitting on the hill of the opposite bank beside Ginny, knees drawn into his chest, a worried look on his face.

Ginny caught sight of Lucien first and nudged Nik, getting quickly to her feet and running down the dune towards the beach.

Lucien checked Nik over quickly for signs for damage; he followed this by inspecting Ginny. Both assured him they were fine.

Esme said, *'Ianvar,'* and everyone's clothes dried almost instantly.

'Let's go,' said Jae.

As one, the group made their way through the slats of the wall surrounding District 6. Everyone kept their weapons out, eyes peeled for any signs of movement. They crept without a sound across the overgrown lawn towards the black shape of the building. Yet even their steps sounded too loud, each gust of wind felt like a whisper of death.

'So, what did happen?' asked Shara, breaking the silence.

Lucien glanced over at her. 'What do you mean?'

'I mean, how did the others come through after you guys?'

'We're not sure,' said Adair, putting a hand on her shoulder. 'We think once we came through Salfar, the Tear just never closed. Others slipped through. Enough that it became noticeable.'

'Do you think humans got onto Salfar?'

Lucien and Adair locked gazes, but said nothing. It was a concern they'd all brought up over the years, but as the Tear had always been housed in District 6, none of them had ever gained answers.

'Stop!'

Everyone went still as a group of heavily armed Enforcers darted out from around a corner.

Before Lucien could react, Esme stepped forward, blue light gathering at the tips of her fingers like the enchantress she'd always been in secret.

'It's been a long time since I've killed anyone,' she purred. 'I'm sorry if it hurts. I'm out of practice.'

And then her fists closed.

The humans dropped to their knees, hands going to their heads as they screamed in agony.

'Go!' Esme shouted to the pack.

No one needed to be told twice; the pack hightailed it out of the vicinity. The only one who lingered was Lucien.

He nodded to her hands. 'When I get my magic back, I'm never losing it again,' he said.

'Amen,' she said with a dark laugh.

When the last Enforcer fell, the siblings turned and darted after the group.

The others had lingered around the next corner and all were staring ahead. There, high above them, a mass of black against the dark horizon, was the sarcophagus over District 6. The humans said it was there to keep in the radiation from a nuclear bomb dropped on the district during the war.

'Let's go,' said Esme.

'How do we get in?'

'The front door,' she said blithely, and blasted the door open with a pulse of blue light.

It was like stepping into a terrarium, a ghost town.

Moving through the still building with wide eyes, the pack kept their weapons out, exchanging glances every few steps.

'Do you know where to go?' he called over to Esme.

She nodded. 'The magic's coming from up ahead.'

Lucien listened hard, but he heard no sounds of anyone else nearby.

The corridors dragged on and on, and every step they took echoed like a threat in the soundless building.

At the end of a particularly long corridor was a door. But it was what was beyond the door that caught everyone's attention. The magic was palpable to them all.

Esme halted in front of the door. There was nothing really remarkable about it except the hum of aether. 'This is it,' she breathed. 'I told you it whispers.'

'That's not magic from Salfar,' said Lucien, feeling the magic coming out of the cracks around the door. 'This isn't where they're getting the clips' magic.'

'No,' said Jae. 'That's new.'

'New?' echoed Ginny. 'New how?'

'I don't know,' said Lucien. He glanced at Jae. 'This is right, isn't it? About where we came through?'

'Yeah, but what happened to the bridge?'

'The bridge was on our side, not this side,' said Adair.

'Was it?' Jae seemed to be having trouble remembering.

'We came out in the forest,' said Naida. 'Which is what this district used to be.'

Tuning them out, Lucien carefully turned the doorknob, bracing himself for something terrible. With haunting creaks, the door opened into a room.

But it wasn't what was in the room that made Lucien stiffen. It was what was outside the windows. He raised a shaking finger. 'You see those trees?'

Everyone nodded.

'Those are from Salfar,' said Adair.

'And that isn't Salfar?' asked Mi, squinting through the grimy windows at the world beyond.

Lucien scowled at the distant sky. 'No,' he said. 'The sun is different.'

'He's right,' said Adair.

'Should we keep going?' Mi sounded as wary as Lucien felt.

'It's that or double back,' said Shim. 'And I'm not getting into that disgusting river again.'

'Hear hear,' said Isha.

Lucien hesitated, running through the options one by one. The intention was never to go back to Salfar, but some place undiscovered lent a whole new series of possibilities. He wondered, idly, how many worlds there were. Perhaps the number was infinite and unknowable. And if that were the case, two worlds wasn't much, was it? Luck of the draw could end poorly twice without affecting the overall statistics, after all.

He looked at Nik. 'What do you think?'

'I say we keep going,' said Nik. 'Anything's better than Westend, right?'

'No,' said Lucien, Adair, Jae and Naida in unison.

'Still, it's the districts or a forest.'

'It's what might be inside the forest that worries me.' But Lucien didn't want to turn back, either. He was sick of the island. Sick of being hated. Sick of fearing for his pack at every turn. A new start was tantalising.

Readying himself with a deep breath, he withdrew his pistol and glanced at the others. 'If anyone wants to go back, talk now.'

'I want to go,' said Shara. The youngest in the group, her voice was still youthfully high-pitched, but her features were too pinched for a girl her age. She had never known plenty, never known opportunity. 'I don't want to grow up in Westend. Let's just go.'

And it was that, Lucien knew, that silenced anyone else's doubts.

Everyone took out their weapons, drew up their hoods, and exchanged final looks of determination before they walked through the door into the room with its window to a forest that was not quite Salfar, but was definitely not Earth. They left the room cautiously.

Outside, everything looked the same. Yet, not.

'Those trees are definitely from Earth,' said Adair, nodding ahead. 'So that's trees from both, now.'

'But the sky's different from Salfar,' said Jae, staring upwards. 'You can see a planet with rings in our skies. It's said that's where the Gods once lived.'

'Whoa,' said Ginny delightedly. 'Can you travel there?'

Carefully side-stepping a large broken branch, Lucien nodded. 'It's a holy pilgrimage to go.'

'To another planet?'

'Yes.'

'*Wicked*,' she exclaimed. 'What else?'

There was something genuinely lovely about her honest curiosity. For so long Lucien had buried memories of Salfar in the back of his mind so that they couldn't hurt him. So that the good memories didn't bleed into the bad ones and end up permanently damaged. But he did miss parts of it. He had loved so much of his homeland.

And so, as the pack made their way through the strange forest, he rattled off stories of Salfar. Of the great machines, far greater than anything ever seen on Earth, made of magic and metal; he told them about the cities in the sky, the rotating islands in the seas, the trees with opinions and the waterfalls that sometimes liked to reverse directions, blasting whomsoever was unlucky enough to be walking on the wrong part of the bank. He told them of the library that was eight miles long and rose twenty storeys in the sky – a description that made Nik moan with longing.

When they reached the outskirts of a city it was late in the day and the world had a monochrome tint. In the distance, great buildings jutted up into the clouds; small specks of machinery flew between them.

'They're advanced,' said Adair, an edge of caution in his tone. He caught Lucien's eye. 'We should be careful. We might not be anything like their natives.'

'I swear, if there's another witch-hunt, I will lose my bloody humour.' Lucien checked his gun neurotically, and again wished that his magic wasn't blocked off. It was like walking around without a necessary limb.

The pack kept close together as they wandered through the streets, mindful of the windows above them. But they seemed to have come into a moderately quiet area and they made it three streets without incident.

'Wait,' said Nik as they rounded the corner of an alley. He was staring at a poster. One of dozens, slapped onto the wall side by side. In vicious neon colours, there was no ignoring the message. 'What does it say?'

The writing was Enesh, Lucien's native language. '"Turn yourself in. It's safer inside."' He nodded to the cartoon printed in bright colours beneath. 'It's calling for humans to come to camps.'

'I'm guessing not summer camps,' squeaked Shara.

'No.'

'That isn't comforting at all,' said Adair.

Lucien glanced at Shim and nodded. She nodded back, gestured to Isha, and the pair of them jogged down the road in the opposite direction, weapons out. Mi and Jae left down a third street to scout the area. But this world was more advanced than their last, the technology more like Salfar's, and Lucien now had to worry about surveillance.

An abandoned building further on proved a good hiding place, and Lucien told the rest of them to wait before setting off on his own.

It took no time at all for his suspicions to come to fruition. Suriias ruled this world, and it didn't seem remotely welcoming to humans.

An hour's wandering around the bustling city brought Lucien to what he presumed was the local government's office. He approached the front desk cautiously, expecting to be thrown out or imprisoned. He hadn't been in a government building in years. Not since long before the war.

At the reception desk sat a Suriia with purple hair, pointed ears, and eyes bright pink. When she raised her head, Lucien realised she was a vylka.

'Good afternoon,' she greeted, the points of her teeth visible behind her smile. 'Who are you here to see?'

'Whomever's in charge,' he said, marvelling at this strange new world where Suriias ruled. 'It's important.'

She gestured for him to take a seat as she dialled a number onto a screen.

A group of several Suriias filed out of a glass elevator. Seeing so many affluent Suriias felt surreal. Most wore a blue uniform. A few wore suits. All stopped dead at the sight of him.

'May we help you?' asked one, sidling over. There was something smarmy about the fellow, obsequious and conniving.

Lucien instantly disliked him. 'And you are?'

'Benjamin Cae,' said the frai. 'Leader of the Unit of Prestigious Hunters.'

'That trips right off the tongue,' he said dryly.

Benjamin didn't seem to find him amusing. 'Where are you from?'

'The continent,' he lied. 'I have a meeting here today.'

'With whom?' asked Benjamin disbelievingly.

One of the Suriias behind him, a black-haired sbura, slid forward and put a hand on Lucien's shoulder with a familiarity that was entirely fake.

'Forgive me for being so late to our meeting,' said the sbura. 'I've been going over the new referendum proposal.'

'Right,' said Lucien. 'Don't worry about it.'

'Benjamin,' said the sbura, turning succinctly to the bewildered frai. 'My office will send the draft in the morning. If you'll excuse us …'

Without waiting for Benjamin to dismiss them, the sbura steered Lucien out of the building.

'I don't know who you are,' said the sbura in a low voice. 'But you're going to get into a world of trouble if you're not more careful.'

'Why?'

'Because everyone can smell the human on you.'

'I haven't hurt anyone.'

The sbura pivoted and stopped him short. He leaned in, lips almost brushing Lucien's ear. 'And if you say that any louder, you're going to arouse suspicion. I know you're not from the continent. Which leads me to believe you're from the wildlands.'

'No,' said Lucien. 'I'm from Salfar.'

The sbura's brow shot up. 'No one's come through the Tear in years.'

'We didn't come through a tear. We came through a door.'

Judging by the sbura's expression, this was clearly not a common occurrence.

Opening the door to one of the flying contraptions, the stranger gestured for him to get in. Too curious not to, Lucien clambered inside. The interior of the machine was as flashy and expensive as the outside, and Lucien, in his threadbare attire, felt wholly out of place.

'What's your name?' asked the sbura.

'Lucien. You?'

'Nithin.'

The name was from Salfar, but the sbura certainly wasn't. He had that born-on-Earth aura about him. Like an animal that had been raised in captivity and didn't know its own strengths and weaknesses.

'Are you travelling with humans?'

'Yes.'

'From Salfar?'

'No,' said Lucien.

'The humans travelling with you aren't on the Register?'

Wary, Lucien said, 'My husband is one of those humans.'

'I understand. My wife is human. But if anyone outside this coach were to know your humans are unregistered, they're not even safe to stand on the roadside.'

Lucien was really, really regretting leaving Westend.

'Lucky for you,' Nithin continued, 'I can add them. I need names and pictures. It's the only way to keep them safe.'

'Safe from what?'

'Us.'

'What's wrong with this world?'

'Humans are all but extinct here.'

Lucien held his gaze, weighing the meaning of his words. Nithin had the weary, sombre look of one who had been fighting an uphill battle with no end in sight for far too long. It was a look Lucien deeply empathised with and he felt an odd rush of trust towards this stranger he didn't know. After a beat, Lucien held out his arm and rolled up the sleeve.

'Can you remove this?'

With a pensive scowl, Nithin took him by the wrist, glancing down between watching where he was flying. 'Who did this?'

'Long story.'

Nithin's eyes blazed emerald as he covered the clip with his hand. The rush of magic that filled Lucien almost knocked him out as the clip tugged angrily out of his skin and into Nithin's palm.

Lucien took several shuddering breaths. It was like he'd been half-breathing for years and now his lungs could finally expand.

'Thank you.'

Nithin nodded.

Soon enough, they landed outside another building, one far less unsettling.

'Bring your human friends to this address and we'll get this done as quickly as possible,' said Nithin, holding out a card. 'My company also has funds set aside for helping human refugees. We can spare a little to see you and your pack settled.'

Lucien took it. *The Lathlak Corporation.* 'Thank you. I genuinely appreciate it.'

'Do you have a place to stay tonight?'

'No.'

All business and efficiency, it seemed, Nithin bobbed his head. 'We'll get one of the larger coaches and go pick up your friends.'

It took less than an hour to gather everyone in one of the meeting rooms at the Lathlak Corporation.

Nithin introduced the pack to his colleagues, three of which were human, and one frai who exuded a remarkable amount of energy.

After sorting out the registration and paperwork, Nithin called a driver for them and the pack were then flown through the city and into one of the nicest neighbourhoods Lucien had ever seen.

Unlike the human cities on Earth made of metal and chrome and brass, everything running off steam power, Courtenz was half in the air, entirely vibrant, neon and loud; a high-powered, industrial world of magic and might which made Lucien baulk internally.

Nik took his hand once they were all inside the house and the pack was left alone to settle in. 'Even if this place doesn't work, isn't trying better than not?'

'I suppose.' Still wary and mindful, Lucien glanced at Adair. 'What do we know about the sbura?'

Adair gestured for them to join him in front of a brightly lit screen. They had had something similar on Salfar; here they called it a computer.

'This is him,' said Adair, pulling up a webpage. 'Lord Nithin Summons. The only son of another Lord Summons. His father was apparently the mastermind behind something called the Human Relocation Programme.'

Lucien made a face. 'That sounds beyond questionable.'

'Yes, it sounds bleak. Proposed after their war.'

'They had a war? We've got that in common.'

'Their war reads worse than ours,' said Shim, peering over Adair's shoulder.

A sick feeling spread through Lucien. 'But Nithin isn't in agreement?'

'Not according to this,' said Adair, still scrolling down the page, eyes darting back and forth. 'He's causing quite a stir. Married a human.'

'He mentioned that.'

Finding nothing about Nithin that was of great concern, the pack broke up into groups.

Wary as they were, everyone wanted to explore the new city. Not wanting Nik and Ginny out in the world until they ascertained the level of risk involved, Lucien told Jae to remain behind with them and the children, and the rest set off for the shops.

Flying machines, flying Suriias and even flying buildings, hovered and thrummed in the air high above them. For Shim and the others who had never seen such technology, it was a wonderous and striking sight. For Lucien, Adair and those from Salfar, it was like seeing a cruder, less advanced version of what they'd grown up with.

Locating the market didn't prove too difficult, although the lifts shot them high into the sky and Isha vomited in her mouth, only just managing to swallow it back down rather than getting sick in the corner.

When the doors opened, Lucien branched off to find the toilets with Isha, and the others split up to browse. How long had it been since he could walk freely? Since no one stopped him or scorned him? Since he wasn't fighting or bartering or begging?

They ended up spending far longer browsing the shops than they intended, although they only bought food and necessities. The money Nithin had given them proved more than enough.

At the house, the others were sitting on the sofa and chairs, watching something called a television. Lucien sat down at Nik's feet on the floor and watched the news broadcaster for almost two hours, curiosity getting the best of him.

The hour was late when his eyelids began to close of their own accord. Bidding the others goodnight, he followed Nik down the hall to the room he'd apparently claimed for them.

Lucien dropped down heavily on the bed.

'Tired?' asked Nik.

'I woke up in an alternate universe this morning,' said Lucien quietly. 'How strange. Stranger still, it's not the first time I've said that.' The difference was, when he first arrived on Earth, he'd had hope. Now all he had was a deep, rotting wariness.

Nik rested his head on Lucien's chest. 'Try and get some sleep.'

Lulled by the calm thudding of Nik's heartbeat, Lucien nodded off almost immediately. But he felt like he'd only just closed his eyes when he rolled over, blinking awake, to find the bed beside him empty.

Frowning, he got out of bed. In the sitting room, he found Ginny on the sofa, watching television; Nik was sound asleep beside her, his head in her lap.

'He couldn't sleep,' she whispered. 'I was awake already.'

Lucien kneeled beside the sofa and brushed Nik's hair out of his eyes.

'Ashby again?' he wondered aloud.

'No, his brothers.'

The sudden rushing in his ears threatened to burst Lucien's eardrums. 'His what?'

Ginny's eyebrows shot up. 'You didn't know?'

'No.'

She nodded sadly. 'A prico attacked them. He hasn't seen them since. I think he said they were twins.'

A prico attacked them.

The surge of guilt and bitterness tasted toxic on Lucien's tongue. He didn't want to pry answers out of Nik. He knew he didn't have the right. But was there a chance Nik wasn't telling him something about Geon? Was there a chance it was Geon who'd—

Lucien shook his head fiercely. He'd seen Geon pull out the eyes of a man they caught mid-rape during the war. And in the fray of battle, Geon never left his side. After, he'd never let Geon out of his sight long enough for anything to happen. He never went anywhere. There was no way Geon could have harmed anyone. The timelines, the brothers. None of it made any sense.

'I don't know much,' she whispered. 'But I know their names. Eun and Hyun.'

'Eun and Hyun,' he repeated, flabbergasted. If there was any doubt, their names erased it. Eun and Hyun were the names of Geon and Jae's brothers who died in their youth. Killed on the king's orders.

He pressed his lips to Nik's forehead before standing and leaving them alone.

Lucien stayed awake the rest of the night, staring out the window, glaring at the neon lights of the city, mulling everything over. Their temporary home was high above the ground and the window was level with many of the flying coaches. He had so many questions and no one to ask. This new world was clearly modelled on Salfar, but not nearly as magical. It was an echo world. Like someone had taken a black and white film, coloured it in neon and added special effects from the wrong decade. Some things just didn't *fit* quite right. The effect was jarring.

But despite the oddity of this second Earth, his mind returned to the first one he'd seen. Which was the real one? Which was the mistake? Why had both fallen victim to bloodshed? Was society the problem, or were the inhabitants? Would fear always turn souls to darkness?

When Lucien was little, his brother Faren told him stories to help him fall asleep. Stories of souls and starlight. He told Lucien often that no Suriia could die of old age, but if killed, if sick, if cursed, a Suriia's soul would fall to the realm of Earth. A second life that was so fragile, death lurked around every corner. But Faren hadn't been afraid. He used to tell Lucien that the third life was one of wind and whispers. A true joining of self to soul, and soul to starlight. And once you became starlight, you became magic itself and one day, you would be drawn back down to the first life, pulled by magic and destiny, and you would return anew.

Faren's theories of starlight had always seemed the most beautiful way to transcend the fear that choked so many. For when spun like silk, such words were the stuff of daydreams and dances. And for so long Lucien had clung to Faren's certainties and blanketed himself in them. But the longer he had to fight, the threat of war constantly on the horizon, the more difficult it was to see Faren's starlight.

CHAPTER TWENTY-FOUR
The Girl, the Camp and the Kiss

The revelation that Nik had brothers was one Lucien revisited again and again in the weeks that followed, but he didn't know how to even go about broaching the subject. Unfortunately – or fortunately, depending on how queasy he felt on any given day – the opportunity never presented itself. The new world had distractions and obstacles aplenty, and Lucien found himself facing complications he could never have conjured up in his mind, not even in his nightmares. Not only were Nik and Ginny in even more danger than before, the plight of humans also seemed to be deteriorating by the day.

Back on their world, the situation for Suriias was unpleasant, but in a holding pattern. It was the added complication of having humans in their home that had propelled them to change. Here, the number of humans still left alive was broadcasted daily on the news like a countdown clock. Machines patrolled the streets, scanned the windows, tracked the coaches. Cameras placed at every corner along the streets meant that someone watched every movement they made. Lucien couldn't relax, not even if he'd wanted to.

The feeling wasn't universal amongst his pack, however. Isha and Mi were settling in relatively well and both secured jobs in Courtenz within the first fortnight. Shara was already talking about enrolling in school at the start of the new year, while Eran had brought home college brochures. For his part, Kalid wanted to know when he could start training again. There wasn't anywhere to spar in this strange new world, and Lucien had the feeling that the Suriias here would view them with suspicion if they did.

Racked with fear, Lucien spent most nights glaring out of the window at the vibrant city and counting every shadow. If they stayed, Nik was in danger; if they went back, Nik was in danger.

Lucien didn't know what to do. But it wasn't long before he was forced to find out.

Weeks into their arrival, Lucien woke with a jolt, the space beside him in the bed once again empty.

For a brief second, he assumed Nik had woken up and was in the sitting room with Ginny again, but then he realised that he couldn't even *sense* him. As if Nik was nowhere nearby.

Scrambling to his feet, he darted out of the bedroom. 'Shim!' he barked.

She appeared almost instantly from the adjoining room, pulling a shirt on. 'Ginny's gone also,' she said.

'I'm going to kill them,' he hissed. 'Anyone else?'

'Shara and Kalid,' said Adair from the other end of the hall. 'Eran.'

'They're *all* dead.'

The coach was missing, but with magic restored to them, that hardly mattered. They tracked them to the edges of the city where the forest began.

Lucien tore through the trees, the others hot on his heels. He tracked his magic to the heart of the forest, far into the mountains, running faster than he had been able to in centuries.

He'd been expecting a longer run, however, when they came upon a standoff in the forest. Spotting the coach Nithin had given them, Lucien motioned to Shim, who slowed at once. He couldn't sense Nik well with the magic of the Enforcers filling the area, but he caught sight of Ginny in the front seat of the coach.

Without pausing, Lucien dropped down between the coach and the Enforcers.

'Lower your weapons,' he growled at the Enforcers. 'Now.'

'These humans are under arrest,' said the nearest Spotter. 'We're taking them all in.'

'They're ours.' Lucien cocked his head to the side. Purple light coloured the air around him and the gun jumped into his hand; in a fluid motion, it was aimed at the Spotter's heart. He heard his pack mimic him. 'We were told we get to keep the ones we've claimed.'

'You have claim only to your husband, Lightblood,' said a second Spotter. 'Not to multiple renegade humans.'

'The humans belong to us all,' said Shim tersely. 'We've been keeping them here. The cities aren't safe.'

'Precisely,' said Lucien. 'You are threatening my pack, Ivor.'

'Humans cannot be part of prico packs.'

'I beg to differ.'

There was a sudden flash of light that blinded everyone temporarily and the last soul Lucien expected to see appeared beside him.

Kol Sinn, Nithin's energetic business partner, in his true form was somewhat less obnoxious looking than when he wore his second self, but Lucien was still hard pressed to find him anything but a hindrance in a conflict. Lucien wondered if he'd ever even thrown a punch.

To his credit, Kol's threat came out barbed and filled with wrath. 'I will report you all to Lord Sinn if you don't leave immediately,' he growled. 'Now.'

The Spotters all exchanged uncertain looks. A few lowered their weapons. No one moved to leave, though.

'You have no authority here, Mister Sinn,' said one at the back, although he did not sound confident. 'This isn't your concern.'

His patience evidently expired, Kol's hand closed in a fist and the Spotter dropped to his knees. He clawed at his neck, unable to breathe.

'Don't piss me off, Vikryn,' Kol continued. 'I can have your job for that little remark.'

Another Spotter inched forwards. 'Are the humans yours or Lightblood's?'

'They received permission from Lord Sinn to keep their humans here,' said Kol acidly. 'Mine along with them.' He relaxed his hand, barely. 'This little show of stupidity will be reported. And be aware that my father will hear of this.' Then, with a snap of his fingers, their identification badges flew off the lapels of their coats and into his hand. 'Now fuck off.'

Everyone held still as stone until the Enforcers' coaches vanished, swallowed by the branches of the treetops.

Ginny broke first, sprinting towards Lucien and jumping into his arms, trembling with relief.

'I'm going to put a bell on you,' he said when she dropped to the ground. 'I'm fucking serious, kid.'

Ginny offered a tentative smile. 'We just wanted to help, Luk.'

'Not a great excuse.'

By this point the others were surrounding them. He didn't see Nik and fear coiled like a snake in his stomach.

'Where's Nik?' he asked her sharply.

'He's not with us.'

Lucien stared at Ginny in horror. 'What does that mean?'

'He took the other coach. With Eran.' Ginny was suddenly on the verge of tears and Lucien didn't have time to wonder where they had even sourced a second coach. He could only juggle so many problems.

'We split up when the group did,' she continued. 'He went after some of the humans being chased.'

'We're leaving,' he said to his pack. 'Now.'

A scarred, skinny, scrawny girl joined them. 'I'm coming with you.'

Lucien glanced at her. 'You sure, kid?'

'They have my friends, too.'

'I'm coming as well,' said another of the humans. Two more followed suit.

'Rose, wait,' Kol begged the girl. 'We can't go running to the death camps. We need a plan.'

'We're not waiting, frai-boy,' said Lucien, irritation mounting.

'You'll put everyone at risk if you run in headfirst!'

Ignoring him, Lucien carried on to the coach, doing his utmost not to think about the last time he'd been in such a camp.

'If they have Nik, they have Eran,' said Naida from the back.

'They'd arrest a Suriia?' asked Ginny.

'For helping?' said Lucien. 'Yes.'

The scarred human girl suddenly joined them in the coach, closing the door firmly behind her. 'Do you have a plan?' she asked breathlessly.

'Rose, was it?'

'Thorn.'

'Thorn,' he echoed. The name suited her. 'I don't need a plan.' He was simply going to kill anyone who had put their hands on his husband.

'Are you powerful enough for this not to be a suicide mission?' she queried.

'Would that stop you?'

'No. I'm just curious.'

'No Suriia born on Earth is as powerful as me.'

His words seemed to give her pause, but her next question came out shockingly well-informed. 'You're from Salfar, aren't you?'

'Yes.'

'Why are you helping humans?'

The politics of humans versus Suriias was not something he had the attention span for now. And there was no explaining how little he cared about such things to someone whose life had clearly been deeply impacted by fallout of a similar kind. So, he settled for, 'I help my pack.'

'Are you sure we're going the right way?'

'Yes.'

'How?'

'I can track him.'

'You get Spotter training, too?'

'I'd rather eat dirt.'

'Then how?'

'He's my husband.'

'A little explanation goes a long way …'

'When pricos marry, they make magical imprints.'

'How?'

'He's had my blood,' said Lucien distractedly, eyes fixed on the terrain below. 'My blood has my magic.'

'So, you're tracking your own magic.'

'Yes.'

Thorn appeared slightly impressed by this knowledge. 'And Kol said he was good at tracking.'

'Frai are useless trackers.'

'I'll tell him you think so.'

'If he doesn't know, he's also markedly unintelligent.'

'He's not.'

'I'm sure he's not,' said Lucien, tempted to make a joke about the frai. But now wasn't the time. 'We're here.'

When he landed, everyone disembarked and spread out, weapons in hand, the magic fuelled by his rage.

Lucien walked straight at the front gates and blasted them open with a wave of his hand. The others sent a secondary pulse of magic at the guards, knocking them flat.

When they reached a set of bolted doors, Lucien unlocked them with a muttered spell. Everyone darted inside, and the lights came on.

The sight that unveiled itself before their eyes was sick. Twisted. Absolutely fucking wrong. In cages that went on and on, dozens of humans had been locked away. Some weren't conscious, others were barely standing; all showed signs of ill health and track marks.

Thorn voiced everyone's reaction: 'What the fuck?'

Lucien raised hands that trembled with fury, and the doors of the cells disintegrated in a blast of glass and metal.

'Nik!' he bellowed.

'Parin!' yelled Thorn. 'Trinity!'

He didn't even pause as he followed the feeling to the eighth cell. Nik was forcing himself to his feet, but he'd been beaten and was struggling.

'You came,' he said dazedly, blood dribbling out of his mouth. 'You came.'

Lucien caught him before he could stumble and pressed his lips to Nik's forehead briefly before helping him out of the cell. Nik's legs could barely keep him upright and he kept stumbling.

Adair and Jae sprinted over to them, eating up the distance in seconds.

'Take Nik,' said Lucien. 'Go, now!'

He turned just in time to see the Spotters arrive from a set of doors at the other end of the building. 'Run!' he bellowed.

Everyone moved except Thorn. The girl drew her gun with remarkable bravery – or stupidity, he wasn't wholly sure.

'Better run, kid,' he called.

'Fuck that.' She took the other gun out of his pocket and aimed both at the Spotters. Grinning at her gumption, Lucien flicked his fingers and she fired.

The Spotters were knocked to their knees and bullet holes appeared in their throats and faces.

All it took was a nod exchanged before Lucien and Thorn were sprinting away from the gruesome scene.

'Where'd the others go?'

'The forest,' said Lucien, nodding to their left. 'I can hear them.'

'All of them?'

'All of them.'

'If we don't make sure this place is gone, they'll figure out it was us,' she said. 'It'll blow back on the others.'

Lucien looked at her, bemused that she assumed he hadn't thought of that. 'I wasn't aiming to leave this shithole standing.'

'What do you suggest?'

He stepped forwards, drawing magic from the world around him, and directed it all back upon the death camp. The electrics began to crackle and fry, the wires snapped and fell, cascading sparks through the air like a lightshow; fire appeared inside the building, bursting through the windows and sending glass everywhere.

'Whoa,' said Thorn, stunned.

They were still grinning at each other when a shot ripped through the air and blood soaked the front of her shirt.

In the forest behind her, a Spotter lowered his gun. Before Lucien could shoot him, Nithin Summons appeared behind him and slit his throat viciously. But where he'd come from, how he'd found them, was a question for later.

Lucien reached Thorn just as her legs gave out, catching her before she hit the ground. Lifting her easily, he carried her into the trees away from the camp. But he couldn't carry her far. She was bleeding too badly.

Lowering her carefully, Lucien pressed his hands to the wound. It did nothing. Against the white snow, she looked so small, the blood spreading out around her redder than a rose.

Her eyes rolled back in her head and he shook her roughly. 'Hey! Hey! Don't! Stay with me.'

She rolled open an eye and coughed out splatters of blood that hit him in the face.

'Hey,' he tried again, brushing hair out of her eyes, utterly failing to keep the fear out of his voice. He had lost too many good souls to stray bullets and bigotry. 'Want to know a secret?' he asked, adopting a conspiratorial tone that he hoped would distract her from the pain and fear. 'This is a nightmare world. It's not meant to be. It's just a nightmare, okay? It isn't real.'

'Feels real.'

'It's a lie,' he promised. He knew it in his bones. Something was deeply wrong with both Earths. And he had a terrible feeling it was all his fault.

A weak, gurgled laugh cut out of her. 'Nightmares don't hurt.'

He wiped the blood from her lips and forced a smile that broke his heart. 'Where I'm from, humans are in charge. Imagine that.' She didn't need to know it was a bad world.

A feeble smile twitched at the corners of her mouth and he was glad he'd said it.

'Now that sounds like a dream …'

Her eyes closed.

She stopped moving.

Her heartbeat slowed, and then ceased altogether.

'Move!'

Nithin Summons was suddenly at their side. Shoving Lucien away with shocking strength, he dragged Thorn into his arms. Emerald light lit up his skin from the inside, like he was suddenly made of glowing embers.

'What are you doing?' cried Lucien, mind slow to catch up through the fog of grief.

Nithin ignored him. He leaned down, took a deep breath, brow furrowed in concentration, and kissed Thorn.

There was no romance to the act. If anything, it looked like it caused him physical pain. Green light spread from his skin into hers like electricity crawling from a broken wire. The rain drenched them both, the blood on Thorn staining Nithin's expensive, impeccable suit.

It was an act Lucien hadn't seen since Salfar. A sacrifice he didn't think a Suriia born on Earth was even capable of.

And then Lucien heard Thorn's heart start beating again.

Nithin jerked back, wiping his mouth, Thorn's blood coating his lips. He barely managed to get away from her before he started to heave, horrible, painful sounds tearing out of him. His hands went to his skull as he let out an almighty roar of raw agony. Green light burst out of him and into Thorn, and then he collapsed, blood dripping from his nose and ears.

Lucien looked from one to the other, too shocked to really process what had just transpired.

'Lucien!'

Adair and one of the humans shot out of the trees towards him. The human lifted Thorn into his arms while Adair heaved Nithin up and over his shoulders.

'Let's go,' he urged. 'The drones are coming.'

Necessity overwhelmed Lucien's confusion and he forced himself to his feet. Sending one final blast of magic at the camp, all but obliterating it, Lucien hurried through the woods behind them to where the coach was waiting. They clambered inside and Shim steered them into the air.

It wasn't long before they arrived at Nithin Summons' mansion. Everyone got out in front of the large marble steps as the front doors opened and two figures bolted down to meet them.

Lucien stepped out of the coach with Adair, who picked Nithin up once more. But the human boy carrying Thorn recoiled as Kol reached out to take her.

'No way,' he said as another boy covered in wretched bruises moved to his side, a gun held warningly in his grip. 'She stays with us.'

'I can help her,' said Kol, the worried anguish in his tone hard to hear. 'Please.'

A girl stepped up behind Kol. 'She belongs with me.'

'She belongs with us,' argued the boy. 'We're her family.'

'Grey,' said one of the others. 'That's Thistle. Her best friend.'

'We're her best friends,' he snapped. 'We didn't abandon her.'

Thistle scowled at him. 'I didn't abandon her.'

'We know what happened,' said the man beside Grey, a glare of equal possessiveness twisting his scarred face.

Lucien sighed, wishing he could easily side with the boys. 'She's going to be unconscious for weeks, if not longer. You'll need magic just to keep her alive.'

Both boys stared at him.

'Why?' demanded Grey.

'Because she died,' he said sombrely.

Everyone's attention snapped to him; Kol let out a choked sound and reached for Thorn again. This time Grey didn't stop him and Kol lifted her into his arms. He didn't look at anyone else as he disappeared into the ridiculously large house.

'And Nithin?' asked Thistle.

'He'll be fine,' said Lucien confidently.

Adair was sagging with exhaustion, so Lucien heaved Nithin up and brought him into the mansion. Thistle led the way upstairs.

After depositing Nithin in his room, Lucien found Kol further down the hall, sitting on the edge of a bed; under the blankets, bruises starting to settle, Thorn slept on. He was sewing shut a gash on her arm where debris had raked her flesh open.

'You've got a good friend,' said Lucien from the doorway. 'He didn't hesitate, he didn't even think it over. It's the rare friend who gives up everything.'

'He's my brother,' said Kol, voice hollow. 'He would have done it even if it killed him.'

Lucien had started to like Nithin already, but now admiration cemented the feeling. 'Tell them I hope they feel better?'

'Will do.'

'And let me know if you need anything.'

'Thank you.'

With nothing else to offer him, Lucien stumbled out of the mansion and clambered into the backseat of the coach. Once they were in the air, he rested his head on Nik's shoulder and dozed for the remainder of the journey.

PART THREE
Sleight of Hand

CHAPTER TWENTY-FIVE
Please Just Kill Me

Autumn's glow dusted the dream, casting everything in a warm hue of rust and honey, saturated in that impossible way that only happens in dreams. Thorn didn't remember getting there. Perhaps she'd always been in the forest, safe amongst the dirt and trees. She was barefoot, the soil soft and cloudlike beneath her, the air warm, the sky cloudy yet kind.

Laughter trilled through the air and she turned – it felt like slow motion – and saw her parents. Her father was chasing her mother, promising to tickle her. Her mother couldn't stop giggling.

Thorn laughed.

'Tor!'

Thistle came out of the trees beside her, smile brighter than a firework display. Wearing only a dress, her feet also bare, she looked like a ballet dancer on the run.

They caught each other in a wild tackle that sent them falling to the ground. But they fell slowly, in no danger of a hard landing.

And then suddenly the forest was a field, and Thistle was gone.

Thorn got to her feet, more curious than concerned.

'Rose.'

Kol was walking towards her. Had he been there the entire time?

He reached out, twining her fingers between his.

'Where are we?' she asked.

'The future,' he said conspiratorially. 'Just us.'

He leaned down to kiss her—

And Thorn woke up.

She was in her old room at Nithin's. There was no sign of anyone. The sun was shining through the window and everything was quiet. Calm. Safe.

She could smell flowers wafting in from the open window; different scents she identified easily after so long around Kol. Belatedly, the events at the death camp came back to her. She remembered getting shot. Hastily pulling her shirt up, she searched the place she knew the bullet had gone in. The scar was pale and ice cold. As if it had been months. She ran her fingers over the bumpy scar tissue, utterly perplexed. How long had she been out of it?

Heart hammering, she scrambled out of bed and went to the mirror. Physically, she was no different. She could *feel* it, though. Something wasn't right.

She stared at her eyes, wondering if she could somehow see into her own soul and detect what the change was. But outside of being even more underweight than normal, she couldn't tell what was different.

Desperate for answers, Thorn tied her greasy, tangled hair back from her face and pulled on clean clothes. Someone had left her father's knife and Kol's iron blade by the bed and she tucked them into her boots, feeling somewhat sturdier having them on her. But her legs felt weak and shaky, and she stumbled as she left the bedroom.

There was no one in the hallway, nor any sounds. Everything was eerily quiet.

She walked to Kol's bedroom, but it was empty, as was Thistle and Nithin's room. Only when she reached the bottom stair did she hear the low hum of voices.

Opening the door to the garden, she stepped out into the chilly, sunny day. There was no snow on the ground, though there was still a cold bite to the air.

'Rose!'

Jerking around, she caught sight Kol, already making his way over to her. She met him halfway and threw her arms around him, burying her face in his neck.

'How long was I out?'

'Almost a month.'

Shock cascaded through her, leaving her limbs weak and noodle-like. That would only be possible in a hospital, or with magic. She leaned back. 'What?'

He appeared to be clinging to his composure and didn't respond to her question. 'I thought I'd lost you.'

'Why does the bullet hole look like a scar?'

Instead of answering, he brushed stray strands of hair from her face, still marvelling at her return. Leaning in, he kissed her deeply.

For a brief spell, it was just her and Kol, and she could imagine them forever suspended in the autumn glow of her dreams.

'Tor!' Thistle's cry broke them apart and Thorn embraced her best friend for several precious seconds before her mounting trepidation at whatever it was Kol had given her caused her to turn to him once more.

'What did you do?'

He shook his head fervently. 'It wasn't me.'

'It was Nithin,' said Thistle, equally as careful with her words. She squeezed Thorn's hand. 'I'm so glad you're okay.'

Thorn disentangled herself from Thistle and Kol and took a step back. 'What did he do to me?'

'I gave you a gift.'

She whirled around. 'What?'

Nithin crossed his arms, looking haughty as ever. He was dressed in a suit like always, his sleek hair brushed back. He was cool, suave, collected. But there was something different about him now. Something she couldn't quite place her finger on.

'Every Suriia can sacrifice themselves to save a human life,' he drawled. 'The cost, unfortunately, is our own power.'

'What are you talking about?'

Nithin held her gaze, and she realised then that there was no surge in his green eyes, no overtly sexual vibe, no ripples of power. He cocked his head to the side, but there was no mockery in his voice when he spoke next. 'I'm human,' he said humourlessly. 'You're welcome.'

The swallow she forced felt filled with razors and sand. 'What. Am. I.'

'Sbura.'

Thorn stared at him, the words failing to make sense.

'He saved your life,' said Thistle. 'It was the only way. It'll be okay, Tor.'

Kol, too, stepped towards her cautiously. 'Rose?'

Thorn recoiled, a feeling crawling over her skin, like spiders trying to get in. Without registering the action, she reached for a gun that wasn't there. 'You made me a Suriia?'

'It was the only way—'

'You made me a *Suriia*?' She all but screamed it.

'Rose, please—'

'Stay away from me!'

Kol's skin turned ashen while anguish darkened his gold-black eyes. 'Rose, please,' he tried again. 'He saved your life. You almost died.'

'She did die,' said Nithin tartly.

Thorn didn't care. She would have taken death. The thought of being the very thing she'd spent her life fearing, hating, hunting, running from made her sick to her stomach and the only thing she could process was her horror. Her hands went to her head. The violation burned through her and she wanted to *take her skin off.*

Thistle stepped up, hands out pacifyingly. 'Calm down. It's going to be okay.'

Thorn looked from Thistle to Kol, disbelief welling inside her, threatening to consume her, and then she bolted.

She didn't hear them yelling for her. She didn't hear Kol following her. The rushing in her ears drowned out all sound. Even weak, even traumatised, Thorn could run.

Scaling the wall of the property took no effort and soon she was tearing through the trees of the forest that led away from Courtenz and back towards the mountains.

The fields and hills were overgrown and wild, grasses tall and rocks everywhere, but no matter how many times she tripped and fell, cutting her palms and knees, she kept going.

Night came into the world and eventually she was forced to pause and catch her breath. And then she broke down crying and sobbed wretchedly for hours. Rage followed swiftly, far easier to let consume her than the feeling of betrayal, and she slammed her fist into the trunk of a tree over and over until her knuckle snapped.

Only the possibility of being caught by lurking Suriias pushed her once more to her feet and she kept going, letting the wilderness swallow her whole.

A river appeared hours later, and she began picking up rocks; heavy ones that would drag her down. When she could barely walk from being so weighted down, she waded into the river.

Icy shock made her cry out as she sank into the depths and the rocks held her under, but as her lungs screamed out in protest, she heard her mother's voice.

Live, my darling. You have to outlive them.

She breached the surface, gasping and sobbing and gagging; she couldn't do it herself. Someone else would have to.

With robotic movements, she went back to the bank and pulled herself onto solid ground. She half-hoped she'd freeze to death, but hours passed and nothing happened, and she finally forced herself to stand.

As the night grew colder, she trudged through the forest blindly, soaked to the bone and trembling badly; she found it impossible to form a coherent thought.

A drone passed by overhead and then continued, uncaring that a Suriia was wandering in the forest alone. Suriias could do whatever they wanted. For the first time in her life, the fact that a drone had passed by without a second glance made her furious. She longed for her gun so she could shoot it out of the sky.

Thorn walked on through the freezing night, shaking with cold and hiccupping. Her lips quickly became so chapped they bled.

Within two days, she was tripping over her own feet. The forest, which had long been her friend, now felt like a mountain she couldn't possibly surmount. Every step sucked the last dregs of her energy from her bones. She hadn't eaten actual food in months – whatever sort of magic they used to keep her alive made her skin crawl, but given everything else, she didn't dwell on it nearly so much as she would have.

On she trudged, across cold packed dirt and over icy rivers, attention drifting from what was in front of her to what was above her. She listened hard, often holding her breath, to see if there was any sound of drones or Scuttlers. But none came. It was like the world around her had gone to sleep and she was still trying to walk her way to the exit door of a nightmare.

When she finally found her friends, she didn't even know how long she'd been walking. She felt numb and desolate and wrong. So very, very wrong.

Parin spotted her first, his thin faced pinched and hollower than when last they'd spoken, but a wonderful sight all the same.

'Thorn!' He shot to her side just as her legs gave out and caught her before she hit the forest floor. 'Thorn! What happened?'

She blinked at him through raw, aching eyes. His grip was warm, steady.

'T, what happened? What's wrong?'

'Please just kill me.' Her fingers curled into the material of his threadbare coat and she looked at him for salvation.

Alarm flared in his leaf-green eyes. 'What?'

'They made me one of them.'

Parin raised his hands, cradling her face gently. With remarkable compassion, he wiped the dirt and blood and gunk from her cheeks. 'Now it makes sense why they wouldn't let any of us see you,' he muttered, not moving even an inch away from her. 'Tell me what happened, Thorny.'

She tried to pull memories out of her fogged mind. 'We got the humans out,' she whispered. 'Lucien and me. Everyone got out. I was shot on the way. Nithin ... Nithin turned me into *this*.'

Tears fell from her eyes and Parin brushed them away with his thumbs.

'It's okay,' he promised. 'It's going to be okay. We can fix this.'

'Please,' she repeated. 'Please kill me. I can't be like this.'

'Stop,' he said firmly. 'We're not killing you. We're going to fix this.'

She was too dazed to register much outside of Parin steering her into his tent and helping her out of her boots and into his sleeping bag. He zipped it up around her and stretched out beside her.

She stared at him through swollen, aching eyes. 'I can't be like this,' she choked out, tears starting to fall again.

'We'll figure it out,' he reiterated. 'Magic did this, magic can undo this. Try and get some sleep, okay?'

'I don't want to sleep.'

'You need to,' he said sternly. 'We'll figure everything out in the morning. And I'll be right here. Trin, too. And Grey. Okay?'

Thorn didn't have the strength to argue.

'Close your eyes,' he whispered.

She shut her eyes and a moment later he started singing. His voice was raspy and deep, but it enveloped her like a blanket, and she drifted off at some point.

Raised voices, thick with outrage, dragged Thorn back to cold consciousness. She got up, head pounding like a drum, skin clammy, and, trying to gather her bearings, stumbled out of the tent.

'You don't know what you're talking about,' Jinx was saying.

'Thorn does.' Parin sounded furious.

Thorn stopped a few paces away. She'd bet her next three meals she didn't want to know what they were arguing about.

'Thorn,' said Pike, catching sight of her. 'What happened?'

She stayed mute, frozen with trepidation.

'Parin says Jinx drugged you,' said Jade, eyes wide with horror.

Thorn stared at the campfire, unable to force the words from her mouth.

'It was a misunderstanding,' said Jinx. 'We sorted it out.'

Thorn's eyes burned, but she didn't contradict him.

Suddenly Grey was at her side. 'What happened?' he breathed, his hand coming to rest protectively at the base of her back. 'You can tell me. He can't hurt you. I'm here.'

'He …' She coughed harshly. 'He slipped me Hazies and then climbed on top of me.'

'We'd been seeing each other for weeks by that point,' argued Jinx, shooting her a censorious glare. 'How was I supposed to know you didn't want to?'

'Shut your fucking mouth,' came Parin's acid retort.

'Whatever Jinx did,' said Genny, 'it doesn't change the fact that she's a Suriia now. She's one of them. She can't stay here. I'm sorry, Thorn. That's just how it is.'

'She's one of *us*,' said Grey angrily.

'Not anymore,' said Sinjin.

Parin cursed furiously before he nodded to his sister. 'Trin,' he said. 'Get our stuff.'

Trinity darted off without protest, clearly in total agreement.

But Thorn was too dazed to really follow what was happening. 'What are you doing?'

'We're leaving.'

'Parin—'

'You're not one of them,' he said resolutely. 'You're one of us. And we're not staying here with this weasel.'

'I'm coming, too,' said Grey, sticking his gun in its holster and going to fetch his things.

Thorn blinked several times, having trouble keeping up.

Trinity reappeared with two bags over her shoulders, and she wasn't alone. Jade had her bag, knife in hand. A murmur of surprise went through the group.

'Jade, no,' cried Jinx. 'You can't!'

'I can,' she said quietly.

'Come on,' said Parin, tugging on Thorn's hand; he held his gun in the other hand, half raised as a deterrent. Against people.

The reality of the situation hit Thorn harder than she could have hoped to put into words.

'Where are we going?' she croaked as they walked away from the campsite.

'Somewhere else.'

Hardly able to process anything, Thorn let Parin steer her through the forest, Trinity, Grey and Jade falling in behind them. The woods were silent, dark and still, most creatures hiding from the winter chill. But every crunch of their boots on ice sounded loud, every drop of melting snow sent a shiver down Thorn's spine.

At some point her legs really did give out. Parin carried her then, and Trinity took the lead. Grey and Jade stayed on either side of them, weapons in hand, eyes scouting the trees religiously. Resting her head in the crook of Parin's neck, Thorn tried not to notice the rush of desire for him that she had never felt until that moment. One she loathed.

I won't touch anyone, she promised herself. *I won't. I won't. I won't.*

She bit the inside of her cheek so hard she tasted her own blood.

They made camp in a cave hours later. Trinity and Jade went to hunt, Grey worked on the campfire, and Parin set up the tent. When he was done, he came to her side and sat down, draping a blanket around their shoulders. Like her, he had new scars. She reached out to trace the angry pink lines on his temple and cheek.

'Camp?'

'Camp.'

'I'm sorry.'

Parin waved off her concern. 'Are *you* okay?'

'No.'

'I mean physically.'

She shook her head. 'I haven't eaten in days. But it's more than that …'

'You need different energy sources now.' He leaned in and caught her eye. 'It's okay.'

A strangled, wheezing cry tore from her lips, and she scooted away from him. 'No, it's not.'

'It is,' he assured her. 'And whatever you need, we're all here, okay?'

'You can't fix this.'

'We'll figure it out. That's what friends are for.'

'I'm not a person anymore. I'm a Suriia.'

'You'll *always* be my best friend.'

'I feel sick,' she admitted. 'Dizzy.'

'It's the lack of energy,' said Grey, joining them now that the fire was crackling. He put his soot-stained hands together and frowned at Thorn's shaking form. 'I met a sbura at a Speak Softly once who told me that a revenant's power source comes from others. But just having power in general requires acquiring it.'

Thorn pressed the heels of her palms to her eyes. And Parin, embodying the role of the brother she'd never had, wrapped his arms around her and held her as she wept.

CHAPTER TWENTY-SIX
The Fragile Threads of Friendship

The jarring ring of the telephone made the pack all start. The technology of the new world still sounded alien and strange. Shim tossed the phone to Lucien and he answered on the third ring. Weird as they were, he appreciated the mobile phones of this world.

'Yes?'

'Lucien,' came a familiar voice. 'It's Nithin Summons.'

Lucien cocked an eyebrow at Shim, who shrugged. Nithin had made it abundantly clear that they were not welcome after he pestered them for weeks on end regarding Thorn's condition.

'What can I do for you?' he asked at length.

'Would you have an hour to come by my house?'

'Why?'

'I have a matter of some urgency to discuss with you.'

Lucien would have declined, but he was still worried about the small human girl who had taken a bullet to the heart and he wanted to see her. 'Fine,' he growled. 'I'll be there shortly.'

Without waiting for Nithin to answer, he hung up the phone.

The flight took no time at all, and soon Lucien and Shim were jogging up the steps of the sprawling mansion. The door opened before he'd even raised his hand to knock and he found himself face to face with one very wretched looking frai.

'What drained the life out of you?' he asked.

Kol waved them in. 'Thorn ran away.'

'What?'

'She woke up yesterday and then ...' Kol knocked back a glass of clear liquid with a scent pungent enough that it tickled Lucien's nose. Straight gin.

Lucien glanced at the clock. It was barely nine in the morning. 'Why am I here?'

'We wondered if you'd seen her,' said Nithin, sauntering into the entrance hall. Gesturing for them to follow, he led the way to an ornate sitting room that smelled clean, floral and expensive. Unbuttoning his suit coat as he sat down, crossing one leg over the other, Nithin motioned politely for Lucien and Shim to join him.

'I haven't,' said Lucien, sitting on the adjacent sofa. 'Why did she run away?'

Kol's confession sounded like it pained him: 'She didn't like how Nithin saved her life.'

'Fair enough.'

This response was clearly not one widely shared. Both Kol and Nithin fixed him with looks of astonishment.

'What? Would you want to be turned into your enemy?'

'We're not the enemy,' said Nithin irritably.

'You are to Thorn.' Lucien held out his hand pointedly. He found their lack of comprehension deeply frustrating. 'I knew her for five minutes and I can say that much with confidence. That girl's never had a day in her life to breathe. Because of the thing you just turned her into. I'd be surprised if she doesn't kill herself.'

'Shut the *fuck* up!' The roar tore out of Kol, unbidden it seemed. He stood and went to refill his glass. His hands were shaking so badly he spilled half of it over his hands before managing to fill his glass.

Nithin eyed his friend with unguarded concern before turning back to Lucien. 'Will you let us know if she contacts you?'

'Why not track her yourself? She said you made a fuss over your skills.'

Without turning around, Kol answered, 'Something tells me if I use magic to track her, she won't forgive me.'

Lucien wouldn't blame Thorn for never trusting another word out of his mouth, although he understood Kol's distress. The situation was bleak all around. He glanced at Nithin, wondering. 'How did you learn that trick? I haven't seen that since Salfar.'

'It's done on Salfar?' Kol's curiosity appeared to have distracted him ever so from his anguish.

'Warriors on the battlefield could offer their immortality to a fatally wounded friend.'

Kol rounded on Nithin, shocked. 'How *did* you figure out how to do it?'

Nithin, oddly, appeared unruffled and nodded to Lucien. 'I read it in the books you gave me.'

'Impressive.'

Not sure what else to say to the odd pair, Lucien promised to let them know if he learned anything and stood with Shim to leave. Yet a feeling gripped him as they walked away. Whether it was compassion or a warning, he couldn't have said. In the doorway, he stopped and turned. 'I don't know what it's like to be in your shoes entirely, Mister Sinn, but I do know this: On our Earth, humans rule and Suriias bleed. I had a clip for years. I could wield no magic. And even still, my abilities far outmatched my husband's. If I wanted to, I could snap his neck without breaking a sweat. The same goes for you and Thorn. The same goes for Mister Summons and his wife.'

Kol's eyes blackened, his teeth sharpening to vicious points. 'I would never hurt Thorn.'

'You can't make that promise to someone who's been hurt beyond repair. And it's not a relationship if they worry what'll happen if you turn them down.' With that, and feeling horrible, Lucien bowed his head and put his hat back on. He'd bought a new one the previous week.

Shim fell into step beside him as they walked out of the mansion. 'I think you just ruined them both,' she muttered as they got into the coach.

'It's true.'

He started the engine and drove away, not sparing the guards at the gate a glance.

'You don't think a human could ever really love a Suriia?'

'Of course,' said Lucien. 'That's not my point.'

Shim's brow furrowed. 'I'm confused.'

'It's two separate arguments. Perhaps there'd be a way to minimise a Suriia's power enough to make it relative to a human; perhaps there'd be a way to maximise a human's power enough to be with a Suriia. But we're from different worlds. We have different rules. And whether we're discussing Thorn or Thistle or—' He choked. 'Or Nik … They've all been abused by Suriias. How could that kind of imbalance ever be okay?'

Shim extended a hand thoughtfully. 'Don't you think they should have some say in it?'

'Of course.'

'And if they don't care?'

'They should care.'

Only Geon had ever cared about Lucien's fears of Astril, his first spouse. Only Geon had disobeyed the rule of law and the king himself to save Lucien from what would have been unending pain. But Geon hadn't been faster than the wind. Geon hadn't reached him before Astril tortured him. And

Lucien would always remember what it felt like to scream, to beg, to *fear*.

As they passed over the city, Lucien let his eyes dart from coach to coach, frai to frai, a nervous flutter in his chest.

'I wonder what life would have been like if we'd grown up here,' Shim mused aloud.

Lucien shook his head. 'Don't do that.'

'What?'

'Torture yourself with what-ifs and maybes. Dwelling will only drive you mad.'

Shim drummed her fingers on her leg. 'If I'd been born here, my parents would be alive.'

'If you'd been born here, your parents would likely have been murderers or apologists,' said Lucien. 'There's nothing admirable about that.'

'They'd be alive.'

Lucien wasn't sure if it was better or worse, and so he left Shim to her thoughts. They returned to their house a few minutes later.

Outside of Adair and Naida, everyone was at home. In the short time the pack had been on this world, their home had become cosy and filled with new messes and smells. But it made for a peaceful reprieve from Courtenz.

'If anyone hears from Thorn, let me know,' he said pointedly.

'Isn't the finicky frai her number one fan?' Isha snorted. She had no time for anyone with money. 'Why doesn't he find her?'

'The frai's the one who lost her.'

Isha rolled her eyes.

'I gave Parin your number,' cut in Ginny.

'You did?' said Lucien in surprise.

'Yeah. Thought they might get into trouble in the mountains.'

'Good call, kid.'

'Really?'

He nodded and winked at her.

With that, he left to find Nik. As usual these days – and most days – Nik was in the bedroom, buried in a stack of books. He didn't even bother to look up as Lucien stepped inside.

'Reading anything good?'

Nik held up his book, but he was too far away for Lucien to read the title. Meandering over, he dropped down beside Nik and tilted his head. The volume was a history of the city.

'You ever get tired of reading?' he wondered, picking up one of the books on the bed and turning it over in his hands. 'Even I don't read this much. And our house had four libraries I put together myself.'

'Books are nicer than Suriias and humans,' said Nik mildly.

'True.' Lucien reached out and brushed the hair back from Nik's face. The move was unintended, and he only realised he'd done it when Nik leaned into his touch.

Not wanting to get caught up, Lucien plucked the book from Nik's hands and set it aside. 'Take a break for lunch?'

'Sure.'

But no distraction proved enough to keep Lucien's mind from drifting to Thorn with increasing frequency and he found himself fretting about the little human girl who almost died in his arms for the rest of the day. And the next one after that.

He didn't really think she'd contact him when Nithin called him over, but Ginny's remark about giving one of the humans their number made it somewhat more likely, and Lucien spent a week staring at his phone until, one evening, it rang.

He snatched it up. 'Hello?'

'Lucien?'

The gravelly, shaky voice flooded him with relief. 'Hi, Thorn,' he said. Everyone in the room turned to look at him. Shara did a silent cheer. 'What can I do for you?'

'Can you come get us?'

'I'm on my way,' he said, grabbing his keys and gesturing to Adair to follow him. 'Where are you?'

'South of the falls, near Lake Ilane.'

'Stay hidden,' he advised, although if Thorn truly was sbura, there was no reason for her to keep out of sight. But it was a code he'd long lived by, one that left him unbidden.

Stay out of sight, stay alive.

A two-hour flight finally brought them to Lake Ilane and Lucien tracked the humans easily enough. He landed in a marshy field and stepped out, Adair just behind him.

One by one, the group appeared from inside the thick cover of the trees. First Grey, gun in hand, then Jade and Trinity, with Parin and Thorn bringing up the rear.

Thorn looked *awful*.

'Need help?' he asked Parin.

'My bag,' said Parin, not loosening his grip on Thorn.

Worry mounting, Lucien took his bag. Despite how exhausted and half-starved Parin clearly was, he lifted Thorn easily into his arms and fell into step beside Lucien without missing a beat.

Back at the house, Jade helped Thorn shower while the others changed into borrowed clothes. When the girls reappeared an hour later, Lucien tracked Thorn's every step. Where Jade looked like a good ten meals and a week of sleep would cure her, Thorn seemed like she was knocking at death's door.

'Humans aren't meant to be Suric,' said Adair under his breath as they watched Thorn from the other side of the room. Lucien rubbed his jaw, fretting.

'We made food,' said Shara, appearing from the kitchen with a tray stacked high. Eran, Kalid and Ginny filed out after her.

Everyone curled up in the sitting room to watch the movie Isha had put on.

Finally having someone else standing guard hit the humans one by one, and as Lucien watched, they all fell asleep, lulled by the sounds of the television, and each other's steady breathing.

Lucien wasn't sure how to go about finding a place for the runaways – it was Nithin who found the pack a house when they needed one. And so, feeling slightly guilty, Lucien left his pack with the humans the next morning and went to the Lathlak Corporation.

The marble floors and low humming music grated instantly on his nerves. He'd never cared much for rich, garish places and his respect for Nithin didn't change that.

He nodded to the receptionist. 'Tell Summons that Lucien Lightblood wants to see him.'

The vryko nodded and pushed a button on a screen before her.

Less than two minutes later, Nithin appeared. He wore his usual suit, his black hair brushed back neatly. He still carried himself the same and if Lucien hadn't known he was human, he likely wouldn't have been able to guess. But he didn't miss the edge of a bracelet around Nithin's wrist that had the same symbol as the blocker Thorn wore.

'Mister Lightblood,' said Nithin, shaking his hand.

They didn't speak further until they were in Nithin's office with the door shut.

'Thorn's safe,' said Lucien.

Nithin sat down behind his desk and put his hands together. 'Where did you find her?'

'I didn't,' admitted Lucien. 'They called us for help. That's why I'm here. I don't know where to start to find them a safe place to stay.'

Nithin's dark brow furrowed and he glanced at the screen beside him. 'Does she know you're here?'

'No. But you're the only one who can help.'

'I'll find a place,' said Nithin. 'It's easier if she's registered as a Suriia. If you can convince her.'

'Can you do that?'

'I know someone who can.'

Lucien nodded thoughtfully. It was still strange to be back on a world where Suriias ruled. Things didn't feel much different, though. 'I'll convince her. If she's doing it for the other humans, she'll listen. But I'm going to ask that you don't tell Kol.'

Nithin appraised him with a critical eye. 'Do you have any idea how frustrating it is to have Thorn leave after the lengths we went to in order to keep her and Thistle safe?'

'Can you blame her? The whole reason she died is because Suriias here hunt humans. She has no reason to believe you're better.'

'She's trusting you.'

'She died in my arms.'

Nithin's scowl only deepened. 'She came back to life in mine.'

'Why was it you and not Kol?'

The answer to that question had ruminated in Lucien's mind for days.

For a few seconds, Nithin allowed the silence to fester, clearly debating whether to return the show of trust. Then, in a soft voice, he said, 'When Kol called me from the mountains, I told him to go to his father. I told him to bargain for Thorn's friends and that I would go to the death camp and make sure nothing happened to her. He's better with his father and I'm better with the Hunters. Bureaucracy and negotiations have never been

Kol's forte. He cares too much and doesn't know when that's going to get him into trouble. It's happened before and he knew that. I convinced him we could play the odds.'

'You sound like you knew what would happen.'

Nithin didn't deny it. 'I had a feeling Thorn was going to do something remarkably stupid trying to save her friends. I didn't want him to see that. I didn't want him to deal with the fallout. And Thorn would never forgive him for stealing her humanity. I, on the other hand, don't particularly care if she hates me.'

Lucien chuckled darkly. 'I can't tell if you like her or not.'

'She's my responsibility. She's the family I chose. I knew what I was signing up for when I brought her home with Thistle.'

'I can understand that.' Getting to his feet, Lucien held out his hand. 'I admire what you're doing here. You just came too late for some.'

Nithin took his hand with the same strength and poise he'd shown as a sbura. 'I didn't come too late for everyone,' he said adamantly. 'And I will make this world better. Not only for the ones like Thorn; for the ones coming. Like my child.'

Fewer announcements could have surprised Lucien more. 'Oh. Congratulations.'

Nithin smiled tightly, but his entire body had tensed. 'Of all times to be human, I really picked the worst one.'

'If you ever need protection …'

'Thank you.' Nithin bowed his head. 'I've increased security on the house and the company. We don't go anywhere without Kol. It's a miracle no one's found out.'

'You should keep looking in those books. Spells work for humans. Some useful stuff in there.'

'You don't need them back?'

'I have them memorised.'

Nithin bowed his head gratefully. 'Thank you, Mister Lightblood. I appreciate your help.'

'Lucien,' he said. 'I've never gone by Mister Lightblood.'

That made Nithin laugh. 'Well, Mister Summons makes me feel far too much like my father.'

'A horrifying thought for me.'

'I know the feeling.'

They exchanged far more pleasant smiles when Lucien took his leave.

He was waiting for the lift when someone called his name. Glancing over, he did a doubletake at the sight of the tiny human woman. Where Thorn was tall, too thin to be healthy, scarred, and radiated mistrust and outrage like perfume, Thistle was short, composed, with twinkling eyes that danced with laughter and light, and a smile that came easily, like she'd never learned that smiles could be dangerous things.

'Hi,' he said, slightly thrown. 'How are you?'

'I'm all right,' she replied. 'Have you heard from Thorn at all?'

He hesitated.

'I just want to know if she's okay,' said Thistle. 'If there's anything I can do.'

'She's okay,' he assured her. 'I'm making sure of it.'

Thistle exhaled shakily. 'She's with the others, right?'

'Right.' Donning his hat, he bowed his head. 'I promise I'll keep an eye on her.'

'Thank you, Lucien,' she said sincerely. 'I really appreciate that.'

He stepped into the lift and pressed the button. When he looked up, Thistle was still watching him and his heart broke for her. 'She'll come back to you,' he found himself saying. 'Best friends always come back.'

He was deeply relieved the doors closed before she could reply. A heavy, stilted breath left him, and he leaned against the wall, Geon's words when he'd saved Lucien from the Tower replaying in his mind, as clear to him now as they had been three hundred years before, determined to undo his tenuously maintained sanity.

I told you I'd be back, Luka. You should see the mess I made. It's literally a bloody mess – you'll laugh at that someday, I promise. But the king lost this one. We're free. I've got you. Don't die on me now.

I've got you.

Even after securing the runaways their own house a sennight later, the ragtag group of humans stayed in the back of Lucien's mind, as if his pack had grown without permission and he was needed in two places at once. He couldn't even quantify why he cared about them, but he did, and he wanted to know how Thorn was doing most of all. She had looked awful when they parted ways. Finally, in the middle of lunch one afternoon a few weeks later, the phone rang from an unknown registration.

'Hello?'

'Lucien?' It was Trinity. 'Something's wrong with Thorn.'

Lucien immediately straightened up, gesturing across the table to Shim. 'What is it?'

'She's been sick. I don't … I don't even know. It's not, like, normal. Can you come over?'

'I'm on my way.'

Thorn was on the sofa, sweating badly and burning with fever when he arrived. He didn't have to ask to know what was wrong. He'd seen it before.

'Sbura's power comes from their magic, which can only be replenished with sexual energy,' he explained in a low voice to her friends. 'Procreation. Even if she's not using her magic, she still needs to draw energy from elsewhere. She'll die if she doesn't.'

'She won't touch us,' said Parin bluntly. 'We've all offered.'

Lucien thought that made them better than most friends, but he couldn't fault Thorn her refusal. 'What about the frai?' he proposed.

'She'd kill us,' said Jade. 'She doesn't want to talk to him.'

'Yeah, but it wasn't Kol who did this,' said Trinity. 'It was the other one. Tristan—'

'Nithin.'

'Whatever. The sbura who married her friend.' Trinity shrugged. 'She was mad at Kol, but she'd probably take him over death.'

Parin snorted. 'She's stubborn.'

'Is she stubborn enough to live?' prompted Lucien, genuinely curious.

'I don't know.'

Lucien made the decision in a split second. Promising to call soon, he got back into his coach with Shim.

Instead of flying home, he made for Soshing River and the large mansion he still found ugly.

'Where are you going?' asked Shim.

'I want to make a visit to the frai,' he said.

'I thought you didn't interfere.'

Lucien shook his head, squeezing the wheel anxiously. 'She's killing herself.'

When Shim didn't argue, he felt somewhat validated in his interference. Landing the coach in front of the gates minutes later, he drove up and they got out. The mansion was as impeccable as ever, although the gardens had wilted noticeably, the flowers losing petals with every brush of wind.

At the door, he knocked twice and Kol answered almost straight away.

'Hi,' he said, taken aback.

''Afternoon,' said Lucien. 'There's a matter I need to discuss with you.'

'Which is?'

'Thorn.'

Kol's grip on the door tightened visibly and his eyes darkened. 'Is she okay?'

'It's not my place,' said Lucien uncomfortably. 'But she's not well. She's not adjusting.' It reminded him of Geon, if he was being honest, and he wanted so badly for Thorn to have a better end.

Sometimes magic killed.

'Did she get hurt?'

'She's sick. She's weak and she's getting worse. She'll die.'

Kol rubbed his face roughly before squeezing the bridge of his nose. 'She won't appreciate my help.'

'Sometimes the ones we love push us away,' said Lucien. 'And sometimes love is knowing when to push back.'

'I'm the reason she's gone.'

'You didn't do anything.'

Kol's laugh was disbelieving and shattered, like a chord had broken inside him.

'You didn't. Her fear and everyone else did that. But she trusted you once. Parin tells me she's in love with you and won't touch anyone else. That's not nothing, Kol.'

He sent a pointed look at the frai before turning and trotting back down the large stone steps towards the coach. Perhaps he hadn't done the right thing in saying as much, but Lucien didn't know how to help Thorn. And someone had to.

CHAPTER TWENTY-SEVEN
An Itch Beneath the Skin

The hour was late, the sun tucking itself away behind the clouds, ready to retire, when Thorn and Parin found themselves alone on the sofa. The day had not been a good one for Thorn. She was having trouble keeping her head up. Her bones felt leeched, her skin like leather and her eyes hurt when she redirected her line of sight. Every single part of her was twisted, ruined, wrong.

Parin rolled his head towards her, his scars making his pensive expression edged and dangerous. 'You have to do something soon,' he noted for the tenth time that day. 'You're getting sicker.'

The needles of disgust in Thorn's stomach only grew more painful. She bit the corner of her finger in agitation. 'I can't.'

'Yeah, but if you die, we're screwed.' He laughed it off, but she didn't miss the hysteria that crept its way into his voice.

'I'll figure something out,' she croaked.

He nodded. 'Another movie?'

'Sure.'

It was when he leaned over her to grab one of the films from the box that it happened. Suddenly, the only thing she could focus on was his proximity. Reaching out without meaning to, she put her hand on his cheek. Green light instantly spread from her fingers into his skin and he turned towards her.

'Do you want to?' he asked thickly.

'Yes,' she breathed.

A knocking sounded on the front door, but Thorn didn't care. The second their lips touched, all sense vanished, and she pulled him down on top of her.

But it wasn't enough.

She helped him out of his shirt and then her own. He kissed his way down her stomach, his fingers tracing lightly over her skin.

'Rose?' Kol's voice cut through the room like a knife and she scrambled away from Parin. They stared at each other for a moment before she stumbled over to the door and opened it.

She really should have remembered her shirt.

Kol took in the sight of her, shirtless, of Parin, trousers unfastened, and his eyes flooded black. He cocked his head pointedly from Parin to the staircase. The indication was clear.

Parin glanced at Thorn, eyebrow raised. 'You good?'

'I'm good.'

He bolted up the stairs without another word.

The silence that followed was broken by Kol slamming the front door shut, eyes still entirely black, teeth elongated. 'Am I interrupting?' he all but snarled.

'Yes,' she said testily, crossing her arms over her chest to stem their trembling. 'What are you doing here?'

'Apparently nothing,' he snapped with surprising viciousness. 'You've clearly found a human you prefer.'

She scoffed.

'What?'

'Your timing is just really impeccable,' she muttered.

His lip curled. 'Busy with Parin?'

'You want to know that my best friend was my last resort? Nithin turned me into a *leech*. I haven't touched anyone until tonight. This isn't my fault.'

She heard his breath catch in his throat and his eyes roved over her with unchecked concern and confusion. In the time since they'd last seen each other, she had lost a spectacular amount of weight. Her cheekbones were now prominent, her collarbones jutted out; she looked like a corpse in bad lighting.

He stared at her in utter, appalled astonishment. 'How are you even standing?'

'Sheer irritation.'

That seemed to hold true for both of them. The dark shadows of stubble on Kol's face enhanced how exhausted he was, too, but she was also entirely certain he'd never looked so beautiful.

'How did you find me?' she asked in an effort not to gape at him. Or do something stupid like kiss him.

'I refrained from tracking you until now.'

'Why now?'

He gestured to her. 'I had cause for concern.'

'Who gave you cause?'

'Lucien's worried about you.'

Thorn didn't even have the energy to be annoyed.

'Why?' he asked after an overly long pause, voice strained.

'Why what?'

'Why haven't you touched anyone?'

'Seriously?'

'Yes, seriously.'

'Because the thought of anyone other than you touching me, makes me sick. Happy?'

Confessing that much made her feel horribly uncertain, but then Kol reached out, brushing her hair back from her face. 'I've missed you,' he murmured.

'Yeah, I've missed you, too.'

'You haven't?' he asked again, and she thought she felt a change in his magic – something she would never have picked up on before. 'Not even with Parin?'

'Not with anyone. Parin and I barely kissed.'

For a second, he only regarded her with an indecipherable expression, and then he closed the distance between them and captured her in a kiss.

The months of absence, of heartache, of bitter longing, built up inside of her and she jumped, wrapping her legs around his waist without thinking about it.

She didn't even notice the world around them change until Kol was lowering her onto her own bed upstairs.

'How did you do that?'

'Magic.'

For once she didn't care. All she could think about was him. And for the first time since they'd met, she didn't hold back. Her mind didn't flit to other worries, or overanalyse the situation and what it would mean. Nor did either of acknowledge the fact that what they were doing was going to change everything. Even if it did nothing to soothe the heartache between them, it would alter everything for Kol.

Regardless, like her, Kol seemed to be taken by another force altogether. He barely let his lips leave her skin, and when he did, it was only to murmur the best sorts of things.

'I love you,' he said, over and over. 'I love you.'

The sick, shaky, gnawing feeling that had eaten away at Thorn since she woke up that morning after being shot finally abated when at last they stilled in each other's arms – which was not a comforting confirmation to gain.

Beside her, as if sensing the return of her tension, Kol began tracing the skin on her collar bone. 'Please don't run away again.'

'I can't run away from my own house.'

'You did.'

'That was Nithin's house.'

'It was your house, too.'

She ran a hand through her hair. It was the first time she'd been able to process thought in a month. Like someone had taken a weighted blanket off her and she was able to breathe easily once more. What that meant made her stomach clench into knots of disgust, and the dual feeling left her reeling slightly.

'I feel bad,' was what she managed.

'For running away? You should. It was mean.'

'No,' she said bluntly. 'I'm sorry I couldn't stop myself.'

He gaped at her, only then realising her meaning. 'You must be the only person in the world who apologises for sex.'

She sat up, looking around for her shirt. 'No one who touches me now has a choice.'

'*I* do,' he retorted, also getting out of the bed. 'And I love you. Human or Suriia. Infuriating or wonderful.'

'You don't know if you even wanted to,' she muttered, feeling close to tears and bizarrely insecure about something that hadn't occurred to her thirty seconds beforehand.

'Sbura magic doesn't overtake frai,' he said, coming over to her side and wrapping his arms around her. 'I promise. *I* wanted to. I've wanted to since you made me that smoothie.'

A slightly hysterical laugh escaped her. 'Are you sure?'

'I'm positive.' He kissed her forehead and held her close. 'I've been in love with you from minute one. Being a Suriia hasn't changed that one bit.'

She tried to hear his assurances and believe them, but the niggle of uncertain doubt remained, refusing to be shaken off entirely. Swallowing hard, she tried to force herself to think about him and not herself. 'Do you want to stay for dinner?'

A flash of surprise lit up his face. 'Really?'

'Yeah.'

She gave him a tight smile before opening the door and leading the way downstairs.

In the kitchen, busy making dinner, the others greeted Kol without reservation, but when he walked over to the sink to wash his hands, Parin caught her eye.

You good? he signed. *I can throw him out.*

I'm fine, she signed back.

Just let me know.

For weeks now, the others had been learning the sign language Thorn and Thistle had made up.

Thanks.

Kol caught the end of the exchange and glanced between her and Parin curiously. He passed no comment, however, and simply walked back over to her side. The kiss he placed lightly on her cheek was only slightly pointed.

'Anything I can lend a hand with?' he offered.

'Carrots,' said Trinity from over by the sink. 'And onions.'

'Pass 'em,' he said, holding out his hands.

As Trinity and Kol sliced vegetables, Jade kept an eye on the simmering pots and pans, and Thorn set the table while Parin did the continuous piles of dishes being accumulated and Grey dried them off and put them away.

Thorn was just placing the last plate down when suddenly there was an arm around her waist. She leaned back against Kol, her whole body seeming to hum at his proximity.

'You look beautiful,' he whispered in her ear, instantly eliciting shivers.

She turned in his arms. 'Setting the table?'

Instead of answering, he kissed her.

A little after dawn the next morning, Thorn woke up slowly, sleepy and content. Her eyes felt the good kind of heavy that

473

only comes after a full night's rest, where every bone in your body has finally managed to relax. Kol's arms were around her and she felt warm, whole and healthy. Lifting his hand, she kissed the back of it.

''Morning,' he whispered behind her.

She rolled over without disentangling herself from his hold. 'Good morning.'

He smiled sleepily; his hair was tousled every which way and he looked adorably handsome. 'I have to go to work,' he murmured, his fingers tracing over her skin. 'But if it's all right, I'd like to come by later.'

She nodded. 'Okay.'

'Yeah?'

'Yeah.'

She brushed black hair back from his gold-black eyes and he leaned into her hand to kiss her palm.

'Does this mean you're my girlfriend again?' he wondered.

'I'm still not okay with what I am,' she told him bluntly. 'I'm not okay with the fact that this was done without my permission.'

'I know. I understand. I'm sorry about that. There wasn't time. Nithin reached you first. He just … did it.'

Fury flared within her, but also … curiosity.

'Why? Why would he give that up for me?'

'Because he loves me. Because he knows how much I love you. Whatever else you think of him, Nithin is my best friend and he'd do anything for me.' The way he said that resonated more with Thorn than the actual words. She didn't have to like Nithin to empathise with how much Kol loved him.

'Okay,' she said at last.

CHAPTER TWENTY-EIGHT
Conflict(ed)

The problem with relationship problems was that they didn't change simply because your location did. The problems between Lucien and Nik that had reared their heads in Westend Circle came back as soon as life somewhat settled into a rhythm in Courtenz. Lucien still couldn't get past how they'd met, and the innate power differences between them; Nik decidedly did not care and kept affirming as such. Both too stubborn to change, they now bickered more than they conversed.

For days Lucien woke up alone in bed, Nik elsewhere in the house and, somehow, despite living together, they didn't seem to see each other much throughout the day. Whether Nik was avoiding him or not wasn't even a question anymore, but Lucien didn't know how best to fix things. It was driving him mad.

On a particularly stormy morning, Lucien awoke to a boom of thunder. Nik was curled up in a chair by the window, reading studiously, his chin resting on the back of his hand.

Lucien admired him for a moment before sitting up and rubbing his eyes. 'Up long?'

'Only an hour,' said Nik, not raising his head. 'How'd you sleep?'

'Fine.'

'Do you want to go get something to eat?'

Lucien shook his head. 'I don't feel safe on the streets.'

'We can't hide inside forever.'

'No,' said Lucien. 'But I'm not taking you outside when everyone on the street wants you dead or harmed.'

Nik finally looked at him. 'How long do you think you can keep me locked up for?'

The acid in his words made Lucien flinch. 'I'm not locking you up,' he replied, hurt. 'I'm trying to keep us all safe.'

'At some point I have to live my life, Lucien. They think I belong to you here? Well, so did the last world. What others think about us doesn't bother me. I'll wear a shirt that says PROPERTY OF LUCIEN LIGHTBLOOD if it'll help you relax and come with me to get coffee before I lose my mind.'

A habitual introvert, Lucien sometimes forgot that others required stimulation from the outside world. Lucien, for his part, could happily go months without speaking to anyone outside of his pack.

'Fine,' he caved. It was a terrible idea, but he knew Nik had a point as well. 'Let's go out. But please, please, stay close.'

'You worry too much.'

'I worry the correct amount,' he muttered irritably.

Outside, the rain was beating down, the air coming frosty and fast, and Lucien tightened his coat around his torso as he and Nik meandered up the path.

There was not a part of the frigid walk that was better than being inside, but Nik's steps seemed lighter already. Yet the serenity of the moment dispelled quickly when they reached the square and the now familiar signs encouraging humans to turn themselves in began to pop up. Lucien moved closer to Nik.

'Should we go back?' he asked, wondering if Nik wanted to. 'Not home, I mean. In general.'

Black hair tossed across his face by the wind, Nik only increased the mess by shaking his head. 'There are no districts here.'

'No, there are death camps.'

'True.'

'It's like all the universe is saying we shouldn't be together.'

Nik stopped him short. 'What's that supposed to mean?'

'It means humans and Suriias clearly aren't meant to mix. Look what happened. The worlds can't have both.'

'That's crap. The problem is greed and power, not predestination. War existed on Earth before Suriias. Didn't war exist on Salfar?'

Lucien nodded heavily.

'There you go.'

'Your argument is that everyone is awful?'

'My argument is that it doesn't matter if you're human, Suriia, mortal, immortal, magical or not. The problem is that those with power want to keep it. And they'll do anything to get rid of those who seek to stop them. The problem is unlearning the inclinations that society brought. The problem is the system, not the souls.'

Lucien huffed. 'You should be king.'

'I hate politics.'

'Even if you could help?'

'I'm a bookworm, Luka. I like books. I don't, and never have, liked anything that involves confrontation.'

They turned up a lane and suddenly found themselves in a jampacked square in central Courtenz. Lucien gripped Nik's hand, the old feeling of magic burning inside him, powerful enough to ward off any unfriendly encounters. That realisation hit another – that like this, he could do even more damage to Nik than he could on Earth. He looked down at their hands, suddenly terrified that just holding Nik's hand would leave him bruised. Perhaps it was a little overly cautious, but it stayed in Lucien's mind. A shadow over every moment with Nik.

No cup of coffee had ever filled Lucien with such disquiet, and he spent the entire time they were in the café alert, ignoring his coffee until it was ice cold.

Shara and Eran were watching a movie when they stepped into the house a couple of hours later, groceries in hand from a detour to the shop.

Lucien began cooking, wanting to keep his hands busy. Wanting to not dwell on the unending questions and confusions running rampant in his mind.

'Anything I can help with?' asked Nik, leaning against the counter beside him.

'Grate some cheese?'

Nik kissed his cheek before opening the fridge. The feeling of his touch lingered on Lucien's skin like a brand.

When the clip had been in his arm, the enchantment between them had felt almost muted. Dull. An ache that couldn't quite be identified. Now it was constant, overwhelming and problematic.

After dishing out all the food, he excused himself and went to his bedroom, desperate to be alone. Unfortunately, Nik decided to follow him.

'Everything all right?'

'I'm not hungry.'

Nik's brow furrowed. 'Seems like there's something on your mind.'

'Having magic back is a little overwhelming, that's all.'

An odd look blossomed in Nik's eyes, and Lucien's stomach tightened with apprehension. 'How so?' asked Nik.

'Everything's more enhanced,' he admitted.

'What could you do?'

'What do you mean?'

Nik nodded towards the books on the wall. 'Could you make one come over here?'

The banal act made Lucien almost laugh. He reached out without even looking and a book flew into his hand. He held it out to Nik with a smirk. 'Easily.'

A smile curved Nik's lips as he appraised the book. Then, setting it down, he reached out, ghosting his fingers over Lucien's lips. 'You seem happier with your magic back.'

'I'm relieved.'

'You like it, too.' Nik searched his face. 'Don't you? It's not a shameful thing to admit to.'

Lucien managed a stiff nod. 'Yes, I like it.'

'See.'

'See what?'

Nik tilted his head, smiling fondly. 'You don't have to hate yourself all the time. Sometimes it's all right to enjoy who you are.'

Lucien couldn't stop himself from kissing Nik at that. Gentle, grateful, restrained. And then Nik moved closer, his hands finding their way under Lucien's shirt, and he pulled back sharply with a gasp.

'Don't,' he said.

'Did I do something wrong?'

'We've been over this, Nik.'

'Yeah, and I never agreed.'

'Tough.'

Nik stepped away, wiping his mouth. 'This is ridiculous. I'm *telling* you it's fine.'

'Well, it's not fine with me,' he snapped. 'So, we're at an impasse.'

'I'm not going the rest of my life without having sex. What happened with Ashby is awful, but I'm dealing with it. I want to touch you. It'd be nice if you wanted to, also.'

Lucien had a hard time wondering if Nik was being intentionally obtuse. 'You think I don't?' he retorted, voice strangled.

'You never touch me. I'm sick of your bloody chivalry. It's starting to feel like an excuse and I'm tired of asking. You're making me feel unwanted.'

A flush of panic spread through Lucien's chest and it was suddenly hard to draw breath, but he didn't back down. He couldn't.

'If you want to be with someone else,' he croaked. 'I understand.'

Nik's hands went to his head. 'You are such a dick sometimes.'

'I don't want you to feel trapped. If you're unhappy, we can come to an arrangement.' But even as he said it, the suggestion made Lucien want to gouge his eyes and heart out.

'I don't want a fucking arrangement.' Nik grabbed him by the shirt collar and slammed their mouths together.

Lucien's hands came up to shove him away, but instead pulled him in closer. He felt powerless in Nik's arms.

Nik broke away, gasping. 'I'm not helpless and I'm not weak.'

'I never thought you were helpless.' In fact, Lucien was slightly offended that he would think so. 'But that doesn't change the facts of the situation.'

'You saved my life.'

'And you had no say in the matter.'

'Are you honestly telling me that we're never going to be more than this? That's not a marriage, Lucien!'

'Coercion is no marriage, either.'

'I'm not afraid of you!'

'You still wake up in the middle of the night and sleep in the front room because you're scared of pricos. Don't tell me you walked away unscathed.'

Nik stepped back, leaving a cold, empty space between them. One filled with far too many questions for a healthy relationship. 'Where did you get that from?'

'Ginny told me about your brothers.'

The words erased the colour from Nik's already peaky complexion. 'What?'

'That they were attacked by a prico.' Lucien shook his head. 'On some level, you'll always be afraid of me, Nik. That's not *fine*.'

Nik knocked a fist against the wall. For the first time since they'd met, he looked almost condescending. Contemptuous, even. As if Lucien couldn't begin to fathom the depths of his own ignorance. 'First of all,' he sneered, 'my brothers weren't *attacked*. My brothers were *tortured*. Right in front of me. My mother was killed because the prico didn't believe her when she said she didn't know where my father was.'

Lucien stared at him in abject horror. 'You said your mother died of sickness.'

'I lied.' Nik almost levelled Lucien with his glare. 'My mother was murdered by a prico.'

Still having trouble processing everything, Lucien said, 'Why?'

'Why what?'

'Why was a prico looking for Geon?'

Nik threw out his hands. 'You tell me! I've never met the bastard! He left us behind to *die*.'

The anguish in his tone went straight to Lucien's soul. Nik had likely been living on the streets his entire life, his family too. However Geon had come across Nik's mother, whatever the real story was, Nik had never had a chance. A childhood. Anything.

'I raised them.' Tears now shone in Nik's eyes. 'We didn't have a dad, so I was their dad. My mother named me after her father, but they were named after our father's dead brothers.'

'Eun and Hyun,' said Lucien numbly. He reached out uselessly. 'Nik—'

'I don't want your pity,' Nik snarled. 'And right now, I don't even want to be near you. I'm sleeping on the sofa. Don't follow me.'

The silence that filled the bedroom was the worst Lucien had ever endured.

This silence felt cold.

CHAPTER TWENTY-NINE
Trust

Ever since Thorn's brief death and subsequent resurrection, the nightmares of her parents dying had become nightmares of herself as their murderer. The worst were the ones where she was a Spotter, hunting humans for sport and locking them away in cages to be drained.

After one particularly vivid nightmare, Thorn sat bolt upright in bed, drenched in sweat and shivering, a scream lodged in her throat. Her own evil laughter echoed in her ears.

Kol sat up seconds later. For the last few weeks he had been spending nearly every night with her and things had been easy. Simple.

'You okay?' His black hair fell every which way, his beard mussed from being pressed against the pillow.

'No,' she muttered.

'Want to talk about it?'

'No.'

'Was it about me?'

'No.'

He kissed her shoulder, his arms coming up to wrap around her stomach. 'Come here,' he said, tugging her back down into the pillows.

'Does it drain you the way it does humans?' she asked when they parted. 'You said I can't sway you – but does the magic drain you?'

'I have a thousand times the energy and recharging my strength is easy.' Leaning down, he kissed her deeply before drawing back, black and gold eyes flashing.

'How do frai get energy?' she wondered. 'Is it just proximity to nature or something?'

'Partly,' he said. 'Our power comes from Salfar. If the Tear was ever closed, we wouldn't have magic at all. We're the only race that doesn't have to borrow energy from others to endure here.'

'Thank fuck.'

Thorn scratched the side of her face as she mulled that over. 'So why is it different for, like, sbura?'

'I don't know,' he admitted. 'Sometimes I wonder if it's not almost our own fault. We're not native to Earth. We don't belong here, not really. Perhaps it's sort of a side-effect.'

It took a great deal of effort not to tell him the Suriias deserved every side effect under the sun.

'I hate that it never feels like enough,' she groaned in frustration, pressing her forehead against his. 'I always … *want.*'

Kol chuckled. 'Do you want me to tire you out?'

'I don't think you could. It's never enough. I never feel … sated.' She grimaced and put her hands over her face, blushing furiously. 'That sounds so stupid.'

'*I* can tire you out,' he assured her, and then he captured her in a heady kiss.

'What does it mean?' she asked when they had to part to breathe. 'Being with me now. You being frai and all.'

He shook his head. 'It doesn't mean anything to you.'

She stared at him, slightly stung. 'Ouch.'

'No, that's not—' He rolled his eyes and ran a hand through his thick black hair. 'I just meant it's only on my end.'

'Do you feel different?'

'Yes.'

Not sure what that meant, she appraised him thoughtfully. 'How so?'

He scooted out of bed and tugged on his jeans, expression turning to one of deep uncertainty. 'Rose, everything about our relationship has made you run in the opposite direction. You've never even told me that you love me. I don't really feel like bearing my feelings to you when all it'll do is scare you away.'

'You think I don't care?'

'I know you do. I also know that every time you look at me, you have to remind yourself who I am, not what I am. And that's shit for me. Even if I understand.'

'Lucien can track Nik since he shared magic with him,' she said. 'Can you do something like that with me?'

'I can track you either way. It's what I'm good at.'

'So that's it? The only thing being a frai does is make you monogamous for life?'

He cracked a grin. 'You say that like it's a bad thing. I don't see it that way. I've had more than enough opportunities. You're the one I want.'

Thorn still couldn't fathom why. 'Is that really it, though?'

'It does ... more,' he allowed, sitting on the edge of the bed and picking at a loose thread in the blanket.

Thorn sat up and crossed her legs. 'Like what?'

'Like ... You sure you're not going to get spooked?'

'I promise.'

Kol nodded, although he clearly felt hesitant. 'Frai only love once. The first one we're with becomes our world. All we see. All we want. It's not only feelings, though. It's physical. Touching anyone else would be sickening. Uncomfortable.

Physically so. We can only have children with the one we choose. And our magic ... our magic is entirely linked to nature until we fall in love. And then it's linked to them.'

Thorn's brow furrowed. 'How so?'

'If you're injured or sick or unhappy, my magic is affected. For the worse. Likewise, the happier, healthier you are, the stronger I am. It doesn't draw from you directly, not like sbura. But a frai's duty on Salfar was to keep the natural world in order. To better the world. You can't do that if you're not paying attention. To your own health, to the health of the one you love most. It all ties together.'

She tucked her hair behind her ears and tried to think of a kind way to ask him if he'd lost his mind. 'Why risk it? My track record for emotional stability isn't good.'

'Because I love you,' he said simply. 'And one day you're not going to second-guess that.'

'Can I ask a hypothetical question without *you* getting spooked?'

He nodded, although his eyes flashed worriedly.

'I'm not going to,' she prefaced, 'but ... Say a frai falls in love, has sex, and then the other one wants to break up. What then?'

In a noticeably quiet, very controlled voice, he said, 'It happens. It's the reason most frai pick frai. There's nothing you can do.'

'That's awful.'

'Most would be driven to desolation or madness,' he muttered. 'Some try and make the best of it.'

She had another, more horrible thought. 'What happens if, like, a vryko rapes a frai who's never had sex?'

'Exactly what you think. That's why it's a death sentence to do so.'

'Unless it's being done to a human, apparently.'

He grimaced in agreement.

Not wanting to start another fight, Thorn reached out and took his hand. 'In my whole life, you're the only one who's ever made me look twice. You're the only one I want. I'm not good at I-love-yous. But I don't want anyone else. I've never thought about anyone else. Parin was a last resort, not because I wanted to.'

His smile took her breath away. 'Yeah?'

'Yeah,' she promised. 'I think you're crazy for picking me, but I pick you, too. So just … know that. I'm not gonna look elsewhere.'

He leaned in and kissed her and she could feel his relief. When he drew back, he asked, 'Do you want to have breakfast before I leave?'

'Sure.'

Kol left for work by midmorning and, not in the mood to dwell on anything but too antsy to sit around, Thorn began cleaning her weapons. She'd been neglecting them of late, not feeling up for much of anything.

She'd only just set aside her gun and picked up her dagger when a knock at the door made her go still. They didn't have many visitors and Lucien always called ahead.

To her astonishment, it was Nithin. His black hair was slicked back and his green eyes, even without magic, were still bewitching. He wore a finely tailored black suit and held himself like all the world was beneath him. She had never seen a human carry themselves in such a way. But she knew Nithin still thought himself a Suriia, just as she still thought of herself as a human.

'Your coach,' he said, tossing her a set of keys.

She caught them deftly. 'You serious?'

'It's a company coach. Don't damage it.'

'Okay.' She tucked the keys into her pocket. 'What are you doing here?'

'I have a proposition for you,' he said. 'May I come in?'

'Ah ... sure.' She waved him in and brought him to the sitting room. They sat opposite each other, both stiff and guarded. Like her, Nithin didn't ever seem to lounge. He was always on guard, always watchful. As if he mistrusted the very air he breathed.

'How have you been coping?' he asked politely, unable to mask the curiosity in the query.

'Poorly. Until Kol.'

'I'm impressed you lasted that long.'

'I don't take without asking.'

His eyes, jade in the dim lighting of the room, turned to slits. 'You know it insults Thistle every time you insinuate that she had no choice in loving me?'

Thorn didn't rise to the bait. 'Now I have first-hand experience and you know what? I still feel the same.'

'You are beyond grating.'

'Should have let me die, then.'

They scowled at each other.

But whatever Nithin had come for finally pressed him to break the standoff. He leaned in, elbows on his knees, fixing her with a look that promised secrets and truths. 'You don't want to be Suriia? I don't want to be human. Help me and we can fix this abominable situation.'

For the first time since meeting him, Nithin had left her speechless. Finding her voice required severe concentration. 'Seriously?'

He inclined his head. 'Yes.'

'I can be human?'

'Yes.'

'How?'

'Salfar knew of Earth before Earth knew of Salfar because Suriias have been here before,' he explained. 'One Suriia has always been able to travel between. It's said she can go to the afterlife, too. And the beforelife.'

'What is she?'

'We call her the Lady of the River. The River isn't water, exactly. It's a link between the worlds that formed out of the Tear between the fabric of reality. Like a long tunnel made of magic. She guards it, watches over it.

'When the war broke out, the lady prevented anyone from coming or going. We are where we are. But she can be summoned. She can grant wishes. If she likes you, or if you do her bidding, she's a chance like no other. She gave Shadow his long life.'

Thorn stared at him. 'Just by asking?'

'No one knows what it was she made him do. He's sworn to secrecy. And honestly, I think we're all too afraid to ask. But she did do it.'

A small chance, then, and potentially an unsavoury one. Yet it was a chance all the same. If the task was abhorrent, Thorn could always decline. All she wanted was a chance. 'Why are you just telling me this now?'

Nithin did not reply straight away and a sick feeling of betrayal welled in the pit of her stomach.

'How long has Kol known?' she whispered.

Nithin hesitated.

'How long?'

'He found out from Shadow,' said Nithin softly. 'A hundred years ago.'

Despite being seated, Thorn felt like she was in freefall. Kol had known the entire time that there was a way she could become human again and had said *nothing*.

'Okay,' she agreed, hands balled into fists of fury. 'Let's go.'

'You're sure?'

'I'm positive.'

He huffed, the austerity gone from his demeanour. 'Thank you, Thorn.'

It was like they'd crossed some kind of bridge, though where they stood now, she hadn't a clue. If there was one thing she believed true about Nithin it was how much he craved his standing and his powers. He wanted his magic back, his immortality, he wasn't lying about that. And she didn't doubt his story about Kol.

'How's Tiz?' she asked.

'Well,' he said at length. Suddenly he seemed almost cheerful. 'She misses you.'

'I miss her.'

'You're more than welcome to come by.'

'Yeah,' she mumbled, thoroughly disinclined at the prospect.

They made a few more attempts at pleasantries, but neither of them excelled at the task and Nithin took his leave shortly thereafter. The air in the room felt thick in his wake.

Mind racing, Thorn went upstairs to Parin's room and slipped inside. He was stretched across his bed, nose buried in a book. Domestic life had been good to him and he was now a healthy weight, his skin no longer chapped and paper-like. 'All good?' he asked without looking up.

She dropped down beside him and pulled her legs into her chest. 'Nithin thinks he can help me be human again.'

Parin set the book aside, delight spreading across his face. 'Seriously?'

She nodded.

'T, that's amazing!'

'Will you help me?'

'Of course,' he said, tugging her into a hug. 'I'm so happy for you!'

When he leaned back, she was still fighting the urge to cry. 'Kol knew,' she croaked. 'He knew and didn't tell me. Nithin did. What do I do with that?'

Parin frowned. 'I don't know.'

'He lied to me. I hate how much that hurts.'

There was really no advice for Parin to offer, but he wrapped his arm around her shoulders and began to read aloud, his deep voice unknowingly battling away the dark thoughts each time they tried to form in the back of her mind.

A few days after their conversation, keeping up the pretence that they hadn't already seen each other, Nithin arrived in Ilkven with Thistle and Kol. There was something else, and it took Thorn a minute to process what she was seeing. Thistle had changed radically in so short a time. But it wasn't just how delicate and done up she looked.

'You're pregnant?'

Nithin's sudden pressing desire to have his power back made even more sense, and Thorn felt an odd rush of guilt. She didn't want Nithin's powers, but he'd need them to keep Thistle safe.

The idea of Thistle being pregnant was an incredibly strange one, too. Somehow Thorn had never imagined either of them having children. She'd assumed they'd die young enough, but together. To Thorn, they were still barely capable of raising themselves, let alone something small and helpless. But Thistle had always wanted children, always wanted a large family. Thorn didn't. Couldn't, she supposed. She'd never bring a child into a world where they'd be hunted. So it was amazing – and odd – to see Thistle now.

Thistle took Thorn's hand and put it against her stomach. 'Surreal, right?'

'Surreal,' she echoed.

When they took their seats, Thorn noticed how Thistle didn't sit beside her. But Grey claimed the space and gave her a small, understanding smile that helped a little. Kol took the adjacent chair, but not before kissing her cheek. It sent a flurry of contradictory feelings through her. She hadn't confronted him yet, but her resentment brewed hotter every day.

'I was thinking we could take a trip somewhere,' said Nithin. 'Hiburn or White Frost or Gradnell.'

Other than knowing the names to be fancy resorts, Thorn couldn't have pretended to have an opinion on any of them.

'Nah,' said Kol.

Nithin sifted his hand through his hair absently and arched an eyebrow, the picture of suave nonchalance. 'You love Hiburn.'

'Thorn wouldn't,' said Kol. 'It's crawling with Suriias.'

Thorn tried to properly maintain her façade when her gut instinct was to agree entirely with his point. 'I'd be more worried about leaving the others,' she replied, gesturing to Grey, Jade, Trinity and Parin.

In a perfect show of disinterest, Nithin snorted and said, 'If I thought they'd be inclined to come, I'd say bring them.'

Grey sat up. He, like the rest of the humans save Thistle, knew the plan. 'Are you serious?'

'My father owns a lodge up there,' said Nithin airily. 'There's plenty of room.'

Parin rocked his head. 'I've never been to a fancy resort before. Is it safe?'

'You'd be under my protection.'

'Fuck it,' said Parin, clapping his hands together. 'I'm in.'

Kol, however, remained unconvinced and caught Thorn's eye. 'We don't have to.'

'It'll give us all a break from the city,' countered Nithin. 'And you and Thistle could spend more time together.' He nodded to Thorn.

She looked from Kol to Nithin, and then to her oldest friend. Thistle was the only human not in the know, and that felt wrong. So many walls had come up between them where once Thorn had only to look at Thistle and it was like they could read each other's minds.

'Sure,' she mumbled at length.

'Seriously?' Kol couldn't hide his astonishment.

Thorn inclined her head ever so, though she found it difficult. Lying to Kol felt fundamentally *gross*.

'Other Suriias will be there,' he said in a low voice. 'You won't like it.'

'Well, if they touch my friends, I'll kill them.'

Kol's expression remained blank, but she could tell it wasn't without effort.

'Nothing's going to happen,' said Nithin, drawing their attention away from the pointed standoff.

'Then it won't be a problem,' she replied coolly.

Nithin's eyes flashed. Even in on the lie, they were hard-pressed to get along. Somehow that was reassuring for Thorn.

Trinity's suggestion broke the tension. 'Dinner?' She stood and held out a hand to Thorn, who took it gratefully and let herself be steered into the kitchen. When they were alone, Trinity turned to her. 'You okay?'

Thorn shrugged.

'It's going to be okay,' said Trinity, drawing her close. 'It's going to work out. I promise.'

'You sure?'

'I'm sure.'

Weirdly, some part of Thorn believed her. There were degrees and directions of optimism, and Trinity's innate goodness proved contagious.

She helped Trinity cook, and one by one the others wandered into the kitchen to lend a hand. After Nithin and Thistle departed, Kol joined her by the stove. He smiled every time their eyes met and kissed her each time he passed by. But she couldn't be happy about it.

And after, when they were alone in her room, Thorn unconsciously started to pace. The stress was making it hard to keep a lid on her unstable magic.

Kol caught her as she passed by a fifth time. He reached out and tucked her hair behind her ear. 'It's okay to ask, you know?' he murmured. 'I can tell how much you need it.'

Her stomach twisted into knots. Half were in desire; half were in disgust. 'It's fucking sick, Kol.'

'It's not sick, Rose. It's who you are now. And I love you as much now as I ever did.'

And then they were kissing, and Thorn forgot everything but the heat of him.

It was almost dawn when they finally wore themselves out enough for Kol to call it a night, but Thorn didn't want to close her eyes. She feared her dreams too much. Now they didn't just haunt her; they *taunted* her.

Instead, she curled up on the window seat and scowled at her hands. For a time, she watched the night pass by, lost in thought.

Kol shifted in his sleep and, perhaps sensing her distance, opened his eyes. 'Rose?'

'Hm?'

'You okay?'

'Human or Suriia?' she asked quietly, hands balling into fists. 'You'd love me either way?'

In a smooth movement that only someone with magic could have achieved, he was suddenly across from her, tucking into the corner of the windowsill. Reaching out, he cradled her face in his hands. 'I would love you in whatever form. On whatever world.'

Somewhat dubious of his conviction, she wondered, 'Even if I was a human guy?'

'Yes,' he said firmly. 'I'm yours. I will always be yours.'

Was it the frai rule, she wondered, or was it just him?

'Kol?'

'Yeah?'

She decided to give him one last chance. 'Is there no way I could be human again?'

He held her gaze, love and sympathy unmasked on his handsome face. And then he said, 'No.'

Something inside her snapped and she turned away, gritting her jaw. *Never trust a Suriia.*

'I'm sorry,' he continued, raising her hand to his lips and kissing her fingers. 'But it's going to be okay.'

It took all her strength not to punch him in the teeth.

When Kol left for work hours later, Thorn remained in the sitting room, immobile with a bitter outrage that she couldn't shed. Kol was supposed to be on her side. Kol was supposed to love her enough to support her even when he didn't like her choices. So why was it Nithin who had offered her the very thing she wanted?

A sudden soft patter of footfalls preceded Parin, who fretted about her more than ever these days and never left her alone for long.

'You okay, T?' he asked worriedly.

'No,' she muttered.

With a nod, he stood and disappeared into the kitchen. He returned with a tub of ice cream, a bag of popcorn and a bottle of rum. Placing them on the sofa beside her, he grabbed a blanket and draped it over her before turning on the television.

The others joined them one by one, and they whiled away the day with a movie marathon. No one spoke much, but no one had to. Moments like these were what Thorn craved more than anything else – quiet, private moments without fear or tension.

Halfway through their fourth film Kol returned. Jade let him in and upon seeing them all snuggled up on the couch, he immediately caught Thorn's gaze, grin broadening.

Her stomach tightened. He was so confusing. He took such delight in seeing her happy, yet he was lying to her.

'Room for a sixth?' he asked, taking off his coat.

Parin shifted wordlessly away from Thorn's side and let Kol take his place.

Folding himself in beside her, Kol caught her in a soft kiss before drawing her into his arms. 'You smell good,' he murmured into her ear.

'Popcorn?' Parin held the bowl out. There was a flare in his eyes that only Thorn could discern, but she appreciated it.

When the movie finished, she bid the others goodnight and trailed after Kol up the stairs, her mind, her heart, and her body all arguing to do something different.

'I have to go out of town for a couple of days,' he said as they undressed. 'Do you want to come with me?'

Thorn cocked an eyebrow dubiously. 'Is it a super fun excursion to the mountains?'

'It's a business trip with Nithin.'

She wrinkled her nose. 'That sounds dreary.'

The acerbic response made him laugh. 'Thistle's going to come. She's been getting involved in the business more and more. Nith wants to make her one of the partners.'

Thorn couldn't think of anything that sounded less appealing.

'Rose?'

'Yeah?'

'What do you want to be?'

'What do you mean?'

'I mean, you're not running anymore. You're not being hunted. What do you want to do with the rest of your life?'

The question made her pick up her father's blade from her bedside table and turn it over in her hands. Holding it made her feel less like screaming.

'Humans are still being hunted,' she growled. 'The extinction countdown is still up.'

'So, do you want to join us at Lathlak? We're trying to change things for the better.'

Setting the knife down, Thorn yanked on her tatty sleep shirt and trousers before replying. 'I'm a gutter rat, Kol.'

He stared at her. 'Don't say shit like that.'

'It's true. I don't know anything about business. And you know what? I don't want to know. I'm not a politician. I'm not a businessperson. I'm not a S—' She closed her mouth before the word came all the way out, but his eyes narrowed.

'You are Suriia, Thorn. How long are you going to fight it?'

'I'm not going to pretend that this life is okay,' she retorted. 'That I'm happy with the way things turned out.'

Kol put his hands on his head, and she realised then that his fingers had sharpened to talons. His wings jutted out and his eyes were blackened. 'How is it that you are now not hunted, your friends are alive, Thistle is thriving, and you have a home, a job and someone who loves you, and yet somehow you're still determined to be unhappy?'

Stepping back, she crossed her arms, outrage mounting by the second. 'Fuck you.'

'No, fuck you, Rose,' he snapped back. 'Nith saved your life. Get over it.'

'No one asked *me* if I wanted to live this way!' she roared. 'Every time I look in the mirror, I see the thing that killed my parents! It's not a privilege to be one of you and no one fucking asked!' Sparks shot out of her hands and she balled them into fists, fearful of her own unknown abilities.

Stricken with guilt, he moved to her side. 'Rose,' he murmured, pulling her into his arms and holding her close. 'Oh, Rose. I'm sorry. I'm so, so sorry.'

Her fury burst like a dam and suddenly she was crying into his chest, so overwhelmed by the sheer amount of everything.

At some point they moved to the bed and she must have fallen asleep because it seemed like only minutes later when she was being shaken awake.

'Rose. Rose, wake up.'

Kol was leaning over her. He was fully dressed, and his bag was by the door. She sat up, rubbing her eyes.

There was a tired, worried air about him. 'I don't want to leave after last night.' He reached out and brushed a strand of hair back from her face. 'I'll be sick with worry about you the whole time.'

She swallowed the razor-sharp burn in her throat and leaned away from his hand. 'I'll be fine.'

'Will you answer the phone when I call you?' he implored, and the tone of his voice sent pangs through her chest. 'Please.'

She heaved a sigh. 'If it rings, I'll answer.'

He kissed her temple. 'I love you,' he said. 'If you remember nothing else, at least remember that.'

She watched him go, mute and bitter.

When his coach had disappeared into the sky, she threw her phone at the door as hard as she could and watched it smash into a hundred pieces.

CHAPTER THIRTY
Knife's Edge

Nik and Eran burst gracelessly through the door well after sunset, gasping for breath and drenched in sweat. Both sported cuts and bruises, their clothes torn, their trousers muddied from running through some unknown filth.

Lucien wasn't the only one who jumped to his feet. He'd been frantic since Nik vanished earlier that morning, but a fight with Adair ended with him agreeing not to immediately track Nik down and drag him back to the safety of the house.

'What happened?' he demanded, calculating the damage with his eyes and feeling increasingly more furious by the second.

'We met some lovely Suriias in the park,' said Nik, rotating his shoulder and wincing. It looked as if someone had dragged him over the pavement. 'They thought I'd make a good drink.'

Lucien's blood went cold. 'Did they—'

'No bites,' said Nik, as if being bitten was of no great concern and not the fact that a vryko could steal his soul. 'Don't worry.'

'Oh, I'm convinced now,' he said caustically before cutting a scowl at Eran. 'You okay?'

Eran bobbed his head, no worse for the wear and cocky as a result. 'Got a few punches in. Been a while since I've done that.'

'Don't get used to it,' said Adair sternly, but he was regarding his eldest son with unmasked concern.

Lucien took Nik by the arm and steered him out of the sitting room and down the hall. In the relative security of their bedroom, Lucien examined him more carefully.

'I'm fine, Luka,' said Nik when he checked the same bruise for the fifth time. 'It's not that bad.'

'Whatever world you're on, you get hurt,' said Lucien furiously. 'I should never have brought you here.'

'I wanted to come. We all did.'

'It was a mistake.'

Nik shook his head. 'It wasn't a mistake. Things are just a different kind of awful here. But that just makes it even more clear.'

'What?'

'That something's not right.'

Distracted by a particularly nasty cut on Nik's eyebrow, it took Lucien a moment to respond. 'What do you mean?'

'I mean, yeah, the two worlds are weird, but doesn't it all feel a bit wrong? Like it's not meant to be like this?' Nik held out a hand. 'You said my father cut a hole between Earth and Salfar. What if doing so literally split Earth in two? And the Tear let some onto one and some onto the other.'

'It's possible,' he agreed. 'I don't know how it's fixable, though. Not without the book, which is missing.'

'What book?'

Lucien waved the question away. 'It doesn't matter now. Someone in Westend has it.'

'Is that dangerous?'

'I hope not,' he muttered grimly. 'But I can only deal with one problem at a time.'

'Isn't fixing these worlds kind of our responsibility? It's Geon who did this.'

'None of this is your responsibility. If anything, you have every right to turn tail and run as fast as you can in the opposite direction. You're under no obligation to anyone.'

'Sure I am.'

'How do you figure that?'

'The problems of the worlds are as much my problem as everyone else's,' said Nik, holding out his hands. 'I'm not the only human who's been enslaved. I'm not the only human on the run. I'm not the only one in love and hitting roadblock after roadblock.'

Lucien swallowed hard at this last remark. 'You've got his stubbornness and determination, I'll say that.'

'Not enough,' said Nik bitterly. 'If I had enough, perhaps you'd want me more.'

'Firstly,' said Lucien, trying not to wince, 'let's leave all suggestions of a likeness between you and your father out of our relationship. Please. For my own sanity.'

Nik wrinkled his nose and nodded in agreement.

'Secondly,' he continued, 'I don't have doubts about *you*, Nik. You can't possibly think that. All hesitations are on my part. Until I'm sure that you feel comfortable, I don't want to cross that line. It's not a place you can ever come back from. If you are ever scared of me, that's it. We're over. And the thought of that makes it kind of hard to breathe around you.'

Nik's glare softened somewhat. 'Do you really think you'll hurt me?'

Repulsed by the mere thought, Lucien shook his head vehemently. 'That's not the point, though. The point is that I could. The point is that you'll always know that. You may feel safe, but what if you suddenly don't? What if I do something that makes you terrified and you think back to Ashby? No, Nik. I'm not risking that. I can't. You love me? I love *you*. And if I ever scare you, we're done. The thought breaks my heart. Don't you get that?'

Nik looked like he wanted to argue, but to Lucien's eternal gratitude, he nodded belatedly.

'It doesn't mean I don't want you,' said Lucien. 'Trust me. I have innumerable filthy thoughts. I just *can't* risk you being scared. I'm sorry.'

Although Nik looked disappointed, a wolfish grin curved his lips. 'Filthy, huh?'

'Oh, yeah.'

'Good to know.'

As they regarded each other, their smiles broadened and the air grew heavy with anticipation and desire.

Abruptly, Nik withdrew the iron blade from where it was holstered at his side. Raising it so that the sharp point was resting against Lucien's chin, Nik inched closer.

'What if I had this?' he queried. 'Are you still more powerful than me if I have this?'

Lucien held his gaze. A low burn was emanating from where the iron brushed his skin. 'One cut and you poison me. Don't adjust your grip.'

'I'm steady,' said Nik. 'But if you were going to attack me, you'd cut yourself.'

'Probably.'

Ever so carefully, Nik leaned in, his lips grazing Lucien's. 'Am I still the weakest one in the room?'

Before Lucien could answer, Nik sealed the question with a burning kiss.

He tasted like temptation, like he wanted to be consumed. And although Lucien was very conscious of the blade burning a mark onto his throat, Nik's hand remained steady, and it didn't nick his skin.

And so he kissed Nik back.

CHAPTER THIRTY-ONE
Tear

Thorn was in the midst of meticulously sorting the kitchen shelves – she always cleaned more when her anxiety worsened – when Kol wandered in. It had been nearly a week since their argument. She hadn't spoken to him at all while he was away, but the days apart had done nothing to make her feel better about his secret-keeping.

He, too, seemed uncertain about where they stood. His hair was wet from a recent shower, and he wore his usual jeans and long sleeve shirt, though he'd swapped his normal black coat for a light grey one. The shade emphasised his dark features and Thorn found herself appreciating his beauty even as her anger flared anew.

'There you are,' he greeted, eyeing her anxiously. 'Trinity let me in.'

She nodded.

'I've been calling you for days.'

'My phone broke,' she replied, stiffer than marble and just as cold.

'Oh.' He cracked a smile. 'I thought you might be avoiding me.'

'Do I have reason to avoid you?'

'I feel like you're angry with me.'

Thorn looked away. She heard him sigh and a moment later he was in front of her, his hands coming to rest lightly on her hips.

'I missed you,' he confided. 'I hated leaving you so upset.'

Staying furious with him when he said things like that was nearly impossible and she gave him a small smile, an act that felt almost like betraying herself.

'I just want to be me again,' she muttered. 'That's not going to change.'

'I know. But what sort of boyfriend would I be if I didn't love you however you are? Whatever you are?'

Wrapping his arms around her and pulling her close, Kol kissed the top of her head. Thorn tucked her head into his chest and closed her eyes. If she didn't, she was going to punch him. But deep inside her chest, her heart fluttered like a stationary hummingbird, flapping its wings relentlessly.

He helped her finish in the kitchen before they wandered upstairs. But the privacy of her room only increased the underlying tension between them.

'Do you want to talk about it again?' he asked, unbuttoning his coat and folding it neatly before setting it onto the empty space on her desk. 'It won't be a fight, I promise.'

If she said anything, she risked saying everything. The fight that was brewing inside her chest was going to burst out of her soon – she could only tamper down her anger for so long. But if she lost her one chance to be human, she'd regret it forever. So she had to be silent, at least until she had some answers of her own.

Rather than answer, she crashed her mouth against his, letting her desire force her common sense to the back of her mind. If she only felt, touched, breathed, and didn't think, then everything in that moment was perfect. And however much he wanted to talk to her, the move served as enough of a distraction and Kol began hastily tugging off his shirt.

Thorn had always been fine lying to Suriias until Kol came along. But it was easier, wasn't it? Postponing heartache.

At least that was what she tried to tell herself.

Dawn crept forth pale and bitter the morning of the trip, as if the weather personified Thorn's mood. She cast the slate skies a scowl of solidarity on the way to the coach Nithin had gifted her. Parin joined her in the front seat while Jade, Grey and Trinity stretched out in the back.

Nithin and the others met them on the outskirts of the city and Thorn followed his coach across the fields, still new to flying and slightly nervous as a result.

The resort was north of Courtenz, nestled in the mountains, and a thick fog set in as they flew over the midlands. The area was so quiet and pristine, none of them could stop staring at the scenery as they neared. About half a mile from the gates, Nithin landed, and they drove the rest of the way.

The road seemed to go on and on, but ornate buildings slowly began to appear; each a refined little cottage hugged on all sides by snow-capped fir trees.

'This is strange,' Trinity observed. 'Everything's so nice.'

Thorn's heart thudded in her chest. 'I can't believe we're willingly vacationing with Suriias.'

'We'll be fine,' Parin assured her. 'Try not to think about it.'

Easier said than done.

At last Nithin parked and Thorn followed suit. But before opening her door, she turned to the others. All four bore nervous expressions. 'Anyone wants to leave, we leave.'

'Deal,' they said in unison.

As one, the group got out of the coach. The mountain air smelled fragrantly of winter pine and the only sounds came from the odd bird or distant laugh from vacationers.

Trinity appeared at Thorn's side and linked arms with her. 'You notice that Grey keeps checking out Nithin?' she hissed conspiratorially. 'He's in love.'

Thorn giggled, drawing Thistle's attention. There was something like jealousy in her eyes, but she tried not to dwell on it.

After checking in – Nithin had rented an entire *cabin* apparently – everyone divided up into groups. Thistle, Nithin and Kol wanted to ski; Jade went to build a snowman with Trinity; and Thorn sat by the fire with Parin and Grey.

'When do we go?' asked Grey once they were alone, each cradling a cup of hot chocolate. The shelves were filled to bursting with packets for instant hot chocolate, marshmallows, teas, biscuits in a dozen flavours, and other luxuries. The Suriias really had capitalised on human discoveries and inventions.

'Tomorrow.'

'Good.'

Parin's brow creased. 'And when Kol tries to follow?'

'Well, we'll be gone before he wakes up. And according to Nithin, there's no tracking in the Tear.'

Parin absorbed this, but then nudged her with his boot. 'What is the plan once you're human again? We can't go back to the house. There won't be any protection for us.'

'I haven't thought that far ahead.'

He chuckled. 'What if we disappeared? Into the woods. Vanish. Would anyone here actually miss any of this?'

'Once I'm human, I'm game.'

'Really?' Grey eyed her sceptically. 'What about Kol?'

'He lied to me.'

'Maybe he didn't mean anything by it,' said Parin softly.

'You don't think so? Would you lie to the people you love?'

They exchanged looks of mutual discomfort, none of them trusting, none of them used to having the luxury.

'See.'

'Love sucks,' Parin concurred, squeezing her shoulder.

'Want to know what sucks more?'

They waited.

'Being *surprised*.' She drew her legs into her chest and propped her elbows up so that she could press the heels of her palms against her eyes. 'I was convinced.'

Their arms encircled her protectively, like siblings.

For an hour they sat undisturbed in companionable silence, eating everything they could find until a knock rapped on the door, and Thorn opened it to find herself face to face with Thistle.

'Hi,' she grunted, slightly surprised.

Windswept from the slopes, Thistle looked more beautiful than ever. Her shiny black hair was tied back from her face, which looked fuller than it used to. 'We haven't done anything just the two of us in months,' she said hopefully. 'Want to go for a walk through the snow?'

It was on the tip of Thorn's tongue to say that the reason they'd spent no time together was Thistle's fault, but Thorn missed her too much to say so.

She nodded and grabbed her coat. Even now, she wore her ratty one. She couldn't bring herself to shed any more parts of her former life. 'It's weird that we can do it now without fearing for our lives.'

Thistle grinned, unburdened by the parade of dark thoughts in Thorn's mind. 'It's better, isn't it?'

'I suppose.'

They made their way carefully down the steps and headed towards the woods. Snow blanketed everything; it was crystalline and gorgeous. Even the animals were hiding away. An untouched world.

'What's it like?' Thistle glanced over at her, skin glowing in the snowy sunshine. 'Being Suriia?'

'It's shit,' said Thorn, kicking at a pile of snow. 'What's it like being pregnant?'

'I'm nauseated and tired all the time. It's nice, though.'

Thorn jammed her hands into her pockets as the cold crept into her bones. 'Feeling sick is nice?'

'I don't like *getting sick*, I like being pregnant. Knowing I have a family. The one I've always wanted.'

It was like someone had stolen the air from Thorn's lungs. 'Lucky you,' she managed. She wanted nothing more in that moment than to cease to exist.

Thistle misinterpreted her change in demeanour. 'Come on. Being Suriia can't be that bad.'

'I'm horny all the fucking time and I get to drain people to stay sane. Colour me joyous.'

Thistle stopped short. The trees surrounded them now, which was a good thing, judging by the fire in her eyes. 'Nithin gave up everything to save your life, Thorn.'

'I didn't want to be saved, Thistle. Not like this.'

'You'd really rather be dead?'

Thorn snapped. 'When was it you forgot our childhood? When was it you suddenly decided we weren't hunted and hated?'

'Perhaps I'm tired of hating! Aren't you exhausted?'

Thorn threw up her hands. 'No!' she roared, her voice strangling on the word. 'Do you know how much I want to eat my own gun these days? More so than I ever fucking did before!'

With a look of utter disappointment at Thistle, she stormed off into the snowy trees.

Trinity and Jade found her a few hours later sitting on the ground, shaking with cold and too angry to move inside.

'Thorn?' Trinity kneeled before her. 'What happened?'

She shook her head.

Interlacing their fingers, Trinity squeezed her hands. 'Do you want to go to the Tear or just go?'

'No,' she said heavily. 'I'm sick of this. I want to be me again.'

They helped her to her feet and the three of them walked back through the woods.

Thankfully only Parin and Grey were outside the cabin when they stepped off the path.

'Come on,' said Parin, beckoning them inside. 'I'm going to make hot chocolate.'

'Where's Kol?' asked Thorn.

'Out with Nithin. Want me to get him?'

She shook her head.

The rest of the afternoon passed in quiet company. The group of scarred, bony, weary friends did not look the typical picture of serenity, but when it was just them, huddled together, legs and arms entangled, they were just that.

Thorn was halfway through her book when Kol walked in, prompting the others to take their leave. He waved to them before bending down to kiss her in greeting and taking a seat on the edge of the bed.

'You and Nithin have fun?'

'He's less graceful these days,' said Kol with a laugh. 'He misses being Suriia.'

'I know how he feels.'

Kol frowned at her words. 'He's still Nith. Anyone who thinks he's different needs their head examined.'

Thorn swallowed her caustic retort.

'Rose? You okay?'

Since she couldn't say what she wanted to say, she settled on the other area of heartbreak still smarting. 'Tiz is *so* delighted to finally have a family.'

'Oh, Rose.' His voice softened, so filled with love and understanding, that she looked up, hating herself for once again being drawn in by just how genuine he could sound. 'That was a rotten thing for her to say,' he continued. 'I'm sorry.'

Thorn forced several blinks to keep her composure. 'It's like I don't mean anything to her.'

'I'm sure she didn't mean it like that.'

'Then she shouldn't have said it.'

'Sometimes we say things we don't mean.'

'Do you?'

'What? Say things I don't mean? Never.'

A fresh flush of fury filled her. 'Never?'

'No.'

'Sure.'

'I'm ridiculously, blunderingly, honest. You've seen it yourself.'

The urge to fight him on the point kept building in her chest and distracted her so thoroughly that she didn't realise he'd moved until he was kissing her stomach.

'What are you doing?' she asked, desire eating her anger instantly. Bloody sbura magic.

'Admiring you. Should I stop?'

'Not unless you want to.'

He kissed her hip bone before looking back up at her. 'Will you marry me?'

Processing his words took a few seconds. 'Are you proposing to me?'

'Yes.'

'Seriously?'

'Seriously.'

'Good timing.'

'I thought you'd appreciate the lack of displays.'

His innate charm brought a smile to her face unbidden. He grinned proudly.

'Well?'

'Will I marry you?'

'That was the question.'

She appraised him critically. All she could think was that he was lying to her. If he was lying about this, what else was he lying about? But still, the thought of spending the rest of her life with him was dangerously tempting.

'Would you live away from the Suriias?' she murmured, wrestling with an outright refusal. 'Would you go somewhere far away?'

Kol sighed.

'That's my condition,' she said. 'I don't want a life with the Suriias. I'm sticking with my people.'

A scowl darkened his face and he moved away from her.

Guilt welled like heartburn in her chest. 'Kol—'

'You know,' he growled, expression dark with anger and hurt, 'if I said half the shit about humans that you say about Suriias, you'd never speak to me again.'

'Well, the Suriias—'

'I know!' he cried, raising his voice at her for the first time ever. 'I fucking know, Rose. We're all fucking terrible! Humans do despicable things, too! Lucien can tell you!' He shook his head and walked out of the room, slamming the door behind him so hard the wood cracked.

Thorn turned and kicked the closet door furiously.

Less than a minute later, the door creaked open, and Grey stuck his head in.

'You hear that?' she grunted.

'Yeah.' He held up a deck of cards. 'Want company?'

'Sure.'

His grin turned catlike and he pushed the door open fully, revealing Parin, Trinity and Jade.

Thorn laughed despite everything.

It was late in the evening when Thistle, Kol and Nithin returned to the cabin. None of them wore wholly casual clothes like the group on the ground, and they could have been a trio of starlets out for a night on the town standing in the doorway side by side, each as striking as the other.

'Anyone up for dinner?' said Thistle, clapping her hands together. 'There's a restaurant up the road and Nithin booked the whole place out.'

Parin whistled. 'It pays to have rich connections.'

'That it does,' said Nithin bluntly.

'Can we dress up?' asked Trinity, eyes wide with hope.

Parin chuckled and tugged on her earlobe. 'You love any excuse to wear a dress.'

'I never get to.'

Nithin, amazingly, winked at her. 'You can dress up. Thistle might even have something for you to borrow.'

Trinity hesitated, glancing at Thorn, but when Thorn smiled and nodded, she grabbed Jade's hand and followed Thistle from the room.

Not interested in dressing up, but desperate to escape the awkward tension, Thorn went to change into a less destroyed pair of jeans and a clean shirt. She had just taken off her top when Kol stepped inside.

'I don't want to spend all of dinner in silence,' he said, walking over to her. 'Can we forget I asked?'

'I've never even thought about a future, Kol,' she said, finding that anger at him was hard to maintain. 'But if I have one, you're the only one I can imagine it'd be with.' *If you weren't a liar.*

His lips twitched and he leaned in, kissing her chastely.

True to his word, Nithin had booked the entire restaurant and other than the servers, there was no one else around. The atmosphere stayed light, largely as a result of everyone but Thorn's banter. She was too lost in thought to engage much with anyone.

It was after everyone had ordered and Thorn saw what time it was, the seconds ticking away on the clock above the hearth, that her mind went to the journey she, Nithin and the rest were about to take. He had eluded to there being a trade of some kind. But what would she have to give? She knew already what she *wouldn't* give. And simply asking sounded far too easy. Her stomach churned.

'It's really strange eating in a restaurant,' said Trinity, interrupting Thorn's spiralling thoughts.

Jade took Trinity's hand and kissed it. 'But you look pretty.'

Thorn nodded in agreement on both matters. 'Do you guys want to leave?'

'No, it's okay,' whispered Trinity. 'It's just strange.'

Across the table, Thistle said, 'One day it won't be.'

Thorn tensed.

'One day it'll be normal,' her best friend continued. 'We'll all be the same.'

Thorn didn't know what to say to her, and instead stared down at her plate. She said nothing for the remainder of the meal, nor spoke much to Kol after they returned to their room. Thankfully, he didn't pester her for conversation.

She listened to him watching television for over an hour, but stayed outside on the balcony until she heard a soft snore.

Not giving herself a second to deliberate, she grabbed her backpack and weapons, and leapt over the railing. Landing on the ground without a sound, she darted into the trees. The snow was falling fast now, and her tracks were covered quickly.

At the end of the property, hidden in the shadows of the trees, she found the others.

No one spoke. It was too cold and the shared anxiety was almost tangible. The group simply slipped into the dark forest like wolves in the night.

More than three hours dragged by before a sign gave any indication that they were on the right route. It told hikers to be careful. They were near the historic Tear.

Shortly thereafter, they rounded a corner and found themselves atop a hill. Far below was the strangest sight: where there should have been a clear view of the trees beyond, the world vanished for several metres. Like someone had punched through the very fabric of the universe. A crackling fog hung around the edges of the Tear. Inside, obscured by the fog, was what looked like another, brighter forest. One without snow.

'What's in there?' asked Parin with all the enthusiasm of a man at the gallows.

'A forest,' said Nithin. 'Unless you're not seeing what I'm seeing?'

'What kind of forest?'

'We're *in* a forest,' muttered Grey.

'A magical one,' said Nithin, ignoring him. 'It grew between the worlds until the lady barred the way. Now only she can travel between the worlds.'

Thorn turned to the others. Her friends. Her family. 'You guys don't have to come. This could end really badly.'

'We're not going anywhere,' said Parin in solidarity. 'We're in this shit with you to the end, babe.'

'It's not like I have anything better to do,' said Grey, winking at her as he drew his gun and checked the barrel.

'Ilkven was boring anyways,' added Jade, nudging Thorn with her elbow.

Trinity clapped her hands together. 'Someone has to keep you idiots from walking off a cliff.'

One by one, they stepped through the rip in reality. In the very fabric of the universe. The forest beyond the Tear was so dark Thorn couldn't even make out the shapes of the trees.

'Do monsters live in here?' asked Grey.

Nithin snorted. 'Monsters?'

'As if you fuckers don't have weird monsters.'

'I don't think anything lives in the Tear.'

Parin made a dubious sound. 'Then why is it so dangerous?'

'Because,' said Nithin drolly, 'nothing *lives.*'

Thorn wasn't the only one who shot him a glare.

The midway world didn't feel real. Like walking through a dream. Was it half Earth and half Salfar? Was it something else entirely? Magic seemed to exist in the Tear, but it was corrupted.

'This world feels dead,' said Parin at one point.

Not even Nithin could disagree.

'Nithin?' asked Thorn, staring at the murky sky that seemed heavy with secrets.

'Yes?'

'Kol ever tell you his theory about levels? Earth and Salfar and shit?'

'Eloquent. And yes.'

'You know how he says on Salfar things were different? That Suriias didn't drink blood and whatnot? Do you think that's because of the Tear? That maybe it makes magic wrong somehow. That some of you guys are just ... messed up?'

She felt impatient for his answer, but it took a long time to come.

Finally, his voice floated through the distance between them like an olive branch, 'I think that's very possible.'

Empathy was a curious thing, and all too often pity took its place, but in that dark and quiet moment, Thorn found that she felt safe with Nithin leading the way.

Halfway through the second day of their trek, Thorn's skin began to itch. Her flesh turned taut and became much, much too sensitive. Even the breeze began to feel too intimate. The effect was like a strange high at first, slightly floaty and bearable, if strange. But the further they walked, the more exposed she felt. Like her skin was raw and chafing beneath her clothes; like she wanted to grab Nithin and kiss him, no matter how little she actually wanted to. Something magical was happening, but she had no idea what it was or how to bring it up.

Unsurprisingly, Nithin was the first to mention it, openly exasperated after watching her sweat profusely and shake for hours. 'Sex isn't about love for a sbura,' he said tartly. 'You can't simply ignore it. You'll get weaker. We should have brought Kol.'

'I'll be fine.'

'You won't.' He cocked his head to Parin suggestively.

'Fuck off.' The thought of sex with anyone who wasn't Kol was enough to make her retch. 'I'm mad at Kol,' she muttered, 'but I'm hardly going to mess around on him.'

'If you think that my suggestion doesn't enrage me, then you're a fool. But you're no good to us like this. You're completely distracted. Ignoring this makes you a hindrance, not a help.'

Thorn's lip curled as her stomach tied itself into knots. 'Why's nothing happening to you guys?'

'The closer to Salfar we go, the more the thrall of magic overwhelms you. You should be using it; allowing it to use you. Right now you're just a grenade in a blender.'

'I would be the only Suriia the *one time* it's not beneficial.'

He snorted in agreement.

The rest of the day was an exercise in frustration and restraint. By nightfall, her patience was threadbare and she wanted to destroy everything in sight. She felt like punching Nithin just for giving magic to her.

More determined than Nithin – or, as was more likely, more concerned about her – Parin took her aside later that night. 'If you won't ask the others, then I'm offering,' he said gamely. 'You look like you're about to claw your skin off.'

She hated how tempted she felt. The consent given on her behalf by a magic that hadn't asked for permission. 'No,' she said firmly. 'I won't do that to Kol.'

'Isn't the whole point of this to become human so you never have to do it again? So you can have a say in your sex life?'

'It's cheating.' Worse, frai only loved once. She couldn't obliterate Kol's heart no matter how furious she was.

Thorn spent the rest of the night crying – and biting – into her fist, trying not to make a noise which would wake the others.

She'd barely nodded off when she felt a hand on her shoulder. The second skin touched skin, a moan escaped her.

To her deep embarrassment, the hand belonged to Nithin. But he didn't seem to have noticed her reaction, or at the very least was enough of a gentleman not to say anything about it.

He raised a finger to his lips in warning.

Instantly on alert, she sat up and looked in the direction he was glaring.

'I thought nothing lived here,' she breathed.

He shrugged.

She didn't have time to get mad. A monster the likes of which she could never have imagined was moving in the distance.

'What is that?'

'Eury,' he whispered. 'He feasts on rotting flesh.'

'Oh, *lovely.*'

'I thought you said nothing lived here,' said Trinity, echoing Thorn, voice quiet but pitched high, like a thoroughly affronted mouse.

'He's technically dead,' said Nithin.

They all shot him scowls of furious exasperation. But keeping their attention off the monster for more than a second was impossible.

It was just so *big*.

Like a body made of bodies. Only some of the bodies were inside out, in pieces, or placed askew.

Grey dry-heaved into his mouth, managing to stay quiet even as his stomach rebelled.

Finally, Eury disappeared into the trees and everyone let out rattling sighs.

'That was close,' said Nithin, wiping his forehead. 'Too close.'

'Anything else we should be aware of?' asked Jade, gaping at him.

'Probably.' Nithin held out a hand. 'I know extraordinarily little about the Tear. It's a corrupt place. Magic never should have come through from Salfar and everything here is twisted. Things that were caught in the middle when the Tear opened.'

Before Thorn could process this, something seized her ankle. She had a split second to reach for her blade when she was yanked into the air.

It took her several moments to realise that she'd been wrenched into the air by a *tree*.

The blast of green light burst out of her and suddenly she was on the ground.

Nithin darted to her side. 'Care to lend a hand?'

'What?'

'I'm being literal. Give me your hand, Thorn.'

She gasped, surprised to find that his grip was as strong as Kol's. Words she didn't understand tripped from his tongue and the pull of magic shuddered through her.

A great, shimmering green barrier appeared in the air between them and the murderous trees.

'How are you doing that?'

'Magic. Obviously.'

Her stomach flipped as the barrier grew brighter and brighter until the light was almost blinding.

And then it vanished. The forest around them was suddenly still and quiet.

'Whoa,' she grunted.

'I've never done that before,' he said, gasping for breath. A small laugh left him then, and he ran his hands over his glistening face.

Thorn wiped sweat from her own forehead and nodded several times. 'Good work, then.'

'How did you do that?' asked Parin, coming up behind them. 'Thought you were human.'

'I was using Thorn's power,' said Nithin.

Thorn did a doubletake. 'I didn't know you could do that.'

'Lucien gave me a spellbook from Salfar.'

'Wait, there are spells?'

'That's kind of cool,' said Jade.

'It is not,' said Parin.

'Whatever.' Grey looked like he couldn't possibly have cared less about potential spellwork. 'Let's get out of here.'

No one disagreed with him.

They walked on until dawn, pausing only for breakfast, and then continued until midmorning when Nithin stopped short and pointed ahead.

'There. The waters.' The river to Salfar didn't look like a river at all. More like a glimmering, blue-black ribbon with shimmering light that danced upon the surface. Magic, every bit of it.

Thorn nodded. 'So … what? Do we have to drink from it or something?'

'We have to summon her first.'

'How do we do that?'

'Magic.'

'Yes, thank you. I meant *how*.'

'Blood and a spell.'

The one thing Thorn would give Nithin was his resolve and determination. In so many ways, it matched her own.

They approached the water slowly, mindful of their surroundings. There had been no other encounters after Eury and the trees, but that didn't mean none were coming.

As everyone held their weapons aloft nervously, Nithin kneeled beside the edge of the river. Then, with remarkable efficiency, cut a line down his arm with her knife.

Blood quickly dripped into the water. As each droplet hit the surface, the angry burgundy dispelled into light pink and then vanished. Then, a sudden gust of what looked like crimson dust puffed away from the water's surface.

'I swear no allegiance to the Cold King,' he declared.

She thought he was going to say something else, but when he didn't, she squatted down beside him. 'That's it?'

'Apparently it's a test. Once you've said it, you're on Salfar's watchlist.'

'Oh, goodie,' quipped Parin. 'Like we didn't have enough enemies. Now King Cold hates us, too.'

'He's dead,' said Nithin.

'My thanks to the timeline on that one, then.'

Before Thorn could chime in, something in the water caught her eye.

Someone was watching them.

She grabbed Nithin's still bleeding arm. 'There.'

The Lady of the River came forth slowly, gliding through the water like she was made of fish or plant. She was unlike any Suriia Thorn had ever seen. Her hair was blue or green, depending on how she tilted her head; her eyes were milky white, her skin blacker than raven's feathers.

The lady tilted her head to the side enquiringly. 'Whom do you swear allegiance to, Nithin Summons?'

'My family,' he said simply.

The lady's impenetrable gaze shifted then to Thorn. 'And you?'

Thorn nodded. 'Same answer. Probably different people and qualifications, though.'

'And what is it you want?'

'I want to be as I was,' said Nithin.

'Same,' said Thorn succinctly.

The lady appraised the pair in turn. Then her gaze went past them, to the others.

'Oh, we don't want anything,' said Parin quickly. 'Don't look at us.'

'Quite content,' Grey affirmed.

Jade and Trinity exchanged smirks.

The lady returned her attention to Nithin and Thorn. 'Only one of you shall receive a gift,' she said, voice discordant and strange.

Thorn's heart hammered in her chest. She was about to speak when she caught sight of the look on Nithin's face.

'Him,' she said abruptly. As badly as she wanted to be human again, Nithin had saved her life.

Nithin turned to her, stunned. 'Why?'

She shrugged even though it burned everything in her to get her next words out. 'You saved my life.'

'Thorn—'

'It's okay.'

For a moment, all he could do was stare at her. Then, quietly, 'Thank you.'

The lady smiled and put her palm on Nithin's forehead. Green light spread between them and he collapsed a moment later, half submerged in the Immortal River.

Thorn dropped down beside him and put her hand over his heart. 'Nithin! Nithin!' She then realised the others had all fallen, too. 'What did you do to them?'

'They will be fine.' The lady waved her hand, unbothered. 'Do you know who the Cold King is, Thorn?'

Parin and Nithin's conversation replayed in her mind, but she knew nothing else. 'No.'

'He's been the Lord King of Salfar for some time. He's not one any of the history books will emphasise emulating.'

'His name does allude to that.'

The lady laughed, the sound beautiful and hypnotic. 'Do you like poetry? Sometimes the poets speak truths best, I find.'

'Sure.'

Words fell from the lady's lips like a song, a story, a warning. *'There is a legend, centuries old, / of the orphan who stole the book of souls / by breaking into the Tower in the dead of night, / and rescuing the prince long kept out of sight.*

'But any villain worth his salt will say, / Be sure you've truly killed your prey. / For as magic bled and townsfolk fled, / The cold king rose again.

'The king searched high and low for the stolen souls, / an impossible task with war taking hold. / But then one night the cold king's spies / told of a boy, who had his father's eyes.'

'Huh,' Thorn grunted.

'All legends come from somewhere – and that poem's more fact than fiction.' The lady's strange eyes took on a curious glaze as she stared across the water. As if she could see Salfar from where they stood. The air around them picked up and the grass danced this way and that, as if the land itself was unsettled. 'Salfar isn't like Earth, Thorn. Different world, different universe. Different rules. The only ones who can rule that world are those with the crown's magic in their blood. They are the caretakers.'

'What's crown magic?'

'Long before recorded history, an ancient queen afraid of being deposed bound her bloodline to the crown, to its magic. Any who rebelled were killed, their souls locked away inside a book. With each soul added, the book's power grew. And the only ones who can wield the power of the book, who can open and close the fabric of reality, and who can declare rulers, are the descendants of her bloodline. A tyrant who reigns can only be overthrown by one of his own.'

'Sounds like an exhausting birth right.'

'Quite. But such is the way of things.'

'I suppose.'

'Do you want to know a secret, little human?'

'What?'

'If the Suriias remain on this world, it will mean unending war and bloodshed.'

A lump swelled in her throat. 'Can it be reversed?'

'It's as your friend said. The Tear is an infection. The two worlds were never meant to be one. This magical mistake grew between what is an afterlife for some; a beforelife for others. And the two cannot be one. But if you leave Earth, all will fall into place.'

Thorn stared at her. 'Leave Earth? Like go to Lucien's world?'

'No,' said the lady. 'Go to Salfar.'

Words fled her tongue.

'It's the only way you will ever be human again.'

Thorn stared at her. 'What?' she rasped.

'Bring the prince home,' said the lady. 'Only when the prince is home, and on the throne where he belongs, will all be righted.'

Thorn was starting to feel really bad for the prince who'd run away from home and now had an entire world sitting on his shoulders because his father was evil and his blood was somehow important.

'Who's the prince?' she wondered aloud. It was probably going to be next to impossible to find him.

'Lucien Lightblood.'

Thorn's eyes narrowed. 'Lucien Lightblood? Who's—*oh.*' She squeaked in astonishment. 'That poor bastard.'

'Yes.' The lady bowed her head. 'If you return the Prince of Salfar, you will be human once more.'

And then she vanished into the shimmering, magical mist that rose off the river. As she disappeared, a final warning trilled across the wind: 'You can tell no one. You must complete this task yourself ...'

Stunned, Thorn sank slowly to the ground, too in shock to think or move or do anything but stare. Lucien was a prince?

Perhaps it made sense. He always seemed like he was running from something too. But that made it worse. She couldn't force Lucien to go back somewhere that he was running away from.

By the time the others came to, Thorn had been sitting on a stump, twiddling her thumbs for hours.

Nithin scrambled to his feet first. He looked around wildly, incongruously unkempt. 'What happened? Where'd she go?'

Thorn waved a hand vaguely. 'Where does she live?'

'I have no idea,' he admitted. 'What did she say to you?'

'Unfortunately, nothing supremely helpful,' she lied.

He stared at her with an empathy she could not have thought him capable of displaying. 'I'm so sorry, Thorn.'

'It's fine.'

'Thorn—'

'Let's go.'

Like a stuck gramophone, the lady's words played over and over in her head as they walked back through the Tear. The Tear was still a marvel, even after everything that had happened, but Thorn couldn't process anything new. All she could think about was how, yet again, being human and being free was out of reach.

'Thorn,' he queried as they walked. 'Why do you seem to hold me less responsible for this than them? It was a choice I made without asking either.'

'Why did you?'

'Save you?'

'Yes.'

'Because you didn't deserve to die,' he said simply, and without any guilt or intent or tactic. For Nithin, all that mattered, it seemed, was an offer of fairness. 'Because you have never been given a chance at all. Because I knew, no matter how much you'd hate me for it, that you should have the chance to say goodbye to Thistle. You should have that, at least.'

Thorn didn't register when they'd stopped walking, but they were now alone in the woods, the others gone ahead into the twisting trees.

He regarded her intently, deep meaning in his cunning eyes. He looked otherworldly even now with dirt on his cheeks, hair oily and curly with sweat. 'Because I want to live in a better world,' he continued ardently, with all the conviction of a king. 'And I want you to be there to see it. To see how *good* living can be.'

She couldn't have said what made her do it; she stood on her tiptoes and wrapped her arms around him. He returned the gesture slowly, and something inside her that had once recoiled at his mere presence vanished as if it had never been.

'I'm glad you took us in,' she said thickly, letting herself realise, perhaps for the first time, that he was on her side. That he cared. 'And thank you for saving my life.'

Nithin's arms tightened around her for the briefest of seconds before he leaned back. 'There will be a good outcome, Thorn. I promise.'

She wasn't sure she shared his hope, but the genuine sincerity was not one she thought came with a caveat this time.

'If there's another way, I'll find it,' he added, urgency deepening his voice. 'I'll help you become human again. No matter how long it takes.'

'You mean that?'

'I swear.'

With a sad smile, she kissed his cheek. 'Thank you.'

They carried on side by side, their mutual animosity a shadow they were only too happy to leave behind.

The trip back to the resort was quicker than the journey to the river, but Thorn felt a rising sickness inside of her with every step. She might have mended things with Nithin, but she couldn't shake her bitter feelings towards Kol and Thistle.

They were barely out of the treeline of the ski resort's forest when Kol and Thistle sprinted over.

'Where have you been?' they cried in unison.

'We got Nithin's magic back,' said Parin before anyone else could answer. 'Doesn't he look nice and green?'

Kol and Thistle both rounded on Nithin, whose smile was sly. His eyes sparkled with magic. It really did suit him.

'How?' asked Thistle, glee spreading across her face. 'How's that possible?'

'Thorn,' said Nithin. 'She made it happen.'

Kol and Thistle both opened their mouths and Thorn held up a hand. She was done pretending. Done hiding. 'Did you, or did you not, know that there was a chance I could be human again?'

She knew already that Kol had lied; what cut the deepest was the same mirror of guilt on Thistle's face. She nodded several times, mouth screwing up with anger.

'Rose—'

'Tor—'

'We're done,' she spat. 'Don't ever speak to me again.'

'Rose!' Kol moved to catch her arm and the sound of four guns being cocked made them all still.

'She said no,' said Jade, stepping up to Thorn's side, her gun trained on Kol. 'Don't push it, bro.'

'Thorn!' Thistle's reprimand shattered through the serenity of the woodlands. 'This is ridiculous!'

Thorn held her gaze through raw, heavy-lidded eyes. 'You finally have your family, Thistle. What do you care?'

It seemed only then Thistle realised what she had said. Her expression crumpled. 'Tor—'

Thorn couldn't have said how she did what she did next, but green light burst out of her and created a barrier between the groups.

Kol had never looked so desperate, nor so undone. Like his entire world was coming apart beneath him. 'Rose, wait! Please!'

'You lied to me.'

Kol turned to Nithin. 'Take it down!'

'No,' said Nithin quietly.

'Nithin, take it down!'

The strangled, desperate sound that wrenched its way out of him tore through Thorn like a bullet, but as she walked away, the barrier stayed up. And at some point, she realised that it wasn't just her magic keeping it there, holding Kol and Thistle back.

Nithin was helping her.

CHAPTER THIRTY-TWO
Plan C

The sunset filled the sky with a fiery kaleidoscope of vivid colour, but Lucien was too preoccupied to enjoy it. Things between him and Nik had marginally improved, but Ginny had been cornered in an alley two nights beforehand and only Adair and Shim's presence kept her from being assaulted. She hadn't left the house since but she was already growing antsy, and he couldn't keep her – or Nik – inside forever.

Unfortunately, his pack wasn't the only one that had a knack for finding trouble. He stopped by Thorn's house after a sennight of silence and heard a story that threatened to rattle his sanity – she had found Geon's Tear. And by the sound of it, she'd met Aosh, who was apparently calling herself the Lady of the River. Only Adair, Jae and Naida shared his horror at this realisation, however. The gap in reality on their world had let out here, but this world let out on Salfar. He didn't know if tears were appearing at random, the spell never undone, the magic never fixed, the rip between the worlds flexing and shifting over the years, but it alarmed him to know that the only thing between his pack and his homeland was Aosh. She'd once *haunted* the castle grounds, for pity's sake. How had she claimed the role of guardian of the Tear?

Thorn had seemed off during their entire conversation, but Lucien couldn't blame her. Aosh was disconcerting for those who grew up whispering her name.

A sharp knock at the door made him start. Leaving the window, he went to answer it, waving at Ginny and Nik to stay seated.

Too his surprise, Kol stood on his front step.

'What are you doing here?'

Kol pulled off his expensive-looking sunglasses, revealing bloodshot eyes. 'Got a moment?'

'Sure.'

Lucien stepped aside to let him in and led the way down the hall to his study. Shutting the door behind them, he walked over warily and took a seat in his chair. 'What can I do for you, Mister Sinn?'

'Have you seen Thorn?'

'I saw her yesterday.'

'And?'

'It's not my job to tattle on my friends, Mister Sinn. If you want to talk to Thorn, go to her house.'

A surge of magic swallowed Kol's irises, eyes flooding to black like someone had tipped ink in them. 'Is she okay?'

'What do you think?'

'I just—'

'You lied to her. Take the consequences with grace.'

Kol squeezed the bridge of his nose, face scrunched up, clearly trying to gather himself. He then opened his eyes, sifted his hand through his hair, and nodded to himself, resolved. 'Will you tell her that I'm sorry?'

Lucien nodded. 'I'm keeping an eye on them. I promise.'

'Thank you.' Kol rubbed his face. 'Did you ever think you'd love a human?'

'I never thought I'd love anyone,' said Lucien bluntly. 'I'd grown quite used to caring only about my family and nothing else.'

'You wouldn't go back, though. Avoid meeting Nik if you could do it again?'

'No.'

Kol smiled brokenly. 'I always hated the laws here. The way they treated humans. But it never felt personal until the night she and Thistle got in our coach. I've never seen so much hatred in anyone's eyes before. And she levelled it *all* at me. Hated me before she met me. And that broke my heart.'

'I know the feeling.'

'Shadow almost *died.*' Kol held out his hands, as if seeking benediction. 'I just wanted her to be safe.'

'I know.'

Eyes glistening, Kol stood and left.

Feeling gloomy, Lucien wandered into the kitchen for a distraction from his melancholy only to find that a conversation he could not have fathomed having in a thousand years was well into swing.

'We should,' Ginny was saying.

'I think so, too,' said Nik, from Ginny's other side, nonchalant as you please. 'Salfar might be the best of all three at this point.'

A noise of astonished horror tore from Lucien's lips. 'We are *not* going to Salfar,' he growled emphatically. Had Geon been alive, the room would be on fire. 'Not ever.'

Ginny didn't mask her shock. 'Why?'

'No. Not happening.'

'It might—'

'No,' came four vehement refusals. Adair, Jae and Naida had come in behind Lucien.

'Why not?' This time Shara wanted to know.

Lucien left the kitchen without a backwards glance, his heart beating so hard it hurt to breathe. He could hear Jae, Naida and Adair stifling the others' protests, but the sound of fast footfalls told him that Nik wasn't going to be shut down so easily.

In their bedroom, Nik closed the door behind them. Lucien could hear the thrum of his heart from the other side of the room. Focusing on it soothed his own racing heart, like using a drum beat to keep time.

'Why won't you go back?' Gentle as they were, Nik's words felt biting. 'Weren't you born there?'

'I ran away from there.'

'Why?'

Lucien shook his head.

'Don't you miss your family?'

'My family is here.'

'You sound like you hate your parents or something.'

'I do,' he whispered. 'My father most of all.'

'Why?'

'Because he wasn't a good father.'

'Wasn't?'

Lucien exhaled slowly. 'Geon killed him.'

'W-what?'

'He killed him,' said Lucien bluntly. 'The night we left Salfar.'

'How?'

'He stole his magic and cut his throat.'

'Why?'

Lucien crossed his arms. The last days on Salfar weren't ones he felt like unlocking from the cellars of his mind.

'It's not like you haven't heard bad stories from me.'

He rubbed his jaw roughly, a shaking, painful breath cutting its way out of him. 'I once had an elder brother. Faren. He was perfect. The way older brothers are to younger brothers. Better at everything and beloved because of it. My father loved him most, my mother loved him most, Salfar loved him most. And I was happy to be ignored.'

Nik's eyebrows creased as he tried to pull the pieces together. 'What, was he like the prince or something?' There was a joking edge to his confusion, but at Lucien's nod, his eyes went wide. 'You're a *prince*?'

'I was. I'm not anymore.'

'What happened?'

'No one cares about the second son. I was of no import. The lands had their heir and he would lead them well. I was free. More or less. I befriended the villagers and got into trouble with the locals. Minor annoyances, but nothing embarrassing for a second son. And then one day, my troublemaking went too far.' Even now, it was hard to remember exactly how it had all gone so terribly wrong. 'Geon, Esme, Naida and I were the best of friends. We did all the stupid things children do. Including going into a dragon's den on a dare.

'Adair was Faren's best friend back then. He was older, smarter than us. He realised what had happened and went to find Faren. They came after us. Naida and I were both severely burned; Adair almost lost his arm; Geon broke six ribs; Faren died.'

Nik was stunned beyond speech.

Lucien nodded wretchedly, heart shattering anew. 'My parents blamed me,' he continued. 'They banned me from seeing my friends ever again. My mother's resentment turned to apathy and abandonment. My father's hatred turned to abuse.

'I was beaten so badly once, I couldn't leave my room for days,' he murmured. 'Geon bribed one of the guards and got in to see me. I don't even know how he knew that something was amiss, but Geon was a loyal friend. He found out Naida's sister died before the rest of us and was there to hold her hand. He discovered that my sister had been attacked by one of the knights and in revenge he cut his throat and left his body in the square, naked and branded. A warning to rapists.'

'Really?'

'Geon's love was extreme and unconditional and forever.' And Lucien missed him *so much* it physically hurt. 'There's nothing he wouldn't have done for any of us. And there's nothing he didn't do. He helped us – Esme, too – escape the palace. We were almost to the neighbouring lands of Kerling when my father's guards caught us.

'We were brought back to the castle. Geon was beaten almost to death. My sister was beaten and returned to her husband. I was tortured and thrown into the Tower. A prison filled with magic that eats at your mind and your soul until you kill yourself.'

Nik stared at him in absolute dismay.

'Geon saved me. He saved us all. The book I mentioned? It has spells – spells that can open a hole in the universe. The only ones who can wield the book's magic safely are the royal family. It's stupid, but it's an ancient rule. Geon stole it and the magic ate his mind. And I think he may have, rather unintentionally, doomed the worlds in the process. He cut a hole in the universe to save us – and war followed us. Slowly, yes, but it's our fault there are two worlds. It's our fault all these generations have ever known is fear.'

Nik looked like he didn't even know where to start with his questions, which suited Lucien fine. He didn't have any answers for him.

'If we go back there, you'll be free,' said Nik quietly. 'You won't have to worry about Enforcers or Keepers or any of the rest of it.'

'Bring you to Salfar? That's taking you from one prison and bringing you to another.'

'You can't protect me here being hunted. You can protect me there if you're not. And I hate it here, Lucien. I really do.'

The desire to do what Nik wanted warred unhelpfully with the urge to shield him from his past. Reaching out, Lucien put a hand over Nik's. 'I can't take you to a world where you won't be safe.'

'I'm not scared.'

'I'm not one to tempt fate.'

'But—'

'Please, my love,' said Lucien softly. 'Don't ask me to go back there. There's nothing for me on Salfar.'

The small endearment made Nik's expression crumble and before Lucien could move, Nik was kissing him. Slow at first, calm and steady, yet each second seemed to increase the confidence of the act.

'That's cheating,' he said thickly when the need to breathe won out and they parted.

Nik smirked. 'If the Suriias are in charge there, then surely they'll know more about magic than we do here,' he reasoned. 'We can see if there's a way to make it so we can be together. So that you don't feel bad every time you want to kiss me.'

Nik traced the sides of Lucien's jaw with the tips of his fingers, and Lucien leaned into his touch instinctually. 'You said he's dead. What's there to be afraid of?'

Everything inside Lucien constricted, but he shook his head. 'I can't risk you.'

'I'm not afraid.'

'I am.'

'Do you trust me?'

'You know I do.'

'I want us to be together,' whispered Nik. 'In a good world. In a free one.'

Only for Nik would he even consider returning. But the thought filled him with more fear than he could combat.

If the Tower still stood … If enemies still lingered …

But then Nik said, 'Take me to Salfar, Lucien,' and a feeling of total deference spread through him.

'Please be sure.'

'I'm sure. Let's find some place better. Who could touch us? Not Spotters. Not Enforcers. Not Keepers. We could live our lives in peace. We can leave these worlds behind and start brand new lives. Together. An ex-prince and a bookworm on Salfar. What do you say?'

Words like honey, and Lucien felt like he might drown in them.

CHAPTER THIRTY-THREE
Salfar

Bring the prince home.

The words reverberated in Thorn's head for days. Not for the first time in her life, she was at a crossroads. But bringing Lucien back to a world he had fled sounded beyond cruel. She passed the days trying to decide what the best course of action was and feeling increasingly like there was only one thing to do.

And then the impossible happened—

Lucien suggested going to Salfar himself.

'I thought you hated your family,' she said in a quiet voice when he finished telling them his pack's plan a few weeks after the first excursion to the Tear.

'I'm terrified of them,' he whispered. 'But we have to try something else. And Nik wants to go.'

Thorn didn't have to wonder how he felt. When Thistle asked to move to Courtenz, Thorn hadn't been able to refuse forever. Sometimes the only way to make the agonising choice was if you were making it for someone else.

'Can we go?' she asked tentatively.

His eyebrows shot up in bewilderment. 'I'd've thought that be the last thing you'd want. Suriia world and all that.'

'There's no place for us in this world,' she muttered. 'There's no place for us in your Earth, either. Wherever we go, someone's going to be in danger.'

'That could be true of Salfar, too.'

'Are you willing to risk it?'

'My husband wants to go. I have to try. For his sake.'

Thorn smiled. 'That's sweet.' She meant it as a compliment, but Lucien didn't seem to take it as one.

'Are you going to ask Kol to come?'

'I haven't spoken to Kol since the Tear.'

'I know. He came to see me.'

She couldn't ignore the clenching in her chest. 'How's he doing?'

'Not great.' Lucien held out his hands. 'Frai don't handle rejection well.'

'Is that my fault?'

'No. I'm just being honest.'

'Would you forgive Nik for lying to you about something like that? For lying about something that you held so dear to your heart that the betrayal feels like someone's taken a shovel to your chest and dug in?'

Lucien rotated his hat in his hands, cerulean eyes fixed on the floor. 'It's not my place to tell you what I would do.'

'Tell me anyway.'

He continued turning his hat in his hands with deliberate slowness. Without it, she thought he looked younger. More vulnerable somehow. As if the hat were part of a persona he adopted like a second self, one to keep his distance from the rest. 'Sometimes the things we do for love aren't kind or rational or honest. I suppose you must ask yourself what lines you're willing to overlook him crossing, and what lines you aren't. It differs for everyone. Would I forgive Nik lying to me because he feared for my life? Yes. Because I've done the same to others and I'm not a hypocrite. Would I forgive Nik anything? Perhaps not. I hope I never have to find out.'

She bit her lip, his words affecting her on a fundamental level. 'I guess of all the reasons to be mad at someone, them saving your life is kind of a weird one.'

'Perhaps,' he agreed with a small smile. 'Whatever you decide, we're leaving tonight at midnight. We're going back to Aosh and we're going to see if she'll let us cross without the book.'

'Aosh and the book?'

'Her name is Aosh. And the Book of Ten Thousand Souls is an ancient spell book that contains, well, ten thousand trapped souls. It's the only way the Tear was even possible. You need to have a ridiculous amount of power to rip a hole in the fabric of the universe.'

'Where's the book now?' The thought of someone random finding a book full of souls made her skin crawl.

'I lost it on my last world. Earth I. Or Earth II, I suppose. To you.'

'You *lost* it?'

'Don't get me started.' He sounded thoroughly putout. 'It was stolen from my study.'

'Why didn't you have it in a *vault?*'

'Because I am the only one who can use it. Geon had to use an ancient spell to do it – a spell no one on Earth would know. He cursed himself in the process.'

Thorn absorbed this, all too aware of just how miniscule her knowledge was on the subject of other worlds and magical spell books. 'Is it safe to bring humans there? What if they change like the Suriias on Earth did?'

'I guess we'll see,' said Lucien honestly. 'Inform your friends fully.'

She walked him to the door and bid him farewell. But she didn't have to tell the others. They stepped into the room right away, clearly having been eavesdropping.

'Better new problems than the same ones that are killing us,' said Grey blithely. He looked beyond tired these days. A house had not brought him peace.

'I agree,' said Trinity. 'Fuck this place. Let's find another.'

'It's not a fix,' said Thorn, heart fluttering at the thought of a new world – and the chance to be human again. 'We're running from the problem, not helping anyone.'

'Are we even equipped to help anyone?' Jade interjected. 'We're nothing. Nobodies. But maybe, somewhere new, we can be *somebodies*.'

Trinity took her hand in solidarity. 'Agreed.'

Thorn smiled at them, surprised by how freely they offered to join her at every turn. 'If you're all sure …'

'I've always wanted to see if I can fly,' said Parin wickedly. 'Maybe that'll be our side-effect.'

Everyone laughed nervously.

As the others set about gathering their things, Thorn left the house and got into her coach. For the first time in her life, she had goodbyes to make – and a final, futile offer to give.

She mulled over what she would say on the flight, but she settled on nothing by the time the familiar mansion came into view.

It took almost ten minutes for Thorn to finally step out of the coach and walk over to the gate. They opened before she even reached them and the nightguard ignored her entirely as she wandered up the drive. Before she could fathom a guess as to why, the doors opened and Kol was standing in front of her.

'I was wondering how long you were going to sit out there,' he said. 'Finally get cold?'

She stopped at the bottom of the steps, holding his gaze, unsure how to feel about him. 'You lied to me.'

'Do you want to know why?'

She crossed her arms, waiting for him to come up with any defence worth listening to. But *oh*, she wanted one.

'Shadow almost died when he went.' Kol descended the steps with purposeful slowness. The weeks since their fight had been unkind to him, and a twinge of guilt bit at her conscience. 'See, the Lady of the River gives nothing without consequence.'

Thorn knew that all too well, but she argued the point anyway. 'She gave Nithin his powers back.'

'Nithin lost his powers and she reignited them. I'm still not entirely sure she hasn't sworn him to some horrendous, impossible task.' Kol shook his head darkly. 'Most Suriia who have gone have *died*. There's a reason no one bothers anymore. Do you know how many come back alive? *One in thirteen.* It's a throw of the dice with that witch! But she told Shadow she'd let him live. Give him a gift. Why? Because some day he would be *important*. That's what she said.

'Shadow was *lucky*, and he wasn't even removing magic. Just tying his life to Ayla's. She didn't want him to do it, for the record. He found out on his own and went without telling her. When we got there, it was too late to save him. The lady let us leave the Tear alive but Shadow was ruined. Ayla had to nurse him back from the brink of death for years. And do you know what it was we eventually found out? The lady made him drink from the Immortal River and it *ate him alive*. He nearly went insane as his body twisted itself inside and out, rearranging in a way that pushed it just that bit more past human. I didn't want that for you. Any of it. Who knows what she'll ask him to do – *what he'll have no say in.*'

The statistics were really quite bad, Thorn had to admit, and it left her marvelling at how much Nithin had risked. Just like her.

She heaved a sigh. 'If you'd *explained*—'

'Oh, you would have listened to me? All you ever do is tell me my kind are scum. You would have picked death.'

'No, I wouldn't have.'

'We both know you'd die before being dependent on anyone else.' Kol's eyes filled with angry tears and he pressed the heels of his hands to them. 'I wanted you to be safe,' he ground out. 'I wanted you to be happy. I wanted you to be whole. I'm trying so hard to give you a *life*, Rose, but it's never enough for you.'

Thorn swallowed the lump in her throat and breathed heavily through her nose for several seconds until she had control of herself. 'I'm sorry.'

His hands fell to his sides. 'For what?'

'Both sides can suck,' she allowed. 'And Suriias can be awesome. Just look at you.'

He eyed her cautiously. 'I never lied about anything else. I swear. I love you.'

Perfect words, and she wanted to believe them. And so, choosing to, she nodded and waved at the door. 'I need to talk to all of you.'

'About what?'

'Are they home?'

'Upstairs with the baby.'

It took a second for those words to process. 'The baby?' she echoed.

Kol nodded and gestured for her to follow him inside. Her heart was hammering so fast she thought she was going to be sick.

Upstairs in Thistle and Nithin's bedroom was, sure enough, a baby. Thistle was fast asleep on the bed, Nithin was standing by the window, the small bundle in his arms.

He looked up when they entered and gave Thorn a small smile. He was himself again, and Thorn was glad of it.

When she reached his side, Nithin placed the baby gently in her arms.

'What's her name?'

'Kali,' he said with a small laugh. 'It was Kol's idea.'

Kol chuckled at her obvious confusion. 'You're the worst student ever, Rose,' he admonished. 'I told you it was a type of thistle.'

Leave it to Kol to always render her speechless. She grinned broadly and gazed down at Kali. She did look so much like Thistle.

'Ask her second name.'

'What's her second name?'

'Rose.' It was Thistle who had spoken. 'Kali Rose Summons,' she continued, sitting up and brushing messy black hair from her face, doe-eyed with exhaustion. 'What do you think?'

Thorn walked over with Kali and sat on the edge of the bed. 'I think I should have been here.'

'You're here now.'

They smiled meaningfully at each other.

When Kali was sound asleep, the four of them relocated to the sitting room downstairs. Thorn claimed the chair by the television and leaned forward on her elbows, trying to figure out how she was going to go about it.

'I take it by now you all know that we found a second Earth,' she began. When they nodded, she continued, 'But it's terrible, too. So, we're trying our third option. Me, Parin and the others; and Lucien's pack, too.'

'But—'

'It's not dangerous this time,' she assured them, cutting off Kol's outburst. 'You asked if there was a deal when Nithin and I went? There was. I have to bring Lucien home. The lady's expecting us.'

Nithin leaned in, concern creasing his austere features. 'Thorn, why didn't you tell me?'

Because it's my task, not yours.

'Because it didn't matter. I want you guys to come with us. This is a one time only, free pass through the Tear. With an honest to goodness prince to keep us safe. What do you say?'

Although Thistle's response was expected, it still broke Thorn's heart.

'I want to give this life a chance,' her best friend whispered, devastated. 'I'm sorry, Tor. I don't want to run anymore.'

Thorn nodded, her face screwing up as she tried not to cry. 'I get it,' she croaked. 'I do.' Her eyes flicked to Nithin, who, to her surprise, appeared profoundly saddened by this news.

'I'm coming,' said Kol abruptly.

Thorn regarded him, curious. Wary. 'Are you sure? We might not be able to come back.'

A sad smile twitched his lips. 'What are boyfriends for?'

In that second, Thorn was no longer angry. She was no longer bitter. A rush of dizzying relief filled her, and she shot out of her chair. He met her halfway and caught her in a bone-bruising hug. He was at her side with no hesitation, and it meant the world to her.

None of them seemed to know what to say after that, but Thorn wasn't ready to leave just yet. Thankfully, she wasn't the only one.

'Do you have time for a last movie?' Thistle smiled hopefully.

Thorn nodded. 'I have until midnight.'

Thistle took her hand, interlacing their fingers. 'Doesn't matter which world you're on,' she said. 'You're my family. And I'm sorry I was such a shithead.'

'I'm sorry I was such a brat.'

Thistle pulled her down onto the sofa and Thorn curled up beside her. No one spoke throughout the film, as if everyone wanted the night to stretch on.

But the credits rolled all too soon and Kol went to pack a bag with Nithin, leaving Thorn and Thistle to say goodbye in private.

Thistle's eyes filled with tears as they stood, still holding hands. 'Will we ever see each other again?'

'Someday,' said Thorn. 'I promise.'

Thistle walked her to the door minutes later; Kol and Nithin were talking in low tones, waiting for them. They exchanged private smiles, and then Nithin yanked Kol into a tight hug.

'I love you,' he said, voice muffled in Kol's coat. 'Be safe.'

Kol tightened his hold on Nithin ever so, as if he wanted to ask him to come, but knew he couldn't. 'I love you, too. Take care of yourself.'

When they parted, Kol pulled Thistle into a congenial hug and Nithin turned to Thorn.

'Don't make too many messes,' he said, but there was a fondness to his tone, and he smiled when he said it.

'Don't be too posh,' she retorted, winking at him. He laughed.

Thorn and Kol left then, out into the cool night. At the door to the coach, she turned back, meeting Thistle's gaze. *I love you,* she signed.

Tears trailed down Thistle's cheeks. *I love you, too.*

With a tremulous breath, Thorn got into the coach. Somehow it didn't feel like the end. The lady's promise rang in her ears, but Thorn couldn't fathom how any of this was going to work out. All she could think about was getting Lucien to Salfar and then hopefully some kind of sense would be discernible. More than anything, she was deeply glad she hadn't had to suggest to Lucien that he go. She wasn't sure she'd be able to handle that level of guilt.

'Want to drive?' she asked Kol, feeling far too sick and distracted to fly herself.

He nodded and took over the controls.

Instead of carrying on toward the city, Kol turned the coach left and a few minutes later they'd landed in a field and he clambered out. Thorn hesitated a second before following him.

'What?' she called, walking over to him, the crisp grass crunching under her boots with every step. 'We're going to be late.'

'Before we're back with the others, I want everything out in the open,' he said. 'I want you to tell me everything on your mind. I'm going to tell you everything on mine. We're not going to go on a potential one-way trip with things left unsaid.'

'Everything is out in the open.'

'Is it? Aren't you mad at me?'

Thorn leaned back against the coach and shook her head. 'I'm angry that you lied to me. I'm not angry about your reasoning. I get your reasoning.'

Although admitting that much was hard.

'Do you trust me?' He held out his hands. 'If we go to Salfar and we're in a world filled with every creature you've ever hated – and probably thousands we've never heard of – do you trust me to have your back?'

'Yes.'

His eyebrows shot up. 'You do?'

'Yes,' she said honestly. 'I wouldn't have come back to ask you guys to come if I wasn't one hundred per cent sure.'

'And going to an all Suriia world doesn't bother you? Why not Lucien's world? Where the humans are in charge?'

'Because it's no better. I want to figure out what went wrong. I want to live in a world where there's no hunting, no fear, no bloodshed.' *I have to return the prince, so I can be me again.*

'Salfar isn't a sanctuary. It's a world a million times more advanced than this one, with beings far more powerful, with magic coming out of the ground.'

Thorn had to force her swallow, but the words didn't make her change her mind. 'It's Plan C.'

He eyed her shrewdly and then, his whole body relaxing, he nodded.

Half an hour later they had picked up the others and were flying to Lucien's. He and the rest of the pack were waiting for them and they got into their coach when Kol pulled up outside.

The flight passed in tense silence and seemed to take an age. When they reached the forest leading up to the Tear, they parked and everyone clambered out, shouldering their bags.

'We sure this is going to work?' Parin asked them. 'No monsters this time?'

'Monsters?' squeaked Shara.

'It'll be fine,' said Lucien. 'Aosh wouldn't dare.'

Thorn had a thousand new questions, but forced them down.

'I'm still boggled we're going to Magic-land,' said Jade.

'You guys sure you want to do this?' Thorn glanced around the group. 'We can stay.'

'We can,' said Lucien, sounding hopeful. 'Say the word and we can go back.'

'Neither Earth is working and something's wrong,' said Eran bluntly. 'We have to try this.'

There was a general murmur of ascent.

And so the group set off down the path Thorn had taken not too long ago with Nithin to beg for her humanity back. And now she was going there to ask to be let into the world of the Suriias.

She wondered if dying had robbed her of all her sanity.

Thankfully, this turn through the Tear revealed no monsters or irate trees and the lady materialised unbidden as soon as they reached the Immortal River, as if she'd been waiting patiently for Thorn to bring the prince back.

'Hello, Lord Prince.'

Lucien stiffened at the title. 'Aosh.'

'You remembered!' She sounded gleeful. 'I was hoping you would!'

'How does a witch get this gig?'

'It's all in the timing, darling,' she purred. 'When you abandoned your post.'

Thorn glanced at Lucien. He was considerably paler than normal. 'We can stay,' she found herself saying.

Lucien looked like he wanted nothing more, but he shook his head. Resolute.

'Follow the Immortal River down to the end,' said Aosh, stepping to the side as a boat appeared in the strange magical waters behind her. 'Salfar awaits.'

'Will going through close the Tear?' asked Jade.

'No. The Book of Ten Thousand Souls opened it. The book has to be used to close it.'

'We don't have the book,' said Lucien.

'You will again,' said Aosh confidently. 'But remember, the book cannot be wielded by any save one with royal blood – or one pure of heart.' She looked at Thorn when she said this, and Thorn's stomach plummeted. Surely this was not the time to be singled out.

'Pure of heart?' said Parin.

'Only those who don't wish to use the book's magic for themselves can even touch it. All others will die.'

'*Lovely.*'

'What about Geon?' asked Adair.

'He never used the magic for himself,' said Lucien softly. 'He used it for us. It was never about power.'

The lady bowed her head. 'Many believe the book a death sentence to simply be near, but they forget that those who do not want it, those who do not want power, may wield its magic. But they will lose their minds in the process – and their souls are locked forever within.'

Thoroughly disinclined to ever go near such a book, Thorn didn't bother asking for more details.

One by one, the others headed towards the boat. She made to follow them when the lady called at her to wait. Kol raised an eyebrow, curious, but went down the bank at Thorn's nod.

'You've done well,' said Aosh when they were alone.

'Does this mean I get to be human again?' she asked quietly.

'You haven't finished your task yet.' Aosh bowed her head, her body starting to fade into the mist. 'The prince must *sit* on the throne.'

'That wasn't—'

But Aosh was gone.

Thorn barely tampered down the myriad expletives that she longed to hurl after the lady.

'Rose?'

Snapping out of her daze, Thorn forced her feet into motion.

The hill was slightly slippery from the rain and she stepped carefully around the slickest patches, reaching the others a moment later.

'What did she say?' asked Kol when Thorn was almost to the boat. He held out his hand and helped her climb in.

'Nothing supremely helpful,' she lied, echoing her words to Nithin from the last time.

'What did Salfar used to look like?' asked Jade when they set off.

'Nothing like either Earth,' said Lucien quietly. 'If you think of how they built up Courtenz, it was a model on Salfar. We discovered technology millennia before the humans.'

This intrigued everyone, and the group gathered around to listen to Lucien's tales. Esme, Adair, Jae and Naida added details here and there. It didn't sound like the wretched place Lucien purported it to be when regaled with everyone else's tales.

But the stories, entrancing as they were, could only last so long. For what felt like days there was nothing but water and fog. The group ate the food they'd brought and tried not to voice their fears that it would run out before they reached Salfar.

'I don't get it,' said Grey at one point. 'Why are we sailing to Salfar when you guys just walked through a hole?'

'Magic isn't stable. It likely morphed and mutated over the centuries. The Immortal River grew out of the Tear, adapting to the gaps in two realities and doing what life does – carrying on.'

'Where was it originally?'

'A bridge.'

'A bridge?'

'We were running,' said Adair. 'Geon didn't have much choice. But we came out in a field on Earth. The first Earth, that is.'

'And the guards followed you through?'

'They waged war,' said Kol. 'The stories of how the Suriias left Salfar and found their way to Earth say that they were avenging their wronged king. They amassed an army and used magic to widen the Tear.'

Thorn's eyebrows shot up. 'Is that really what you were taught?'

He grimaced. 'I didn't say I believed it all.'

Not sure what to believe either, Thorn gazed up at the muted, blank sky and leaned back against the side of the boat. She wondered what Thistle was up to, and how fast Kali was growing. She wondered how Nithin was getting on at work. And, oddly, she wondered where Jinx had ended up. Jade never spoke of him, and Thorn didn't want to ask. But she thought of him often.

Time passed with continuing monotony. It was like they were idling in the middle of a great lake. No waves came, no creatures in the water, no birds in the sky.

And then, suddenly, a shore.

One second there was nothing but water and fog, and the next a great mass of land stretched before them.

Thorn looked at Lucien. 'Is this Salfar?'

Lucien, whose complexion had drained of blood, barely managed a nod.

'So, going by Kol, our souls lived here once,' said Trinity softly. 'I wonder what we were.'

'I think I could fly,' said Jade.

Trinity giggled. 'Because you're always dreaming about flying?'

'Exactly!'

Kol laughed; when he caught Thorn's eye, he looked slightly uncertain, but she smiled, and he relaxed.

When they reached the rise, the group stopped dead. It was unlike anything Thorn could have imagined. A world of impossible things. Homes floated in the distant sky, trees walked about without warning, the grass changed colour with the wind. There was a tower that disappeared into the distant clouds – and unless Thorn was very much mistaken, it was switching levels.

The third storey removed itself from the building to become the tenth, the fifth to the eighth, the first to the seventh.

'The Tower,' said Lucien, following her line of sight.

'That doesn't sound good.'

'It's not.'

From their other side, Isha said, 'It looks weirdly empty, no?'

Thorn appraised the city before them. Everything seemed alive with magic, but Isha was right. There didn't seem to be anyone in sight.

'I don't like this,' said Trinity warily. 'Something's off.'

'It's okay,' said Jade, taking her hand and giving her a reassuring smile. 'We don't want to encounter loads of Suriias, right?'

'Perhaps not,' said Jae. 'But it's strange that there's no one.'

Everyone exchanged wary looks before continuing, eyes and ears keen for any approaching Suriias.

There was no one on the road, no one in the fields, no one anywhere.

'This world is so peculiar.' Thorn turned in a circle, slowly taking in each new sight.

'I like the plants.'

She looked over at Kol, who was squatting on the ground, eyeing an odd-looking flower. It made small *humm*ing noises every few seconds, like it was a creature. 'You glad you came?'

He reached out and traced a finger over the petals, they quivered and then changed from scarlet to navy to black. 'Are *you* glad I came?'

'Yes.'

They smiled at each other.

'Think this place is going to be better?' she wondered as they stood and carried on after the others.

'It's looking better so far,' he said, squeezing her hand.

The further into the city they got, the stranger it was. Soon enough homes began floating above them; others stood of their own accord, legs of brick and mortar and metal working together magically to shuffle them about in odd formations.

'The houses are as arrogant as their owners,' she heard Naida explain to Grey. 'Some always want to be on display, some want the best spot in the sun, others want to be nearer to the river.'

'Do the houses fight?' asked Parin, clearly joking.

'Sometimes,' said Jae.

Thorn exchanged a wide-eyed look with Parin.

They reached the heart of the city but still they came across no one.

'This is so fucking creepy,' said Grey.

'It's *too* quiet,' said Ginny.

Thorn's attention drifted from house to house, window to window, garden to garden. It didn't look like a dead town. Nor an abandoned one. It was a deserted one. As if everyone had been there the day before and was now simply gone.

'Come on,' said Adair, nodding left. 'This takes a roundabout route through the city.'

Everyone followed him, hands gripping tight to their various weapons.

'That's the castle,' said Lucien hoarsely, moments later. He was staring ahead at the massive white stone castle that made Nithin's mansion look like a shack.

'We can avoid it,' said Kol, apprehension audible. 'Go elsewhere.'

'It looks empty,' said Nik.

Thorn frowned. It *did* look empty.

'Did all the Suriias leave Salfar?' asked Trinity. 'Where is everyone?'

'I don't know,' said Lucien. 'I don't know what happened.'

Thorn grimaced at the castle. 'I'm more than all right with bypassing the castle.'

'Agreed,' said Lucien.

She saw Nik take his hand and kiss his knuckles. 'Everything's going to be okay,' he assured him.

She smiled, but she couldn't quite believe him.

'We're not going to find out what happened to anyone if we don't start somewhere,' said Grey. 'Might as well go in.'

Not convinced, Thorn made a face. 'Let's stick to the forest.'

'Agreed,' said Lucien.

'Let's try the castle,' said Shim. 'It's been three hundred years. Likely no one who knew you is alive or around.'

'It's the best place for answers,' agreed Esme.

Thorn eyed Lucien, Jae and Adair, who all looked like they'd rather spend the afternoon licking dirt off their boots than go anywhere near the castle.

'Let's just keep walking around until we find someone,' said Jade. 'Surely there's *someone*.'

'Or everyone's gone for a reason,' said Grey.

A shiver crawled up Thorn's spine. 'What do you mean?'

'Like they're running,' he muttered. 'From something headed this way.'

'Comforting.'

With no clue as to what the best course of action was, they moved into the castle with slow wariness, looking at every shadow. The walls had a thick layer of grime on them; the air was heavy with damp and dust. It was like no one had stepped inside in years.

Parin turned to Lucien. 'Did Geon kill the whole castle?'

Equally as perplexed if the look on his face was anything to go by, Lucien shook his head. 'I don't know ...'

'Geon never talked about it,' said Jae softly. 'He just said he'd killed the king.'

'Well, something's not right,' said Parin. 'It's like a bloody tomb in here.'

'Maybe the spell that opened the Tear killed everyone in the castle,' said Isha.

'But why wouldn't a new king have come in?' asked Jade. 'Isn't that how it works?'

Lucien shook his head. 'Only those whose blood the crown recognises can sit on the throne. And we're the only ones meant to wield the power of the book. I say *wield* because no one was ever supposed to *absorb* the souls' magic.'

'That's a crap rule.'

'Agreed.'

As they reached the top of the stairs, the group exchanged perplexed glances.

'Throne room?' suggested Nik.

Grey nodded, holding his knife tightly. 'Which way?'

Nik looked at his husband, who was still peaky with shock, and took his hand. 'There's no one here. It's okay.'

'It doesn't feel right,' said Lucien quietly.

Nik kissed his cheek. 'Come on. Let's figure out what happened.'

Still visibly hesitant, Lucien steered him down the corridor to their left. Everyone else followed.

Every step the group took echoed ominously against the stone walls and Thorn found herself gripping her gun tightly, her fingers starting to go numb.

'The castle's empty,' said Kol reassuringly from her other side. 'It's okay.'

Thorn nodded but didn't holster her gun.

They stopped outside a large pair of wooden doors that had intricate designs carved into the woodwork. Lucien took a deep breath and pushed the doors open.

As one, the group stepped into the throne room. The hall was made of dark red stone. It was warm, rather than cold. Almost stiflingly so.

But the heat was not the most off-putting part of the scene.

At the other end of the room was a large chair.

A throne.

As Thorn watched, a figure began to take shape. One so terrifying he sent a shiver of alarm through every member of their group.

'That's my father,' said Lucien.

And, just like that, it was as if someone removed a mask from in front of her eyes. The empty room was empty no longer, and she could see dozens upon dozens of Suriias in every corner, lining the walls, floating above them. There were figures of all shapes and sizes, each one a fiercer, more frightening version of their Earth-born counterparts. She spotted ghuls, vrykos, vylkas, pricos and many more besides. All armed. All dangerous.

The king's spindly fingers twitched on the arm of the chair as he sat up, eyes dancing with magic and madness and might. 'At last,' he drawled in a voice of icy wrath. 'I admit I lost faith in you.'

Thorn's attention snapped to Lucien. But Lucien wasn't watching his father. He was staring at Nik.

Nik, who had bowed low before the king and was holding out a book. A book that seemed to be whispering, the cover glowing an odd kind of light. 'My lord,' he said. 'Forgive me for the delay, it took longer than expected.'

The king raised his hand and the Book of Ten Thousand Souls flew to him.

And then a blinding light engulfed them all.

PART FOUR
These Days of Ruin

CHAPTER THIRTY-FOUR
Everything Goes Wrong

SALFAR
After the Tear, 335

When Lucien was little, his older brother Faren would comfort him from bad dreams. Their parents had never been supportive, even then, and so it fell to Faren to soothe his brother's fears. And he did it happily. The sort of child every parent should hope for; a sibling who would give anything to his brother without thought or resentment. Whenever Lucien cried, Faren appeared at his side; when he was hungry, Faren brought him to the kitchens; and when their mother was indifferent and their father cold, Faren offered love and safety.

Until the day Faren died saving Lucien's life.

Children's stories filled with dragons were not sufficiently terrifying, not on Salfar, not on Earth. They spoke of adventure, of daring, of saving wayward wanderers from hungry creatures. Children's stories left out the carnage and the violence. They left out the crying families and the wailing lovers. They left out the tears and the bones. So many bones in just one cave. And the Crown Prince of Salfar joined them without hesitation – his last breath spent driving a blade through the dragon's heart.

For hours after his brother's death, Lucien sat in the cold cave, cradling Faren's body, unable to move, his friends around him, just as broken by their grief as he. Looking back years later, Lucien pinpointed that day as the end of his childhood.

In the years that followed, life became its own kind of nightmare for Lucien. One that only Faren could have saved him from. Lucien had been a timid child, a penchant made all the worse by confrontation or arguments. Prone to running whenever anyone raised their voice, Lucien had been called 'fragile' for most of his youth. His father, mad with grief, began to search for a way to bring Faren back to life. Yet the only thing the Book of Ten Thousand Souls could not do, it seemed, was resurrect the dead. Faren was in his next life, and there was no bringing him back. But the king's madness consumed him, and his fury at Lucien turned to abuse.

What saved Lucien from total despair was crossing Geon's path one day. Nothing had ever drawn Lucien's attention like the starving boy who lived in a rundown cottage in the forest. He had dirt encrusted skin and sunken eyes from a lack of nutrition. His teeth were dirty, some missing. His first words to Lucien were, 'Do you have anything to eat?'

Without thinking about it, Lucien had given Geon the cakes in his bag.

Geon all but inhaled them. 'That was good,' he said when he was done, licking the crumbs from his fingers. 'What's wrong with your face?'

Lucien was all too aware of the purple bruise stinging his eye and cheek, but he shrugged. He doubted the starving boy would find the prince's plight very moving. 'Are you still hungry?' he asked instead.

Geon bobbed his head. Then he gestured at the ramshackle home. 'My siblings, too.'

Lucien held out his hand. 'Come with me.'

It felt good to help Geon and his family. For the first time in his young life, Lucien became the leader, the fixer – a feat that so often only rears its head when it's done for someone else. For Geon, Lucien put himself between starvation and cold, and later between his father and the court. He would have put himself between his best friend and the whole world if that was what it came to. Unfortunately, Lucien's father had other plans for him.

Long after Geon saved him from the Tower, opened the Tear, and lost his mind, Geon's cries would drag Lucien from his own nightmares and he buried his trauma as he tried to keep Geon from harming himself. For a time, he almost convinced himself that the Tower had simply been a nightmare. That his father was a bogeyman from his dreams that he'd made up one night to scare himself with but who wasn't real. But of course, his father was real. The Tower was real.

Somehow, though, not even the torture Lucien endured in the Tower achieved the same level of internal agony as the feeling that hit him like a battering ram when he realised that Nik was working for his father.

No one moved as Nik straightened up, attention on the king. The change in his demeanour was so stark it stole the air from Lucien's lungs.

'What took you so long, Nikolas?' The king's voice boomed around the throne room.

'I trekked two worlds to find him,' said Nik deferentially. 'Two wars. Forgive me.'

Breneth's icy stare shifted to Lucien. 'Welcome home, Lucien,' he said icily. In the centuries since Lucien had last seen his father, the horrible tone of his voice had not changed. It needled its way through his ear and into the marrow of his bones. His skin suddenly felt hot, uncomfortable. He couldn't draw a proper breath. The air itself felt toxic. Like one more gasp would be Lucien's last.

'Parin? Jade?'

Torn from his impending panic attack by his friend's cries, Lucien turned to Thorn, the rising hysteria in her voice crawling beneath his skin like some kind of tick.

'Trinity!' Thorn all but screamed her name. 'Grey! Ginny!'

Lucien looked around rapidly. All he saw were Suriias. No humans. As if the light had swallowed them whole.

'Ginny!' he bellowed.

'She's gone,' said Shim, stumbling back in shock. 'They're all gone.'

'How?' squeaked Shara.

'What the fuck?' Thorn sounded close to total despair. She rounded on Nik. *What did you do?*

'It was the book,' he said softly.

'All is as it should be,' said Breneth, each word like a stab of ice. 'Everything was in place, all I needed was—'

Thorn raised her gun at the king. Guards instantly slithered out of the shadows like wraiths. They wore the same uniforms as the last time Lucien had seen them and the memory of them bringing him to the Tower flashed painfully through his mind.

Kol caught Thorn's hand and shook his head. The air around them shuddered as he used his own magic to form a shield. His eyes blackened, his teeth and fingers sharpened. But they were markedly outnumbered. As strong as any of them were one on one, none of them – not even combined – could have a hope of besting the king and his guards.

It took a monumental effort for Lucien to finally turn back to face his father. 'How are you even alive?'

'I'm not so easily bested as Geon hoped.'

'Pity,' spat Jae.

'Your mother gave her life to save mine,' said Breneth, still addressing his son.

Lucien and Esme stilled. The idea of his mother sacrificing her life for his father was not nearly so touching as seeing Nithin save Thorn.

'She's dead?' he croaked.

'Yes.' Breneth shrugged, unbothered by the loss of his wife. But then, for Breneth it had never been about love. He'd married her only for the throne. For bloodlines.

How disappointed he had been when his options were Lucien or Esme.

Beside Lucien, his sister stood statuesque and poised to strike, the magic inside of her so built up that the very air around her hummed in anticipation of an explosion.

Lucien wasn't a good older brother, but in that moment he wanted to be. Putting a hand on Esme's shoulder, he levelled a glare at their father.

Breneth huffed, amused by his daughter's hatred. 'If it isn't my precious daughter,' he crowed. 'I see you've done nothing to better yourself.'

'Hoped I was dead?'

'It makes no difference, Esriana.'

Before Lucien could jump to her defence, Adair's vicious retort cut across the room. 'You will show her respect, Lord King, if you wish it returned.'

Breneth sneered at Adair. 'I'm not running an orphanage, little lord. You're free to leave and return to your pitiful plot of land. What's left of it, that is.'

Adair, who hadn't acted the role of lord in centuries, exuded nothing but endless disdain. 'As a lord, I am entitled to a place in your castle. As are my guests. Deny me, and we'll have a problem. And from the looks of it, a problem is something you can ill afford, Lord King.'

Where Lucien had always hid behind Faren, and later Geon, Adair had never feared the Lord King of Salfar. Lucien envied him deeply.

'We should have stayed home,' said Shara, her whisper a soft plea in the throne room.

Lucien nodded to Adair, who nodded back. Whatever was happening, whatever was going on, Adair stood ready to act, and his assuredness meant more to Lucien than anything else in that moment.

'We need to go,' said Thorn, putting her arm around Shara's shoulders. 'Now.'

The rest of the pack murmured or nodded their agreement.

Anticipating movement, the guards closed ranks around them, weapons drawn.

'Nikolas is indebted to me, Lucien,' said Breneth. 'He's not leaving this castle.'

In that instant, Nik looked, oddly, small. It was a strange stance for a turncoat.

Lucien glared at the top of his head. 'One chance, *Nikolas*.' He said Nik's full name like a curse, and Nik flinched.

'I can't.'

'Why not?' Even as he asked, Lucien was entirely certain he didn't want to know the reason. The silence which followed stemmed either from a refusal to relay a deep sense of loyalty to the king – a conclusion that made Lucien thoroughly ill – or because there was something Nik could not say for fear of repercussions, which in turn made Lucien feel remarkably murderous.

He turned back to his father, heart moving at a sickening pace. 'How do you know Nik?'

'Your little friend's son works for me,' his father said, although he didn't seem delighted by it. As if Nik's loyalty was a tiresome practicality.

'He's my husband.' It came out automatically, and Lucien winced on his own words.

Breneth's chilling eyes flicked to Nik. 'Did you think this would spare them your failings, Nikolas?' He stood and the room grew darker, frostier, the shadows creeping in all around them. 'You were meant to bring him home *two centuries* ago.'

'Apologies, my king.'

Lucien wasn't the only one who choked.

'Clean yourselves up,' Breneth told the group, waving a hand glibly. 'I expect your presence at dinner.'

'Eat me,' said Esme.

Breneth's eyes flashed and Esme dropped to her knees, a scream of pain tearing out of her. Adair caught her before she hit the floor. One of Breneth's talents had been known to enemies as 'needling'. It turned the air around the victim to knives and pierced them until they went insane.

'Enough!' Lucien put himself between his sister and his father. 'Stop it!'

'Stop being so taxing, Lucien,' his father drawled, but he relinquished his hold on Esme.

She collapsed against Adair, fingers gripping his coat so tightly they were white. She was wheezing, soaked in sweat, and shaking violently. Adair kept his arm around her waist protectively, blue light curling around his fingers in warning. Few could wield ice burns like Adair could.

'Your duty is to Salfar,' said Breneth, forcing Lucien to look at him. 'And you failed. Your absence and the loss of the book almost destroyed our world. The magic turned toxic and defective. You have a lot to answer for.'

Lucien glanced out the window. The landscape that stretched into the distance echoed the Suriia-run Earth more than the human one, only now his homeworld looked like a haunted ghost land with secrets in every corner.

'Geon emptied the Tower of all its prisoners,' his father continued. 'They laid waste to us for years.'

Lucien was still at a loss as to why he was supposed to care. Most of the prisoners hadn't deserved the Tower. Even those who did, *didn't*.

'My heart breaks for your guards,' he said coldly.

'Oh, Geon killed the guards. The prisoners killed villagers.'

The words sent a chill down Lucien's spine, and he had to force himself not to react.

'Go,' said Breneth at length. 'I have too many things to do to worry about you right now. Salfar will now be filled with the Earth-born Suriias. There will be chaos on the streets. Make yourself useful and perchance I'll let you keep your husband.'

Lucien held his gaze defiantly. 'Everyone with me is off limits. They're part of my retinue and you will not touch them.'

Breneth waved a hand as if such a request was tiresome.

Relying on his father's adherence to title and decorum – which was not much to rely on at all – Lucien seized Nik's upper arm and steered him out of the throne room. The others followed, all still bearing arms. Thorn looked ready to murder everyone.

It was a strange sensation, being disgusted with his husband. He could have gone his entire life without experiencing such a feeling. His legs felt brittle, his lungs corroded, his heart tight, and only growing tighter.

Halfway down the cold corridor, away from prying eyes, he stopped short and rounded on Nik.

'Who was your mother?' he demanded. 'And don't lie to me again.'

'Janna,' said Nik, far less certain now than he'd seemed before the king.

Lucien's hands went to his head as memories of Janna, Geon's girlfriend, tumbled through his mind. Geon had wanted to marry her but she'd turned him down.

'When the king found out he was my father,' Nik continued, oblivious to Lucien's thoughts, 'the guards came to our home. They killed my mother. Right in front of me. They took my brothers away – I was brought before the king.'

'But you *were* human,' said Lucien, still completely lost. Nik had been breakable. He hadn't imagined that.

Nik's hands went to his head, too, gripping tightly to his black hair, and he bit his lip so hard Lucien could smell his blood.

Lucien stared at him. 'What?'

'You were forced to give up your powers,' said Thorn softly from beside them.

The weight of those words sank into Lucien like a sickness.

'Yeah,' said Nik. 'I never wanted to be human.'

'How is that possible?' asked Jae.

'I gave your father my magic in exchange for sparing my brothers,' said Nik, the tears falling down his face. 'My magic only came back now – when I returned the book to him. For years I've been effectively human.'

Lucien stared at him. 'He's the prico who attacked your brothers?'

'Yes.'

It just kept getting worse.

After a wretched silence, Kol cleared his throat. 'Where are your brothers?' he enquired.

'They're in the Tower.'

The very ground beneath Lucien's feet felt like it was crumbling.

Jae, who had been taking in his nephew's betrayal with heartbroken silence, interjected, 'How did you end up with Ashby?'

'The first Earth I went to was theirs,' said Nik, nodding to Thorn. Her eyes widened in astonishment. 'At the time, the Suriias were just starting to take over. I thought finding Geon would be easy. But then the war broke out and everything was bedlam. And I couldn't find a way to the other Earth. I didn't even know about the doorway until they began building the camps and someone fell through.'

'That happened?' asked Kol.

Nik nodded. 'The government of your world have known about the doorway for a long time. But they didn't fear the world where the humans were in charge. Then your world started rounding humans up. Putting them into death camps. I looked human … Resistance movements were quashed, uprisings easily combatted … we were overrun. I went through the door to the other Earth. This was before the humans put a lock on District 6.'

'How are you even still alive?' There was a bite to Kol's normally light tone. 'That was centuries ago.'

'I gave the king my powers, not my immortality. His wife gave him both. But they're not the same.'

Kol's brow creased. 'I suppose that makes sense. Shadow was never given powers, only immortality.'

'How did you get the book?' Lucien hadn't stopped turning the months over in his mind. No moment jumped out at him. 'Did you go through my things?'

Nik's silence was answer enough.

'That's why you spent all your time in the libraries,' he concluded, stomach curling as the realisations made his skin tighten and his body shudder. He felt inexplicably violated. Like finding out someone's been watching you without your permission. 'How did you even touch it? The book—'

'It doesn't have any effect on those without magic. I was safe until my magic was restored.' The shame on Nik's face didn't suit him. 'I'm sorry.'

'You could have told me the truth.'

'How? You would never have come back here to your father and I had to save my brothers.'

'That's the difference between you and Geon. He never once doubted the depths of what I would do for him. He trusted me. I trusted him. And all I've learned today is that I'll never trust your word again.'

His fury cut Nik to the bone and Lucien couldn't stand it. Stepping around Nik, he walked away without looking back. He knew Shim would stay with Nik and he couldn't be around him at the moment. Everything felt off-colour, off-centre, off-balance.

As his feet took an old familiar route out of the castle and into the gardens, Thorn fell in beside him. They exchanged a look and he saw faith alive in her dark eyes. Faith that he would come up with something. Lucien didn't have the heart to tell her he had no answers.

They stopped on the crest of the hill. Salfar stretched out before them. A strange new world even to him. He didn't know how to be a prince. He never had. And he could not be anything with his father in power.

'Lucien?'

He glanced at her.

'You okay?'

'Did you ever forgive Kol for lying?'

'No,' she said. 'I just want him around more than I want to stay mad at him.'

Lucien let out a shaking sigh and crossed his arms over his chest to obscure how badly they shook. 'Might take me a while to get there.'

'I'm still getting there,' she admitted.

They sat on a bench surrounded by hedges and trees. The world here was busy, everything moving with purpose, even the leaves on the wind.

Adair appeared with Kol a few minutes later. 'Shim and Jae are going to stay with Nik,' he relayed.

Lucien let out a timorous breath and nodded. 'We'll bring everyone home,' he said, more to himself than to them. 'We'll get Nik's brothers and we'll deal with my father.'

'Exactly,' said Thorn. She squeezed his hand. 'And I'm helping.'

'We'll all help,' said Adair.

He gave them a tight, grateful smile.

'Are we staying here?' asked Kol.

'I have to,' said Lucien heavily.

Kol merely nodded. 'Okay.'

'Luka.'

He glanced over his shoulder to see Esme walking towards them. 'Are you all right?' he called, still worried about the effects of their father's magic upon her.

'No.' She joined them by the bench, murder unmasked in her eyes. 'But if we can't leave Salfar, let's make it what it should be.'

He frowned. 'What do you mean?'

Esme leaned in, her lips close to his ear. Her next words sent a shiver of foreboding down his spine. 'I'll never bow before him, but I'll bow before you.'

He leaned back sharply. 'What?'

A dangerous gleam had entered her eyes. 'We could do it, big brother. We could be free of him. You would be in charge. I'll be at your side. I'll keep you safe. I'll keep Nik safe.'

'I don't want to be king.'

'Do you want him to be?'

They both knew the answer to that.

'What do you propose we do?' he asked quietly.

'Leave that to me,' she said. 'Shim might be your second, but we both know I'm your righthand.'

Memories of the Suppression flashed grimly through Lucien's mind. Long before she left, Esme had stood at his side through war and torture. And she fought bloody, but unparalleled.

'Do you trust me, Luka?'

'Yes.'

She gave him a wicked, cunning, sisterly smile, one filled with threatening promise, and then disappeared into the night.

'Should that worry us?' asked Kol, staring after her.

'Probably,' said Lucien.

Adair shrugged. 'Sometimes the only way to beat evil is with madness.'

Thorn nodded grimly. 'What now?'

'Now we pretend we don't want to kill the king,' said Adair.

'I'm not sure I'm that good of an actor,' said Lucien heavily.

Exchanging unhappy looks, the group wandered back into the castle as a unit. He brought them to a far wing where everything was covered in a fine layer of dust and mould, but it was quiet. Cosy, in an abandoned sort of way.

'You two can have this room,' said Lucien, pushing open a door. It squeaked loudly on its hinges and a cloud of dust billowed out. 'If you want,' he added with a grimace.

'I've slept beside a rubbish bin,' she replied. 'Bit of dust is nothing.'

'We'll fix it up,' Kol assured him.

Relieved, Lucien turned to Adair. 'Should we find the others?'

'Yes.'

He looked back at Thorn. 'We'll be back in a bit. Unless you want us to stay?'

'No, go.' Thorn waved him away. 'Might as well settle in. If there's one thing I've learned, it's that planning takes time.'

'Very true,' said Lucien.

He and Adair took their leave and closed the door behind them. Alone for the first time in days, they both paused for a brief moment, the day hitting them like a battering ram.

'Luka—'

'I can't.'

'Sure.'

Adair didn't press, and they carried on down the corridor in silent solidarity.

CHAPTER THIRTY-FIVE
A Lesson in Madness

The king's warning that there would be chaos in the streets proved prescient. Although the identity of the instigator of the first spark would probably never be known, for weeks on end, fires lit up the towns and cities of the kingdom, each causing another. It seemed like everyone was angry, for some reason or other. Anger had crawled its way into everyone's hearts and boiled their blood, and no one wanted to be the first to stop. To step back. And Thorn couldn't blame them. The fear for her friends built itself into a kind of painful armour, like holding a sword that burned her hand at the same time. She was able to carry on, but it hurt. Constantly.

New arrivals came to the castle every day to ask what had happened, why they couldn't go home, and why Breneth seemed to think he was in charge. Breneth put this final line of questioning to rest after obliterating someone with a wave of his hand.

Thorn could safely say she'd never come across anyone so chilling, but she didn't suggest leaving the castle behind just yet. Not until they had everyone. Not until their friends were home. Not until she was human again. And apparently Lucien had to be on the throne before that was going to happen.

Something Thorn hadn't expected, however, was encountering Suriias from Earth that she'd somehow avoided while living in the city.

Like Yang.

Thorn thought she was seeing things at first. The tall, muscular vylka hadn't changed much since the last time she'd seen him. When he ran with Jared. He wore the same suit, light brown with too many buttons.

Yang, perhaps feeling the weight of her glare, turned and locked eyes with her. They were in the forest behind the castle, the road largely deserted.

Thorn's hand dropped immediately to her knife.

'Well,' said Yang, loud enough for her to hear even from some distance away. 'This is a surprise.'

She held still as he strolled over, as haughty here as he had been on Earth.

'I didn't think they let humans onto this world,' he drawled. 'Did you come up from the sewers, sweetheart?'

The knife was suddenly in her hand. 'Call me that again and it'll be the last time you have a tongue.' For some reason, though, her words came out stronger than she felt capable of. Like Yang had turned her from twenty to eleven and she wasn't strong and capable, but small and scared.

Yang's hand snaked around her throat in a blink and he yanked her close. His rancid breath made her gag involuntarily. 'I've always regretted not taking my turn after Jared finished with you,' he purred.

Childish fear had locked Thorn's limbs temporarily and before she could gather herself, a hand seized Yang's and ripped him away from her. Thorn collapsed on the ground, gasping for air.

Like some kind of guardian conjured from the earth itself to protect her, Nithin had Yang pinned to the ground, green light encircling them both. And then, as if the light were made of a million tiny insects, it burrowed into Yang's eyes.

The screams would echo in Thorn's ears for years to come.

When Yang finally quieted, dead, Nithin shot to her side, inspecting her throat worriedly.

'Are you okay?' He winced sympathetically as his fingers brushed over the burgeoning bruises.

'I'm okay,' she croaked. 'Where did you come from?'

'The other side of the bloody island,' he muttered, helping her to her feet. He was soaked in sweat and bleeding profusely from a cut on his head. 'What happened?'

'The Tear's closed,' she said. 'It sent everyone back to the world they're apparently designated for.'

Wrath distorted Nithin's features. 'Who closed it? You?'

'No, Nik. He was working with the king this whole time. He betrayed us.'

'He what?'

'Yeah.'

Nithin's hands went to his head as he absorbed this information.

The break in conversation allowed Thorn to properly take in his appearance. He looked like he'd been in a fight or two along the way. Messy, dishevelled, bloody and bruised, Nithin was far and away from his usual sleek, suave, calm self.

'What happened to you?' she asked, mystified. Worry made her reach out and start examining a nasty-looking gash on his forearm. Dirt and debris had caked into the dried blood, threatening an infection. 'We need to clean this.'

'It's bedlam out there. Everyone's got their magic and immortality back, only half of them were oppressed for a century and the other half did the oppressing for much longer than that and now there's fighting everywhere.'

'Kol's mentioned.'

'Where is he?'

Thorn waved vaguely at the gates. 'Out with Lucien and some of the others. They're working on starting a life here.'

Nithin searched her face knowingly. 'But not you.'

'I'm going to find my friends and I'm going to be human again. Aosh said that it was possible.'

'How?'

'I don't know yet,' she admitted. 'But apparently getting my wish is taking a while.'

Nithin's brow furrowed deeply. 'Why didn't you tell me?'

'I didn't want you to feel bad for not having to do anything for your wish.'

He sighed, but his hand came to cover hers where she was still examining his wound. 'Let me take care of this sack of shit and then you can show me where to clean up. Then we'll figure out how to do all that.'

Her heart leapt. 'You're going to help me?'

'Of course,' he promised. Squeezing her hand reassuringly, he let go and gestured to the body. 'What about this?'

Taking Yang's body to the forest and depositing him there didn't take more than an hour, and soon they were in Thorn and Kol's room, clean and donning fresh clothes, catching each other up on everything that had happened in the days since they'd parted ways on Earth.

Twilight had just arrived when a knock at the door interrupted them. The door creaked open and Adair leaned his head in.

'Oh, hello, Nithin,' he greeted, taken aback.

'Adair,' said Nithin, bowing his head politely.

'The king's requested everyone's presence at dinner,' said Adair. 'And Lucien and Esme have to go. I figured we could provide a buffer.'

Thorn nodded. 'Did Kol not come back with you?'

'Lucien said he got caught up in something.'

'Oh, okay.'

'You should change,' he advised. 'Can't go to dinner in jeans. Trust me.'

Thorn peered down at what she was wearing. 'I don't have anything else.'

'Talk to Esme,' he said. 'Nithin, do you want to borrow something from me?'

'Yes, thank you.'

They parted ways and Thorn went to find Esme. She didn't feel remotely comfortable in the castle, but the king appeared to be leaving them alone for now. Although Thorn would bet her best knife his word was as good as his temper.

The stone halls weren't empty, much as she wished they were. Guards dotted the corridors like dark shadows, the kind that appear in the corner of your eye but never quite actualise. There was something almost spectral about them and Thorn got a bad case of shivers every time they passed by.

Thankfully, it didn't take long to find Esme. She was in her bedroom, poring over a book. The princess cut a fearsome sight, even without weapons. A faint scent of smoke and oil radiated off her skin even from across the room, and the beds of her fingernails were visibly dirty.

'Still think we can get rid of him?' asked Thorn after closing the door.

'Of course we can,' said Esme. 'If you think I'm going to let him get away with this, you don't know me.'

'I know you. You're like me.'

Esme cocked her head to the side. 'Is that right?'

'Scars are calling cards, baby,' she teased, feeling a surge of kinship with Esme that she hadn't predicted.

'I like that.' With a wink, Esme strolled over to her wardrobe and plucked out a dress. She tossed it to Thorn. 'Put this on. It's short enough not to trip you up if you need to run.'

'I appreciate that.'

Thorn stripped in the corner and tugged the dress on, glad that it didn't require lacing. The sleeves were long, with three loops at the end for her forefinger, pinkie and thumb, but the dress wasn't. It fell just to her knees, light and airy.

'You look good,' said Esme, eyeing her appreciatively. 'You sure you like that frai?'

'Yeah, he's grown on me.'

'Pity.'

Giggling, Esme grasped her hand and steered her out of the bedroom and down the corridor. 'Try not to let anything my father says tonight get to you,' she advised. 'We'll only have to put up with him for so long.'

A few of the others were there already, although there was no sign of Nik. Nithin stood by the fire with Adair and Naida.

Thorn walked over to Lucien. 'You okay?'

'Fantastic.'

The king entered then, his mere presence sucking the joy out of the room.

Thorn put her hand on Lucien's back in solidarity.

'I see you've found yourself someone new,' said the king, scrutinising Thorn.

'My husband's absence does not erase his existence,' said Lucien acidly.

'You need an heir whose blood is fit for the throne. Nikolas is not an option.'

'Neither am I,' said Thorn irritably. 'I've already got someone.'

The king's eyes, like lazurite stones, glinted in the candlelight. 'Ah yes, the frai. And where is he?'

'Late,' said a voice from the doorway.

Kol had arrived. He hadn't changed and the day clung to him, dust and sweat marks on his clothes, but he still held himself like a dignitary as he walked over to Thorn and Lucien, more poised than Thorn could possibly have hoped to rival.

'Sorry I'm late,' he said to her, kissing her temple before turning to face the king. 'Good evening.'

'At least you look the part of a prince,' said the king. 'Pity my son fails so greatly.'

Thorn bristled on Lucien's behalf. For his part, Lucien remained silent, staring at the floor determinedly. It was then Kol caught sight of Nithin. His mouth opened, but a subtle headshake from Nithin waylaid a reunion.

The *ding* of the dinner bell saved them from further torturous conversation, and Thorn sat down between Kol and Nithin. Kol kept cutting sidelong glances at his best friend, but seemed to guess now was not the time for personal conversation.

Dinner was a thoroughly uncomfortable affair that involved listening to a lot of odious court discourse, none of which Thorn had any interest in. She was delighted when the king retired, and they were all free to go.

Kol went straight to Nithin's side and the pair splintered off ahead of the others, deep in conversation.

Thorn trailed after them, keeping pace with Lucien, Esme and the others.

'You okay?' she asked Lucien. He hadn't spoken unless spoken to all evening.

'Fine.' It sounded like a lie.

'We're going to figure this out.'

Lucien clearly didn't believe her. 'You can always go,' he murmured. 'I know how much you hate being here.'

'I'm here for you.'

Lucien sent a grateful smile her way. 'What if nothing changes?'

'Then you're still my friend,' she promised. 'And I'll still be here.'

It was true, she realised. Whatever else happened, Lucien was as much her friend as Thistle and Parin, Jade and Grey, Trinity and Ginny. And she did not abandon her friends.

'What we need to do is get the book back,' said Esme.

Everyone stopped and turned to her.

'We don't want to open a new Tear,' said Lucien. 'Look at what happened last time.'

'We don't need a Tear. The book has other spells. If we can get the book, we can take the crown from Father and do a simple travelling spell.'

'A "simple" travelling spell?'

Esme smirked. 'You could do it. If you had the book, you could go to Earth, get Thorn's friends and come back.'

'No,' said Thorn, though it pained her. 'Lucien has to be on the throne.'

They looked at her curiously.

'Why?' asked Lucien.

She hesitated, and then decided to spill. 'Because once you're on the throne, Aosh will make me human again.'

'When did Aosh say that?' asked Lucien. 'Before we left?'

'No, when Nithin and I came the first time.'

He appraised her thoughtfully, but he didn't seem angry. 'Sometimes,' he whispered, 'you're too much like Geon.'

She smiled sadly. 'Yeah, but he saved his best friend's life, right?'

Tears filled Lucien's eyes and he turned away to hide his cracking composure.

'Let's find the book first,' said Adair. 'That's problem one. Whatever else happens, the king should not have that power.'

To this, at least, everyone could concur.

Hope of a solution to the painful balancing act their lives had become was the only thing keeping them from disintegrating in the weeks that followed. As Lucien resumed his princely duties – as far from his father as he was able, shadowed always by Jae, Shim, Naida or Adair – Thorn and Nithin threw themselves into finding the book. And while Thorn wasn't sleeping *well*, Nithin was close to not sleeping *at all*. His eyes were permanently red-rimmed, his hair was now always tousled, messy and matted, and he often wore the same set of clothes for days on end before Thorn or Kol reminded him to change. In contrast, Kol settled into life on Salfar with remarkable ease. That he could so easily come to terms with their new life bothered Thorn, but she kept that much from him. It wasn't his fault, after all.

It was perhaps for this reason that she didn't tell him about how much she still ached to be human. She'd grown capable at wielding her magic, and she no longer felt wrong in her own skin, but she didn't feel right, either. Like she was playing a role that didn't belong to her. She'd told him they were looking for the book, that Lucien could use it to bring Thistle and Kali to Salfar. It was enough of the truth that he understood her endless hours away and didn't question the desperation she showed that rivalled Nithin's.

But as the days passed, she spent less and less time with him, and an undercurrent of tension developed between them that neither was inclined to pick at. This proved all too true one night, three months after the Tear had closed, when Kol returned from a day of helping Adair in the town and greeted her with a tentative smile. One that used to come so much more easily.

'How was your day?' he asked, taking off his coat and hanging it on the back of the door before walking over to kiss her.

'Spent time with Nith.'

Kol dropped down into a chair and began unlacing his boots. 'How's he doing?'

'Shit.'

'I still can't believe how quickly it all fell apart.'

'I can,' she muttered. 'Nothing falls apart slowly.'

'I suppose.' He reached out, brushing her hair gently back from her face. 'Do you want to do something tomorrow night? Just the two of us?'

'Yeah, maybe. Nithin wants to try a library about half a day's ride from here. We can do something when we're back though? Unless you want to come.'

'I'm helping Lucien sort through the claims first thing.'

'Claims?'

'Too many Suriias, not enough places to sleep, lots of entitlement, lots of upset.'

'Ah.'

Kol bobbed his head, but he suddenly turned sombre. 'Be careful?'

'Always am.' They gazed at each other for a time, but neither said what was on their minds. Neither wanted to fight again over matters that tore them both in two internally.

Long after Kol had fallen asleep, Thorn crept out of their bedroom and dropped out of the window. Ducking low, she darted through the gardens until she reached the edge of the castle's grounds.

Nithin was waiting in the shadows. Even in the dark he looked wretched. There were deep circles under his bloodshot eyes and his skin had an unhealthy cast.

'Ready?' he asked.

'Ready.'

The forest at night was still frightening for Thorn. Even the forests on Earth, though they'd had some magical elements, hadn't been nearly so magical as the Tyl, which she'd learned the day before was the actual name of the forest that surrounded the castle. This was a forest of woodland creatures who could talk, birds who sang like people or chirped songs that summoned the rain; there were toadstools that followed you, threatening to trip you up, and trees that wanted to give you more helpful directions. And though she'd heard about them from Lucien, it wasn't until she actually saw a unicorn with her own two eyes that she actually believed him.

Careful not to disturb the woods, Thorn and Nithin moved like shadows through the trees until they saw Lucien and Esme waiting in the grove they'd been using to meet up for private conversations. The siblings cut a fearsome sight even in the barest light off the stars and moon above.

The four walked on in pairs, mindful of listening vines or chatty berry bushes. Only when Esme signalled that it was safe to talk did they stop.

'I found it,' she announced, drawing a map out of her bag. She placed it on the ground, tracing her finger across the corner. Wind kicked up as she spoke, sending shivers across their sweat-slicked skin and raising the hairs on all their arms. 'It's in the Tower.'

Thorn's stomach plummeted, but she sought out for a solution regardless. 'Geon did it last time. How did he do it?'

'He had the power of the book first,' said Lucien darkly.

'The Tower is insanity built vertical,' added Esme. 'Those who go in don't come out. The only reason Geon got you out is because he absorbed the book's power. So, if Thorn can get in and get the book, she can use the power to get out again. Only a few guards are needed for the Tower. It's its own security.'

Thorn nodded thoughtfully. 'So long as you guys can keep everyone at the castle, I like the plan.'

'I don't,' said Nithin bluntly. 'It has a remarkably slim chance of actually succeeding and it might be our only ploy. What if it goes wrong and we're stuck in there forever?'

'What if we try a thousand different options before finally deciding to just go for it and break into the Tower?'

Nithin pinched the bridge of his nose. 'Well, when you put it that way.'

'Anyone who isn't our bloodline will be driven insane,' said Lucien, an edge to his voice. 'Worse, if you do this, your soul is trapped inside the book when you die. You're one of the thousands. It should be me or Esme.'

'It won't do that to me,' Thorn declared with a confidence she couldn't remotely justify. 'Aosh told me that I'd be human again. I just had to get you back on the throne. If I have the book, we can get rid of your dad and I'll go back to Earth for Thistle before going to see Aosh. And Earth is for humans again, Luke. You're a prince here. You have power to protect our friends here. What power do you have back on Earth?'

'She's right,' said Esme. 'How about we do it later tonight? Luka and I can keep everyone at the castle while you two can go to the Tower.'

'Sorted,' agreed Thorn.

Nithin concurred, although his reticence was not well tampered. Looking five seconds away from puking on his boots, Lucien nodded after grave hesitation.

The dawn was still far off when they reached the castle and everyone parted ways to get a few hours' sleep. But Thorn barely managed two hours of shut eye before it was time to stumble out of bed again for breakfast. After eating, Kol left with Adair to help Lucien on matters of court. They invited Thorn and Nithin, but both declined.

The rest of the day took too long to pass. Thorn paced around anxiously, watching the skyline. There were flying creatures in the distant skies, but she wasn't sure they could be called *birds*. Perhaps they were avian cousins. Magical, if the fact that one species appeared to be changing size and colour depending on where it found itself in the sky was any indication.

It felt like living inside a storybook. Whether it was a book with a good or bad ending, Thorn wasn't sure. But it didn't feel quite real. Somehow real life was living in a shed, powerless, Thistle beside her. The last year didn't feel like it had happened to her.

Thorn and Nithin were in one of the libraries with Isha and Mi when Kol, Lucien, Naida and Adair wandered in from a side door at dusk. The long day of paperwork and meetings had left them all visibly drained.

Kol went straight to Thorn's side and kissed her. 'How was your day?' he asked when he leaned back, threading his fingers through her hair as if marvelling at being able to do so freely. He kissed her again for good measure, laughing lowly, before finally nodding at her to talk. His happiness made her heart hurt.

'Uneventful,' she said, gesturing to Nithin. 'We did more research.'

'Anything?'

She shook her head at the same time Nithin said, 'Nothing.'

It didn't feel good lying to Kol – *again* – but Thorn knew that what she and Nithin were willing to risk wasn't something Kol would be willing to risk. Namely, their lives. Kol was sensible.

'Something will turn up,' said Kol bracingly.

Neither replied.

As Thorn wasn't in the mood to fake pleasantries with a king they all wanted to kill, she skipped dinner in favour of wandering the grounds with Nithin and Kol. Kol chatted about his work and Nithin asked all the right questions, but Thorn couldn't pay attention. The Tower consumed her thoughts.

When they returned to their quarters, Nithin bade them goodnight, but sent Thorn a small nod when Kol turned around.

A little after midnight, Kol sound asleep, she slipped out of bed, dressed, and met Nithin in the hall. The castle at night felt like a separate villain, a hulking, haunted structure with spies and traps everywhere. Outside, the air was painfully frigid, and their breath left them in dense white clouds.

Only when they were halfway down the road did she finally speak. 'Esme says the Tower moves,' she whispered. 'Apparently, it's on the south side of the city tonight.'

'About an hour, then?'

'Think so.'

Despite their desire to find a way back to Earth, neither of them could hide their reticence when they finally reached the Tower.

The hulking structure was made of a type of black stone that looked like it could withstand an earthquake and left all who gazed upon it trembling with disquiet. But the size wasn't the worst part – the shifting levels stopped both in their tracks. Ever moving, changing, its stone walls creaking like it was strangling ghosts in every nook and cranny only added to the bizarreness of the enchantment that kept the storeys splitting apart and shifting back into place amid the other rows. There was no clear path up or down, no rhyme or reason to it other than making it an impossible ascent. Only a madman would attempt it.

'Wow,' said Thorn, stomach knotting as she watched the eighth level rise to replace the twelfth, the twelfth level shifting back down to the sixth, and so on. 'It's even worse up close. Lucien said it was *easier* to get in …'

'There are doors,' said Nithin, pointing up at a rotating level that did indeed show a door as it turned. 'If you watch, they line up on rotation. We'll have to jump from door to door.'

'And not fall to our deaths in the process.' Even as good a climber as she was, the odds weren't great.

'That would hinder things.' Nithin eyed her uncertainly. 'I can do it, Thorn. I can use the book.'

'No,' she said firmly. 'No, I was told I had to get the prince on the throne. This is my deal.'

Unhappily, Nithin acquiesced, and they set off down the steep hill towards the distant bridge.

'Do you think anyone else knows the book is in the Tower?' she wondered. 'Why hide it in the very place where it was used to open the Tear last time?'

'I've found that those with power love to display it, and often they believe themselves impossible to best.'

Thorn had found that to be true as well. 'Are you worried about the guards at the gate?'

'Do you want to know something about sbura?' he said rhetorically as they carefully picked their way through the slippery grass. 'We manufacture desire. We can distract our enemies with their own longings.'

Not sure where he was going with this, she simply nodded and followed him. When they reached the front gates, there was no sign of any guard presence, but of course that meant nothing.

Nithin held out his hand. 'Together?'

'Together.'

Hands clasped, they sent a blast of green light at the gates and the doors blew off their hinges with an ear-rattling *bang*. A terrible, thunderous screeching sound cut through the air and made the hair all over Thorn's body stand on end.

As the gates crashed open, dark shapes instantly descended from above and dropped onto the ground around them.

Without missing a beat, Nithin threw out a blast so powerful that Thorn felt herself weaken as he siphoned not just his own magic, but hers as well. The pulse didn't knock out the guards. Instead, a strange, disconcerting cast fell over each one. A dreamy look, like each was enthralled. As if enchanted – and perhaps they were – they stumbled around, oblivious to their surroundings.

'Internal desire,' he explained with a hint of satisfaction. 'I can make them dream whatever I want.'

'Can any sbura do that?'

'No,' he admitted. 'I've been studying Lucien's spells.'

To the left of the now distracted guards were stairs, and she beckoned to him as she set off.

On the top stair, she pushed the door and almost fell off the side of the building. There was nothing but empty space beyond the door. Nithin caught her by the arm and pulled her back.

'The floors change, remember?' he cried. 'Be careful!'

And so the long game began. The first few rooms were filled with a different sort of horror, like each one was a torture chamber of some kind. One room housed a pool, with blood instead of water; one room was filled with screams; one had no floor at all and they clung to the doorway tightly, trying not to fall in. They couldn't see how deep it went, magic making it possibly limitless. As soon as the next floor passed, they jumped, and tumbled into a room that held a table covered in empty bottles, needles and blades. Empty cages lined the opposite wall and blood stained the ground. Exchanging unhappy grimaces, Thorn and Nithin hugged the wall and headed to the opposite doorway.

The rooms that were the hardest to get through were the ones with actual prisoners inside. These floors had cells that reeked of filth and decay, and sometimes hands stretched out of the bars, desperately trying to get out; other times they passed by prisoners who held no life at all in their eyes. When Thorn tried one of the cell doors, she was blasted back and burns snaked across her hands.

They made it through one level after another, but at the end of every room was another door. Another jump. More than once, they misjudged the distance of the jump and almost tumbled to their deaths. Only Thorn's years of climbing and running gave her any sort of an edge. Nithin had only magic on his side, but each bit of magic he used to correct a misjudged jump seemed to exhaust him more with every level. There were no guards, but there were no locks or keys or windows, either. Only doors. What became increasingly clear was that much of the Tower hadn't been used in years. So many levels showed signs of abandonment, rot, disrepair, and she wondered how deserted Salfar had been after the Suriias left.

It felt like five or six hours had passed before they reached a floor with nothing in it but a podium. They advanced slowly, both gasping for breath, covered in cuts and bruises, drenched in sweat from the endless climb.

'Why isn't it guarded?' she breathed. 'There's not even an enchantment.'

'Well, if touching it means death or madness, I'd imagine that deters most from trying.'

Thorn swallowed hard. 'Okay. Let's do this.'

Without waiting for him to agree, she moved towards the book. Her heart felt like a hummingbird inside her ribcage. She counted every step she took towards the podium. As she drew nearer, horrible whispers, like a thousand angry snakes, began snarling into her ears, warning her off. The air began to bite at her, angry and alive with far too much magic. It took all her strength to keep moving closer.

In front of the podium, she stopped. Raising her hand, she pushed gently against an invisible ward. Her fingers slipped through the magic slowly; it felt thick, like the air had turned to water. She half expected to die the second she touched the book, but instead the whispers that had warned her away began to *scream*, filling her ears like the roar of an angry fire.

'You need blood,' she heard Nithin say, voice distant.

Thorn raised her knife, the knife Kol had given her, and sliced down the length of her arm – a more practical move than slicing her palm. She let the blood drip onto the book. It didn't stain it; the book absorbed each drop.

'My blood for your help,' she whispered, placing her hand back down.

At once, ten thousand ancient souls coursed through the tips of her fingers and latched onto every fibre of her being. Angry whispers instantly began to swirl around her head. Some from the souls, some from the magic. But sussing out her own thoughts was near to impossible. They hungered for revenge against the ancient queen who trapped them there. They wanted to be let loose. They wanted to wreak havoc.

She shook her head, trying to clear her mind.

'Thorn?' Nithin was at her side. 'Are you all right?'

'Fine,' she managed. 'Let's go.'

Stowing the book in her bag, she followed Nithin to the doorway. He kept glancing back at her, the concern unguarded in his green eyes.

Thorn didn't realise just how different having the magic would be until she opened the door, wishing for a staircase, and the Tower went still. The levels locked, all movement ceased, and a staircase appeared before them.

'Huh,' grunted Nithin, stunned.

Thorn was too dizzy to react, but with Nithin steering her down the steps so that she didn't accidentally faceplant as she fought to keep her thoughts clear, she was cognisant enough to be relieved.

Until they got about three floors down and found the next room filled with waiting guards. None of them looked distracted by desire this time, but they appeared stunned by Thorn. Could they tell that she'd absorbed the magic? Did they even know that was possible?

Thorn's eyes danced over the guards and the whispers in her mind started anew. Louder, louder, louder.

The voices piled on top of each other and made no discernible sense. Thorn's hands began to glow, magic coursing through her without thought or direction. It expelled from her like a tsunami and the guards were blasted through the wall. Their screams echoed as they fell to their deaths far below. The way clear, she made to move, but Nithin held her fast.

Turning her towards him, he cupped his hands on either side of her face. For what felt like a precarious amount of time, they simply gazed at each other. And then she felt it. Magic spreading between them. She felt none of the forced desire that Gemini had pressed upon her, nor any thrall she couldn't pull back from. Only a strong connection that filled her with strength. Her thoughts were, briefly, clear.

When his hands fell, he raised an eyebrow. 'You good?'

'I'm good,' she said, glad it wasn't a lie.

On they went.

Two levels down, they came upon more prisoners. This time, the doors of the cells crumbled as Thorn passed. She wasn't conscious of doing it, but her fury at the sight propelled the magic anyways.

And then she passed two prisoners that made her pause, double back, and stare. There, in the far corner of the disgusting cell, were two men who looked remarkably like Nik.

'Who are you?' asked one, voice raspy.

'Here to get you out,' said Thorn. 'Want to go?'

The brothers wasted no time.

With Thorn's magic working almost independent of her will, getting out was laughably easy. The doors opened, the stairs cleared, and any guards who came upon them were either blasted back viciously or simply disintegrated – this latter result left her immobile with horror, and she only moved on when Nithin put his arm around her shoulders and steered her away from the grisly sight.

Outside in the courtyard of the Tower, everything lay open. If any guards remained, they did not come near.

Thorn, Nithin, Hyun and Eun walked across the bridge without being accosted.

And then the whispers began biting at her mind, hissing, screaming, wanting her to use her magic. Let them loose, let them play.

Only Nithin's grip on her arms kept her grounded.

'I'll get Lucien,' she said when they reached the castle hours later, barely managing to string two thoughts together. 'You guys wait here. We don't know where the king is right now.'

'Be careful,' said Nithin thickly. 'I mean it.'

'You too.'

Leaving them in the shadows of the garden, Thorn set off at a run, glad that for now the voices were leaving her thoughts alone. When she reached the far wing of the castle, she went straight for Lucien's room. He leapt out of his chair, clearly having been waiting for her. Whatever distraction he'd utilised seemed over and she didn't bother asking. It didn't matter now.

'We've got Nik's brothers. By the garden. Go.'

Lucien shot out of the room without another word. Esme, who had been in the corner, went to Thorn's side.

'Thorn?'

Thorn tried to focus on Esme's face, head spinning, whispers whispering. 'I took the book,' she rasped. 'I've got the magic. It really hurts.' The laugh that left her was pained, and far from humorous.

Esme's smile turned triumphant. 'Then you can kill the king.'

The whispers all had different opinions on that, but all wanted the Lord King to suffer, and so they fell quiet as Thorn and Esme made for the throne room.

Thorn had no trouble quelling the guards' response – they simply fell to the ground. Immobile.

Inside the throne room, the king turned to face them. His icy eyes widened at the sight of Thorn.

'How—'

She waved a hand, and his mouth sealed. It was so easy, it terrified her.

'Pin him down,' said Esme, eyes on her father.

Thorn glared at the king, wanting him locked to the throne. And then he was.

'Finally.' Drawing a dagger from the sheath at her waist, Esme advanced on the king. A taunting smile tugged at her lips as she plunged the blade into his chest. 'Siphon the immortality out of him, Thorn,' she instructed. 'Don't let him keep anything.'

Thorn had hated and feared magic all her life. As she stood over the body of the king, green light dancing around the tips of her fingers, a thousand whispers in her mind, she found that that feeling had not altered one iota.

When at last the king stopped twitching, now a husk in splendid finery, Esme removed the crown from the king's head. 'Thank you, Thorn.'

Thorn stared dazedly at her. 'The spell?'

'Here.'

Esme took the book from Thorn's bag and flipped through it before pausing on a page near the back. Tearing it out, she handed it to Thorn. 'Only heirs to Salfar and those with the book's power can use it. But when it's not a Tear, someone has to stay behind to anchor it. Magic requires magic on both sides, and there's no magic native to Earth.'

Thorn nodded, although her heart sank. She could only pray Aosh kept her word.

'Are you sure?' asked Esme. 'The worlds are fixed now, Thorn. Humans there, Suriias here. Is that so bad?'

'Even if I could live with it,' she whispered, 'Nithin needs his wife and daughter. I have to get Thistle for him. For her. Whatever happens to me, they're a family. They need each other.'

As if on cue, thudding footfalls preceded Nithin's arrival.

She held up the ancient piece of paper as he strode over to her. But worry darkened his green eyes, and she could sense his guilt and reservations.

'I'm okay,' she lied. 'It's okay.'

Then, with a reassuring nod, she took his hand, and looked down at the spell.

CHAPTER THIRTY-SIX
The Reluctant King

The Tower had stood for longer than recorded history. No one knew exactly when it was built. Or, if they did, they certainly weren't telling. What little Lucien did know came from his own experiences locked inside its walls and he was one of the lucky ones. He was only inside for mere days before Geon broke him out. Seeing Nik's brothers brought all the memories back with the force of a tsunami. Their sanity was in ruins, their minds forever unsettled.

Hyun was standing, motionless and wide-eyed; on the ground at his feet sat Eun. They looked like revenants: dead bodies reanimated without souls.

Lucien walked over slowly, but he didn't reach touching distance. Shim, who had followed him out of the castle, stayed back cautiously. A few paces away from them, he crouched down on his knees, hands where the twins could see them. 'My name is Lucien,' he said, careful not to raise the register of his voice even an octave. 'I'm your brother-in-law.'

Eun tilted his head, clearly listening, but Hyun didn't react. His fingers twitched at his sides, though it seemed involuntary.

'Nikolas is here,' he continued. 'And we're going to keep you safe.'

'No such thing.' Eun sounded shredded, his eyes ablaze with fear.

'I was in the Tower, too. I know how you feel. All I can say is that you won't ever have to go back there again.'

'If the Tower stands, there's always a chance.' Eun put a hand on his brother's shoulder; Hyun leaned into him, grounding himself with the comfort of his twin's proximity.

'The Tower won't stand,' said Lucien.

That finally got Hyun's attention.

'You think you can bring down the Tower?' The disdain, disbelief and derision that punctuated those words could have stopped a stampede.

'You can help me do it,' he added. 'The king doesn't have the book anymore.'

The brothers straightened up in unison, shells becoming bullets as rage overwhelmed their fear.

Lucien held out a hand, calling magic to him. He watched as blue light, conjured from the universe, gathered in his palm. Having magic come so freely on this world was a luxury he was still readjusting to. Even on the second Earth, magic had felt muted, trapped against an invisible barrier. Now it came to him like inhaling air, filling him.

He wasn't expecting Eun to take his hand, but the second they clasped hands, something changed. Images flashed through Lucien's mind, horrible, twisted, grim recreations of everything Eun had seen in the Tower. Of everything that had been done to him. Being tortured by shadows was more horrific than description suggested.

As the nightmares faded, his unquiet magic siphoned out by Lucien, who could better compartmentalise its warped fury, Eun managed to regard him clearly for the first time. 'Where's Nikolas?'

'In the castle,' said Lucien. 'Do you want to see him?'

'No,' said Hyun. 'I want to destroy the Tower.'

The twins' determination spoke to the very fibre of Lucien's being, and he nodded. 'Let's get Esme,' he said to Shim. 'She'll know where to start.'

'I think she stayed with Thorn.'

'Do you want to come with us?' he asked the brothers.

They nodded in tandem and followed Lucien and Shim towards the castle.

The grounds were deceptively quiet. The guards that had littered the paths and watchpoints perpetually were no longer at their posts.

'I hope they didn't go after Thorn,' said Shim quietly.

'That,' said Lucien, 'or they're at the Tower.'

Taking on the entirety of his father's army sounded less fun than having all his teeth pulled by a dentist who didn't believe in painkillers, but Lucien's pace didn't falter as the group made their way through the eerily deserted corridors.

The doors to the throne room stood open as they approached.

And then he saw it—

Esme sitting on the ground, an empty throne behind her.

In her hands was their father's crown. Beside her was the Book of Ten Thousand Souls.

She was blood stained, her skin off-colour. Traces of magical light slithered over her flesh, remnants of far too much being expelled at once. She'd clearly used her magic to subdue the guards, but he was relieved to note she hadn't harnessed the book's powers.

Lucien stopped short, more astonished by the crown in her hands than by the state of her appearance. 'What? How?'

She stood and strolled over, exuding delighted cunning with every step. 'Well, if it isn't my big brother, the Lord King of Salfar.'

Shim, Hyun and Eun all looked to Lucien, who choked. No words had ever sounded less plausible or more terrifying.

'You'll have to get used to me saying it,' said Esme with a laugh, holding out the crown to him. 'It's true.'

Lucien didn't move to take it. 'I'm no king, Ez.'

'That's what will make you better than him.'

His nose wrinkled as he appraised the crown. 'Can I abdicate to you?' he asked hopefully.

'I'm your savage little sister,' she said proudly, a glint in her cobalt eyes. 'You're the good one who gets the worse job.'

Her words prompted a small, semi-hysterical laugh to escape his lips.

'You can't be worse,' said Shim. 'I mean, really.'

'A ringing endorsement,' said Lucien.

Ignoring his protests, Esme stood on tiptoes and placed the crown on his head. 'It suits you,' she affirmed. 'My king.'

Lucien felt like vomiting.

'The Tower?' said Eun.

He nodded. 'We'll go now.'

'I'll go,' said Esme. 'I'm itching to raze something.'

'Esme—'

'I won't start a forest fire,' she assured him. 'I'm exceptionally good at controlled explosions.'

Not sure how to process that, Lucien watched her leave the throne room with Eun and Hyun, both of whom were clearly just as hungry to do some damage.

'Go,' he said to Shim. 'Keep an eye on them. Someone with a level head needs to.'

'Yes, boss,' she said. 'Er, well, king.'

She left the throne room, laughing at the expression on his face.

Not wanting to be in a cold room filled with too many memories of his father, Lucien left through a side door and headed down to the gardens. When he was in the furthest corner of the backgarden, hidden from view of the others, he sank onto the ground and put his head in his hands. The crown felt hard and unforgiving beneath his fingers.

Did he wear it? Take it off? Fling it at a tree?

Suddenly overcome by the urge to be anywhere else, he didn't linger in the garden and instead wandered down the path, across the grounds, and on through the backwoods towards Geon and Jae's old home.

The woods thickened as he walked, and it seemed like no one had come this way in a long time.

The sight of Geon and Jae's small shack made him want to cry. He had so many happy memories in that home. He couldn't believe it was still there.

'I miss him, too.'

Lucien spun around. Jae was leaning against a tree, shrouded in the early hour's gloom. From a distance, he looked like Geon.

Chest clenching, Lucien whispered, 'I don't think I'll ever stop looking over my shoulder for him.' He swallowed the sudden lump in his throat. 'I don't know what I did to deserve him.'

'You gave him a home.' Jae waved at the ramshackle building that hadn't housed a soul in years. 'Our parents were gone, and we were starving to death and you gave us a home. You gave us friendship. The second you offered Geon your hand, you had his loyalty. You had mine. You still do.'

'It's mutual.'

'Good.'

With a resolved nod to himself, Lucien took the book out of his coat. Without the magic of the souls, it didn't feel like anything dangerous. But it was cursed. When the souls were done with Thorn, they would return to the book once more, trapped and listless, far too many locked within, waiting to be used by those who could so easily abuse.

'Will they be able to get them back? The humans?'

'I hope so.'

Jae pursed his lips. 'She reminds me of Geon. Ready to die or go mad for the ones they love.'

'We don't deserve them.'

Jae placed his hand on Lucien's shoulder. 'Some day you'll realise that Geon never viewed what happened to him as a sacrifice. No part of him regretted it or second guessed his choice. What he gave you was a gift – the gift of his life, which he only had to offer because you saved it once already.'

Gift or sacrifice, Lucien still felt like Geon was the better one. The stronger, kinder, lovelier one.

Words, however, escaped him. He led the way into the house, careful not to disturb the creatures and critters that had made the shack their home since the brothers vacated centuries ago.

They found a bowl under the unusable basin and Lucien carefully set it on the old dining table. He placed the book in the centre of the bowl and stepped back.

'Do you know what's ironic?'

'What?'

'The book cannot be destroyed by anyone other than the king,' he murmured. 'I couldn't have destroyed it until Breneth died.'

'Let's buy Esme something really nice,' said Jae with a rueful laugh. 'A new set of knives, perhaps.'

'She can have the whole bloody army.'

'Well, that's going to be terrifying.'

Lucien stretched his hand over the book. Pale blue fire, which burned cold, gathered like a controlled tornado beneath his palm. The pages caught gradually, and then all at once, and soon the Book of Ten Thousand Souls was nothing but ash, its whispers with Thorn, waiting to be released for good, its spells and secrets lost forever.

Lucien's first move upon returning to the castle was to get rid of any and all with loyalty to his father. He didn't trust the old castle guards and wasn't about to trust them with protecting the new household.

The pack helped with that. Isha and Mi especially took great glee in escorting them out of the castle. Adair and Shim volunteered to elect new guards, a task Lucien was only too happy to pass on.

Soon enough, the castle held only friendly faces and was much, much quieter.

'Can we decorate?' Shara asked at dinner a couple of nights later. Most of the pack were gathered around the table, all finally smiling. Seeing their hope made the fear in Lucien's chest far less acute. 'It feels like a tomb – and smells like one, too.'

Lucien ruffled her hair. 'Do you want to oversee the redecorating?'

She bobbed her head.

'Job's yours.'

Across from his now gleeful sister, Eran leaned in. 'Can I ride one of the unicorns? There's a whole bunch in the castle's stables.'

Beside him, Adair caught Lucien's eye. They both vividly remembered the day Lucien had been dragged over rocks after his unicorn was spooked by a passing dragon.

'We'll see,' he said at length.

Adair mouthed his gratitude.

Naida leaned in, her long black hair falling in front of her too-thin shoulders. 'May I make an observation?'

Everyone waited patiently.

'No one's hunting us,' she said. 'None of us are illegal. This is the first time ... *ever*, that that's been true.'

Lucien raised his glass. 'To having a home.'

'To a quiet reign,' said Adair.

The remainder of the evening was spent in easy company, but he'd only just closed his eyes when someone called his name and he woke to see Jae leaning over him, an anxious look on his face.

'It's Hyun.'

Lucien shot out of bed and followed Jae quickly to Nik's room down the hall.

The sight that unfolded before his eyes was one that made sense only to those who understood madness.

Taking it in with practised efficiency, Lucien walked past Nik and Eun, both of whom were trying to soothe Hyun, and stepped through the barrier of magic Hyun had attempted to put around himself. One that wasn't strong enough to keep Lucien out. He put his hands on either side of Hyun's face and whispered the words of the sleeping spell he'd memorised for helping Geon to sleep.

Seconds later, Hyun collapsed into his arms, limp and defenceless. Lucien picked him up easily and turned to face the others.

'Which room is his?'

'This way,' said Naida, waving for him to follow.

Lucien brought Hyun to his bedroom and set him down gently. Eun moved like a wraith, slipping through the shadows, and then ending up in the corner beside Hyun's bed. Soundless, watchful, mistrusting. His dark eyes didn't leave Lucien until he'd stepped away from Hyun.

To Naida, Lucien said, 'Don't let him out of your sight until you change shifts. And remember that his magic is nothing compared to yours. It's all defensive.'

She nodded.

Not wanting to see Nik, Lucien departed. He was almost to the door when he *felt* Nik approach. He stilled automatically but he didn't turn around.

Nik's whisper sent a chill down his spine. 'Thank you.'

'I don't need to be thanked for looking after my brother-in-law,' he replied, unable to keep the bite out of his voice.

He stepped into the corridor, but Nik darted out after him.

'Luka, *wait*,' he begged, catching up and stopping in front of him. 'Please look at me.'

Lucien rolled his eyes toward Nik, finding it easier to be furious. 'Why?'

'Because.' Nik sounded so broken that Lucien hissed under his breath and before he could stop himself, he had pulled Nik close and was kissing him. Tasting him. Pushing him back against the wall.

'I love you,' Nik said against his lips.

It was like being doused in hot water.

Lucien recoiled, heart galloping, and took several gasping breaths, trying to gather some semblance of control. He took in Nik – lips swollen, shirt unbuttoned and rumpled, hair tousled and falling in front of his eyes – and forced himself to turn and walk away.

If he didn't, he'd fall to his knees and offer Nik his heart, his soul, his kingdom – anything. And what sort of king would that make him?

CHAPTER THIRTY-SEVEN
Jailbreak, Baby

EARTH

The world Thorn and Nithin returned to was not the world they had left behind. It was nothing like Salfar, either. It was a mixed up world of two timelines and a mixture of technologies and inventions.

The pair stood atop the hill that looked out across the fields of Itannera, where the skyscrapers of Courtenz once loomed above the world. Now there were no buildings in the sky. Everything was open and untouched. Under better circumstances, Thorn would've loved it.

'How do two worlds become one?' Nithin wondered aloud.

'No idea,' she muttered. 'And I'm not hankering to find out.'

She hoped, though, that this time would be better. Humans would remember the pain of both worlds. Would they ensure it never happened again? Would they learn from their mistakes this time?

She glanced at Nithin. 'Lucien told me that there were witch-burnings on his world when they realised magic was real. Let's not get burned.'

'Agreed,' he said.

They set off down the hill at a jog, the grass brushing against them with every step. But using the magic to get them to Earth hadn't expelled nearly enough, and the whispers continued scratching at Thorn's mind.

Shivers cascaded across her skin, but amidst the inane babble of ten thousand souls, she heard one louder than the rest. She tried to focus on the voice, but couldn't.

'Thorn?' Nithin was in front of her. When had they stopped running? 'What's wrong?'

She couldn't detach herself from the swirling hissing in her brain, like an itch that only grew worse and could never be soothed. 'Whispers.'

Why did speaking hurt so much?

He reached out, putting his hands on either side of her face. His eyes blazed with magic and suddenly she felt a great pull between them. Like he'd slipped inside her skin and was cleaning out her insides.

The whispers died to a low hum and she managed to nearly ignore them. Green light crackled in his irises, flaring as he absorbed large quantities of the magic swirling inside of her. With a nod to Nithin, she stepped back, shaking and sweating. Nithin, too, looked like he'd just taken Hazies.

'You okay?' he asked, brushing damp black hair back from his eyes.

'I'm okay,' she croaked. 'Let's just find Thistle fast.'

The fields were mostly empty, save for the odd animal, and they came across no external complications as they trudged through the marshlands.

'Of all the worlds we've found out about,' she said, picking her way through the wet, mucky grass, 'which is your least favourite?'

'For me? Undoubtedly Lucien's Earth.' He glanced back at her. With muck on his knees and hands, sweat giving his skin a glistening sheen, circles under his eyes accentuating the gaunt, haunted quality so many sleepless nights had done to him,

Nithin looked nothing like her first impression of him. He looked, she realised, no different than her.

'Yours?' he prompted when the silence had gone on too long.

Thorn rubbed her jaw roughly, now angry at herself as much as by their predicament and said, 'Our Earth.'

'Between the two as it stands?'

'I'm not sure yet,' she admitted. 'You'll probably say Salfar.'

'I want to be wherever Thistle is.'

'Did you really read something about human engagement rings?' she wondered, mulling over everything Thistle had said about him.

'I did.'

She laughed. 'I told Thistle that was bullshit.'

Nithin's lips twitched. 'You certainly didn't help my case whatsoever. She never ceased worrying about what you'd think or say, and often when she had a problem, she'd discuss what you'd do and why it was always the right thing to do.'

'I'm really glad she met you.'

'Thank you.'

Smiles exchanged, they carried on. For most of the day, all they did was walk, following gut feeling more than anything else. When night came and they'd exhausted themselves, they made camp in the corner of a cluster of trees.

But as the quiet set in, so too did the whispers, and she wrapped her hands around her ears, desperate to block it out.

'Thorn?'

It was louder than the whispers.

Calmer.

Not hissing.

Not chaotic.

And then strong hands drew her hands back and she was looking at Nithin.

'Get them out,' she begged, tears falling freely down her face. 'Get them out. Get them out.'

Worry deepened the creases on Nithin's dark, angular face. Taking a resigned breath, he leaned in and kissed her. It wasn't romantic. It wasn't sexual in the slightest. But he held her, unmoving, calm, and her magic slowly ebbed.

The whispers died down.

She drew back with a rattling gasp. She wiped her mouth, her whole body shaking. 'H-how?'

'It's easier to siphon magic that way,' he muttered, clearly not delighted at having done it.

'Thanks,' she said, feeling as awkward as he looked.

'What are you going to do?'

'You mean if this doesn't kill me or make me crazy?' Thorn drew her legs into her chest, resting her chin on her knees. 'I never saw a life past protecting Tiz. But now Kol ...' If she thought about leaving him forever, she'd lose her composure completely.

'I can't say what I would have done,' he muttered, 'but I hate Nik for allowing this to happen. We were so close. Everyone was with who they wanted to be with. And then ...'

Thorn wasn't sure how she felt about Nik's duplicity. Would she have done it any differently if Thistle were in the Tower? She doubted it. Judgement was easy if the choice wasn't yours. 'Will you promise me something?'

He nodded. 'Anything.'

'Don't let Kol be lonely.' Her voice cracked on his name.

'I won't,' he swore. 'I'll tell him how much this broke your heart. I'll tell him how brave you were.'

She closed her eyes, but she felt him wrap his arms around her. 'Nith?'

'Yes?'

'Thank you.'

He kissed the top of her head and adjusted his embrace, holding her close in a way that was immensely reassuring. 'You're welcome, Thorn.'

And, just like that, the whispers stopped.

The trilling of birds woke them a little after dawn. Without anything to eat, the pair simply started walking, their boots picking up dew with every step. There was no hum of magic in the world, no thrum of machinery or industry. It was a quiet world, before the churn of modernity hit. That last grasp of calm before development. It was the sort of world Thorn would love in other circumstances and she wondered what the new world would be like. How everything would go this time around. Perhaps what everyone needed was just a fresh start.

They soon found a dusty path that wound its way towards a town. Every house or building they passed looked somehow ancient, shabby, dull in colour, muted. It was hard to wonder if the world had not simply gone back in time, reverting itself to whatever it had been three hundred years ago, before the Suriias arrived.

Nithin seemed to be making the same observations. 'I think reversing the Tear sent Earth back to how it was. What year did Lucien say? Nineteenth century to humans?'

'Something like that.'

Green aether swirled around his fingers as his agitation mounted. 'This could get interesting.'

'Don't be too green,' she advised.

'Right back at you.'

They were at the end of the street when Thorn heard voices. Not whispers, voices. She caught Nithin before they rounded the corner and yanked him into the shadows.

Across the street, several men in uniform stood gathered, smoking long cigarettes and talking in loud tones. Squinting, she only just made out the name on their uniforms.

'They're Enforcers,' she breathed. 'Fucking figures.'

'What?'

'That becoming Suriia didn't help for shit.'

The low chuckle that left him made her smile ruefully. At the same time, the whispers itched in the back of her mind anew.

Not wanting to worry Nithin or force him to siphon the magical overload out once again, she kept it to herself.

Once the men had dispersed, the pair made their way through the town, heads bowed and trying to remain inconspicuous.

'Your lack of a dress really stands out,' he whispered.

'I'm getting—' Thorn stopped short. There, in the shop across the street, was Ginny. 'Nith,' she breathed.

He followed her gaze and his whole body seemed to relax.

Not wanting to draw attention to themselves, they followed Ginny several streets over to a large house. When she approached, an awfully familiar face appeared in the window above, waving to Ginny welcomingly.

'Parin.' His name left Thorn's lips a cry of joy.

That left five to find.

Not wanting to risk getting into trouble, Thorn and Nithin stayed hidden on the other side of the road until the day wound to a close.

Only when the night swallowed the sun and the cold had long set in did Thorn and Nithin scale the wall. It was easy to do, the stone coarse and cold beneath her fingers, but no match for the boost magic gave her.

She tapped once at Parin's window, praying no one else would hear the sound.

Inside, someone scrambled up, cursing, and she knew it was Parin going for his weapon.

And then he appeared.

'Thorn!' Yanking open the window, he hauled her in and into his arms. 'Thank fuck!'

She tightened her grip around him. 'You're here,' she murmured, reassuring herself that if they were okay, surely the rest were, too. 'You're here.'

Nithin didn't join in the reunion. He was too distracted by the cot in the corner. In a flash, he was at the cot, reaching in and lifting out a small, sleeping bundle.

Kali.

Thorn almost burst into tears right then and there. She looked at Parin, a lump in her throat. 'Thistle?'

Parin shook his head. 'She was taken to the asylums. We're working on it.'

'Asylums? What are asylums?' The word did not conjure joyous imagery.

'Places for the ones they call crazy.'

Her eyebrows shot up.

'Cos, you know, loving a Suriia is proof of insanity.'

As she tried to process this, the whispers grew louder and louder. Thorn blinked hard, trying to force the voices away. She could never tell who was whom, or why some preferred to speak at random moments and others just kept up running monologues. It was like having a carnival inside her mind and she *wanted them out*.

'Thorn?'

She didn't realise she'd been gripping the roots of her hair, staring off into space. Nithin was in front of her, a calm hand on either side of her face.

'Everything okay?' asked Parin, watching her worriedly.

'She's fine,' said Nithin. 'It took a lot of magic to get here.'

Parin reached out and squeezed her arm. 'Anything I can do?'

'No, I'm fine,' she lied, forcing a smile to her face. In truth, Nithin's arm around her waist was all that kept her upright. 'Tell us what you know about where Thistle is.'

'It's this huge building on an island. They patrol the waters and there's a fence around all of it. We've been trying to figure out a way on. Rumour is that if you pay the right sailor, you can get across, but that doesn't broach the problem of getting over the fence and then getting back out. Let alone even finding her.'

Thorn ran her hands over her head, thinking quickly. 'Nithin and I can do it.'

Nithin nodded.

'They might not have the same tech, but they have magic detectors. Ones made on the human world. They'll sense you coming.'

'Then we'll be the distraction,' said Thorn. 'If they sense a Suriia, we'll give them one.'

'Are you sure?' asked Parin.

'I'm sure,' she said, forcing herself to focus on him. On his face. His words. Not the voices creating chaos in her mind.

She didn't realise how tightly she was balling her fists until she gasped in pain and realised that she'd cut open her palms.

'Where're the others?' asked Nithin.

'Ginny's here,' said Parin. 'Trinity, Grey and Jade, too. But Shadow's at the asylum with Thistle.'

Thorn's heart sank.

'We'll get them out,' said Nithin. 'As soon as possible.'

Parin smiled in relief. 'It's really good to see you guys.'

When he'd left the room, Nithin rounded on Thorn. 'Is it getting worse?'

'They never stop talking,' she whispered. 'I can't focus on anything. It's like having a riot in my mind. They're all telling me to do different things. No one can agree.'

Nithin looked pained on her behalf.

'It's only for a little while,' she said, feigning an upbeat tone. 'Once I send you guys back, it's over.'

They were still regarding each other when the door opened, and Thorn was suddenly in Grey's arms. Trinity, Ginny and Jade appeared behind him.

'All right,' said Nithin after a long moment of silence. 'What do we know about the asylum?'

'It's half a day's walk to the shore,' said Parin. 'There's a good stretch of ocean between the mainland and the tiny island where they're keeping them.'

'Do they have boats?' asked Thorn.

'We'll have to steal one.'

She shrugged. 'Won't be the first time.'

Everyone agreed to catch some shut eye before they set off. For her part, Thorn couldn't sleep. She stood by the window and stared out at the silent night. This new world was so quiet, but would it remain so? Salfar's future was bright under Lucien, but Earth's seemed much more uncertain. The asylums were a bad sign, but surely the Enforcers couldn't hold onto much power for long. After all, there was no more magic for them to fight against.

Thorn looked over her shoulder at the others. Nithin was sleeping with Kali on his chest. Parin and Ginny were on the ground, arms around each other. The sight of them made her smile, albeit sadly.

Her last night with them and she couldn't begin to say goodbye.

So, she stood, she watched, she waited.

The island cut a black mark across the horizon, the asylum a terrifying, jagged figure atop it. The brick was almost orange in colour, but a faded, ill-looking orange. Like time had taken issue with the asylum's very existence and done its best to corrode and chip away at it.

From where she crouched, Thorn looked at Nithin, barely tamping down her nerves. 'The Tower, the asylum or the death camps?'

He grimaced. 'Don't forget the districts.'

'How could I?'

Commandeering one of the boats was easy enough, and soon the group were rowing towards the asylum. Each stroke of the paddles, each lap of the waves against the ship, sounded ominous.

'I never realised how much we took for granted with technology,' said Nithin, shouting over the lashing rain, his black hair plastered to his face.

'Do you miss it?'

'I miss coaches!'

A bark of laughter tore out of her and he flashed a grin.

The bank took an age to arrive in front of them, but at last the group jumped over the sides of the boat, landing with squelching sounds. On the shore, water flooded into Thorn's boots and she started to shiver unconsciously. Nithin looked like he'd just gone swimming in his clothes.

'Disgusting,' he grumbled.

'Could be worse.'

'I can smell my socks from here.'

'I take it back.'

The rain hammered down with steady gusto, worsened by the sea and winds, but Thorn would take the added cover of dark clouds and heavy rains to obscure them from view of any watchers above.

They picked their way up the bank, mindful of the sharp, slick rocks and puddles likely much deeper than they appeared.

Thorn found a path halfway up the hill and they took it to a bridge that led to another path, this time paved, and soon enough a gate appeared ahead. The asylum loomed beyond. The architecture was even more sinister and unwelcoming up close.

'It looks like a building someone came up with in a nightmare,' said Nithin. 'Who designs windows to look like that?'

Thorn couldn't disagree. The jagged edges, the bars, the fact that every single one was the exact same and that they went on and on and on …

A flash went through her mind. Another prison break. One she hadn't participated in yet remembered like it was her own.

With a wave of his pale hand, Geon opened the doors, wood and metal falling to the floor around him chaotically, although not one bit of dust even touched him. He raised an eyebrow at the sight, impressed by the magic that now sang in his veins, aching for release. Magic that had been confined for too long. Now, brewing inside Geon, the souls wanted to play.

The smell of the Tower hit him instantly and his stomach rebelled. Damp and mould, death and decay.

Less than two paces into the Tower, guards dropped down to meet him. They moved through the shadows like wraiths.

He killed them with a wave of his hand.

Their bodies slammed against the walls and he heard the uproar of the other prisoners.

A flush of vindictive wrath swept through him and Geon opened their cells.

Snapping back to herself, swaying on her feet, Thorn raised her hands. The doors of the asylum blasted into splinters.

A cluster of people appeared, dressed in hospital clothes, their skin unhealthy, the bags under their eyes like bruises.

Geon's words left her lips: 'Enjoy your night.'

Wicked laughter started from one and then spread like an epidemic from patient to patient.

The prisoners hooted and hollered as they dashed into the night.

Geon ignored them. He took the stairs two at a time, dispensing the guards as they appeared.

The topmost cell could only be opened by the king's magic. One wave of his hand and the door was in pieces. He stepped quickly over the mess and into the cell. There, in the far corner, beaten half to death, was Lucien. He had never looked so small, so helpless.

'Tor!'

Thorn's attention was snapped from Geon's memories to the present. It wasn't Lucien. It was Thistle.

She had stumbled out of a cell near the middle of the corridor. They crashed into each other, both with grips tight enough to bruise.

'I knew you'd come,' cried Thistle. 'I knew you'd come.'

Thorn closed her eyes and breathed in. Even dirty, Thistle still smelled like home.

'Thistle!' Nithin's cry made Thorn pull back so that he could draw her close.

Thorn looked around, eyes darting over the humans. 'Where are the others?'

'They took Shadow,' said Thistle, urgency evident in her tone. 'They've been experimenting on him.'

'Why?'

'He's an immortal human. They want answers.'

'Where?'

'I'm not sure,' said Thistle. 'Downstairs, maybe.'

'I'll go,' she said to them. 'Get everyone outside to Parin and the others.'

Thistle's eyes widened. 'Kali?'

'Fine,' said Nithin, kissing her temple. 'Perfect.'

The words were like medicine and Thistle let out a shaking sigh of relief, sinking into him. Thorn squeezed her arm before turning and bolting down the corridor.

Two guards appeared in her path, but all Thorn had to do was wave her hand and they were blasted out of the window and onto the cold wet ground of the courtyard below.

Downstairs, past a set of sealed double doors that barely slowed her, Thorn found herself in what she could only imagine was a torture chamber of sorts. The instruments on the walls and tables were jagged, pointed or serrated; the figures strapped to the beds lay unmoving, bloodied, bruised, vacant. She unlocked their straps with a flick of her fingers as she passed by. She didn't pause, though. Not until she reached a bed with a familiar looking face.

Shadow was strapped to the mattress, eyes bloodshot and unfocused.

Thorn untied him, but he blinked dazedly at her and didn't react. 'Shadow, wake up,' she said, shaking him. 'You have to get up so you can go to Ayla, okay?'

He didn't move.

'Shadow!' she yelled. 'Wake up!'

He reacted slowly, as if only just registering her presence. 'Thorn?'

'Yes,' she said, grabbing him by the arms and pulling him as hard as she could until he stood up. 'And you need to listen to me – if ever there was a moment to just make your legs work, it's right now.'

To his credit, Shadow tried. He stumbled along beside her as they made their way down the corridor. But they were moving much too slowly.

'Thorn!'

Grey came streaking down the corridor from the opposite direction. He reached them and lugged Shadow's other arm over his shoulder.

Able to move faster now, they made their way up stair after stair.

When they reached the entrance, they found themselves trapped by four guards.

A green blast of light shot from Thorn's hand and slammed into them, knocking them through the door and out into the hammering rain. She didn't even have to think.

'Nice,' said Grey.

In the courtyard, a few of the patients milled about, uncertain and scared. All had a connection to a Suriia, all would be hunted or questioned or killed.

Unless they were under Lucien's protection.

'Hey!' she shouted at them, waving them over. 'Come here!'

Wide-eyed and wary, the patients shuffled over.

'Everyone take hands,' she said; Grey and Parin quickly helped those who were too dazed to comply.

'Ready?' she called when everyone was linked.

'Ready,' said everyone but Nithin.

He held her gaze and gave her a barely perceptible nod. Grim acceptance of what was about to happen.

'How are we avoiding creating a new Tear?' asked Thistle.

'Magic,' said Thorn airily.

'Of course.' Thistle sounded exhausted at the thought of more magic.

Thorn took her hand, and then Nithin's, as if she were going with them, and looked around the group.

She was aware of the rest of the guards on the island. Every single one. She could feel them trying to claw at her magic like hungry wolves.

In the far recesses of her mind, a voice whispered the words of the spell, and the magic of ten thousand restless souls refusing to be controlled, burned through her.

The last place her focus fixed, oddly, was on Nithin.

Time felt suspended in that brief moment as she let go of first Thistle's hand, and then Nithin's. For so long she'd hated everything about him. There was a time when she'd have traded his life for a human stranger without thought. But now he wasn't simply her friend. *Family* wasn't strong enough to define them, either. What term did you assign to someone who protected your sister unprompted and without aim? Who looked after you even when you hated them? Who took your side and followed you to another world? Who had saved your life over and over?

There did not seem words great enough to assign to how she felt about Nithin Summons.

He nodded, tears blurring his emerald eyes; she nodded back. It broke her heart in a way nothing else could. The feeling was something altogether different from romantic love, but of great, indelible importance.

'Good luck,' he said as the magic left her in a dizzying surge, and he vanished along with Thistle and the rest of her friends.

The power of Salfar now cut off, each soul was ripped from her one by one, sending her to her knees. Where they were going, she didn't know, but she watched them leave, like shadows on the wind.

One soul, however, lingered.

He didn't quite take form. He seemed like something made of fog, ethereal and unreal.

Thorn knew who he was before he even spoke. 'Geon,' she whispered, unable to stand. Blood drizzled from her ears and eyes, the magic leaving her body a ruin of itself. She was dying. She knew that much.

'Hello,' the ghost said. His accent was like Lucien's, but slightly more guttural, and distorted in this form. 'It's good to talk properly.'

'It's good not to have you in my head,' she said with a strained laugh.

'I'm sorry for that.' Regret creased his handsome face.

'Not your fault.'

'Still, I know how it feels.'

Sadness twisted Thorn's mouth as empathy bubbled inside her. 'I don't know how you lasted so long. Another day of that and I would have given up.'

He bowed his head, ebony hair falling in front of his face. 'I liked your memories of my sons.' Anguish laced the confession. 'I never meant for any of that to happen to them.'

'I know.'

'I wish I could tell them how sorry I am.'

Would he ever be able to? What became of ghosts? Yet despite all her questions, the one she asked was no longer relevant.

'Did you know what would happen?'

'I knew it would open a gateway. I thought we'd be able to come back eventually. Once we were strong enough. But the choices I made happened in the space of a day. I only knew the book was powerful and that if I had it, we could win. I knew Lucien would be able to use it once he was king. I just had to save his life first. I didn't know about the whispers. Or the wars that would follow. I thought Nik would be safe until I came back. No one knew he was mine.'

'What about Hyun and Eun?'

'Janna and I were having an affair. We had loved each other our entire lives, but she didn't marry me. Couldn't, I suppose. I was a joke in the king's court.

'Her husband was a wretched brute who couldn't have children and beat her for it.' Geon's features, made of brush strokes of light, scrunched up with fury. 'He went to war when she fell pregnant with our first child. He came home, saw Nikolas, and believed him his. Things were fine for a while and he left her alone.'

Fine was undoubtedly relative, but Thorn could see how things might have been painfully complicated, especially under Breneth's reign. 'Watching him raise Nik must've been hard.'

'Horribly so. We planned to run away when we were found out. Breneth arrested me, but Lucien intervened and agreed to an arranged marriage he'd been resisting. Everything fell apart after that. Lucien's marriage was rotten and helping him distracted me from Janna. I never knew she was even pregnant with the twins when I left.'

'I'm so sorry.'

'I'm sorry, too. It's not enough. It won't undo the damage. But I wanted someone to know. I never meant for anyone to get hurt. It was all for Lucien. Everything.' Geon sounded so broken, so desperately in need of some understanding, and Thorn wished she could reach across the ghostly divide and embrace him somehow.

'I know,' she promised. 'And I won't forget.'

'I'm truly sorry about your parents,' he said earnestly. 'If I could undo that, I would.'

'I believe you.'

Bowing his head, Geon disappeared like fog on a fast wind.

Even the dead, it seemed, had places to be.

For a time after he'd vanished, off to some next unknown, Thorn stayed on the ground, blood leaving her slowly now, unable to stand.

Just as Thorn began to fade, her head pounding painfully, her body weak and broken, the battering rain calmed, the wind died down, and suddenly she wasn't on the island at all.

She was on the bank of a river, and Aosh stood above her.

'Hello, Thorn.'

CHAPTER THIRTY-EIGHT
The Unenviable Plight of the Frai

SALFAR

The sudden blast of light left Lucien temporarily blind, but after blinking several times, shapes began to form. And, amongst them, Ginny.

He pelted across the throne room at the same time she did and caught her in his arms.

'Thank you!' she cried.

'Welcome home, kid.' He hadn't let himself wallow in his grief, but having her back made the anguish hit him retroactively. All the fear, all the possibilities, now felt like nightmares he'd entertained and could now banish.

When she dropped down, Lucien inspected the other arrivals.

'Shadow?' Kol, who had been with him and Jae, was staring at the man in bewilderment.

Lucien did a quick headcount and fixed his attention on Nithin. 'Where's Thorn?'

The question was quickly echoed, far more hysterically, by Kol.

Thistle, having come to the same realisation as them, whirled around, her reaction an unknowing mimic to Thorn's when she'd first arrived and it was Thistle who was missing. 'She was right here! Tor!'

The awful words echoed around the room.

'She's not coming back,' said Nithin quietly. He was soaked to the bone and covered in muck. More than that, a strange kind of brokenness seemed to be weighing him down.

Kol stumbled back a step at his best friend's words. *'What?'*

'We knew it going in.' Nithin sounded so hollow. 'I was going to do it. She wouldn't let me.'

Kol choked.

'Is she dead?' asked Grey.

Nithin hesitated. 'I don't think so.'

'What does that mean?'

'Someone had to stay behind to cast the spell, but I don't know what it did to her.'

'The book's gone, too,' said Lucien. 'We destroyed it. There's no power to go back.'

Kol fell onto his hands and knees, gasping as horrible, heart-shattering sobs tore out of him with wild, uncontrollable abandon. Like the very air he breathed was poison to his lungs.

Thistle dropped down beside him and pulled him into her arms, tears streaming down her face. He didn't appear to notice her at all.

Parin made a noise that was truly devastating, and he pointed at Nithin. 'You're fucking lucky you're holding a baby or you'd be dead. Selfish prick.'

And then he stormed off.

Lucien watched the vitriol lash Nithin like a whip, but he didn't crumble. He seemed in shock. Returning his attention to Kol, who Thistle and Shadow were trying in vain to soothe, Lucien wondered if there was anything anyone could do for him. He didn't think so somehow. Was it kinder to leave him behind with his own kind? If Thorn really was going to be human again, she would die and he would live on alone on Earth with no one else like him. With no magic save his own.

Was that crueller than heartbreak? He couldn't have come up with an answer if he had a hundred years to think on it.

He'd known a few frai over the years who'd lost their partners. They never recovered. In many ways, the frai had the most power, the most enviable abilities. But Lucien didn't think the trade was worth it.

Shadow eventually coaxed Kol out of the throne room, but he was hardly able to function and just looking at him made Lucien's heart hurt. Something fundamental seemed to have cracked inside the frai.

'He's not going to try and open the Tear again, is he?' Adair sounded like any more stress might be his undoing.

'No,' said Lucien. 'There's no way to reopen the Tear. And Kol's no murderer. Which would be the only way to get that much power into one source again.'

'So that's it, then?' asked Isha. 'Suriias on Salfar and humans on Earth – bar our friends – and no moving back and forth?'

'That's how it was always supposed to be.'

Lucien's mind, as it was wont to do, went to Geon. Right or wrong, Geon was the best friend any of them could have asked for. Thorn, too.

He would miss her dearly.

The biggest problem with bringing three worlds together was that three vastly different groups all felt their problems were more pressing than the other two. Every day brought more stories of fighting, disturbances in the town, reports of stealing, and other sorts of things Lucien had little to no patience for.

There was no going back for anyone, it seemed, for even those alive who remembered the days before the Cold King could not inhabit the mindset of their younger selves after so much loss and war. Salfar, like the Earths they had left, needed to heal in its own time. Burials were announced alongside investigations, calls to tamper down the use of magic rose at the same time petitions began for everyone to learn more ancient, powerful forms of the craft. Some wanted to research the Tear and the Book of Ten Thousand Souls; others argued digging at a centuries old wound would only cause it to fester.

As the kingdom struggled to come together, every day feeling like a victory, each night Lucien went to sleep exhausted, his mind racing until darkness consumed him.

He'd always preferred to lead by delegating and spent the first days of his reign simply appointing Suriias to various positions. He kept the pack close, trusting them more than anyone else, but old friends from before the Tear slowly came out of the woodwork. Kol's sister Ayla even found her way to the castle.

But there was one matter he put off until there was nothing else on his list to do.

And so, many nights of procrastinating later, and after pacing for almost an hour, he managed to swallow his fury enough to find himself in front of Nik's door.

Jaw clenched, he raised a hand and knocked.

It creaked open after a few seconds. The mere sight of Nik was enough to send Lucien reeling, and he had to take a moment to gather himself.

'May I come in?' he asked curtly.

'Of course.' Nik stepped aside and gestured him in.

In the short amount of time they'd been in the castle, Nik had made the room his own. It seemed his penchant for reading hadn't been entirely for show. The shelves, table, bed and floor were strewn with books. Incense burned on the mantle, clothes decorated the floor, and papers with scribbles all over them covered surface after surface.

Stilling in the centre of the room, Lucien turned to face him. 'How are you?'

'Fine,' said Nik softly.

'Your brothers?'

'Bad.'

He hadn't expected much else, but it still pained him. 'If they need anything, tell me.'

'I will.'

The silence stretched on to a painful degree and Lucien wanted to set it on fire. Suddenly, he had to know. 'Did you know who I was when you did the spell?' he queried, heart in his throat. 'Our marriage?'

After a pregnant pause, Nik nodded. 'But that doesn't mean my feelings aren't real. They are. I didn't want to love you. I didn't mean to. But I did. I do. Love you, that is.'

'I want to believe that.'

'It's true.' Nik closed the wretched distance between them and took his hands. 'I'd hated the idea of you for years. I won't lie about that. I hated you and my father and everyone else involved because I blamed you for what happened to my brothers. But none of that was your fault. And I fell in love with you despite believing it.'

'Is that right?'

'Yes.'

'Why would I believe that?'

'It's *true*,' cried Nik. 'I fell in love with you in Westend. I didn't want to betray you. But what was I supposed to do? Forget my brothers? It was you and the book for their *lives*.'

'You manipulated me.'

'Yeah,' he said, and Lucien was grateful he didn't deny it. That he had enough respect for Lucien not to do that. 'But your father swore up and down that you wouldn't be harmed. That I wasn't bringing you home to death or the Tower. He swore before the court that he was getting his son back and the Tear would be ended, and everything would be all right. I promise, Luka. I struck a deal for my brothers. I couldn't turn my back on them. But I love you. I brought you here – yes, intentionally – but with the belief that we could be together. That you'd love me as much as I love you and we'd be able to make it work. I want a chance to live the life that was snatched from me. That was stolen from my brothers. And I want that life with you.'

Lucien felt his anger crumbling. Would he have done differently? Until he was forced to, he'd never know. 'I don't forgive a second time,' he murmured. 'Don't make me regret this.'

Nik shook his head vehemently. 'I'll never lie to you again. I swear.'

'All right. Then I forgive you.'

A noise of utter elated relief escaped Nik and he threw his arms around Lucien.

It was as he held Nik, the feeling of contentment spreading through him, like a balm to apply to the wounds of the years, that he knew what he had to do.

Promising Nik he would be back later, Lucien headed for the room down the hall.

He knocked twice before stepping inside. The air in the room felt thick with grief and despair. Kol was on the other side of the room, hands hung at his sides, staring out the window with a dazed, slightly disconnected look on his face.

'I'm sorry,' said Lucien when he reached him. 'I'm so, so sorry, Kol.'

Kol didn't answer. Already he looked like he was fraying at the seams.

'Do you know what it says about how much she loves you – the fact that she overlooked her history enough to trust you? Don't ever doubt how much she cared for you, Kol.'

The sudden scent of blood tickled Lucien's nose and he glanced down. Kol was digging his fingernails into his skin hard enough to draw blood. He didn't even seem to notice he was doing it.

'It's not like I don't know her,' he croaked, mouth twisting, as if the words hurt to form. 'What she's like. How far she'll go for Thistle.'

'Does it bother you?'

'Does it bother me that the woman I love doesn't mind dying for her friends?' Kol choked in strangled despair. 'What does that make me?'

'Relatable.'

Tears welled anew in his bloodshot eyes. 'I tried to summon Aosh, but she didn't appear.'

'I thought you liked plans and rational discussions, frai-boy.'

'And look where that's left me.' Kol fixed him with a near-mad look of beseeching need. 'Where did she go?'

'The Tear's closed. Salfar's under my protection. She'll come if I call for her or if Salfar is in trouble.'

'Will you summon her for me?'

'It could be suicide.'

'Please.'

With minor hesitation, Lucien gestured for Kol to follow him.

Neither spoke on the walk out of the castle, across the grounds, through the fields, and onwards to where they'd first come from Earth.

Sure enough, when Lucien called, Aosh appeared out of the mist, half figment, half form.

'A lost prince and a lost love,' she observed, her white eyes shifting from one to the other. 'How truly upsetting.'

'I'll give you anything,' said Kol desperately. 'Please send me back.'

'There is no back. Only the new world. A messy world. One with the lore of more histories than it knows what to do with.'

'Please,' he begged.

Aosh tilted her head to the side, although whether she was curious or mocking, Lucien couldn't tell. 'Anything?'

'Yes.'

Aosh stepped to the side, raising her arm. Nothing appeared. It was simply a bright white glow of light. A doorway to another place, although Lucien couldn't tell if it was to Earth or somewhere with a test.

Kol looked at Lucien fearlessly. 'Tell the others?'

'I will.'

'Thank you.'

'We don't know what's on the other side of that.'

'I have to try.'

'I would, too.'

With a parting nod, Kol walked into the light. It dissipated, and with it went Aosh, and Lucien was left standing at the side of gentle waters, fog slowly rolling in, a chill carried on the wind nipping at his skin. No matter how hard he looked, he could see no sign that once a tear in the fabric of reality had existed between the worlds.

He prayed that they would find each other. He prayed that Earth was better now. Yet the fate of Earth only reminded him that he was now in charge of the fate of Salfar, a heavy responsibility he had never yearned for. Faren, by far, would surely have been the better king. Faren could silence a throne room; he could command armies; everything about him was kind, assured, regal. Lucien didn't know how to even begin emulating such a figure. And his love and guilt and anguish over his brother's death made everything that much more difficult.

A light rain began to fall, and in the distant forest he heard gryphons call to each other; the dancing fish in the river began to swish about, delighted by the movement of the water on the surface. The smallest of wistful, fond smiles curved his lips as he gazed at the forest. Three hundred years away and he'd never let himself miss it. Missing it would mean thinking of Faren, of his parents, of Astril and the Tower. But now that those shadows had passed, he could look at Salfar and recall his childhood, the days spent exploring with Geon, Jae and Esme. The adventures they'd had and the joys they'd shared. After all, it was never the land, nor the world, that was the problem. It came down to fear or ignorance or greed every time. But all things had their time. Even evil couldn't last forever.

'You coming back?'

He didn't turn around. 'Soon.'

Nik appeared by his side a second later and Lucien raised his arm, drawing him in close. Now that things between them had settled, the questions answered and the truths exposed, he found himself truly content with the state of his marriage for the first time.

He marvelled at that a little bit, and kissed Nik's forehead, reassuring himself it wasn't a dream.

Nik followed his gaze out across the water. 'Is he gone?'

'He's gone.'

'Think he'll find her?'

'He seems to think he's a better tracker than I am,' said Lucien with a wry chuckle. 'I think he'll be fine.'

'That's good.' Nik gestured over his shoulder. 'Are you all right with all this? Being king? We could go. I'd leave with you if you wanted. I promise.'

Lucien smiled at him, glad to hear it. Not too long ago he would have jumped at the suggestion. But for the first time, Lucien wasn't afraid to go home. He tightened his grip slightly around Nik. 'I may make an awful king.'

'You made a really good boss.'

'I think there's a slight bit of difference.'

Nik leaned into him and turned his head so that their eyes locked. 'I believe in you.'

'You do?'

'I do.'

'Good to know.'

They stood, locked together by the water's edge, until the cold winds of evening propelled them back to the castle. The grounds were silent except for the passing strand of conversation or echo of laughter. It was a quiet night.

The first of many.

EPILOGUE
Our Bright Tomorrows

EARTH

Thorn chose not to return to the cities. She stayed clear of the villages and towns, too. She left the new world and its changes behind and set off into the mountains of the continent. At the very least, this new old world had no drones, no Scuttlers, no one searching for anyone. As far as the human world was concerned, magic was a thing of the past. The fairy-tales of a life that would soon seem like the stuff of legend and myth.

She walked until the air held still and the forests sounded serene, the water of an adjacent river shimmering as the sunlight kissed the surface.

She had been sitting on the edge of the river one afternoon, staring off into the distance, when she heard someone in the forest behind her.

Straightening up, she turned around, hand going instinctively to her knife.

She froze.

Kol stood only a few paces away. Just like always, he wore his long black coat, but his hair was messier than ever and visibly matted with sweat, his beard unkempt and long. 'Hi, Rose,' he called.

It was then she noticed the real difference. His eyes were a dark, dark brown, but there was nothing catlike about them.

Kol was human.

She stared at him, unable to move. 'H-how?'

'I traded everything.'

Her eyes burned with the promise of tears. 'Kol ...'

'We can't go back,' he continued, stepping closer, hands in his pockets, clearly anxious about her reaction. 'We can't use magic again. It's just us; human. If that's okay?'

'Are *you* okay with this?' she wondered, searching his face for clues.

'I told you,' he said softly, stopping in front of her. 'Back with you is forward for me.'

A strangled sound tore its way from the very heart of her and she nodded several times, tears stinging her eyes. 'I really love you.'

The smile that spread across Kol's face could have outshone the brightest star in the night's sky. 'Finally,' he teased.

She kissed him.

finis

Printed in Great Britain
by Amazon